T0203270

Praise for Jessica

The Last Caretaker

"Strawser's latest fast-paced page-turner (following *The Next Thing You Know*) grabs readers at the start and doesn't let go. For fans of Sally Hepworth and Liane Moriarty."

—*Library Journal*

"Strawser presents a fresh premise and compelling plot. The twists are unexpected, and Katie is pulled along through the adventure until she finds the courage to stand up for herself."

—*Booklist*

"Ms. Strawser, author of Book of the Month bestseller *Not That I Could Tell*, gives readers a master class in distrust through the eyes of Katie . . . Part of the human experience is learning moral and ethical boundaries, yet some situations are dicey, and what is right is less certain. To risk the courage to move forward and through situations—even and especially in the unknown—is a learned skill. Ms. Strawser navigates these waters with nimbleness, and readers might finish the book with a new sense of right from wrong—or, at the least, question their own beliefs, which is the power of a good book."

—*Pittsburgh Post-Gazette*

"You're never sure who to trust or where everyone's loyalties lie in this latest from the very talented Jessica Strawser. Deftly written with an undercurrent of unease, *The Last Caretaker* is a relevant, harrowing mystery with page-turning suspense, a powerful storyline, and relatable characters that readers will think about for a long time to come. Strawser's fans will love this!"

—Mary Kubica, *New York Times* bestselling author of *Just the Nicest Couple*

"Riveting and evocative, *The Last Caretaker* takes its cast—and readers—down a path of discovery and strength, all while telling a story rich with grace and determination and yes—soul-deep hope. Turn off your phones; you will be reading this one in a single sitting."

—Kelly Harms, national bestselling author of *Where the Wind Takes Us*

"A powerful and atmospheric tale that is equal parts emotion and suspense as a woman takes over as caretaker of a remote nature reserve, only to discover the barn is part of a dangerous underground network for victims of domestic violence. In *The Last Caretaker*, Strawser perfectly captures the perils of living in an isolated part of the world and the desperate measures some women must take in order to survive. A richly emotional page-turner with an important message."

—Kimberly Belle, internationally bestselling author of *Dear Wife* and *The Personal Assistant*

"Riveting, harrowing, timely, and important. The story of a woman fleeing a difficult past who stumbles upon a network of safe houses for domestic violence victims, *The Last Caretaker* is that rare combination of page-turning thriller and an issue-driven book with deep resonance. I couldn't put it down, I can't stop thinking about it, and I know it will stay with me for a very long time."

—Michele Campbell, internationally bestselling author of *It's Always the Husband*

"Jessica Strawser's powerful page-turner *The Last Caretaker* takes us on a dark, winding journey that forces the protagonist to grapple with how far she would go to do the right thing, and at what price. Katie's new job as a residential caretaker in a nature reserve is not what it seems . . . far from it. Strawser expertly tackles the mysteries around caretaking at the Grove Reserve with unputdownable twists and turns, proving that while life can get messy, the trick is being strong enough to handle the knocks at your door. Brava!"

—Lisa Barr, *New York Times* bestselling author of *Woman on Fire*

"*The Last Caretaker* is as full of life, beauty, and menace as the nature reserve in which it is set. This masterfully constructed novel explores just how much we're willing to risk to do what's right. Jessica Strawser's writing drew me in and refused to let go until the very last page."

—Laura Hankin, author of *The Daydreams*

"*The Last Caretaker* is a relevant, absorbing exploration into the dark side of relationships. Strawser's skillful insights capture what it means to be a caretaker—what it's worth and the impact on ourselves and those around us. A powerful read from start to finish, thought provoking, and unputdownable."

—Rochelle B. Weinstein, *USA Today* bestselling author

"*The Last Caretaker* is the best kind of book: important, surprising, brave. You'll want all your friends to read it."

—Ann Garvin, *USA Today* bestselling author of *I Thought You Said This Would Work*

The Next Thing You Know

"Uplifting, hopeful, and full of wisdom about surviving loss, embracing life, and offering and accepting forgiveness."

—Barbara Claypole White, bestselling author

"Jessica Strawser does it again—first-rate storytelling, a fresh, unique premise, and a didn't-see-that-coming twist, resulting in a book that's unputdownable! Strawser spins a wise, thought-provoking story that crackles with tension and intrigue. Perfect for book clubs, *The Next Thing You Know* will have you pondering end-of-life issues, and guessing the final, shocking twist."
—Lori Nelson Spielman, internationally bestselling author of *The Star-Crossed Sisters of Tuscany*

"A breathtaking, emotional, and compelling novel, *The Next Thing You Know* is a poignant look at love and hope, and the importance of living every moment with no regrets. Unflinching and unforgettable, this one will crack your heart open and slowly stitch it back together."
—Christina McDonald, bestselling author of *The Night Olivia Fell*

"A magical tale of love and loss . . . bittersweet yet ultimately comforting."
—*Publishers Weekly*

"An emotional, powerful, and page-turning read."
—Megan Collins, author of *The Family Plot*

"[A] deft exploration of connection, death, and grief."
—*E! News*

"This novel is brave and affecting, and should come with a box of tissues."
—*BookTrib*

"Grab the tissues."
—*People*

A Million Reasons Why

"*A Million Reasons Why* is a fascinating foray into the questions we are most afraid to ask: What constitutes family, what are our obligations to those we love, where does American health care fail the most, what secrets are unforgivable? And in case you need another reason to read this book: there are two massive twists you'll never see coming."

—Jodi Picoult, #1 *New York Times* bestselling author of *Small Great Things* and *A Spark of Light*

"Don't miss this searching, fraught family drama by a master of her craft. Jessica Stawser gives us a twisty plot, combined with deeply emotional content, in a novel that examines the most profound questions of our hearts. This is a story that will stay in your heart long after the last page is turned."

—Susan Wiggs, #1 *New York Times* bestselling author

"From the opening line to the heart-healing ending, *A Million Reasons Why* is an immersive and startling novel of great compassion with plot twists that will take your breath away. When all we know is turned upside down and inside out, who do we become? Strawser isn't afraid of the bigger questions, and this beautiful exploration of family, loyalty, and love will both break and heal your heart. Powerful, poignant, and profound—don't miss this compelling novel from a master storyteller."

—Patti Callahan Henry, *New York Times* bestselling author

"*A Million Reasons Why* is the emotionally gripping story of two half sisters, each with her own secrets, who find each other as adults. It's deftly paced and surprising, and Strawser's characters are so layered and flawed and human that I came to care about them deeply. Heartbreaking yet hopeful, this astute exploration of the bonds and limitations of family is a perfect book club pick."

—Joshilyn Jackson, *New York Times* bestselling author

"*A Million Reasons Why* is a heartbreaking, absorbing story with an irresistible premise: a random DNA test reveals you have a sister you've always wanted, a potential lifesaver. Strawser skillfully explores what it means to be family, to rethink the pivotal hinge points in a person's life."

—Angie Kim, bestselling author of *Miracle Creek*

"A powerful and poignant tale with characters that burrowed their way into my heart and will stay with me for a long time."

—Colleen Oakley, bestselling author of *You Were There Too*

"Strawser once again displays her nuanced understanding of all the corners of the human heart."

—Sonja Yoerg, *Washington Post* bestselling author of *True Places* and *Stories We Never Told*

"Through richly drawn characters and a few satisfying plot twists, Strawser handles difficult questions with thoughtful, page-turning prose. A must-read!"

—Susan Gloss, *USA Today* bestselling author of *Vintage*

"A standout novel . . . seamless writing style, complex characters, and a layered plot. The high concept will attract book groups and fans of Jodi Picoult."

—*Booklist*, (starred review)

"This emotional family and medical drama from Strawser will appeal to fans of Jodi Picoult and Liane Moriarty."

—*Library Journal*

"Riveting . . . a provocative family tale."

—*Publishers Weekly*

"A thrilling story of what happens when a long-held family secret comes to light . . . [Strawser] shows that no one is ever truly a villain or a hero, but instead, we are all a beautiful and messy mix of both."

—Associated Press

"A compulsively readable slow burn that is sure to touch the heart of everyone who reads it."

—*Booktrib*

Forget You Know Me

"Gorgeously written, suspenseful, and full of characters who feel like old friends. I loved this book and didn't want it to end."

—Michele Campbell, author of *It's Always the Husband* and *She Was the Quiet One*

"It's been a long time since I've been so lost in a book that when I looked up, I had to remind myself what day it was. I'm delighted to say that this happened several times as I read this book. From the very first page of *Forget You Know Me*, I was putty in Strawser's hands. From her portrayal of the changing nature of adult friendship to the seemingly harmless secrets we keep in marriage, *Forget You Know Me* is that book you can't put down and can't stop thinking about when you are finished."

—Sally Hepworth, *USA Today* bestselling author of *The Family Next Door*

"A fantastic, tautly paced novel that will have you racing to unravel its many questions and half-truths."

—Liz Fenton and Lisa Steinke, bestselling authors of *Girls' Night Out*

"Friendships crack, marriages erode, and dangerous deceits rise to the surface in this twisty, emotionally complex, powder keg of a tale."

—Emily Carpenter, bestselling author of *Burying the Honeysuckle Girls* and *Every Single Secret*

"Sinister, sophisticated, and teeming with secrets . . . completely irresistible."

—Hank Phillippi Ryan, bestselling author of *Trust Me*

"A taut and immensely satisfying novel of domestic suspense. Come for the sinister premise, stay for the insightful portrayals of a friendship crumbling apart, a marriage strained to its breaking point, and at least one character who finds themself suddenly—and dangerously—in over their head."

—Kathleen Barber, bestselling author of *Are You Sleeping*

"Masterful."

—*Publishers Weekly* (starred review)

"Strawser is a clear master of the craft."

—*Booklist*

Not That I Could Tell

A Book of the Month Club Selection

"Full of slow-burning intrigue, Strawser's second novel will appeal to fans of Liane Moriarty's *Big Little Lies* and Jennifer Kitses's *Small Hours*."

—*Booklist*

"*Not That I Could Tell* is a psychological thriller of the highest order, as well written as it is structured. That means the magazine Strawser once edited might well be covering her from the other side, and deservedly so."

—*Providence Journal*

"[An] engrossing, taut tale."

—*Publishers Weekly*

"In *Not That I Could Tell*, Strawser tackles the secrets of suburbia, domestic abuse, and friendship in a gripping story about a neighboring family gone missing. The characters are unique, engaging, and relatable, and the ending is both surprising and poignant. Fans of Liane Moriarty will adore Jessica Strawser; she's a huge talent!"

—Kate Moretti, *New York Times* bestselling author of *The Blackbird Season.*

"In *Not That I Could Tell*, Strawser has wrapped a mystery into the fabric of a tightly knit community. When Kristin, recently separated from her husband, leaves in the middle of the night after a night of drinking with her girlfriends, her neighbors can't help but wonder: Did she leave of her own accord? Or if she simply ran away, why? When her soon-to-be ex moves back into their house and more secrets about Kristin are revealed, her friends begin to question whether they knew anything about her at all. Well-drawn characters, a perfectly cast neighborhood, and a great puzzle; what more could you want in your next read?"

—Catherine McKenzie, bestselling author of *Fractured* and *The Good Liar*

"In Jessica Strawser's sophomore novel, *Not That I Could Tell*, we're transported to Yellow Springs, Ohio—a charming small town and the sort of place where neighbors are friends and nothing terrible ever happens. Until a woman and her children go missing and the residents of Yellow Springs realize they don't know their neighbors as well as they thought. As the lies build and secrets unravel, you'll probably stay up too late to finish the book as it speeds toward an edge-of-your-seat conclusion. Ultimately a story about the power of instincts and the strength of women, *Not That I Could Tell* is full of satisfying suspense and one to add to your "must-read" list!"

—Karma Brown, internationally bestselling author of *Come Away with Me* and *In This Moment*

Almost Missed You

"A taut psychological thriller . . . Strawser's imaginative story is a three-pronged domestic drama that rivets the reader; explores the vagaries of fate; touches on politics, PTSD, and pregnancy; and leaves the reader breathless."

—*Richmond Times-Dispatch*

"Fans of smart women's fiction mixed with a fast-paced plot should not miss this startling first novel."

—*Library Journal*

"Strawser's exploration of marriage, its expectations, and motherhood are spot-on, making for an absorbing read."

—*Publishers Weekly*

"A book worth losing sleep over, this novel takes readers on a winding emotional journey that delves into the complexity of human relationships, guilt, and forgiveness. Told from alternating voices, the layers of the story are woven together chapter by chapter, slowly coming together like the pieces of a puzzle to reveal the bigger picture."

—*RT Book Reviews*

"Once in a great while, along comes a novel that defies the odds, a true mystery that bars no holds and plays no tricks, leaving the reader both deeply moved and thoroughly astonished. *Almost Missed You* is just such a book, a debut that asks if we can ever really know another human being, by a writer's writer with talent to spare. You may not have heard of Jessica Strawser today, but by tomorrow, everyone's going to be talking about her and about this story."

—Jacquelyn Mitchard, *New York Times* bestselling author of *The Deep End of the Ocean*

"*Almost Missed You* is a skillful, insightful debut: a deft exploration of the mysteries of marriage, the price we pay for our secrets, and just how easy it is to make the worst choices imaginable."

—Chris Bohjalian, *New York Times* bestselling author of *The Sandcastle Girls* and *Midwives*

"*Almost Missed You* is an emotional powerhouse of a novel, filled with complex relationships and difficult choices, the secrets we keep, and the lies we tell to those we love while hoping to shield them from harm. Strawser's tale of guilt, blame, redemption, and forgiveness is a must-read for anyone who enjoys a well-told, compelling exploration of the human heart."

—Garth Stein, *New York Times* bestselling author of *A Sudden Light* and *The Art of Racing in the Rain*

"*Almost Missed You* is the sensational debut novel by the gifted Jessica Strawser, who has expertly woven a tale of a marriage in crisis with elements of daring, danger, mystery, and secrets that will surprise and delight you. You will revel in the triangle of Violet and Finn, the perfect couple until they weren't, and Caitlin, Finn's best friend, who is pulled into the drama while hiding a secret of her own. This is a rich read that will keep you turning pages long into the night. Glorious!"

—Adriana Trigiani, *New York Times* bestselling author of *All the Stars in the Heavens*

"Taut, emotional, satisfies with its gripping blend of painful secrets and fateful connections."

—National Book Award and PEN USA finalist Deb Caletti

"Jessica Strawser writes from the heart."

—Lisa Scottoline, *New York Times* bestselling author

"Jessica Strawser's richly textured debut novel never lets the reader forget that love is a complex equation in which attraction and affection are balanced by the cost of forgiveness, the obligation of friendship, and the pain of loss. Compelling fiction from a brave new voice."

—Sophie Littlefield, bestselling author

"A thought-provoking debut about the true cost of emotional stress fractures and the jolts that finally crack them open. Strawser's novel is layered with secrets, and will stay with you long after you finish reading."

—Therese Walsh, author of *The Moon Sisters*

"Jessica Strawser hits all the right notes in her memorable debut. With twists big and small, the story is at turns heartrending, unexpected, and delightfully devious. *Almost Missed You* will give book clubs plenty to argue about, and the reader much to contemplate."

—Michelle Gable, *New York Times* bestselling author of *A Paris Apartment* and *I'll See You in Paris*

"In *Almost Missed You*, debut author Jessica Strawser meticulously weaves together a kidnapped child, friends in turmoil, and a Craigslist ad into a tangled web of secrets, lies, and unexpected alliances. This heartbreaking page-turner will make you question how well you really know everyone you hold dear."

—Amy Sue Nathan, author of *The Glass Wives*

"*Almost Missed You* is a rare sort of a book, one part page-turner, one part love song to motherhood, and one part examination of the things we owe each other in friendship. It is by turns tender, sharp, and thoughtful, and always impossible to put down. Book clubs will love this tale of friendship, marriage, and the things we do for love."

—Barbara O'Neal, author of *How to Bake a Perfect Life*

CATCH YOU LATER

ALSO BY JESSICA STRAWSER

The Last Caretaker

The Next Thing You Know

A Million Reasons Why

Forget You Know Me

Not That I Could Tell

Almost Missed You

CATCH YOU LATER

A NOVEL

JESSICA STRAWSER

LAKE UNION
PUBLISHING

This is a work of fiction. Names, characters, organizations, places, events, and incidents are either products of the author's imagination or are used fictitiously. Otherwise, any resemblance to actual persons, living or dead, is purely coincidental.

Text copyright © 2024 by Jessica Strawser
All rights reserved.

No part of this book may be reproduced, or stored in a retrieval system, or transmitted in any form or by any means, electronic, mechanical, photocopying, recording, or otherwise, without express written permission of the publisher.

Published by Lake Union Publishing, Seattle

www.apub.com

Amazon, the Amazon logo, and Lake Union Publishing are trademarks of Amazon.com, Inc., or its affiliates.

ISBN-13: 9781662510236 (paperback)
ISBN-13: 9781662510243 (digital)

Cover design by Faceout Studio, Jeff Miller
Cover image: © Leonardo Alpuin / Arcangel; © Highlander, © Brian Fulda / Stocksy

Printed in the United States of America

In loving memory of Martha Strawser,
who was always up for a drive to the ocean,
no matter how far.

1

Mikki

October 2016

The thing about living near the interstate was, it never let you forget where you were.

Highway noise was a constant background thrum. Louder at night, when you most wanted quiet. Louder in the barren landscape of winter, when you most wanted to migrate someplace warm and peaceful. You could seal yourself inside, muffle all that mechanized rumbling, but the only way to drown it out was with more noise: the TV, a fan, music, headphones. Most people said they got used to it, didn't even notice it anymore, but Mikki found it maddening to have silence out of reach. She'd catch herself standing at the windows of the tiny apartment she shared with Lark, glaring at the endless stream of headlights in the distance, just as she was now.

To her, the thrum wasn't so much a nuisance as a reminder.

When the biggest thing your town had going for it was the interstate, you couldn't help but feel like you should be on your way somewhere.

Everyone else was.

"Catch," Lark called, and Mikki turned just in time to grab the apron Lark had tossed her way. Lark was already wearing hers. When they'd first started working the Travel Stop night shift together after high school, it had seemed like a great coup. The shift began after the owner's preferred workday of 11:00 a.m. to 7:00 p.m. So they slept as late as they wanted, clocked in after dinner, and got off at 3:00 a.m.—which often equated to getting paid to stay out all night, flirting and goofing around. They played by their own rules and had only two: say yes as much as possible and keep your eyes open for a ride out of Becksville.

It was fun for a while, stripping down to swim in the moonlight, watching sunrises from rooftops, mildly trespassing in mildly interesting places—abandoned buildings, new construction, sites that were reportedly haunted or storied or cursed. Their rules were no secret, which meant people liked to push them. Test them. And why not? When nothing else passed for excitement, might as well create your own. In a city, Lark Nichols and Mikki Jensen might not have stood out, but here they joked about passing for "small-town pretty." And if you were under the impression they were down for a good time, up for anything, well, you were in luck—and so were they. They never hurt anyone and most of the time managed not to get hurt back.

There was only one problem: staring down their thirtieth birthdays, they were still here.

And they were really stuck now.

Lark smoothed the apron over her midsection. "How long, do you think, before anyone starts to notice?" she asked.

"Oh, months," Mikki said with more confidence than was warranted. She was no stranger to the anxiety of peeing on a test stick and holding her breath, hoping for a negative line to appear. And she'd babysat lots of infants over the years, growing up in a town where no one could afford maternity leave. But she was foggy on the specifics of the nine months between a non-negative test and the swaddled bundle toted home from the hospital.

That was about to change. Everything that happened to Lark also happened to Mikki, and vice versa. Mikki had never resented it before—in fact, she'd long considered her best friend the only thing she had going for her—so she figured she didn't have a right to start resenting her now. This time next year, Lark would be a single mom, though she wanted to keep that news between them for as long as possible. And Mikki would be . . .

Well, she'd be here. Same as always, only different. Because she'd have to do the one thing she had never once done, not even during the worst moment of her worst day.

She'd have to resign herself to staying put.

"Nini will notice soon," Lark said. "She notices everything."

Mikki's grandmother, Nini, had been practicing her whole life to embrace the role of cranky old lady. As far back as anyone could remember, she'd been flat-out mean, but now that she'd progressed in years, people laughed her off instead of getting bent. Apparently, she'd earned some unspoken seniority to do as she pleased and come across as endearing.

Of course, when she was the only family you had, it was less so.

"Would you go to Nini for any kind of life advice?" Mikki asked, gesturing in the general direction of Nini's house down the street. Formerly Mikki's mother's house. Not that it had actually belonged to any of them. It was a miracle they had yet to be evicted.

"Life advice from Nini? Hard no." Lark shuddered.

"Then she's not someone you should ever take criticism from."

Lark pulled back and looked at Mikki with admiration. "That's good. You could start a line of bumper stickers with that one." Lark was always telling Mikki to put things she said on bumper stickers. Like *that* was the million-dollar idea that would save them.

"And give up all this?" Mikki gestured around their living room slash kitchen, stifling in the freak autumn heat wave. From the side window, their catawampus air conditioner splashed a stream of condensation onto the peeling vinyl floor, and Lark laughed. No matter how hard they tried to perk up the room—painting each wall a different color, combing yard sales for cute castoffs—it still looked like an uninspired space over a garage, unintended for habitation. Because that's what it was.

"If only we had an in with someplace a lot of drivers came through," Lark mused.

When she joked about the Travel Stop this way, it never sounded like a stretch. Which was how Mikki had always known Lark was more content there than she let on.

"Speaking of," Mikki said. "Pete's on the rampage about being on time. You ready?"

"Ready." Lark pointed at Mikki's phone on the end table on her way out the door. Mikki had plenty of messages waiting, but none she felt like responding to. Nini had been barraging her with excuses to postpone her neurology screen, as she did every six months, because Nini hated her specialist as much as she hated the hour-long drive to his office, the closest one they could find. Meanwhile, Mikki's on-again, off-again boyfriend was in an "on" mood while Mikki was firmly in the "off" position. And Pete was nagging her to "just think about" switching to the early shift, which she'd already told him was the only thing sadder than the late shift. Worse, when she hinted that the only switch she was interested in was to *manager*, Pete had texted, I think that's more Lark's speed. When she'd asked what that was supposed to mean, he'd said Mikki was the obvious choice today, but Lark seemed more likely to stick around for the long haul. Like it wasn't backward to tell someone she was "too good" to get a leg up.

All of which was why Mikki strode purposefully, stubbornly, even joyfully past her phone. "You're the only person I want to talk to," she called after Lark, "and you're with me."

Mikki would play it back later, wondering, *What if.* Of all the unforgettable moments ahead on this night—and the days that would follow—she'd think about this one quite a lot.

But not half as much as Lark would.

2

No one had bothered to come up with an original name for the Travel Stop. After Pete bought it from a franchise that deemed business too slow, he changed the logo to a *T* and an *S* that looked like some flunky had spent ten minutes tops on the design in exchange for a six-pack.

Not that it mattered. Most of their customers just wanted gas—truckers on one side, cars on the other. Those who ventured inside were after the bathroom and maybe cigs, lottery tickets, or a soda. Without full-service showers or a restaurant menu to define them as a true truck stop, nobody ever used the few café booths to do anything but tie a shoe or wait on the microwave. Obvious drug transactions were shooed outside, where dealers had to take their chances with the state troopers on patrol. After dark, the flow of customers became a trickle, and Lark and Mikki found doubling down to cover the shift themselves vastly more appealing than spending every night with even the least objectionable coworkers. At first, Pete resisted letting "pretty girls" work alone after hours—until they proved as efficient as the four men who predated them.

Sure, they'd had incidents with customers getting handsy, but Mikki talked a mean game. Literally: she'd learned from Nini. If that failed, the troopers on rounds were only a call away. The women had comped enough coffees to see to that.

Usually, Lark and Mikki took turns—one behind the register, one on rotation—restocking shelves, cleaning restrooms, collecting trash.

Lately, though, Mikki had ceded the front counter to Lark, whose first trimester made her sensitive to strong odors. Lark claimed she didn't know what smelled worse: the bathroom, the diesel fumes, or the hot dogs under the heat lamp.

"Sludge coffee," Mikki grumbled now, as she emptied the hours-old grounds from soggy filters. "That smells worst." As usual, the day shifters had left the dregs burning on the hot plates, but there was no point complaining to Pete. People weren't exactly lining up to work there.

Lark shot Mikki a sympathetic look from the register. The first few hours had seen steady traffic from stoned patrons heading to some concert, but coming up on midnight it was just the two of them. Lark fiddled with the radio, finding the classic rock station, but Mikki wasn't listening so much as watching. She couldn't deny that despite everything, Lark was glowing.

"Whatcha thinking about?" Mikki teased. "Baby names?"

Lark shushed her. "That's bad luck—I'm only eight weeks. I was actually thinking about . . . Don't be mad." She raised her petite frame on tiptoe, like inches could add confidence.

"Don't you dare say Chad."

"Okay, I won't say it, but . . . Do you realize he finally gave me something I wanted? For the first time since I was seventeen, when I think of him, I don't feel bitter. Only grateful."

They'd been best friends since kindergarten, yet still, Lark's capacity for forgiveness could amaze Mikki. Granted, sometimes Lark was *too* forgiving. Like on the rare occasions her old high school boyfriend stopped in town to visit his parents without his wife and kids along. "Our say-yes-as-much-as-possible rule should never apply to Chad," Mikki had scolded Lark, time and again. *Don't remind me,* Lark would moan, and Mikki couldn't bring herself to pile on top of her shame.

Lark wasn't the type to go for a married man. It was just that when it came to Chad, she'd never known how to say no—and shouldn't have had to. He was the one Mikki faulted. Once every year or two, he'd roll through on some business trip with his quarterback good looks and the gleam of his white-collar suburb all over him. He'd have dinner with his folks and then show up on a barstool at the Neon Moon, looking for one last trip down memory lane before morning. Lark would always cry when he left, kicking herself for feeling so used, for letting herself be. But whenever he came back, there she was, right where he'd left her.

"Will you still be grateful when he runs into you in seven months and wants to know where your kid came from?" It was a delicate point, but they couldn't avoid it forever. Becksville barely qualified as a town—more like a couple of isolated blocks where news traveled fast. "He's in finance, you know. He can add and subtract. And so can everyone else who knows the history with you two."

Lark nodded, resolute. "I'm thinking the key is to get out ahead of it. Start a false rumor about myself and some mystery guy." In the month since Lark had realized her situation, she'd never once considered hitting Chad up for money—at least, not out loud. Whether that was honorable or stupid, Mikki didn't know.

"Is this a bad time to remind you what a terrible liar you are? You have never once successfully covered for me. Remember prom? How you got me grounded? Hell, remember last week? When all I asked was for you to tell one tiny fib to Nini?"

"This is different," Lark demurred. "I'll be keeping *myself* out of trouble."

Mikki shook her head. Lark had one of those faces—and the warbling voice and restless body language to go with it. You could have the intuition of a brick wall and still tell exactly what she was thinking. Lark wouldn't stand a chance, lying to or about Chad, unless he was content to play dumb. Which, luckily or unluckily for Lark, he might be.

"Let's just tell everyone I'm the father of your baby," Mikki suggested.

Lark's glow brightened. "The only one we need."

Maybe someplace else, Lark and Mikki could have actually passed as a couple, but never here, where everyone saw them as sisters. Once the rest of Becksville found out Mikki was about to become Aunt Mikki, it would go without saying she'd stay in the apartment as long as she could. Until Nini's mild cognitive impairment diagnosis began stretching the definition of *mild*. At which point Mikki would have to move back in with her.

There was no one else to do it. Which was becoming a recurring theme.

Sometimes Mikki felt like a character in a slapstick cartoon. All she'd ever wanted was to get out of this town, yet every time it seemed within reach, a piano fell from the sky or the road dropped off a cliff or a fuse was lit on the TNT hidden in some essential hatch of her escape plan. Whereas Lark, in this animated fantasy world, was more like Snow White. Her deadbeat family had lost interest in her long ago, but she'd made do, stuck in the middle of nowhere with a bunch of misfits. She didn't fuss, and you might even catch her humming.

Mikki didn't like the idea of Lark settling into her status quo; they both deserved better. But it was true Lark had always wanted to be a mom. Mikki suspected she needed to prove to herself that she wasn't doomed to repeat her family legacy of neglect.

The door from the automobile side of the plaza chimed open, and their heads turned in that habitual glance-up to clock the man who'd entered and make sure he didn't have a gun.

Then Mikki did a double take to check out the wheels parked behind him.

Not their usual fare. Certainly not the car—a gleaming silver BMW convertible. And not the guy either. He looked about their age or a little older, and the words *well-off* came to mind . . . but felt wrong. His worn jeans and tee were cut almost too perfectly, along with everything else about him, from the artfully windblown haircut wisping out from beneath his ball cap to the physique that could only be coached by a personal trainer. He looked exhausted, but more fed up than sleep-deprived. Sweaty. Rumpled. Disheveled in the manner of someone who's rarely caught out of sorts. Fumbling with his own car keys like he'd never seen them before.

Lark's eyes found Mikki's, brightening with a dare as the man approached the coffee station where Mikki stood and surveyed the dismal offerings: *He's all yours.*

"Could you please point me toward your freshest caffeine?" he asked politely, with not nearly enough skepticism, considering.

The trucker-side door chimed, and in strolled one of their regulars, Stan, whose wardrobe consisted entirely of Rolling Stones fanwear. Today he sported the Jagger lips in a Warhol-inspired grid. "They're my raaaaaainbows," he sang to her and Lark by way of greeting, and they waved. He'd buy two Mountain Dew bottles and talk Lark's ear off at checkout until another customer lined up behind him. Any given night, this could take two minutes or twenty-two.

Mikki turned back to the stranger standing in front of her. "Long night?"

"Sticky night. I finally buy my dream car and the AC gives out after . . ." He shook his head. "Forget it. You wouldn't believe me if I told you. The universe is having a laugh at my expense today."

Hmm. Maybe Mikki had been mistaken about which car was his. "The BMW?" He nodded. "But that's a convertible. Who needs AC?"

"Maybe if I wasn't driving all the way to Florida. The novelty of driving with the top down wears off a few hours in. I mean, the highway noise alone . . ."

Now *that* Mikki could relate to. Even if his car was fifty grand nicer than hers, broken AC notwithstanding.

"I'm about to make a fresh pot if you want to use the restroom, get a snack, whatever. You could use a big fountain cup, pour it on ice?"

"Great," he said. "Thanks." But he didn't wander away. Instead, he leaned back against the counter, stretching his arms overhead as he watched her fill the carafe at the drink station's little sink. Mikki didn't know why she felt so self-conscious. Other than . . . Most people in this sort of mood weren't up for a chat. In fact, most of them didn't even bother to be kind.

"Where you coming from?" she asked.

"Michigan."

"All the way to Florida, huh?" She retrieved grounds and filters from the cupboard beneath the counter and caught Lark watching. Usually she didn't mind Lark overhearing most of her life, but tonight she was oddly glad her friend was too far away to eavesdrop.

"Amelia Island," he specified. "Destination wedding. Why celebrate for one day when you could mastermind a whole long weekend with a preset itinerary?"

"Ah, one of those," she said, switching on the first percolator and starting on the next carafe, making her way down the row. The last wedding she'd been to had involved baked beans and Styrofoam plates at a fire hall, but she could picture the kind of affair he was referencing, thanks to reality TV. Surely if this guy fit that mold, he could have flown there first class. "How come you decided to drive?"

He gave a little laugh. "Selective memory, I guess. I usually regret it a few hours in, but in theory, I prefer doing things myself. I'm very committed to having no one else to blame when everything goes wrong. Which it inevitably does."

"That is commitment. It's taking, what, eight or nine times as long to get there?"

"Good math. You've made the drive too?" He seemed suddenly eager to know if she'd been crazy enough to attempt it. Or maybe he just wanted a detailed report of road construction.

"No. I've looked into it, though."

"For vacation? Or your own destination wedding?" If he was fishing to find out if she was single, he did a good job of casting the line—like he really would rather talk about her than him—and again, she felt self-conscious. Because she really would rather not.

"I just want to see the ocean." Her face colored, instantly. Why hadn't she made up something, anything, that didn't make her sound like some bumpkin who'd never left Ohio? "Anyway. I can tell you how long it takes to drive most anywhere from here."

He looked amused. Also, dubious. "Is that so? How about . . . Toronto?"

"Little over six hours, depending on wait times at the border crossing."

"Memphis."

"Nine hours, but you gain an hour changing time zones."

"Washington, DC."

"Eight and a half."

"Savannah."

"Just under twelve."

"Key West."

"Twenty-two."

He looked impressed, and she grinned. "Look 'em up if you want. They're correct."

He made no move for his smartphone. "Cool party trick. Ever been any of those places?"

"Not yet."

That was what they'd learned in her high school gifted program, for all the good that had done her: growth mindset. To harness "the power of yet" when discussing things you hadn't mastered but hoped to. She had the mindset, all right, but growth was another story.

She'd reached the end of the row, and the air was growing fragrant with the fresh brew. He helped himself to the biggest fountain cup and headed for the ice.

She held out her hand. "Do you trust me? I can make you the Mikki Special. It's a pretty good dupe of a coffeehouse frappé."

"I trust you completely." He looked a little surprised at his own sincerity as he handed over the cup and thumbed toward the restrooms. "Okay to step away while you make it?"

"That's for the best. This is going to look weirder than it tastes."

She glanced at Lark, who was humoring Stan while he loudly griped about the price of gas being the president's fault, though he knew as well as they did that theirs was the cheapest on this stretch between Dayton and Toledo. Anyway, if he wanted to blame a politician, it should be Ohio's governor, whose taxes on diesel were among the highest in the country.

Mikki began building the frappé: a squirt from the so-called vanilla cappuccino machine, which melted the ice into a creamy puddle, followed by a swirl of cola slushie, then ice cubes, fresh coffee, creamer, then more ice, coffee, and creamer, mixed in rotation with one of those long, wide straws with a scoop at the end. By the time he returned, she was snapping the lid on.

He took a sip. "You're not kidding. Pretty good for a travel stop."

"Years of practice."

There was nothing left to do but head off to pay, but he lingered, scuffing the linoleum with his sneaker. "I was thinking. About all the drive times you mapped out?"

"Yeah?"

"I've mapped out a lot of routes I haven't taken, too, but more like on a life map instead of actual roads." He took another pull through his straw, as if waiting for her to answer, though he hadn't asked anything. Mikki wasn't sure what to say. "Point is, I hope I didn't insult you by calling that a party trick. I know exactly how to get to a lot of places I've never gone. And it wasn't easy, planning trips I didn't take."

The skin on Mikki's forearms began to tingle. Usually this happened when a guy was about to ask her on a date—the preemptive nerves, the *do I want to?* But this was more like finding out alien life could be surprisingly sensitive. What do you know; some do come in peace.

"You didn't insult me," she said, flashing a genuine smile. "But thanks. Safe travels." She bent to close the unused coffee and filters back in the cabinet.

"I don't suppose you'd want to come with me?" he asked. "I can bring a plus-one."

She straightened, sure she'd misheard, but he was still standing there, just . . . looking at her. She blinked. "To the wedding?" He nodded. "In *Florida*?"

He shrugged. "My sister is always telling me to be more spontaneous. And if you've seriously never seen the ocean, well, we can fix that. What do you say?"

She laughed. "Good one."

But he didn't break. Just crossed his arms and broadened his smile. Surely he wasn't serious?

"Tempting," she said, as if gamely going along with the joke. "But silly me, I didn't think to pack a suitcase when I left for work tonight. My loss." She looked down at her sneakers and jeans. Under her apron, she wore a gray V-neck T-shirt. No makeup. Hair loose and unwashed.

"We can buy whatever on the way," he said. "Anything you need to be comfortable, and dresses for the wedding events too. My treat, of course."

She laughed, more nervously. "What? Just walk out of my shift?"

But he appeared to be warming to the idea. In a too-casual way, as if he were trying to talk her into pizza for dinner, rather than an all-night drive to a multiday formal function.

"It's kind of perfect," he mused. "I didn't want to drag a date to this, but I've been dreading going alone, and I like talking to you. I can't promise the wedding will be fun, but you can check the beach off your bucket list." He gestured toward the convertible. "I'll even put the top down if you want."

He was taking this too far to be kidding. She looked down at herself again. Even if this was some romantic gesture, Prince Charming rescuing Cinderella from the Travel Stop, she had no godmother around to transform her. At best, this was a fairy tale. As in, not reality. Creepy, even.

"Oh, God." He looked suddenly panicked. "I just realized how that might've . . . I'm not some creeper. I promise to be a perfect gentleman. I'm sure the resort is fully booked, but I reserved a suite. You could take the living room—the pullout has a nicer view than the bedroom. Oceanfront balcony."

She'd have rolled her eyes at the *gentleman* bit, except this guy wasn't setting off alarm bells, which was a feat, considering. Through the windows, his BMW gleamed in the floodlights. Could she just . . . get in? Leave with only the clothes on her back, à la *Pretty Woman*?

Mikki shook her head. A *prostitute* came to mind, yet she was considering it?

"Is this one of those things where you could use a date to make an ex jealous or something?" She was pretty sure that had been a movie too. With a *male* escort.

He laughed, and the awkwardness faded a little. "Not looking to reenact the plot of any rom-com. Honestly, I just didn't have anyone I wanted to ask, and now I do. We could keep it platonic, I wouldn't want you to . . ." He blushed. Actually blushed. "I just think we'd have fun."

Fun. Okay. If she kept asking questions, he'd realize how crazy this was. How long he'd be stuck with her, a complete stranger. What a mistake that could be. For either of them.

"How many days would I be gone?"

"Let's see. If you call in sick, say it's a nasty flu, I could have you back Monday evening . . . Unless you want to stay longer, which I could be talked into."

Talked into? She gaped at him, incredulous. It was barely an hour into Thursday. He really was one hundred percent serious. What world must he live in, where you could drop everything for five days at a moment's notice? Too good to be true. Completely impossible.

Wasn't it? *Could* she call off sick? Could she spare the hit to her paycheck and manage not to get fired, knowing Lark would do a notoriously terrible job of convincing Pete or anyone else that Mikki was legitimately too ill to drag herself to work?

Maybe. Pete had already told her she had no future here, so what was the point of trying not to piss him off?

"I don't doubt we'd have fun," she said. "But I can't accept. I'd want to pay my own way, but it's not in my budget. I don't want to be a charity case. The clothes alone . . ."

Honestly, her place was close enough to ask him to swing by so she could pack a bag. But if he saw where she lived, he'd change his mind. If she didn't die of embarrassment first.

"Let's not overthink it," he said. "That's not how being spontaneous works—so I've heard. Besides, it's hardly charity when I'm begging you to keep me company in a heat box on wheels. More of a trade."

Mikki wavered. Since when did she overthink anything? There were only two rules she'd ever committed to, and this was a clearcut two-for-one-deal. *Say yes. Keep your eyes open for a ride out.* Ten years ago, even ten weeks ago, Mikki would have found the idea of saying no blasphemous. She wouldn't have cared if she got fired, or even if he brought her back at all. And she would've had faith that even if the guy turned out to be a creep, she'd handle it.

But things were different now. People were counting on her. Lark, with a baby on the way. Nini, with those disoriented moments she couldn't shrug off anymore. Each time she called Mikki by her mom's name, Mikki knew her days of going where the wind blew were numbered.

What if this was it? Her last chance to say yes to one last adventure?

"I know this is crazy," he said, like he knew what she was thinking. Or maybe he was thinking it too. "But why not?"

Why not, indeed? What was the worst that could happen? She could hear Nini's voice answering for her: *You'd become the subject of one of those true crime shows, except the only mystery would be how anyone could be stupid enough to get raped and murdered like this, of all the ways. You're practically signing up for it!*

Then again . . . What was the *best* thing that could happen if she said yes? That answer was just as vivid: she could have the time of her life.

If she went, she was reasonably sure she could handle herself. But if she stayed? That was real, inescapable danger, because she'd never know what might've been.

And living with that really could kill her.

Lark was frowning at her over Stan's shoulder, aware something was up. Lark wouldn't like this. But she didn't have much room to argue. When Mikki got back, Lark would get over it. Besides, so much of success in this world boiled down to who you knew. If Mikki could be the perfect plus-one, this could be more than just an invitation. It could be an opportunity.

And an opportunity for Mikki was an opportunity for Lark. When she needed it most.

Before Mikki could change her mind, she pulled her apron over her head and looked up at him shyly. "I don't even know your name."

"Chris Redmond. Nice to meet you, Mikki." He jiggled the ice in his cup, beaming. "Let's make one of these for you and hit the road."

3

Lark

March 2024

"What's our dream tonight?" Dove asked, snuggling closer and blinking up at Lark through long eyelashes. Every night, Lark tucked in her sleepy, pajama-clad daughter and left the bedtime stories to Nini while Lark headed to work her shift at the Travel Stop. And every night, Lark promised to meet Dove later, in their dreams. Most of their plans involved sliding down rainbows and riding unicorns together, and not once had Dove complained their dream blueprints hadn't materialized into the real thing. Eight hours from now, Lark would tiptoe back in to kiss her sleeping daughter's forehead and wonder if Dove really was off in the safe, billowy dreamland they'd concocted. It was a lovely thought, though Lark wasn't picky. She'd settle for any sleep at all in the few hours between clocking out and waking up to get her first grader off to school.

"What if we met beneath a beautiful waterfall?" Lark suggested. "A warm, clear waterfall that empties into a perfect swimming hole, with flowers and trees all around. We'll have matching pink swimsuits and a big swan raft to float on and a fuzzy blanket for a picnic."

Dove considered this seriously. "Can there be cookies?"

"The best homemade cookies you've ever had. And ice cream."

"Ice cream would melt at a picnic."

"Not if we don't want it to." Lark pulled her daughter in for one last squeeze. "That's what's so wonderful about dreams. No rules."

Lark had given up on rules long ago. It had been a while since she'd had one of her recurring nightmares, but they never really left her, hovering on the fringe even when she was awake, ready to move in if she let her guard down. In one, she was at the Travel Stop in the dead of night, and all the gas pumps were full of cars and vans and trucks and even buses that sat empty, their drivers nowhere to be seen. Lark ran panicked from one vehicle to the next, screaming Mikki's name, flinging open the doors, banging on the windows, peering into the back seats, terrified at what she'd find there. But she never found anything or anyone. She just ran in circles through the parking lot alone, checking the same places over and over, lonely and scared and frantic for someone, anyone, to come help her find something that wasn't there.

Maybe that was the real reason she liked to leave her daughter with such a happy picture before bed. The more details they could agree upon, the easier it was to keep the image with her, crowding out the shadows with all that bright, sunny hope.

"It's a waterfall date," Dove said. "I'll meet you there."

"Do you have a book picked out for you and Nini? Don't forget to mark it off on your reading challenge for school."

"Who could forget," Nini grumbled from the doorway, waving a sticky note. "There are reminders all over the house. How will you monitor my memory function if you never give me a chance to think for myself?"

"No need," Lark deadpanned. "With any luck, I'll puppet you through the motions indefinitely, and no one will be the wiser."

Nini ignored her, which was her version of getting along just fine. The main thing that set Nini off was being overly nice, so Lark behaved accordingly. Still scowling, Nini stuck the yellow square note teasingly to

Dove's forehead. *Please Remind Dove Reading Worksheet Due Tomorrow* it read. "This one was on my toothpaste. What's next, my false teeth?"

Dove giggled. "You don't have false teeth, Nini."

"Not yet. Only part of my head that hasn't been scrutinized by overpaid medical quacks."

Lark grinned, ceding her spot on the bed so Nini could climb in. Mikki's grandma was growing closer to child size herself with each passing year. She was already in her flannel nightgown and would probably fall asleep as soon as Dove did, though the sun was still setting. The gray March days were inching longer at last, but spring had yet to reach Ohio. "Be good, you two," Lark said. "Call if you need me. I could be home at—"

"A moment's notice," Nini and Dove chimed in unison, and Dove giggled again. The two of them had mastered the art of acting annoyed by their nighttime routine while obviously loving it. Lark flashed them a thumbs-up and made for the door. Better to leave them smiling.

She fiddled with the broken zipper on her puffy down jacket, grabbed her purse and phone—always, *always* her phone—and twirled the ring on her left hand, a new habit she hoped she'd never tire of, as she strode to the car. The sparkle of the tiny diamond chip caught the light of the dashboard, gleaming white and red as she started the engine. The distance to the Travel Stop was so short that driving felt silly, but it was the only way she felt comfortable leaving Nini and Dove alone together, even if they did spend most of the time fast asleep. Aside from cutting down travel time, it ensured she never had to worry about Nini getting behind the wheel.

This phase of Lark's life felt like she'd struck a deal with the universe: neither of them would rock the boat with needless risks. Lark was determined to keep her end of the bargain.

She'd come to think of her life this way—in phases—for the past seven and a half years. Life After Mikki was too big of a catchall to process otherwise. The first phase, pure shock, had been the most all-consuming: the confusion, the shame, the guilt, the failure to get police or media to take her seriously when they assumed Mikki had every reason to stay gone. The exhaustive viral "Find Mikki" campaigns to raise funds to hire a private investigator who came up empty, not so much as a license plate number or a face beneath the ball cap on the surveillance video. Then, reluctantly, had come the survival phase: having no choice but to go on in a world where Mikki wasn't coming back. Where they might never know what had become of her. Where everyone whispered that Lark was to blame for "letting" her go, as if anyone *let* Mikki do anything. As if she'd ever once asked permission.

That survival phase might have gone on forever if Lark's daughter hadn't arrived late that June, ready or—most definitely, in Lark's case—not. She'd known she had to learn to breathe again for the baby's sake, to do what was best for an infant who'd be wholly dependent on her for not just nourishment and shelter but also security and comfort and love. So began the inhale-exhale phase. At first, Lark had barely been able to function. When she did venture out into the startling bright summer, no one could look her in the eye, Nini least of all.

Eventually, of course, she and Nini had admitted how much they needed each other. Just not out loud. The further they moved past the shock of losing Mikki, the closer they tied their lives together, until they ushered in the longest, closest-to-content phase: acceptance. Separately and together, each in her own way, they'd gotten used to what life looked like now, understanding they could never go back, no matter how much they still wanted to.

And now, at last? The biggest surprise. Her favorite phase of them all, still unfamiliar, like a stiff new pair of jeans or a factory-scented car fresh from the dealership: happiness.

She was still amazed at how much and yet how little effort it required. Don't throw your weight around. Don't tip the boat over. Look around you and marvel at how calm the waters are.

"It's about damn time," Nini had cheered, in a rare moment of affection, when Lark announced her engagement. If Mikki could have seen it, honestly, she'd have fallen over. "And don't worry about me. I'll figure something out. Turn me over to Medicaid."

"You're not going anywhere," Lark had told her. "We're family."

Okay, so she had said it out loud. And it had only taken her . . . going on eight years. Long enough, evidently, for Nini not to take off running when she heard it.

Lark knew some people thought it an odd choice, to keep working at the Travel Stop after everything that had happened. The Travel Stop would always be The Last Place She'd Seen Mikki. People came right out and asked sometimes if it was hard to face. But that was just it. The Travel Stop was The Last Place *Anyone* Had Seen Mikki—the person who'd taught Lark, shown Lark, that you could bear anything in this world as long as you had one true friend. How could she ever leave it?

Now, she turned in beneath the TS sign and spotted Heath's cruiser parked out front. Even though it looked just like all the others—a gray Dodge Charger, winged Ohio State Highway Patrol emblem on the doors, blue lights on top—his seemed somehow friendlier. More reassuring than intimidating. But probably only to her.

Heath jumped out holding his hat, rushing to open her door. He'd been raised by his grandfather, and as a consequence, sometimes seemed like a seventy-year-old trapped in a forty-year-old's body. He took chivalry equally seriously—whether he was dealing with Lark, Dove, or Nini—and it never really stopped catching them by surprise. Nini would swat him away, biting back her smile. Dove would giggle and curtsy like a princess. And Lark—well, Lark would fall headfirst all over again.

"Hey, gorgeous." He leaned in for a quick kiss.

"Hey, yourself. Why are you in uniform so early?"

"Had to go in for a meeting with the post commander. Thought I'd catch you on my way home."

"Long day. Can I grab you a coffee?"

They owed their relationship to Travel Stop coffee. For years, Heath had routinely circled the parking lot on his patrol of the exit, venturing in for the occasional caffeine boost. On slow, quiet nights when the rest of the world slept, he'd find Lark with her inventory clipboard and pay her some compliment: on the warm chocolate chunk cookies they'd started stocking, on the new haircut she'd given herself. Sometimes she'd find an excuse to walk with him to the parking lot, where they'd keep talking under the stars until his radio went off. Her coworkers always teased that she was doing her nightly good deed, letting speeders pass this stretch of highway without a ticket. But they were just as thrilled to keep Heath here longer than was necessary. Customers were on their best behavior with him around.

"I can grab my own coffee," he said, like always. "I don't need special treatment."

"Oh," she said, kissing him again, "but you do."

Someone cleared his throat loudly, and she turned to see Sergio, her night cashier, tying his apron on his way to clock in. She liked Sergio. He was always on time and his register was never more than a few dollars off, which could not be said for most of the staff. "Hey, Boss." He tipped his Cincinnati Reds cap, then grinned devilishly at Heath. "Hey, Becksville 9-1-1."

Heath had made the mistake of having a sense of humor about this *Reno 911!* joke once, and now he was doomed to repeat it on demand. He pulled the mirrored sunglasses from his pocket and slipped them on with a reporting-for-duty nod. Sergio howled with laughter.

"So listen," Heath said, once Sergio had gone inside. "About that meeting I'm coming from. We're getting some new cubs to train, finally. And Phil Stush is retiring."

"No kidding? Wow." Lark didn't know why she was surprised. Stush *was* getting up there in age. But he'd grown synonymous with the job, the kind of trooper who was hard to picture in, say, swim trunks.

"Yep. Sergeant pulled me aside after because he thought I might be interested."

Lark wasn't following. "Interested in what?"

He pulled off the sunglasses and folded them back into his shirt pocket. "In working mornings."

Mornings. Lark's mind did the quick math. He meant the shift from 6:00 a.m. to 2:00 p.m. that followed Heath's longtime stint on the shift that staties called "midnights." Mornings, Heath usually spent sleeping. Mornings, Lark faithfully divided, first waking to make Dove breakfast, pack her lunch box, and put her on the bus, then attempting to nap while Nini puttered downstairs to the drone of daytime TV.

"Why would your sergeant think that? Are you interested?"

Heath looked at her intently. "You tell me. Once I sell Granddad's house and we're married . . . a change might make sense for all of us. You do an amazing job monitoring Nini, but you're constantly worried you're on borrowed time with her." Lark could tell he was choosing his words carefully. She constantly worried about a lot of things, including being judged by people who thought Nini's "borrowed time" was already up. Nini's doctors were adamant that mild cognitive impairment was *not yet* dementia. In fact, studies showed spending time with a child would help keep her sharp, doing both Nini and Lark more good than harm. The key was for Nini to keep her screening appointments, and for Lark to watch for signs of decline. Stay on it.

Lark had an elaborate system. She wasn't just on it, she was all over it.

But she was hyperaware nobody else could know that from the outside looking in.

"True," Lark said. "But I'm not sure we need a plan B yet."

"No," he agreed. "If we had one before we need one, though, I think you'd worry less. Say I do switch to days when I move in. You could handle mornings at home. After school would be our family time, all of us together through dinner, and then I'd be home nights. We'd have it all covered."

Family time. The words warmed Lark. Creating a plan B before she needed it was, frankly, a luxury she'd never been able to afford. The idea that someone cared about her worrying less, enough to actually do something to help . . . This was more than a luxury. It was a dream. Heath's granddad's house was all but condemned; it wasn't an option to live there, and they didn't expect to get much for it. But once they'd combined expenses, she could stop worrying that Nini or Dove would bankrupt her with a broken hip or a high fever that landed one of them in the hospital.

Heath was a creature of habit, though. She'd never once heard him complain about working nights. He had a system, too, which was part of what made them work: they understood each other.

"But you hate mornings," she pointed out. "Even on your days off."

"But I love you," he said, like it was that simple. "I know it's not something we've talked about, but if I want dibs before the cubs all get assigned, I have to decide fast. Think on it, okay?"

She nodded, and he wrapped her into a long hug right there where everyone could see, a very un-trooper-like thing to do. Lark found herself blinking back grateful tears. Who *was* she? After years of stoic determination, of being the woman who never let anyone see her cry, she'd spent the past two weeks easily and often reduced to a puddle. When Heath had gotten down on one knee and asked if she'd have him, if she'd let him devote the rest of his years to her and everything that came with her, Lark had cried so hard she could barely speak.

Then, like the dolt she was, she'd asked if he was sure.

It was one thing—one *enormous* thing—for Heath to sign on to raise her daughter as his own, though Lark knew he loved Dove already. But it was quite another thing to assume responsibility for her long-gone best friend's grandma. Lark had already accepted how unlikely it was that anyone would sign up for that. It was part of the acceptance phase trade-off.

"What a question," Heath had said, so kindly that Lark blubbered harder. "What about me right now seems unsure?"

Nothing did. That was just it. It barely made sense. "I love that you see me as a package deal," Lark told him, wiping at her cheeks. She had to speak clearly. To be *heard* clearly. "But this package, it's a lot. I don't want you to get all the way in and realize . . . I'd hate for you to be thinking all of this has to become your problem . . ."

"It'll never be my problem," he said. "If you say yes, it'll be my *privilege.*"

That's when she'd heard Mikki's voice chime in. The way she always used to. The way she rarely did anymore. *Lark, look at this man. Listen to his beautiful words! Say yes, already. That's the rule.*

Now here he was, making good on everything he'd said within a matter of weeks. Lark had a fleeting thought that, as much as she'd always wanted that white dress, she'd just as soon make it official right here in the parking lot. Why not? She'd marry him yesterday, follow him into tomorrow. It wouldn't matter who took what shift or how they shared the load, only that she had a good, caring person to share it with. Not just the load but her life.

For the first time since Mikki.

Lark pulled back from the hug and smiled up at him ruefully. "If Nini ever caught on that we were conspiring to babysit her, she'd hate it," she said.

"What's the difference," he said cheerily. "Nini hates everything."

～～

Inside, Lark nodded to Sergio and his surlier counterpart Cam, both of whom were with customers, and headed for the back office, where she spent most of her working hours now that she'd been promoted to night manager. Pete said she had a knack for handling vendor orders and putting out fires he was too busy to deal with during the day, but it was obvious her job consisted of stuff he didn't want to do, which was fine by her. All she cared about was the pay raise that came with it. And even if her staff was a little rough around the edges, she'd earned their respect. They thought it was gritty and tough that she was the only manager who'd ever opt to refill the squeegee stations in the rain instead of lending a hand at the register. They didn't need to know the real reason was she didn't like being in the exact spot where she'd stood the night Mikki walked away, the only place where she'd still catch herself staring at the door.

It wasn't like Lark actually expected Mikki to magically reappear. Even if Lark hadn't entirely given her up for dead like everybody else seemed to, she *had* given up on the idea of her coming back. The Travel Stop still stocked the "Mikki Stickies" bumper stickers she'd printed with the leftover "Find Mikki" funds, but only because she'd ordered too many. The stickers bore the last words Mikki had said to her—Catch You Later—with their exit number in a retro Route 66–style design. But even those had lost meaning, the old inside joke that all her Mikki-isms belonged on a bumper sticker. The idea that Mikki would see one out on the road one day and recognize the signal that she was wanted and forgiven back home.

These days, watching the door was more of a muscle memory, a reflex. Even if Mikki's presumed death was ever confirmed, Lark knew she'd keep on looking. It was *that* hopelessly, senselessly ingrained.

But Lark was determined to leave hopeless and senseless behind her. Most nights, she hid at her desk, catching up on admin for a few hours, then went out to see how she could pitch in.

So it was tonight. She was embroiled in a lengthy email exchange about their soft-serve machine breaking yet again. An hour flew by as she worked through the messages waiting in her inbox, then another lost to inventory spreadsheets. The computer's desktop was set up to show the footage from the security cameras running in the background, a grid monitoring the Travel Stop from various angles, so she could keep an eye on things. It was a slow night: every time she minimized her Excel file for a cursory check, she saw the guys just lazing around. She was trying to think up a task to give them—as soon as she finished reconciling Pete's delayed candy shipment—when Sergio knocked on the office door.

"Boss? There's some guy here asking for you."

She didn't look up. "What guy?"

"Dunno. Never seen him before."

"Okay, let me finish this before I lose my place. Tell him to take a seat; I'll be out."

She checked her math and saved her file, glancing at the video feed to see if she recognized whoever had asked for her. She didn't see anyone sitting in the café booths, but a man at the self-serve counter was pouring coffee into a cup meant for fountain drinks.

She squinted at him, already half out of her chair.

Then she dropped back into it. Looking again.

It couldn't be.

Lark's heart began to race, her breath catching in her throat. She enlarged the feed's fish-eye view of the inside of the store, garish in the fluorescent lighting.

The man stood surveying the surroundings like he wasn't really interested in the coffee. His expression looked almost too friendly, almost too familiar.

Just like the last time she'd seen it.

The only other time, until now.

She seized the laptop with both hands, face inches from the screen. She had to be sure. Couldn't risk being wrong about something like this. Not ever, but especially not now.

Not when she'd finally stopped being the Lark who was barely holding it together.

Her palm was sweaty as she reached for her phone, clutching it to her chest. She kept to the shadows as she inched toward the STAFF ONLY doorway, where she'd have a clear view into the store with no camera lens between her and her mark.

She had him in her crosshairs now, clear enough to confirm.

Any lingering doubt disappeared. It was the man who'd driven off with Mikki.

It was impossibly, finally him.

With shaking fingers, she dialed the dispatch number she knew by heart.

Then she threw up, right there in the hall.

4

Mikki

They'd driven only about ten miles, but it was plenty far for Mikki to be rethinking the impulsiveness of her decision. And plenty close for it to feel reversible.

Only ten miles from Lark. Only ten miles from home. Only ten miles from the phone she'd left on the living room table, tonight of all nights.

She'd forgotten all about it until Lark had reminded her. *This isn't like all those other times you've said yes on a whim, Mikki. I can't go along.* But by the time Lark had started making a scene over her phone, Mikki had been pulsing with anxious energy—Lark red-faced in the garish lighting, Chris patient in the car, Mikki more and more annoyed by Lark's resistance to the very rules she'd helped create. Mikki wouldn't back down over a technicality.

She was used to having a phone, yes. It was a nice safety net, yes. But that was not the same as *needing* it. In fact, she'd always relished the freedom of those childhood summer weekends when her mom had driven them out to join friends set up at some campground. Back then, it wasn't a worry that no one could reach you; it was the whole point.

Did it even count as a vacation if you remained tethered to everyone and everything back home? Mikki wasn't going out of her way to spend her one and only beach trip obligated to check in like a teen on curfew.

It's better this way, she told Lark. *It'll force me to live in the moment.*

But as the miles ticked by, she was more than in the moment. She was, in every second, being carried away toward the unknown, by the unknown. Did she truly want to be? She could ask Chris to pull over and let her out. Unless he was a psycho, of course. In which case she was already trapped. She tried not to picture him cackling and engaging the childproof door locks.

"It's a little late to be asking this," Mikki said, "but what happens if you don't like me?"

"I'll take my chances," Chris said, sounding as relaxed and polite as he'd been in the store.

Mikki poked her fingers through the inch of open air at the top of her window, like the molecules might bond her to something outside this car. Chris hadn't exaggerated about the broken air-conditioning: it had felt too stuffy with the windows closed, but now it was hard to have a casual conversation over the rush of air.

"I'm putting a lot of trust in you, you know," she chided, half-teasing. Mikki trusted only one person, and she'd just left her standing, bewildered, under the brash lights of the Travel Stop. Mikki had tried not to look back, but she couldn't help it.

"Likewise." Chris tilted his iced coffee, almost empty, and his profile lit briefly in the headlights of a passing car. If he was having second thoughts of his own, they didn't show.

He glanced over, met her eyes. Registered her anxiety.

"What if we get it out of the way?" he suggested. "Disclose our most unlikable qualities up front. You tell me yours; I'll tell you mine."

"What could possibly go wrong," Mikki quipped.

"Come on," he said. "Everybody has something. For starters, obviously I'm hard up for a wedding date. So whatever you say is unlikely to change my mind."

She laughed, despite herself. "Okay. The most unlikable thing about me, at this moment?" She wondered what he expected to hear. Some personality trait—being clingy or needy? (She wasn't.) Some physical quirk, like snoring? (She didn't.) The only thing that came to mind was the truth. Was she really going to answer honestly?

Apparently she was.

She took a deep breath. "My best friend is pregnant, and I'm kind of mad at her for it."

He glanced over again, looking interested. "Why's that?"

"Well, when a man and a woman are attracted to each other . . ."

"Ha. I mean, why are you mad?"

Mikki shook her head. Now that she'd said it aloud, it seemed truer. Maybe if she could find the words to explain it, she could make peace with it too.

"I know it's not about me, but it affects me, and it's the result of some unstellar decision-making on her part. Even though, improbably, she's happy about it, which should make me happy for her, but I'm not there yet. So yeah. I've never admitted it before, and I'll deny it if you tell her, but I'm mad. At least, I'm disappointed. But I'm trying really hard not to be."

Chris shook his head. "You monster," he said. "And you're trying *not* to be? Disgraceful."

He clearly thought it was nothing. Like when an employer asks what your weakness is in a job interview, and you say you're "too much of a perfectionist." But Chris was wrong. Feeling resentment toward Lark, of all people, wasn't nothing.

It was everything.

"Her name is Lark—she's the one who rang up your coffee. And when she didn't want me to leave with you, I blew her off." Still, Chris didn't react. "I'm being selfish," she clarified. "Maybe, partially, because I'm secretly mad."

He nodded, signaling before pulling into the passing lane to get around a sluggish RV. Flashy car notwithstanding, he seemed like a careful driver. "Selfish," he repeated thoughtfully. "I see that. I mean, listen to you, already worrying this resentment will come between you two, even though, if she just found out she's pregnant, you have plenty of time to work through your feelings before the baby arrives. And maybe a few days of distance is actually a good way to do that. Very selfish. Also, worrying *I* won't like *you*, instead of the other way around. Self. Ish."

He shot her a very likable look then.

She couldn't help smiling. "Glad that's out of the way. Your turn. Most unlikable thing about you. Go."

He nodded solemnly. "If we must. I'm a piner."

"A what?"

"I pine over things. I drive myself and everyone around me crazy with my inability to let go. For example, I have more than one ex-girlfriend I'm not over, which, yes, I know how contradictory and hypocritical that sounds."

"So . . . you're a romantic? Every girl might be the one who got away?" He shrugged. "Does this have to do with those routes you mapped out but never took?"

"Yes and no. There was the marrying Julia route, which my mom called 'irresponsible, if not impossible.' That's the real common thread: the routes aren't all women, but they're all things my family talked me out of."

"Like what else?"

"Well, the liberal arts route, which my dad called 'a waste of my marketable skills' and 'a snub to his legacy.' Although now that his legacy really is . . ." He cleared his throat. "Now that he and my mom are gone, I understand more where he was coming from. The route I'm really stuck pining after is the digital nomad route. You know, where you have a job you can do remotely and forgo a permanent address? Live in one country six months, then three months somewhere else, immersing yourself in the world one city at a time? I really could've done that."

"What did they say was wrong with that?"

"Obviously it would have made me a drifter. The men in my family do not drift. They pick a direction—or one is chosen for them—and stay the course."

Mikki half smiled. "All the way to Florida, broken air-conditioning be damned?"

"Exactly."

"Well, you detoured to get me."

"I did, didn't I? Look at us, drifting."

They exchanged a smile and fell into silence for a few miles. Or a few moments. Time and distance melded together, rolling on this way.

"Sorry about your parents," Mikki ventured. "I'm not sure grieving counts as pining, for what it's worth."

Chris nodded. "Well, my brother and sister would make a distinction. They're grieving. I'm pining. Maybe because I was on shakier ground with the family in the first place. Losing both our parents was bad enough, but it's not just that. We've lost . . ." He caught himself, and Mikki took note there was something he wasn't ready to share. "We've lost a lot," he picked up, clearing his throat. "You'd think it all might have brought my siblings and me closer, but instead, there's this rift over our family business. We've inherited a lot of responsibility, and we can't agree on where to go from here. You hear about families torn apart over wills and estates, and you think it's privilege at its most disgusting, and then it happens to you. They say business isn't personal, but ours is. Fast-forward one miserable year I won't get into, and we're still at a stalemate. My brother is drunk and depressed, my sister is in full Type A mode, and I'm avoiding everyone."

Again, he seemed to catch himself, as if he'd said more than he intended—though he was being so vague, all Mikki could discern was that some tragedy had occurred. And tragedy, she could usually spot a mile away. Except with Chris, she hadn't spotted it until she got in his car.

Maybe that was what privilege really afforded you: a veneer. Tinted windows. Photo retouching. So you had to look closer to see what was beneath, unlike Mikki, who had nothing to hide her mess behind.

"So," he went on, "I pine. For the way things were and how we'll never get that back. They call it survivor's guilt, but survivor's torture is more like it. And unlike you, I'm not trying to stop. The worse it gets, the more I lean into it, like maybe the answer is to pine harder. To pine all the way."

He sighed, frowning. Only then did she know for sure that his breathless, wildly improbable, self-aware monologue was entirely sincere.

Okay. So she'd had this guy pegged wrong. Broken air-conditioning in a luxury car was not his biggest problem after all.

"You monster," she said finally, echoing his response. He glanced over at her, clearly expecting something different, and she rolled her eyes for effect. "Pining *all the way*," she said. "How do you sleep at night."

"I don't," he deadpanned. "Piners are terrible sleepers. They're more inclined to call you at three in the morning to see if you're pining too."

"Perfect," she said. "I get off work at three. Call anytime."

His smile turned more genuine, and right then she decided: no more second-guessing. She didn't know what to make of Chris Redmond, but she felt some connection between them, against the odds—the kind that's tough to fake. It wasn't necessarily chemistry . . . She didn't know what it might turn into. But no sense in ruining it by doubting herself, or him.

Besides, he'd made an insightful point about some distance being good for her and Lark. He made it sound natural and healthy, not knowing their idea of taking a break from each other was spending an hour apart running errands. *Of course* Mikki hadn't had a chance to work through her feelings about Lark's pregnancy. Lark was always right there, needing her to be supportive.

Which Mikki would be. As soon as she got home.

For now, for the first time, it was okay to be disappointed. Chris was the only one to see it, and he wasn't holding it against her. Getting this most unlikable thing out of the way hadn't been such a bad idea.

"So," she said, changing the subject. "This is your dream car, huh? I've never been in one before."

"Was," he grumbled. "Was my dream car."

"You're forsaking your love just because of the AC?"

He laughed. "Not quite. It's a long story."

She reclined her seat at an angle, crossing her ankles. "Good," she said. "We have a long stretch of time to fill."

5

Lark

Lark hugged the cinder block wall, grounding herself in the cool touch of the glossy, painted stone. In something solid and immovable that was right where it was supposed to be.

She felt as if she were hovering over her body, watching in horror and fascination.

Was this happening? Was it real?

For all the thousands of times she'd imagined Mikki strolling back through the door, she'd never once thought to picture this man daring to reappear—because those odds had been much closer to zero. It was far easier to accept that she'd never see him again.

She had to go out there.

There was no telling how long it would take law enforcement to arrive. She'd called the highway patrol because they always came fastest. And they knew her. They wouldn't let him get away. *We're proactive,* Heath always said whenever anyone tried to reduce him to a traffic cop. Troopers lived in a state of being ready for anything; more often than not, they intervened unbidden, intercepting a staggering volume of criminal activity that had nothing to do with traffic offenses.

Deputies are reactive. They came when you called, but the county sheriff was twenty miles away. They'd show up eventually—Would they still even have her original missing person report on file?—but for now, she needed a first responder.

The dispatcher clearly hadn't known what to make of Lark's call. *You've got eyes on a suspect? In a missing person case?* Lark had spoken firmly, with purpose, but the dispatcher was breaking it down into questions, as if giving Lark a chance to change her mind. When Lark had hissed to please just hurry, the dispatcher had turned stern, admonishing her to under no circumstances approach the suspect.

Fat chance of obeying those instructions. They'd been read off a script that had nothing to do with Lark and what she was up against, what she'd been through.

After hanging up, she called Heath and got voicemail.

That settled it. Lark would do more than approach. He'd asked for her, after all. She'd get him talking. Keep him talking. She'd do whatever she had to do so he didn't leave.

She watched him sip iced coffee from their largest cup, like he had on the night Lark could never forget.

Why could he possibly be here?

Only one way to find out. She looked harder at him, committing him to memory, in case things went sideways. He was much tanner than she remembered—far too tan for the Midwest in March. And that moneyed look about him was gone. So, too, was the look of exhaustion that had seemed so disarming. He looked more like someone who'd been on vacation for years. Refreshed. Suddenly, she fought the furious urge to rush at him, to scream. *How dare he, how dare he, how dare he?*

In an alternate universe where she did not have a child and a fiancé and a future urging caution and restraint, this was the moment she would jump on his back and claw out his eyes, like a woman possessed. Like the rabid animal he'd turned her into when he took away the only person, *her* person, who'd kept her together.

In this universe, she steeled herself, straightened the name tag pinned to her button-down, and marched right up to him, unable to wait a second longer. She saw the recognition on his face: He remembered her too—of course he did. Sergio said he'd asked for her. Yet before, he'd only spoken to Mikki. That night. *The* night.

Maybe this *was* a mistake. Lark would be powerless if he changed his mind and decided to bolt. She'd be made infamous all over again by her complete ineptitude.

But he didn't bolt. Instead, he did the most inexplicable, nonsensical thing of all.

He smiled.

"I can't believe it," he said. "You're really still here. Lark, right?"

Her mouth fell open, but no sound came out. Lark's body started to tremble, with rage or fear, she didn't know. She felt both and neither, excitement and hope and utter confusion. She listened for that faint voice that sometimes whispered what Mikki would say, making her feel so sure, for a passing instant, that her friend was still out there, thinking of her. But now, she didn't hear or feel or sense Mikki at all. Only her own disbelief on repeat.

How was this happening? Why?

"Lark, right?" he repeated, and she crossed her arms over her chest with a nod. His grin widened. If he registered her shock, he was reading it wrong.

"I knew this was the same travel stop; I knew it," he said, as much to himself as to her. "I wasn't sure of the exit number, but as soon as I saw it . . ." He cleared his throat, ran a hand through his hair. "I know the odds are slim, but I have to ask. I don't suppose Mikki's around?"

Lark's heart pounded in her ears, drowning out the radio, the chatter, the hum of the refrigerator case. Dark splotches clouded her peripheral vision, until all she could see was the man standing in front of her, and the world around them fell away.

She still didn't understand why he was here.

But she knew he was a liar. The worst kind of thief, cheat, criminal. And he was going to pay.

6

Mikki

"Hang on," Mikki told Chris. "Let me make sure I have this right." She found it perplexing just how much she was enjoying this story that, under other circumstances, might have made her want to punch someone in the face. "You're thirty-five," she confirmed.

"Correct."

"Yet this is your first car that wasn't a hand-me-down? Your whole life, you've been driving your parents' luxury sloppy seconds that were always showroom quality but not your choice of make and model?" Mikki said this as neutrally as she could for someone who paid hard-earned money for decidedly unluxurious, secondhand clothes, home goods, purses, even shoes. And whose own car broke down on a quarterly basis.

"Correct." To his credit, Chris seemed to understand his punchability in this moment. Unless she imagined it, he actually ducked a little.

"I still don't get why," she persisted. "I mean, if you didn't like those cars, even though they were obviously very nice, why not say no thanks and buy your own?"

He cleared his throat. "I believe one thing that unites all Midwesterners—regardless of tax bracket—is that we are, for better or worse, duty bound to drive any automobile as long as possible, testing the extent of its roadworthy life as a point of pride."

Mikki had to laugh. In Becksville, nothing got you bragging rights like hitting two hundred thousand miles on an odometer, even if it was attached to an indistinguishable frame of rust. And in the college town where her mom used to work, student lots were full of beige Lexus sedans the tuition-paying parents had obviously bored of driving, cars far nicer than any teenager needed, much less appreciated.

Besides, Chris had lost his parents—recently, from the sounds of things. She wasn't about to take issue with the fact that they'd been generous with their offspring.

"You know what?" she said. "That actually does track."

Chris nodded. "Natural as saying 'Ope!' when you bump into someone at the grocery."

"You betcha." Mikki giggled. Although again, that nervous feeling nagged at her. That he was exactly the sort of easy-to-talk-to man she shouldn't have accepted a ride from. The kind whose neighbors shook their heads on the news as bodies were exhumed from his backyard, saying, *He seemed so normal.* Mikki pushed the thought away. "Okay. So while doing your Midwestern duty of driving all those beautiful automobiles that were not to your personal taste, you got to coveting this specific one."

He assumed an exaggerated dreamy expression. "The BMW 4 series, 440i xDrive sport convertible. But I still take my Midwestern duty seriously, so I couldn't buy a new one. I needed a unicorn: low mileage, extended factory warranty. Plus, I wanted mineral-gray metallic, with the premium packages. I mean, check out the head-up display."

He hit a button, and the GPS navigation appeared on the windshield, like a hologram glowing over the dark road. Mikki had never seen such a thing. "Very Batmobile."

"I won't bore you with the tour of the features, but you get the picture. I couldn't believe it when this car came up on Autotrader. I kept rereading the listing, looking for the catch. But I didn't see one. I was so optimistic, I took an Uber an hour away to meet the guy for the test drive. At first, I didn't regret it. One look and I was sold. He owned it outright, and I was paying in full, so we went right then to transfer the title. That's when the trouble started."

"What trouble?"

"First, we'd forgotten it was Sunday. We found a bank at a grocery store that posted afternoon hours, so we went there for a notary, but they were closed."

"And you're stuck an hour from home with no way back and don't want to make the round trip again?"

"Exactly, and neither does he. He lives an hour in the other direction, and his wife is already on her way to get him."

"So what did you do?"

"I told him my buddy was a notary, and if he wanted to fill out his half of the title, I could take care of the rest."

"He trusted you to do that?"

"He was super cool about it, actually. Said he'd leave the purchase price blank so I could write down whatever I felt like paying taxes on. And then we shook on it, I paid, and his wife pulled up to the curb to give him a ride home."

"I'm still not seeing the issue."

"Neither did I, until I saw her."

"The wife?"

"The wife. Otherwise known as my ex."

"Oh, no. Not the one you've been pining for? I mean, one of the ones?"

"*The* one. As in, I can't even sit in this car without picturing her in it. With *him*."

Mikki pulled a face. She pictured her own ex, whose texts she'd been ignoring all day until they'd prompted her to up and leave her phone at home. Mikki's romantic track record resembled a flat line on a heart monitor, each relationship persisting with hopeless urgency until someone called the time of death. Ted was a nice, aptly named teddy bear of a guy; it wasn't his fault she couldn't seem to conjure much more than ambivalence toward any man who felt at home in Becksville. Ted worked the front office of the motel behind the Travel Stop, and she could always tell he was on duty by scanning the lot for his Silverado. Funny how closely you came to associate people with their cars. She'd never see *any* blue Chevy truck without thinking of him. It was a nice truck and all, but if she won the same model in those prize drawings at the mall, let alone the exact one he'd been driving? No, thanks.

"At least they're grown-ups?" she reasoned. "I'm sure it's not like they were getting busy in the back seat."

"For the love of BMW, Mikki, can you *un*say that? Not helpful."

"Sorry." She couldn't resist. "At most," she added, "they probably just held hands across the front, right here." She gestured toward the gearshift and cupholders between them. He shivered visibly, but his mouth twitched toward a smile. She decided to risk it. "I mean, I suppose they probably kissed in here at least a few times . . ."

"Stop this instant," he said, but he was smiling for real now.

"You don't think he would have proposed in this car, do you? I mean, it *is* a very nice ride. Makes a certain promise of the kind of life you're signing up for." She ran her hand admiringly over the dash. "I must admit, it helped me decide to come along with you. Do you ever wonder . . . if you'd had this car back when you were dating her . . ."

He burst out laughing. "Well, we've established you can narrate my innermost thoughts with surprising accuracy. You are now caught up on the first several hours of this drive, up until we met. So you can stop the recap if you don't mind."

"Wow. I see what you meant about the universe having fun at your expense."

"I never overpromise," he said cheerily. "Underpromise, overdeliver; that's my motto."

"So I, uh, guess you don't want the car anymore?"

"I cannot get rid of this car fast enough," he confirmed.

"When *was* all this?"

"Yesterday."

"No."

"Yes. I don't even want to bother with the title transfer now. Or the registration. Total waste of time when I'm not going to keep it. But I had an impatient buyer lined up for my old car, and I didn't want to back out and screw him over too. So here we are."

"Which is why your license plate is propped inside the back windshield?"

He shrugged. "It's temporary, right? Figured I'd try to get by with my old tags until I sort this mess out."

"At the very least, you should bolt that on. You could get pulled over."

"I'll risk it."

She gritted her teeth. Spoken like a cis white guy who can afford a ticket. "Won't you take a loss if you resell right away?"

"It'll be worth every penny. Anyway, I need to get through this wedding before I have time to deal with it. And I need to get there, obviously. So."

So, indeed. Mikki's grasp on the situation clicked into place.

"That's part of why you invited me, isn't it? You didn't want to ride alone in here."

That smile again—a little shy, a little guilty. "It was too quiet. Too easy to picture her in the passenger seat, rubbing it in mercilessly. Which I felt sure *you* would never do."

Mikki pulled a face. "Sorry! Low-hanging fruit."

"Yeah, yeah."

"I thought it might be one of those things you have to laugh about to get through."

"You thought right," he said more quietly. "Thanks again, by the way. For coming along." He looked at her again, a little longer this time, and Mikki felt herself blush. Usually people only *really* looked at Mikki if they were trying to place her. Strangers were always saying she reminded them of someone, but they'd give up trying to figure out who. *You just have one of those faces, I guess.* Mikki thought that summed things up: she was indeed almost someone.

"I still can't believe I talked you into this," Chris added. "But I'm glad I did."

Mikki found herself smiling back. Chris was easy to find endearing, even charming, between his self-deprecating stories and his *why not* attitude. Coincidentally, he used the same two coping mechanisms that had kept her going all these years since her college plans hadn't panned out. It was reassuring, in a way, knowing she could still relate to someone so different from her. Her disappointments had not *completely* transformed her into a bitter shrew after all.

To the contrary, and against the odds, she and Chris had a vibe—she just couldn't put her finger yet on what kind.

But she didn't need to. They had plenty of time to figure it out . . . and no time to get attached. Because this trip was only going to end one way: with her right back where she started.

Stay in the moment, she reminded herself. And this time, it didn't feel quite as scary.

She wanted to remember every second of this. It was going to have to last her.

7

Lark

2024

Lark looked the man in the eye for the first time since she'd rung up his iced coffee a whole lifetime ago, mere steps from where they stood now—a memory she'd recounted so many times it no longer seemed real.

He paid cash, didn't say much. Then I saw that Mikki was holding her apron. She looked kind of manic with excitement, like a kid who's discovered a new toy she has *to have.*

That's when I started getting this terrible feeling.

Facing him now, Lark swayed a little, waiting for the dizziness to pass, until the sights and sounds of the Travel Stop returned to full color and volume around her, grounding her back in this place she'd never left. He'd trapped her here, was what he'd done. He might as well have chained her to the counter.

Now, he wanted to know if Mikki was *around*.

"The last time I saw Mikki," she said evenly, "she was leaving with you."

She registered his surprise, then confusion. He squinted as if trying to remember the name of some obscure movie. For a blistering instant, she thought he might deny Mikki had ever left with him. *I don't know what you're talking about,* she braced for him to say, even though he knew exactly. He was the *only* one who knew exactly.

When Mikki had first said she was "tagging along to a wedding in Florida," Lark thought she was kidding. Then, of course, she'd immediately tried to talk her out of it.

"Mikki," Lark had said, reasonably. "You know nothing about this guy. Just because he drives a nice car does not mean he isn't bad news."

"You know I read people pretty well. Plus, he has a sister."

"There are lots of creeps with sisters." She grappled for someone Mikki hated. "Chad has a sister."

"What I mean is, he seems respectful. Besides, what about our rules? Saying yes, looking for the ride . . . You used to hold them sacred."

"I hold you sacred," Lark had countered, tears stinging her eyes. Damn pregnancy hormones. All she could think was that she couldn't let this happen. It was all she could do not to say, But what about me? *She wasn't jealous, exactly . . . or was she? She didn't want to go. But she didn't want to be left behind.*

And just like that, she'd understood where Mikki was coming from. Why she had this now-or-never look. Soon, Lark would be venturing into the unknown herself—motherhood and all that came with it. And Mikki was too good a friend not to stick with her.

"Lark," Mikki had said evenly, "what I'm about to say . . . Promise not to read judgment into this, okay?"

Lark had nodded, suddenly nervous, her emotions swirling too fast to get ahold of.

"I need this," Mikki said softly. "Please."

This had become Lark's defense for "letting" Mikki go. First with the police, and later in the court of public opinion, neither of which looked upon her favorably. *She said she needed to go. She begged. How could I stop her?*

It was the scene she could still imagine people trying to piece together. *At the very least,* she'd heard them whisper, *she could have gotten the driver's name and number. Or found out what resort or even what town they were headed to, literally anything more specific than "Florida" and "wedding" and "ocean." Or bothered to notice the car had no license plate. I heard she didn't even check that her friend had her cell phone.*

Never mind that, among other things, she *had* asked Mikki for specifics, and Mikki had rebutted her like she was a helicopter parent. Lark never corrected any of the rumors because the truth would have sounded worse. She was still waiting for people to forget. Mercifully, it was starting to happen. A few of her newer staffers didn't even seem to know about Mikki. They didn't speculate or look at her sideways or even ask about the bumper stickers on the counter.

Now, this . . . The driver reappearing out of nowhere, the police on the way, and whatever came next . . .

It was going to change everything.

"Are you saying," the guy asked slowly, "you haven't seen Mikki for over seven years?"

Lark clenched her fists. "That's exactly what I'm saying," she snapped. "When is the last time *you* saw her?"

To his credit, he looked so thrown off by this information that he hadn't yet considered how it might implicate him. "Um. Four or five days after you did? We spent the weekend at the wedding, and then she planned to drive back here in a rental car. The concierge had arranged it. We said goodbye at the hotel."

Rental car? *Concierge?* They couldn't be talking about the same Mikki. "I thought you were supposed to drive her back?"

"I was. But I sold my car."

"You *what?*"

"Long story. But she was fully on board. We parted ways on good terms." Seeing her recoil, he rushed on. "She was excited to get back to you. I can't believe she would've done anything but come straight home."

Lark had waited all this time for someone, anyone, other than her to echo these words.

I can't believe she would've done anything but come straight home.

But hearing the words from the last person to see her? It was the opposite of comforting.

"She didn't even have her phone," Lark protested. "You let a woman drive hundreds of miles alone, with no way to check on her?" She flung out all the accusations that had ever been hurled in her direction. Hitting their proper target at last.

He lifted his hands. "Hey. I only spent a few days with her, but I don't think anyone ever *let* Mikki do anything."

Lark wanted to laugh. Those words had also been her own defense, verbatim.

But this was something else.

"You drove her all the way down the East Coast and abandoned her? You set the scene for her to vanish—no, for both of you to vanish without a trace. You didn't even have tags on your car." The more Lark talked, the harder it was to control her volume. "You hid your face beneath a hat when you came in, and no matter how many times that surveillance photo was shared online, nobody could ID you. It was like neither of you ever existed. Don't you dare pin that on Mikki being headstrong. You expect me to believe your whole shady setup happened by accident?"

"Surveillance photo?" he stammered, going pale. Sergio and Cam were openly staring now, the few customers in the aisles craning their necks to see.

"Look," he said, "I have nothing to hide. Starting with my name. I'm Chris Redmond. Maybe we could go somewhere, sit down, and I can explain . . ."

Chris Redmond. It was strange, putting an ordinary name to such an extraordinary dread.

"You're crazy if you think I'm going anywhere with you," Lark said coldly. "But you got the last part right. You're definitely going to explain."

The chimes sounded on the door, and a pair of uniformed troopers entered, hands on their holsters, looking around uncertainly.

Lark raised her hand like a kid in class and met Chris's eyes defiantly. "I'm not the only one with a lot of questions for you."

8

Mikki

2016

"Are you sure you won't let me find you a mall?" Chris looked dubiously at the red and white bull's-eye sign above them. "Nice of you to be low maintenance, but there's no need."

They were walking laps around a Target parking lot just across the South Carolina state line, stretching their legs and waiting for the store to open. After driving all night, they'd pit-stopped fifteen minutes too early. But for Mikki, it felt right on time. This wasn't just an errand; it was a milestone. Never before had she felt this Carolina sunshine on her skin. Never before had she tipped her face back to drink in this Carolina sky, animated by this Carolina breeze. Moments ago, as they'd zipped past the Welcome Center, she'd gawked at the rows of palmetto trees. Not plastic props for some tacky tiki party, but real-life palms. *Real life.*

Now, out of the car, she marveled that the highway noise was the same backdrop she was used to, yet it no longer sounded like being left behind. Months from now, on a lonely day back home, she'd close her eyes and tune in to this soundtrack, comforted by the memory of this far-away morning filled with possibility. If any arbitrary halfway point could sound so familiar, maybe all those halfways were connected in other ways, too, leading somewhere after all.

"I can get what I need way faster here than at a mall," Mikki told Chris. She used to make exactly two annual mall trips with her mom—for holiday shopping and back-to-school sales—and it was never the fun treat it was meant to be, watching her mom sweat the price tags even for items on clearance.

Chris still looked skeptical.

"Seriously," she said. "Think how many different things I'll need to get." She began reciting aloud the list she'd mentally compiled as he drove. "Swimsuit, makeup, sandals, basics like underwear . . . Even a duffel bag to put it all in." She felt her face color, maddeningly. What was she embarrassed about? No one could last four days without *underwear*. Plus, he'd offered. But it was impossible not to feel like a freeloader when she couldn't buy any of it on her own.

"Okay," Chris relented. "It's a beach wedding, so *maybe* you could get away with sundresses? You'll need nice outfits for the welcome reception, rehearsal, ceremony, and day-after party. I should warn you, this crowd—they're the type to show up in stilettos and act surprised no one paved the sand for them."

So he had thought about it. He'd also found the gentlest way to hint a big box store might not pass for high class. Mikki was reminded of her teenage August afternoons munching soft pretzels by the fountain in the food court, convincing her mom she didn't care about name brands splashed across her clothes. The difference was, now she meant it. Plus, the idea of being unleashed in Target with actual spending money really did fill her with giddiness.

"Do not underestimate my ability to make Target work for *any* occasion. Even faux designer wedding attire. Plus, while I'm trying stuff on, you can get a screwdriver to attach your license plate."

Mercifully, Chris let her change the subject. "Again with the license plate. All those troopers coming through the Travel Stop must have rubbed off on you."

"Aren't you even a little worried that the car might look stolen? Or that your name isn't on the title? If you put the top down, there won't even be a back windshield to prop the license plate in."

"It's nothing that couldn't be straightened out with a phone call."

"Oh, yeah?" she challenged. "What if, as soon as you drove away, your ex said to her husband, *Do you realize who that was?* What if he regretted selling you the car as much as you regretted buying it? He had fond memories of his BMW, and now it belongs to someone who used to screw his wife. So when he gets the call, he says, *Gosh, Officer, that so-called sale wasn't notarized, never happened, but that name sounds familiar . . . I think this man may be obsessed with the woman I married. Word on the street is, he's pining.*"

Chris howled. "That's quite a reach," he said. "You win. I'll buy a screwdriver."

"Why, thank you."

"Hey," he said, more quietly. "Whatever you want to wear is fine with me. I just don't want you to think I don't find you worthy of better than Target. That's all."

Mikki was oddly moved, but her "Travel-Stop tough" was one of the only things going for her. "I appreciate that, but I worship Target without shame. Besides, if none of the other guests would set foot here, they'll never recognize where my dazzling ensembles came from."

They were lapping the front of the store, and he nodded at the café sign. "When your house of worship opens, I'll grab us breakfast. Meet me there when you're done."

"Perfect." She glanced at her watch. They still had a few minutes to burn, so they rounded the corner for another lap.

"So. How long have you worked at the Travel Stop?"

"Too long."

"Yeah? Thinking of moving on?"

The only thing worse than people thinking Mikki couldn't do better than the Travel Stop was people thinking she didn't want to.

"If thinking about it could move me on, I wouldn't still be there."

"Where would you be?"

She shrugged. "I'd have gone to college, for one thing."

"Why didn't you?"

The sound of their sneakers on the pavement turned awkward. And he didn't deserve awkward. He was trying to be friendly. "Honestly? I just don't like talking about this—or anything else to do with my mom."

"I get it. I don't like talking about what happened to my parents either." He didn't point out that he *had* talked about it, albeit in vague terms. But he didn't have to.

"It's not like that," she said. "I just don't want you to think less of me."

He shook his head. "I of all people would not judge you by your parents."

"You would, though. It would be in the back of your mind, and . . . Can we just not?"

He snapped his fingers. "She was a carjacker, wasn't she? She forced you into child labor, unscrewing license plates. This explains everything."

Mikki couldn't bring herself to laugh. If he knew the real story, he wouldn't have made the joke. "Look," she said. "I don't expect you to understand how I came to be wasting my life on night shift. I'm sure you're wondering why I don't quit my dead-end job, get out of my dead-end town, and work up to something better. But take my word for it that it's not that simple."

"You're right. None of my business. I'm sorry." They'd reached the end of the parking lot, and he pointed to the storefront as they circled back. "Go-time anyway. It's eight o'clock." He pulled his wallet from his pocket and right there, conspicuously alone in a sea of empty chalk lines, held out a wad of folded bills. "This enough, you think?"

Mikki recoiled, eyes wide. Was he *crazy*? She made no move to take the money. Instead, she picked up her pace and lengthened her strides until she'd put distance between them, leaving him scrambling to catch up.

"Wait," he called after her, breathlessly. "What? What did I do?"

She kept going. "Besides handing me a stack of cash in an empty parking lot in full view of the interstate? Are you *trying* to make me look like a drug dealer? Or a sex worker? I'll spare you the lecture on how many patrols I see for this exact thing every day."

"Sorry," he panted, on her heels. "Didn't cross my mind. But we're not doing anything wrong. Who cares how it looks?"

She wheeled around to face him, and he almost crashed into her.

"I care," she said. "Same as I care about the license plate. You want to know about my mom? If she taught me anything, it's that being accused of wrongdoing can ruin your entire life. And your daughter's life. And the scary part is, it doesn't matter whether you did it, or if anyone bothered trying to prove you did or didn't. Not if you're working class in a small town with limited employment. Where I'm from, being suspected is as good as guilty, which makes your family guilty by association. So I've learned to care how it looks. But lucky me, you're not like everyone else. You're going to be the only human on this planet who doesn't think less of me because of her. Right?"

He was stunned into silence. *Well done, Mikki.* He'd tried to hand her a shopping spree, and she'd launched into a panicked rant. She couldn't have sounded more ungrateful.

He cleared his throat. "Sorry. I should have backed off. And I should have been more aware of how things looked. Or how they felt."

Mikki sighed. She wondered what his family business was. He'd make an excellent mediator. Or human fire extinguisher. "I shouldn't have snapped at you like that. I only made it worse anyway. Now you want to know what she's been accused of, and . . ."

"No. You tried to politely draw a boundary, and I pushed it. Don't apologize. And now I'm trying to figure out how to hand you the money at all without feeling like I'm paying you off. I botched this all the way around."

She looked into his eyes and saw that he meant every word. Somehow, it was harder this way. Because he was right: she had tried to draw a polite boundary. But with the forced intimacy of the road trip, polite was only going to get them so far. Eventually, they'd have to be honest.

"My mom," she said quietly, "got fired the year I graduated high school, accused of stealing from her employer. When she couldn't find work anywhere else, she spent my entire college fund on opioids. By the time I realized, every penny I'd saved was gone."

He paled. "Mikki. Oh my God."

"The college where I'd enrolled *was* her employer, and her discount was the only way I could afford tuition in the first place. Next thing I know, I'm withdrawing, we're canceling the big celebration graduation trip we'd planned to Florida, and she's gone. Not only did she leave me to take care of myself, but she also saddled me with a mountain of debt and her pain-in-everyone's-ass mother, who is going to need a caregiver before long." She raised her eyes to meet his. "For the record, I don't mess with drugs, and I've never stolen anything. But not everyone believes that. They think I'm wild. They figure the apple doesn't fall far."

His mouth fell open, but what could he say? She'd just told him the one person who was supposed to want better things for her had been the one to snatch it all away. She'd overshared, as if trying to rub his nose in his own sheltered naivete, when it was clear that outside of Becksville, she was the sheltered one.

This was the real reason she was stuck. She always got in her own way.

Tears pricked her eyes, and she looked down at the broken pavement. She didn't know what would happen next. She didn't know what she wanted to happen next. She just knew she didn't want *this* to be happening now.

"I'm glad you told me," Chris said finally. She looked up at him, feeling self-consciously hopeful. "I'm so sorry that happened to you."

"If you've changed your mind about taking me with you . . ."

"I haven't. Hey, take your time in there, okay? One should never rush through a house of worship. I'll grab a café table up front and wait as long as you need." He held out the cash more subtly, tucked between his knuckles in his cupped hand, like a peace offering.

This time, she took it.

〰️

In under thirty minutes, she selected two strappy dresses that came to midcalf, one flowery, one silky, plus an ankle-length sheath with billowy sleeves. She built outfits from there: dressy heeled sandals, smart flats, a sleek cardigan, a tailored blazer, linen pants, silk camisoles that could be layered or worn alone, earrings, a clutch, an oversize purse that could double as a beach bag, plus basics for the pool, including sunglasses and a floppy straw hat. As an afterthought, she grabbed some separates that could pass for either a casual lunch or a workout, lest she end up overdressed, then headed to the beauty aisles for toiletries and makeup. She stayed focused, checking through a mental list, anxious to get back on the road despite Chris's assurances to take her time. It was hard not to feel unsettled by their argument, even if it had felt necessary in some undefinable way, like clearing the air.

Walking past the electronics department, she paused. This was her chance if she wanted to buy a pay-as-you-go phone. Chris could hardly object to her wanting a safety net—they were far from home and had already had their first argument. Plus, Lark had begged her to check in and would be worried if she didn't.

On the other hand, if anyone had shown too much temper so far, it was Mikki. And she was starting to see the truth in Chris's theory that this break would be good for her and Lark. Usually Lark was the one person Mikki could be herself around—and self-censoring her emotions for Lark's sake these past few weeks had strained Mikki in ways she hadn't wanted to acknowledge. What if Mikki didn't even know who she was without Lark?

If she kept Lark an easy text or phone call away at all times, she might never find out.

A display had several laptops set up for customers to demo, and Mikki pulled her cart up to the first one and opened the web browser. Before she could second-guess herself, she went to her webmail account and entered her username and password. She knew it was risky to log on to an open network, but she was willing to gamble that security for a different peace of mind. She started a message to Lark with the subject line "checking in."

Hey, girl!

Had a quick chance to borrow a laptop on a quick stop for provisions to let you know all is well. Been driving all night, now, and still on track to arrive after lunchtime. I can't believe in a few hours I'll be like that Zac Brown song you like: toes in the water, butt on the beach. Even if it doesn't live up to the hype, the anticipation is half the fun.

Wanted to say sorry again for leaving in such a rush. Carpe diem, and all that. I know you're not a fan of this plan, but please don't worry. Everything is as promised, no red flags. He's nice. I'm going to take this chance to stay in the moment on this trip, okay? Embrace not having my phone, party like it's 1999. But it really is safe to assume all is well. I'll tell you all about it when I'm back Monday night. And I'll bottle up some sand and sea for you!

xo -Mikki

She read it over and then, satisfied, hit Send. She wasn't sure it would make Lark feel much better, but it did the job of due diligence. Hell, maybe once Mikki was in Amelia Island, a few drinks in, surrounded by strangers, she'd want nothing more than to call her best friend. But this way, if she didn't, she'd have made her apologies in advance.

At checkout, her haul was more than she'd ever spent in one transaction, even with twenty-three dollars left over, and her body didn't know how to feel about it. Her stomach was empty, her nerves frayed, but her feet bounced with sleepless energy. She rolled her change into her palm, gathered her bags, and headed to the café by the exit, scanning the seats for Chris.

The tables were dotted with customers, and she took them in one by one. Then, more slowly, again.

This was where he'd said he'd be. She was sure. Her eyes flicked to the restrooms, the customer service desk, the bins of impulse buys: no Chris.

Her heart dropped, her feet slowing as the store closed in around her. Why *would* he stay, after all she'd told him? This was exactly what she'd been afraid of when he'd started asking all those questions. *Why* had she opened her big mouth? She'd known better.

This had always been a danger: Chris could change his mind at *any* stage of their journey and just . . . strand her. She turned another circle, telling herself not to jump to conclusions. He was probably using the restroom or grabbing a toothbrush he'd forgotten to pack. And even if he had bailed, better to have done it here than all the way in Florida.

Or was it? Because now she'd have not even one moment at the ocean, and no way home either. What would she do? Call Lark, ask her to please disregard the email she'd just received, and beg to trade a new Target wardrobe for a ride? It wasn't Lark's style to say *told you so*, but Mikki deserved it. Rescuing her would cost gas money they couldn't afford, even without a baby on the way.

Air. She needed air.

Mikki burst out the automatic doors onto the sidewalk, trying to quell her panic.

But there at the curb, Chris stood surveying his handiwork: a newly attached license plate. Two large coffees steamed next to a bag of breakfast takeout on the trunk. He didn't register her panic, didn't blanch when he saw her loaded down with so many bags, and didn't ask for the total or his change. He just said, "Oh, good, you found me," strode over to lighten her load, asking if she was ready.

Mikki had never been readier in her life.

9

Lark

The first time around, when law enforcement questioned Lark, they did a thorough job of making her feel like a world-class idiot. The worst part was that she couldn't even claim they were being unfair. All they did was point out what Lark, by then, already knew.

The facts were these: a grown woman voluntarily—happily—got into a stranger's car and didn't return. The authorities needed a reason to suspect foul play to justify investigating. And Mikki not getting in touch didn't qualify as a reason. Especially not when everyone they asked said the same thing: that Mikki told anyone who'd listen how much she wanted out of Becksville. So she'd finally scored not just a ride but a date with a good-looking guy who appeared to have money. The real mystery would've been if she *had* come back. The lack of details on the surveillance video could be an unlucky coincidence. And so what that the plates weren't bolted onto his car? A clean-cut guy in his pay grade probably wouldn't even get a ticket if he got pulled over.

That was the problem, though. A clean-cut guy in his pay grade might not get a second look at all. From much of anyone.

Lark hadn't reported Mikki missing until the day after she'd promised to return. One of Lark's trooper friends took the initial report when she pulled him aside—*Do you have a minute? Can I tell you what happened? Is it too soon to worry?* He didn't think it too soon. In fact, he hinted it might be too late, the trail already days old. He turned it over to the sheriff's office. *What else can you tell us?* They wanted to know. They read the email Mikki had sent. They pointed out that taxpayer money did not fund wild goose chases to hunt down people who simply didn't want to be found. In fact, not to be harsh, they said—*not to be harsh*—but some people might argue that anyone careless enough to behave as Mikki had didn't deserve to be rescued. *We understand you're upset. We want to help. Call us when you have more to go on.*

Eventually, the staties took pity on Lark and put out a BOLO, alerting highway patrol to *Be on the Lookout* for a silver BMW convertible, newer model, and do a welfare check on any thirty-ish female passenger inside. "We like you and Mikki," they all said. "You're the only people who are always happy to see us." But by then, a week had passed, and the alert was active only in Ohio. With no way to know if the car had headed to Florida at all, where it was by now, or whether it might be traveling northbound or southbound, they cautioned Lark that even if she could get a missing person report to be taken seriously, cooperation with other state agencies could be spotty at best.

Now as then, the lobby of the sheriff's station was no place to be at this time of night. It smelled of the dirty mop water soaking in the corner, and every square inch—from the leak-stained ceiling to the scuffed-up walls—looked dingy in the poorly lit dark. The only people who'd been brought in during the two hours since Lark arrived were obvious DUIs, belligerent and reeking of tequila.

Lark sat on a ripped vinyl chair, holding a Styrofoam cup of coffee that had gone cold. Aside from the blast of the air vent above her head, it was quiet enough to hear the distant chatter and laughter of the meagerly staffed office beyond the reception desk, which irked her.

Who could laugh at a time like this? And what was taking so long?

Heath sat stoically beside her, which she should have found more comforting than she did. His uniform drew mixed reactions in the sheriff's station—some nods of recognition, some looks of confusion—and his usual air of authority had morphed into unspoken tension.

Contrary to popular belief, there wasn't much animosity between the troopers and the local cops; in a sparsely populated area like this, they often responded together to serious roadway emergencies. "Road dogs," they called themselves collectively, and when their paths crossed on duty or at the hardware store, they were more likely to clap each other on the back than to trade jabs. But the higher-ups could be territorial about their jurisdictions and issue directives that made things awkward. More than once Heath had arrived at a fender bender only to find a deputy passively waving traffic around the wreckage and the drivers annoyed it had taken Heath so long to arrive, unaware he needn't have been called at all.

Heath's trooper colleagues had called him immediately after they'd arrived at the Travel Stop. But they'd also called the deputies once they realized who'd handled—or mishandled—things the first time around. Chris had come to the station voluntarily, but the longer Lark waited in the lobby, the more she regretted involving any cops at all. She'd had a chance to *make* him talk, to deal with him herself. And instead, she'd handed him over, relegating herself to the wrong side of a closed door. It was torture, imagining what he might be telling them or, worse, refusing to say. The old man at the reception desk had already suggested more than once that she "head on home."

Going home was not an option. She was the only person Mikki had—at least, the only one with reliable faculties about her—but she wasn't biological family. Which meant they were under no obligation to call her with an update. Dragging Nini out of bed seemed premature, and in the meantime, who's to say the deputies wouldn't accept Chris's explanation—some longer version of the bullshit he'd fed her at the Travel Stop—and let him walk?

Lark couldn't let that happen.

He had to know *something* that would lead them to answers about Mikki at last. He had to. He was their last and most unexpected hope. All the others had faded.

Here, stationed by the exit, she could tackle him herself if she had to. And if it came to that, she would.

Heath squeezed her hand, and she looked up to see one of the officers beckoning them into the long hallway bisecting the various rooms of the station. She stood up so fast her purse fell from her lap, spilling its contents across the floor.

"I've got it," Heath said instantly, kneeling to scoop up all her detritus. Lark crouched beside him and held the bag open impatiently, face burning, tears stinging her eyes. "It's okay," he said, so only she could hear. "You're okay. We're all on the same team here. They'll wait."

She took a deep breath, then another, until she was sure the tears wouldn't fall. Then she got to her feet and followed the officer to an open doorway at the end of the hall. It looked like an ordinary office conference room: none of the two-way mirrors or bare dangling light bulbs she'd seen on TV. His partner sat at the table, nodding at Lark and Heath when they came in. Chris was nowhere to be seen.

Lark tried to swallow her panic. Surely, he was still here somewhere. They wouldn't let a "person of interest" cowardly slip out some back door, would they?

The deputies reintroduced themselves, shaking hands with Heath, who explained that he was Lark's fiancé, though they already seemed to know. Lark repeated their names to herself: Deputy DeLue was the one who'd come out to get them, a fatherly type who seemed so casual he might have been at a ball game. Deputy Rodgers was the one who'd taken the lead on the scene at the Travel Stop, younger and more fit, with the decency to arrange his face into a look of concentration, if not concern.

"Can we get you anything?" Rodgers asked now. "Apologies for the wait. We realize emotions are running high. That's why we thought it best to keep parties separate for now."

Lark shook her head, then nodded. No, they couldn't get her anything. Except for her friend back, please. And yes, they might have been right about the separation thing, given that she'd been fantasizing in the lobby about body-rushing Chris to the floor.

"Obviously we'll do more digging, but the basics of his story check out. We've already gotten the bride on the phone to confirm the location and date of her wedding, and she positively identified Mikki's photograph as the woman Chris brought as his guest. She was adamant she hasn't seen or had any reason to think about Mikki since."

Lark forced a deep breath. All this time, she'd worried that she'd put her friend in a car with a psychopath, that there had never been any Florida or wedding at all. That Mikki had ended up raped and starved in a basement or shed somewhere. While Lark wasn't about to believe every word of this, no questions asked, or to let Chris off the hook, hearing the probability that Mikki had made it to an honest-to-God destination wedding was a relief.

Still. Nothing about this could *check out* in two hours, after she'd been wondering and worrying for going on eight years. If she'd known any of this back then, maybe the PI she'd hired wouldn't have been such a waste.

"But now you know where she went," Lark reasoned with the officers. "Even if this Chris guy is telling the truth, you know the exact day and place Mikki was last accounted for. These are the leads we've been missing. Surely someone who was there knows something. The concierge or car rental might have a record? You can interview wedding guests and staff and—"

"We can do some of that, yes," he cut in, his tone obviously leading up to a caveat.

"What do you mean, *some* of it?"

"Hang on. For one thing, it was a long time ago, and that's a real issue. Witnesses are unreliable even moments after an incident. Plenty of people can't remember what they had for breakfast, or what their kids were wearing when they got distracted and separated in Walmart.

And when it comes to businesses keeping records, they often don't go back that far."

"But we can try. I mean, no one was ever able to follow Mikki's trail even a little bit."

He ignored that. "For another thing, there were circumstances we were unaware of."

Heath cleared his throat, sensing, perhaps, that Lark's calm was about to run out. "What kind of circumstances?"

"Turns out Mikki came into some money. Quite a lot of it. Enough to buy a ticket pretty much anywhere and set herself up nice. Which doesn't usually lead folks back to beautiful Becksville, as we're all aware."

Lark felt stricken. All that time out in the lobby, she'd been expecting to hear some testimony. Some evidence. Not a predetermined conclusion, as if Mikki's disappearance was open and shut. The room was freezing cold, but her face felt hot with the exertion of trying to keep up.

"Mikki had people here who she loved," she said. Even to her own ears, it sounded like she was trying to convince herself. Just like it had every other time she'd repeated it over the years.

"Her mother is an addict, correct? Had some past employers threaten to press charges too." He shuffled some papers in front of him. "Theft of company property?"

"That's true, but—"

"Mikki ever use, that you know of?"

"No." Lark seethed. "Never."

"And the mom's whereabouts now?"

What was he getting at? "No one knows."

He let that sink in. Like it meant something. "Back at the Travel Stop, you mentioned she'd sent you an email. Can you forward that to us, assuming you still have it?"

"You have it on file, but I'll send it again. The email clearly says she's coming back."

"But she never sent another one, nor did she reply to any of yours. Correct?"

Lark couldn't bring herself to nod, knowing it would elicit insufferable looks of pity. "I knew Mikki better than anyone. Yes, she wanted out of Becksville, and like you said, everyone understood why. That's the thing. She wouldn't have left like this. Not without telling us." Her cheeks burned. This would be easier if it weren't so obvious she was the abandoned party—and less sure by the second that any of this was true.

"Understanding someone's reasons doesn't mean we have to agree with them," the deputy said, matter-of-factly. "Clean breaks can be easier. We see this sort of thing."

Lark shook her head. "Moving to a nicer town is not a satisfactory explanation for falling off the face of the planet," she insisted. "And what do you mean, she *came into some money*? Like, he paid her to be his date?"

The deputies exchanged a look. "Not exactly," DeLue said. It was the first thing he'd volunteered, and she could tell he regretted it as soon as she turned her gaze on him.

"Then what?" she asked.

Rodgers cleared his throat. "Look, I've probably already told you more than I should have, with the investigation technically ongoing." *Technically?* Lark's heart flinched. "I understand you've been through a lot, and I've owed Heath here a few favors, so I'm extending the courtesy. But let's give it a rest for tonight. Mr. Redmond is cooperating. He's agreed to stay in town for a few days while we dig a little deeper, and that alone tells me his story will probably check out. Like you said yourself, why would he come back here otherwise, let alone stay?"

"Like *you* said yourself, if he's so sure she 'came into some money' and didn't look back, then why would he be here in ratty old Becksville, looking for her?"

Rodgers was unmoved, while DeLue looked at her with such overt sympathy she wanted to claw her eyes out. Or maybe his. "He seemed just as eager to talk with you, not that we necessarily recommend it," he said. "But I'm not sure there's much precedent for this situation. So you can add that to your list of questions to ask him."

Lark gripped the table's edge, her bewilderment and anger redoubling. "I want to know if *you* asked him. And assuming you did, since it's your *job*, I want to know what he said."

"Because of you," he said flatly, getting to his feet. "He thought there was a chance—emphasis on 'chance'—she'd be in Becksville because of you."

They stared at each other across the table while an awkward silence descended like fog. *Because of you.* She'd heard these words ad nauseum since the night she'd "let" Mikki walk out the door. But the tone had shifted from that old, tired blame. This wasn't a *because of you* that spoke to love or the good kind of loyalty. This *because of you* carried duty, regret, sacrifice.

"Speaking of which," he said, "one other tidbit that might interest you." She raised an eyebrow. A *tidbit?* Is that what they'd reduced this to? "Your friend didn't go by Mikki at the wedding. Chris knew her real name, but they used a cover story about how they met. Can't say I blame them, wanting to dodge questions about linking up at a travel stop. Funny, though, that she'd change her name too. Maybe she just didn't want anyone finding her on social media and blowing her cover."

Mikki did always love dreaming up elaborate backstories for drivers passing through the Travel Stop. Lark could almost picture it, Mikki assigning herself a different meet cute with the smooth convertible driver, creating a whole character to play as she danced by the ocean under the stars. And the picture was so much rosier than anything else she'd imagined that the fog began to thin, and she found herself smiling. "What name did she go by?"

He leveled his gaze at her. "Everyone at the wedding knew her as Lark."

Whatever Lark had been expecting, that wasn't it. She looked from one deputy to the next, trying to gauge their expressions, but both appeared carefully neutral. Why did she feel like she was the one who'd been caught in a lie or done something wrong?

There was only one lie she'd ever told about the last time she saw Mikki. And it had nothing to do with this.

Heath took Lark's hand. His palm was clammy, and she understood he didn't think this boded well. At a minimum, Mikki using an assumed name supported the theory that she didn't want to be traceable. But using Lark's name, of all the choices, what did *that* mean? Was it a final homage—a goodbye, an apology, in case Lark ever tracked Mikki this far? Or was it something less friendly, like the words still echoing in Lark's mind?

Because of you.

"Any idea why she'd do that?" DeLue asked. "Use your name?"

Lark shook her head.

He looked meaningfully at Heath, then back at Lark. "You did the right thing by calling us. We understand you live with Mikki's grandmother now?"

Lark nodded. "She's . . ." She never could figure out how to put this so people could understand. "She's struggling with early stages of dementia. She's fairly independent, but she shouldn't be the first point of contact on anything. I wouldn't leave messages at the house with her, for example, and expect anyone to get them."

"Understood. Terrible disease, dementia. Hard on loved ones too." He held her gaze for a beat too long, as if to emphasize his earlier point. *Sometimes clean breaks are easier*—drop the burden and hope somebody else would pick it up. Lark's heart kept sinking, so deep she pressed a hand to her chest to check that it was still beating. *I am*, it thumped beneath her palm. *I am, I am, I am.* "And Mikki has no other family?" he asked. "Or surrogates? Maybe your parents?"

"No. My parents were killed by a drunk driver twelve years ago." She didn't mention that the driver had been her dad. Or that her parents had never been interested in parenting anyway.

Or that she wouldn't have withstood any of it without Mikki.

The deputy softened. "I can see this is upsetting. I want you to keep in mind, no matter what happens next, that what you said about having a lead now that you didn't have before? That's still true." He cleared his throat. "As before, if we determine there's no probable cause to suspect foul play, there's only so much we can do. But at least this time there are other resources to pursue the kinds of answers you're after."

She bristled. "Are you already suggesting I hire my own investigator?"

"Absolutely not. That would be premature and, frankly, get in our way. I am suggesting you take this one step at a time, and yes, bear in mind we are not the be all and end all of investigative options. Besides, if we find nothing criminal, that's good news. Right?"

Heath got to his feet. "Thank you, sir. We appreciate all you're doing."

Lark waited until the door shut behind them before she exploded. "They've already made up their minds. This is unbelievable."

"They haven't. He was just trying to prepare you for the possibility . . ." When Heath saw the look on her face, he didn't bother finishing the sentence.

"I've done *nothing* but prepare for possibilities. Now I finally have one, and they want me to prepare to let it go? While I'm in the same zip code as Chris Redmond?" Every time she said the name, it solidified the idea that this elusive person was real. Not a figment of her imagination after all. Maybe that was what she was waiting for: for someone in authority to acknowledge that she'd been right. That they were sorry for doubting her.

"About that," Heath said. "I'm glad Redmond is cooperating, but I don't love the idea of him hanging around. We'd best steer clear. Let's give the sheriff's office a chance, see what happens."

Give them a chance? They'd squandered years of chances. "But the cops didn't ask me to steer clear," Lark protested. "They encouraged me to talk to him myself, like maybe if I do, we can settle this without them."

"*I'm* asking you." He stepped right up to her, dropping his voice low. It seemed impossible that mere hours ago, they'd been discussing a change in their work schedules as if *that* would be the thing to shake up their lives. Lark still felt more grateful for their closeness than ever—for the reassurance of having him on her team—but she also felt further away, pulled sideways into a lifetime of history he could never really understand.

The truth was, no matter how much love they had between them, she'd need to spend decades with him before their history together could ever match the sheer volume of memories she'd had with Mikki.

"I know we didn't know each other back when this happened," Heath said, echoing her thoughts. "I know what it did to you, though. I know how badly you want Redmond being here to change things. But the way to change them is not to march to his hotel and make demands. For one thing, I don't trust him. For another, I saw how those deputies looked at you when they asked about Mikki using your name."

His eyes scanned the room, as if checking that no one was listening. "He's not the only one they'll be watching closely in the coming days. His story ties up pretty neatly, but if you do anything to draw scrutiny, they might decide yours does too. You have a daughter to think about." He tucked her hair behind her ear. "*We* have a daughter to think about."

Lark couldn't bear to look at him anymore. She pressed her face into his chest, and he wrapped her in his arms. But even as she nodded that she understood, his starched uniform rough against her cheek, she was thinking that she didn't need Heath's permission to go see Chris Redmond on her own time. She didn't even need to find out what hotel he was staying in.

Becksville had only one.

Heath kissed the top of her head, and she reassured herself that she hadn't actually agreed—not in words.

Maybe, if she didn't think about it too hard, this wouldn't count as the second lie she'd ever told a man in uniform.

10

Mikki

Back on the interstate, Chris steered the BMW through the last of the slow-weaving morning commute, and Mikki stayed quiet so he could concentrate, downing the croissant he'd chosen for her, which was warm and stuffed with bits of salty ham and gooey white cheese. After a night of caffeine and sugar, real food brought her back to life. She scanned both sides of the pavement for another glimpse of a palmetto tree, but the landscape here was mostly tall pines that looked like they were growing on stilts, elongated bare trunks with tufts at the top.

"So," she said, once they were going again at a good clip. "Whose wedding are we headed to, anyway?"

The wait for his answer went on a beat too long. Then he looked at her with an exaggerated cringe, as if he were about to make some horrible confession.

"It's Kim's," he admitted, holding the cringe.

She stared back blankly. Another ex? "Who's Kim?"

Chris looked back at the road. "My sister."

"Your *sister*?" Mikki inhaled a flake of croissant and began to cough. Not once had he implied, from the moment he'd shown up in search of a fresh pot of coffee, that this event was anything other than an obligation on his to-do list. She'd assumed whoever's wedding it was had been of little consequence, perhaps an old childhood friend or a distant cousin. Mikki was stunned. The brother of the bride would draw a lot of attention. And so would his date.

She downed her coffee until she stopped sputtering. "You didn't think to mention this before now?"

"I've been trying not to think about it, honestly."

"Why do I get the feeling she won't be thrilled her *brother* is bringing someone she's never met?"

"You'll be a pleasant surprise. They all expect me to bring only my miserable self."

Mikki wagged a finger at him, realizing. "You're using me as a buffer. So you don't have to be alone with them."

"Hey, now." He bumped her knee gamely with his fist. "I'm not *using* you. I'm taking you on an all-expenses-paid trip to a luxury resort, as advertised. You don't have to buffer anything you don't want to."

"Is this about shock value?" she asked, defensive. "Making a statement by bringing some rando to a family occasion?"

"Of course not. My siblings aren't nearly as easily scandalized as our parents were. And if I did want to shock them, I'm perfectly capable of doing it without some *rando's* help."

Mikki fidgeted in her seat, turning it all over in her mind. It didn't sit well with her, but she was hardly in a position to argue.

"Speaking of my parents, though," he said, turning serious. "You were honest with me, back in that parking lot, and I owe you the same. There are some things you should probably know going in. My family isn't on the most ordinary terms right now."

She nodded. When he'd mentioned his parents' death before, it had seemed recent. And sudden. "Okay," she said, balling up her sandwich wrapper. "I'm listening."

He took his time deciding where to start. "Growing up, I was at odds with my family more than I'd have liked. Kim's the oldest, and she was the overachiever from an early age, already masterminding all the things we'd do when our turn came to take over my parents' business. And my younger brother, Cooper, was . . . not a freeloader, but looking for the path of least resistance to continue reaping the benefits he'd grown up with. For me, I don't know. I'm the most easygoing one, so my parents took it personally when they were the ones I couldn't get along with. The more focused they were on the Redmond brand, the less comfortable I was with the expectations. It just didn't feel like *me*, and they'd say, 'How can it not be *you* when it's your actual name?'" He sighed. "I never knew how to explain. It was never about me judging them, though. I was never ashamed to be a Redmond." He cleared his throat. "Until they died."

Ashamed didn't seem like a word he'd throw around lightly. She'd never heard of any Redmond brand. Maybe it had all been a cover, and he'd discovered they were in bed with the mob, or swindling people in some white-collar scheme, or outsourcing labor to a sweatshop, perpetuating some exploitation or discrimination or harassment or . . . what?

"Did you find out the business was . . . not what you thought?" She chose her words carefully. "I don't think you've actually said what your family business entailed."

"That's the running joke," he said. "It doesn't entail anything beyond investing in other people's businesses. We don't even have a real flagship. Dad just added the headquarters onto the house. Basically, my family came to this country with old money and made good decisions about what to do with it. Dad wasn't a shrewd investor, but he was a smart one, which he learned from his dad, who learned from his dad. Although sometimes I wonder how much is actual business savvy— combined with privilege—and how much is luck. I've never understood it enough to know the difference. Maybe luck is more entwined with everything than we think."

"It definitely is," Mikki said. She'd been riding a locomotive of bad luck for years. The Redmonds' luck sounded much better. But in both cases, the track had to run out eventually. "So why don't you want to be an investor?" she asked.

"Bores me to tears. Kim is like my dad: she can talk to someone about their pet project—a restaurant or hotel or product—and feed on their excitement. For her, it's enough to fund the thing. But I never wanted a job backing things other people are passionate about. I want to be the one with the passion."

Mikki saw nothing wrong with helping other people pursue their dreams. She knew plenty of folks that would make a world of difference for. But she was in no position to judge. "It wasn't enough for your parents that Kim and Cooper actually wanted to take on the business?"

He shook his head. "We were growing too fast. Plus Dad was quick to point out Cooper was basically filling a chair at the boardroom table. I'd argue that he let Cooper coast, that they accepted Cooper for what *he* was just fine. And Dad would say, *But he doesn't have the brains for this. You do.* Cooper overheard one of those arguments once and didn't speak to anyone for a week. He cared what my dad thought of him way more than he cared whether it was true."

Mikki nodded. Honestly, the brother's contentedness to go along until he was called out put her in mind of Lark. "Is there something specific you want to do instead?"

"Lots of things. But it seemed pointless to figure out what, given my parents' expectations." He looked over at her. "Is there something specific *you* want to do? Or is the goal just *anything but the Travel Stop?*"

He had a point. Mikki's brief enrollment had been at the College of Art & Design, but she hadn't declared a major, knowing only that she liked arranging things in a way that pleased her.

"Anything but the Travel Stop," she admitted.

He nodded. "Anything but investing." Mikki sympathized with his predicament, but she still didn't understand what about his family warranted being called "shameful."

"But everything they invest in is on the up-and-up?" she prodded.

"I'm not saying they're perfect, but my family has integrity. Had integrity. Before the wrongful death lawsuit. Or I should say, before the wrongful death."

Wrongful death. Mikki swallowed hard. She waited.

"Kim and Cooper are quick to say there was no malicious intent," Chris said, "but we couldn't deny my parents were negligent. Which is ironic since Dad always prided himself on being so damn singularly focused. Too focused, it turns out."

"What did they neglect?"

"They ignored an evacuation order for a wildfire," Chris said. "Remember that super dry summer, the one before last? Bad lightning storm. High winds. Terrible combination. Compound that with the fact that Michiganders aren't accustomed to fire threats the way, say, Californians are. In their defense, it spread so fast, they weren't the only ones not to take the warnings seriously. But they're the only ones I know of who were so distracted, trying to close a deal, that people paid with their lives. Five employees they could have sent home but didn't—people who spent their entire careers working for us, who we thought of as extended family, with families of their own. If Kim and I hadn't been out of town, working the other end of that same deal, we'd have been casualties too. Or maybe we'd have smacked sense into everyone. We'll never know. Our estate was a total loss—the home, the corporate headquarters, and seven lives lost, not including the poor horses, alpacas, greyhounds, and Monet, our French bulldog."

"What about Cooper?" she asked. "Where was he?"

Chris winced. "Running an errand. He tried to get back in, but the road was blocked . . . The police had to restrain him." He shook his head. "I can't imagine what it was like to watch it all burn, knowing they had no way out. He still can't talk about it."

He cleared his throat. "I'll tell you this: the victims shouldn't have settled. They could have gotten more if it had gone to trial. Redmonds aren't used to paying for their mistakes, and when they do, it's always with money. Which is probably why I'm the sort of man who is tone-deaf enough to hand a wad of cash to a woman I just met in the middle of an empty parking lot."

Mikki felt a twinge of remorse for being so hard on him. They'd had the lawsuit coming, certainly. Still, it sounded to her like he'd paid plenty. Maybe other people had, too, but that didn't invalidate his grief. In fact, it seemed to add to it. "I'm so sorry, Chris."

He shook his head. "Through all of this, not once have I heard Kim or Cooper admit to finding it hard to look in the mirror and like themselves anymore. I guess it's just me."

"It sounds like it was just a terrible tragedy. For all of you," Mikki offered. "You said yourself there was no malicious intent. Surely if their employees had really thought their lives were in danger, they'd have left even if your parents insisted on staying."

"You don't need malicious intent to be negligent."

"No," Mikki agreed. "But negligence is more forgivable than malice." *I should know,* she thought. Surely it would be easier to swallow if her mom had ruined her entire life by accident, instead of knowing damn well what she was costing Mikki and doing it anyway. "If you owned up to it when you settled, you've done what you can. Right?"

He took a long moment to answer. "You're not the only one who sees it that way. Somehow my siblings have maintained all their sentimental feelings about that land, the brand, all of it. Even Cooper, who was there . . . They want to rebuild exactly where it was, exactly how it was. Kim keeps playing the *legacy* card, like that's reason enough. Like, so what if all this acreage that's been in our family for generations is basically the scene of a crime? I can't bring myself to set foot there again, let alone construct a new house, offices, all of it. Not to mention that the legacy itself . . ." He winced. "Cancel culture has not been kind to the Redmond brand since the fire. And it's hard to know how much of it is just people piling on, trying to garner sympathy and attention and financial backing elsewhere, and how much has any truth to it."

"What are they saying?"

"Toxic work environment, lack of transparency since the fire, stingy terms that don't help our clients as much as we claim, calling us out for not funding the most deserving or diverse start-ups . . ." He sighed. "My parents were beyond reproach, and then suddenly we very much weren't. I'll hand it to Kim that she's pulled us through—she'd already been working on things like diversity initiatives for years—though it's debatable whether our reputation is intact. I think Kim managed to come off as this shrewd but savvy businesswoman who isn't here to make friends, but honestly, she used to care about people a lot more. I guess this has changed us all in our own ways. She bucked up, Cooper fell apart, and I . . . well, I froze. Every time I think about dipping a toe back in, I'm just exhausted and overwhelmed by it all."

"But the three of you are still co-owners? With an even split?"

He nodded. "For now. She's made it known she and Cooper are ready to green-light a full-speed-ahead rebuild, and the only thing stopping them is me. They're convinced it all blows over if we forge ahead. Which apparently involves Kim whisking two hundred of our closest friends away for an elaborate four-day wedding to show how perfectly fine everything is."

"Are you not on board because you'd rather rebuild someplace else, or because you want to do it some other way? Or not at all?"

"Doesn't even matter. They think rebuilding makes an important statement, and it's not a statement I'm interested in making, and we've never gotten beyond that. We're at an impasse."

"Can you sell your stake?"

"That's like asking if I can live with my parents rolling over in their graves. I guess I'm at an impasse with myself too."

Last night he'd alluded to a sibling rift, inheriting responsibility, disagreeing about where to go from here. But this was much more than an argument over who got to keep Grandma's crystal goblets. No wonder they were on tense terms. And Mikki was about to walk right into the middle of it on his arm. "Is this the first big event since your parents . . . since the tragedy?"

He nodded. "If I'm honest, this has to do with why I was coming alone. I have a lot to sort through to figure out how to be with people who know all the ugly details. Strangers are easier. So I invite a stranger and then go and tell her anyway." He shot her a sheepish smile, and Mikki did her best to smile back. If he really believed they'd escape scrutiny at this wedding, he hadn't thought things through.

But he'd admitted he hadn't wanted to think about any of it. And that, she could relate to.

"Maybe this is what you all need," she offered. "To spend time someplace no one will be talking business."

"I don't know. Plenty of our associates are on the guest list. But even without them in the picture . . . It still doesn't feel right to be celebrating anything together."

So this is what he'd meant by survivor's guilt. *Survivor's torture,* he'd called it.

"I hope it's obvious I'm not comparing this to your situation with your mom," he said. "You didn't say if she's alive or dead, but this must all seem . . . I do realize it's a luxury to have the option to rebuild or to sell."

"Nothing about your story sounds like a luxury. Even to me." Her eyes drifted out the passenger window. All night, she'd been catching the ghost of her reflection illuminated by the dashboard. Now in the bright day, it was a relief to look through it and focus on what was on the other side.

"I don't know if she's alive or dead," she admitted. Rural Ohio was ravaged with overdose deaths. The whole country was. "But it's evident she no longer cares if I'm okay. Which tells me all I need to know."

"What about your dad? Is he in the picture?"

"My mom divorced him when I was three, and he tried to claim I'd never been his anyway. His temper is . . . Let's just say he's not the kind of guy you approach for any kind of help once he's finally out of your life. Not that he has anything to offer anyway."

Before Mikki knew it, she was telling him the rest. How her best shot at college had been through her mom getting a job at a small university forty miles away. How everyone wanted to work there for the family tuition discounts, and her mom was one of the few who'd pulled it off. How ecstatic they were when she was hired, because they *knew* Mikki was good enough to be accepted—early decision—and she was. How Mikki took over making dinner every night while her mom sacrificed hours to the lengthy commute. How they'd agreed on a reward, a beach trip, a splurge to commemorate all they'd achieved together before Mikki got down to the real work of being the first in their family to get a degree.

How for the first time maybe ever, everything had gone to plan.

Until her mom got escorted from the campus by armed security. That was what happened when you were suspected of stealing petty cash from your employer. *Petty cash*. Not some grand embezzlement scheme. It all crashed down during Christmas break of Mikki's senior year, the season for faith and wishes and miracles, twinkling lights mocking them from every corner.

Mikki's mom swore she hadn't done it. But once people thought the worst of you in Becksville, one of two things happened: either you went to your grave fruitlessly pleading your innocence, convincing no one, or you went ahead and became what everyone already assumed you were. Might as well, with no path to redemption anyway.

Her mom chose the latter. Once she was unemployable, she fell in with an unemployable crowd. Once she could no longer afford to drink away her sorrows on barstools, she moved to couches, snorting and injecting away her sorrows instead. Mikki would never know whether there'd been any truth to the original accusations, but it no longer mattered: There was truth to them now. She must have figured that without the tuition discount, Mikki couldn't make college work anyway. Mikki hadn't told her yet how hard the school counselors were helping her hustle for financial aid, how close she was to some need-based scholarships. Mikki had wanted it to be a surprise. But before she could unveil her plan to save the day, her mother had drained their account—and Mikki's future along with it.

She didn't expect someone like Chris to understand a story like that. Telling him left her feeling the way she had while admitting she'd never seen the ocean. Like she needed to defend her choices, though her lifestyle didn't stem from choices at all. At least, not from hers.

"You get stuck in this cycle where you can't ever seem to get ahead," she finished. "When one lucky break could make a huge difference, but the breaks aren't going your way."

"We see a lot of that in my line of work," he said. "You never know who is just one layoff or unlucky diagnosis away from having to sell everything just to stay afloat."

"Or one natural disaster away," she conceded.

"Touché. I can empathize with what it's like to stand on a patch of scorched earth where your family used to be, surveying the destruction."

Mikki thought about how it wasn't just a metaphor to him. The disturbing image was as real as her own memory of standing in front of the bank teller, crying that there must be some mistake, slumping onto the counter, afraid she was going to be sick right there between the worn velvet ropes of the lobby. The bowl of red-and-white mints crashing to the marble floor, scattering plastic-wrapped candies and broken glass, a shard grazing her ankle, drawing blood. How she'd locked her eyes on the exit, running and sliding for the door.

"I guess for me," she said, "it's more like the fire is still burning, and I'm frantic to find a way out. I don't know if my mom will catch up with me again, or how or when."

"Good thing we're headed for the ocean," Chris said. "Fire can't touch us there."

His eyes held Mikki's for as long as either of them dared before looking back at the road.

"I guess we understand each other better now," Mikki said quietly.

Chris placed a warm hand on her knee. As quickly as she registered the touch, it was over, but the feeling of his hand lingered. She didn't dare dwell on the warmth it left behind. Chris was beyond out of her league—they weren't even playing the same sport. She didn't know what to make of the complicated swirl of emotions his touch was conjuring, but the tangible connection between them was oddly reassuring. If only because it was so undeniably solid. Real.

"I guess we do," he said.

11

Lark

2024

Nini kept Mikki in a box. Literally. She stored all her mementos of grandparenthood on her top closet shelf, where she needed a step stool she was no longer capable of climbing to reach them. Lark had never been able to make sense of the things Nini had saved anyway. A menu from a Dairy Whip where Mikki had worked before it went bankrupt and stiffed her out of her last paycheck. Her final report card from high school, still crumpled from Mikki's enraged discovery of the first and only C she'd ever gotten, courtesy of the distracting drama with her mom. A parking pass from a visit to a campus Mikki had never moved to after all.

If Lark didn't know better—and honestly, she didn't—she'd think Nini remembered Mikki by her disappointments, which seemed unfair. The disappointments may have been more numerous than the successes, but they didn't define Mikki. Certainly not more than the things that were notably absent from that closeted box, like Mikki's college acceptance letter or that amazing clay cardinal she'd sculpted in art class or pressed flowers from the bouquets she and Lark used to pick walking home from the bus stop.

All the belongings Mikki had left behind found their way into storage eventually, and some Nini had donated, grousing that they didn't have the space. But Lark would never pack in her own memories. She kept all her pictures of Mikki out in the open, even now, because Mikki had hated being boxed in more than anything. She talked to Dove about "Aunt Mikki" the way an adoptive mother might speak to her child about her birth mother: as a woman who had love for them both, wherever she was, who'd done her best under tough circumstances and deserved their appreciation and respect.

Sometimes, when the plumber or furnace tech stopped by, or a friend dropped in to borrow a dish for a potluck, Lark could tell all those reminders of Mikki made people who'd known her uncomfortable—averting their eyes, stammering that they couldn't stay. But for her it was the opposite, sometimes the *only* comfort in her day, like putting *Friends* reruns on TV for company while you cooked dinner. It wasn't Lark's job to protect people who'd rather forget. Or to protect herself from reminding them. Lark knew what people thought. She'd overheard plenty.

It's almost like she's taking Mikki's place, moving in with her grandmother, leaving those pictures up. Do you think it's because she feels so guilty she didn't try harder to stop her?

Maybe there's something else not quite right about it. Those girls were too close. What's the word they're always throwing around those talk therapy shows? Codependent.

Can you be codependent with someone who's probably been dead for years?

Her favorite photo lived on the powder room mirror: a faded childhood snap of her and Mikki around Dove's age at their first sleepover, holding up matching pink-and-turquoise toothbrushes, goofy grins stretched ear to ear. Dove had a different favorite: a candid of Lark and Mikki on the makeshift stage at Neon Moon's karaoke night, grinning at each other as they belted into their mics, singing their go-to duet "Islands in the Stream."

"I love her dress," Dove would say, standing on tiptoe to pull the frame off the living room mantel, holding it close to her face. The dress had been one of Mikki's favorites, a royal-purple A-line with a fun swing to it. "I don't guess it comes in my size?"

Lark couldn't bring herself to tell Dove the dress was bagged in the attic crawl space. She didn't think she could handle seeing her daughter play dress-up in that particular one. She and Mikki had found it on a day trip to Dayton in high school. In the photo, the camera had caught her midtwirl, and she and Lark were grinning so widely they had to have been near the end of the song. Usually the regulars at Neon Moon would groan when the opening notes played. *Again? Can't you two sing anything else?* But by the end, it would have turned into one big singalong, everyone cheering and hooting gamely. Lark and Mikki always traded off who got to be Dolly Parton, though whoever sang Kenny Rogers's part would inevitably get the loudest applause at the end, and they never lost track of whose turn it was. But no matter how hard Lark looked at that instant frozen in time, she couldn't remember who'd been whom that night.

It bothered her more than it should have.

That was the photo she went for now, slipping into the house in the dark early morning, breathing in the familiar smells of living with a very old person and a very young one: The Vicks VapoRub Nini rubbed into her arthritic joints. The sugary stickiness Dove left lingering on abandoned lollipop sticks. All preferable to the sour air of the police station. She crossed to the mantel and stood staring at the freeze-frame of her and Mikki together in the spotlight. Dove loved this picture because they looked so carefree, so happy, but the truth was, Mikki hadn't been. Carefree and happy in that moment, maybe. In her life, no.

What did it mean if Chris was telling the truth? If Mikki really had "come into some money"? If she'd rented a car, their best hope was for the car agency to have a record of when and where it had been returned. The deputies had warned it might not. But a missing car—that would stay on file, surely. Mikki wasn't a thief; after what happened with her mom, it was one of two things she'd vowed to never be. So if the car had disappeared with her, that could only mean trouble: wreckage submerged in a river somewhere, or Mikki's travels intercepted some other way that hadn't produced an accident report.

But what if Mikki hadn't picked up the car after all? If she'd bought a one-way ticket instead—hopped a bus, train, boat, something that'd take her as far as she wanted without requiring ID?

We parted ways on good terms, Chris had said. *She was excited to get back to you . . . I can't believe she would've done anything but come straight home.*

What if he'd been right that she'd been excited, but wrong about the reasons why?

Did it absolve Lark of something—of anything? Or did it make it all more unthinkable, in a different way?

Her head spun with it all.

Deputy DeLue had called out all her insecurities, maybe without even realizing it. *If we find nothing criminal here, that's good news. Right?*

Of course she didn't want any harm to have come to her best friend. Of course ruling out foul play was ideal, what everyone had all but given up hoping for.

But she also dreaded knowing, once and for all, without a doubt, that Mikki really had left her like that and for good. Even if Mikki had been following the rules Lark had helped write, it still would mean that the very same night Mikki had promised to be "the father of her baby," she'd changed her mind without so much as a goodbye, trusting Lark would understand.

Some days Lark did. Some days she didn't. But never did any conceivable option ever feel like "good news."

The unknowing was terrible. It was also safe, not having to face any one outcome, keeping some secret speculation just for herself—that there must be some understandable, forgivable explanation for all of this. Which, of course, made no sense. Because if an explanation could fix everything, then why didn't Mikki just reappear and give it already?

Maybe the deputy had known exactly what he was asking: *That's good news, right?* Maybe it hadn't been rhetorical. Maybe Heath was smart to advise Lark to bite her tongue, to wait and see.

Maybe Lark was foolish to ignore him.

But she had to get out of her own head. And the only other place she wanted to be was in Chris's.

She didn't know how long she'd been staring at the photo before Nini shuffled in. Her baby-blue housecoat was zipped to her neck, the ruffled trim fraying away, and her terry slippers were an exact match for the wall-to-wall carpet, flattened gray pile badly in need of washing.

She took one look at Lark and stopped. "What is it?" she asked sharply, clucking her tongue as she clocked that Lark was still in her work clothes, clutching her phone and car keys like she was scared to put them down. "You haven't slept? What's happened?"

How did you tell a woman who sometimes forgot what year it was that you might be on the verge of rewriting your most painful, most personal history together? How did you break it to her gently, explain it clearly, temper her response?

"There is something," Lark conceded. "Want to sit down?"

"I've been lying down all night." Nini put her hands on her hips. Even half-asleep, she clearly fancied herself one step ahead of Lark. Some days, she wasn't wrong.

Lark dropped onto the arm of the couch and steeled herself with a deep breath. There was nothing to do but say it. "You won't believe this, but . . . the driver who left with Mikki? He came back last night."

Nini's eyes narrowed. "What do you mean, *came back*?"

"He walked right into the Travel Stop. Claimed he was looking for her."

"Well," Nini scoffed, indignantly. "I doubt she wants to talk to him again."

Lark's heart slowed, the way it always did when Nini had one of her episodes. These split-second waves of confusion usually happened in anxious situations, or under pressure, and would leave as quickly as they'd come. Lark had grown adept at playing these moments off, gently steering Nini back to what was real, but in this case, the anger where she'd expected surprise jarred her off balance.

"I'll never understand it," Nini muttered, shaking her head. She crossed to the front window and tied the curtains back, revealing a morning barely lightening into a dreary day. Usually she kept the curtains closed so she could pretend she wasn't home, unless she was watching for a delivery man. "Never understand it," she repeated. "Never understand it."

"Nini," Lark began, hesitating. It was always tricky to start over with Nini. Anything she perceived as condescending was a surefire way to set her temper off. "You're right—it is hard to understand what this means. I can't tell you how surreal it was to see him again, to talk to him. His name is Chris Redmond. The police have him, and they're trying to get his side of the story."

"His side of the story?" Nini scoffed. She looked properly disgusted by now, but still not properly surprised. "He has a lot of nerve, showing his face here."

Lark cleared her throat. "He didn't seem to have a clue anyone thought he'd done anything suspicious. He says he took Mikki to that wedding and that was the last time he saw her. He says she was supposed to rent a car and come back on her own."

"On her own?" Nini shook her head. "Some date."

Nini wasn't wrong, even if she was missing the entire point. "He hasn't given us much to go on, but it's something. Deputies are going to see how much of his story they can confirm."

Nini looked cross but also scared. Lark wondered if part of her brain was running the same thought cycle hers had. She envisioned the skeletal frame of a vehicle engulfed in flames, so badly burned that neither the car nor the driver had been identifiable, until this lead prompted a recheck of certain records. *What if knowing did not turn out to be better than not knowing after all?*

"He has a lot of nerve, coming back here," she repeated. "This is all his fault."

Lark stared at Nini, agog, wondering if she'd heard her wrong.

"All his fault," Nini repeated, squinting out the window as if he might creep up on them at any moment.

But Nini had only ever blamed one person for what had happened to Mikki, and that person wasn't Chris. Not even when people were speculating that he'd been the worst kind of human, all premeditated evil, no moral compass.

Nini had only blamed Lark. And though there was plenty of blame to go around, Lark had never pled her case. She'd more or less agreed.

"It will be interesting to see if the police see it that way," Lark said, carefully.

"What about Heath?"

"What about him?"

"Well, he's the only one of them I trust." Nini blinked, as if someone had pressed a reset button on the conversation, and Lark saw the clarity come into her eyes. The reality of the situation finally sinking in. "How long has it been now?" Nini asked. Then realizing how this might sound, she quickly added, "I don't like to count."

"It'll be eight years this fall." At least now they were having the same conversation, oriented to the same point in time.

Lark tried to shake off the odd exchange. She should have anticipated this. Nini's moments of confusion often involved Mikki, whenever the stress of losing her resurfaced. Once, Dove had opened an improbable Christmas gift from Nini that was *exactly* what Mikki would have picked out herself if she could. It was a sequin pouch almost identical to one Mikki and Lark had used to pass notes in junior high—until they got very publicly busted, which had become an inside joke in hindsight: *things teenagers think are subtle.* The gift was nothing the very unshiny, unsparkly Nini seemed likely to choose on her own, and it felt like a sign. When Lark had hugged Nini tight, saying it was little moments like this that made her feel like Mikki was still watching out for her, Nini had gone misty-eyed.

"Well," she'd said. "She wanted Dove to have it."

Outwardly, Lark had let it go, passing the basket of muffins she'd baked for Christmas breakfast. But inwardly, Lark had hung on to the words. She'd let herself think, *Maybe.*

Maybe Mikki really had passed over into some adjacent dimension or spiritual plane where she could whisper her wishes into the universe and make them known. Maybe Nini's so-called declining cognitive function had simply shifted to a different frequency. Before Mikki had vanished from her life, Lark hadn't believed in guardian angels, or a sixth sense, or any other woo-woo cosmic synergy. Now, she was less sure. Once, in a deathly cold winter when their heating bills were sky-high, her car had chosen the wrong moment to need a costly transmission repair. She'd been terrified they wouldn't make their utility bill—until Nini had won $1,000 on one of her scratch-off tickets. Another time, Dove had been sick for almost an entire month, and a whole case of canned chicken noodle soup had been delivered to their doorstep by mistake. When Lark contacted the manufacturer about the error, they told her they didn't even have record of the shipment, so she might as well keep it. "Fortunate accidents," Nini called them, but to Lark, they felt like glimpses of grace, the universe encouraging her to hang on.

Lark didn't know why these little signs always made her think of Mikki. Maybe Lark was reaching for the idea that somehow, whether or not they were both still walking this world, they remained connected—a confirmation of their bond.

The one everyone else had come to question.

Or maybe it was that Mikki was the only one who'd ever cared enough to want good things for her. At least once a year, Lark would pick up the house phone, say hello, and find that no one was there—and always, without fail, she'd stay on the line, wondering if any part of Mikki, even some undefinable essence of her, was on the other end of that silence. Once, she'd even tried to speak to her. *I miss you so much,* she'd said. *I just want you to be okay.* But then a series of tones had played, like a spam call failing to connect, and she'd felt foolish for her pleading. The next time it happened, she'd yelled instead: *Why are you doing this? You're missing everything!* Not that she expected Mikki to actually hear her. But it had felt good to vent. Besides, if Mikki could hear, she'd know what Lark really meant. *I love you. I'll forgive anything if you just come home.*

Now, Nini stomped her slipper onto the carpet. "What a load of hogwash," she said. "This man expects us to believe anything he says, when it took him eight years to check up on her?" Lark almost smiled. Even with her blips of disorientation, Nini would be a more effective interrogator than any sheriff's deputy. "How long might this take?" Nini persisted. "For the police to get answers out of him?"

"I don't know," Lark said. "But I'm going to do my best to speed things up."

Dove appeared in the hallway, dressed to the nines for school, as usual. She was a strong-willed kid who'd insisted on picking her own outfits since she was old enough to proudly pull on pants backward. She wore a satin dress purchased for church on Easter Sunday, three beaded necklaces she'd made from a craft kit, and scrunchies covering her wrist halfway to the elbow. She began to twirl, oblivious to any tension in the room, and threw her arms around Lark's legs.

"Did you love the waterfall, Mama? Wasn't it the best picnic ever, ever, ever?" Dove tipped her little face up and giggled at her mom's blank expression. "Remember?" she said. "Meeting me there, in our dream? You were right about the rules: the ice cream didn't melt!"

It seemed a million years ago when she'd painted that picture for her daughter, but the details flooded back: the raft, clear water, sparkling sun, a place where ice cream didn't melt and the world was as simple as you wanted it to be.

Lark dropped to her knees and hugged her daughter back.

"How could I forget," Lark said.

12

Mikki

Mikki must have drifted off. When she woke, the vibration of the car had gone quiet. Through the windshield, she could see Chris leaning on the hood, ripping the tags off a picnic blanket he must have bought during her shopping spree. Their car sat alone in a small strip of parking spaces, cracked concrete with faded paint lines surrounded on all sides by mounds of high grass bowing in the wind. Mikki looked closer, and goose bumps erupted on her arms, even in the heat of the car. These weren't *mounds* of grass. They were dunes.

She was here.

She opened the door to a cacophony of sound. The rippling of seagrasses in the breeze. The cries of gulls overhead, swooping beneath billowy, fast-moving clouds with patches of blue sky showing through. The pulse of rushing water that could only be waves somewhere nearby, out of sight. All of it loud, vibrant, and yet peaceful, most notable for what she didn't hear.

No highway.

She cocked her head, listening, to be sure. She detected not a single whoosh of street traffic, not a plane overhead, not a bit of radio or a buzzing lawnmower or any sign of human life at all, beyond the man turning to grin at her now.

Wherever he'd brought her, they were utterly alone.

"We're not at the resort?" she asked, pulling up to stand, rubbing the sleep from her eyes.

"We're not far. I thought the first time you see it should be somewhere more out of the way. Without an audience." He closed his eyes and inhaled appreciatively, and she did too. The air was salty, weighted with moisture, like after a drenching rain. "We're in no hurry," he told her, gesturing to the worn wooden boardwalk through the dunes. "After you."

She unlaced her sneakers and peeled off her socks, leaving them on the trunk of the car, and Chris did the same. Then she started across the sand-strewn pavement, trying to keep her cool.

She'd taken only a few steps before impatience kicked in. He'd brought her here so she wouldn't have to act any certain way. They'd been driving for hours. She'd walked off the job. She'd waited her whole life.

Glancing over her shoulder, she caught Chris's eye. He gave a go-for-it nod.

Then she took off in long, free strides. The boardwalk was rickety beneath her bare feet, but she didn't slow to inspect for splinters or loose nails. Wild and free, she crested the ramp and kept going, even as the blue-gray horizon of the Atlantic rose in front of her. She picked up speed, sprinting down the other side, hair whipping out behind her, tangling in the wind, and the emotion flowed out of her in bursts of laughter—or maybe she was choking up, crying too. Her feet hit warm, soft sand. Behind her, Chris let out a whoop; she heard his feet slapping the wooden boards and realized he must be running after her, but she couldn't wait up. She beelined for the water's edge, where the sand turned firm and damp, then straight into the foam, turning parallel to the waves, running alongside them, the denim of her jeans soaking through to her ankles. She filled her lungs, spread her arms, looked down the coast, and saw no one between her and the rise of high buildings in the distance. She slowed and spun in giddy circles, stopping at last to face the water, chest heaving, to stand in awe.

It was exactly what she'd expected.

It was more.

She had never felt so small and so big at once. So close to a higher, spiritual power, yet so grounded, alive and part of something more immense than she'd ever imagined. In that moment, she understood that she could be entirely insignificant in the scheme of things and simultaneously capable of anything.

Chris came to a stop beside her, breathing hard and laughing, throwing an arm around her in a sloppy, happy half hug.

"What do you think?" he asked, joy radiating from his eyes, his smile, his warm hand on her shoulder. He was inseparable from this milestone, and she didn't mind a bit. He'd been kind to bring her here. She wouldn't have wanted to glimpse it through a hotel lobby with tourists and employees milling around, or in the presence of anyone who required restraint, and he'd had the foresight to know this. She blinked back tears, words failing her, so overcome with gratitude that she couldn't imagine he didn't see it, couldn't imagine he didn't know.

"It never gets old," he told her.

At last, she found her voice. "You promise?"

~~~

They spread the blanket on drier sand and sat back on their hands, staring at the Atlantic in companionable silence. Mikki hadn't expected to find such rhythm to something that looked, at a glance, random and feral. She watched the sets lining up to roll in, fixed her eyes on the rising crests, counted the seconds until they crashed into a fantastic roar of foam. It was mesmerizing.

She wasn't a strong swimmer and had a deep respect for the deadliness of water. But she found the gentle slope of it enticing, a literal pull to wade into the force of nature, to become a part of it and leave familiar, solid ground behind.

She wondered how far out she'd dare go. Every day, perhaps, a little farther. Wasn't that how it always was when faced with a new boundary crossed?

"Thank you," Mikki said finally. "Whatever happens from here, it's already worth it."

"I'm glad," Chris said. He had his hands folded behind his head, his eyes closed, looking, for the first time, content. Mikki's gaze drifted back to the waves: it was hard to imagine driving all this way only to close your eyes and miss even one second of this. If she could last this entire trip without sleeping, she would.

"So," she said. "Fill me in. What else should I know? Who's the groom?"

"Jeff Winscott. One of our more successful clients. Owns a chain of elite athletic complexes used by club sports all around Michigan."

"Is that a conflict of interest? Do you think he's the one pressing her to rebuild?"

"Nah. He'll be fine no matter what happens. They're a good match. I like him."

"Okay. So the only match here that really doesn't fit is going to be me?"

He sat up on his elbows. "Who says you don't fit?"

"Please. At the very least we'll need a cover story."

"Why? What do we have to cover?"

"For starters, I assume you're not going to tell everyone you picked me up on a coffee break on the way."

He shrugged. "What's wrong with that?"

"Besides everyone wondering what kind of nut would actually say yes to that?"

"That sounds like more of a you problem," he teased.

Mikki swatted sand onto his feet, and he laughed.

"Okay, I get why you'd ask, but you're overthinking it. It's not like I'll be passing you off as my new girlfriend with everyone cooing and wanting to know how we met. I'll just say I decided to bring a friend, last minute. I think we can avoid the third degree."

"They won't find it strange that you suddenly have a friend they've never heard of?"

"Not if you're a newer friend. Like I said, I've made myself scarce lately." He caught her eye and grinned. "You look disappointed. Why do I get the feeling you *wanted* a cover story?"

It was almost a compliment that he seemed confident she could blend into an out-of-her-league crowd. If he'd been the one to suggest a cover story, she might have even feigned offense.

But maybe this wasn't about either of them having doubts. Maybe what she really wanted was a few days off from being pathetic Mikki who's *still* stuck at the Travel Stop. Who has only one true friend. *She's got potential*, people used to say. *She's going places.*

Now the only thing people said was that she *used to have potential, used to be on her way out and up.* Like it was already too late. Like potential was a thing other people could steal away.

She didn't want to let that be true.

"Let's try this again," Chris said. "Let's make it fun. Who do you want to be?" He gestured toward the ocean. "The world is your oyster."

"Someone whose plans panned out," she admitted. "Who nobody thinks is *just* a service worker or *just* a junkie's daughter or *just* anything."

"Done. I moved to a new townhouse over the summer. So . . . you're a neighbor? We hit it off over beers by the pool. You had vacation time about to expire, like all workaholics do."

"None of your actual neighbors are here?"

"I haven't even met my actual neighbors. What about your name? Keep it, change it? Is Mikki short for something?"

Mikki's name was one of the top three things that drew plenty of incorrect assumptions about her. "When my mom was pregnant, my parents were convinced I was a boy. By the time I was born, they'd been calling me Mikey for months."

"So they switched from Michael to Michaela?"

"One would think. But no, they went ahead and named me Michael anyway. They thought they were hilarious."

Chris seemed to be taking care to keep his expression neutral. "And your nickname . . ."

"I was Mikey when I was little, but I hated being confused with a boy. So in high school, my friends started calling me Mikki. I didn't think it would stick, but it did. Even at home."

"And you prefer it?"

"Honestly? No." She laughed weakly. "But no one assumes I'm a dude. Only a Disney mouse."

"So I guess Minnie is out for your alias, huh?" She scrunched her face, and he laughed. "Hey, be whoever you want. No one knows you here."

Mikki went silent, considering. On the one hand, she didn't want to go on this adventure as someone else, when she could finally go on one as herself.

On the other hand, the name had never really been hers. Only a sour reminder that she hadn't been what anyone was expecting. And look how that had turned out.

"Maybe it's a bad idea," she said, "to use a name I won't answer to?"

That's when she knew. The only name, besides her own, that always made her turn.

"I could be Lark," she said. "She might get a kick out of that. Like a part of her came on this trip after all."

He didn't even bat an eye. "Lark it is. Lark, my neighbor who . . . does what for a living?"

What could Mikki speak knowledgably about? Truckers, gasoline, inventory, retail, food service? "Imports and exports?" she joked.

"Oh, that's perfectly preposterous. No one will question you, either, because they'll worry it makes *them* sound stupid." He shook his head.

"A girl named Michael. Can I just say . . . All your stories are a little sad."

"So are yours. Right down to your nightmare dream car."

"Let's make a pact," he said. "This trip is the one story we're both going to share, right? So let's make it count. Let's promise each other this story will *not* have a sad ending."

Mikki stuck out her hand, and they shook on it.

They had a deal.

13

Lark

The Yes, Please! Motel relied on its monopoly on Becksville's overnight lodging market to stay in business. Lark hadn't been inside for years, but she remembered the lobby as a bold contrast to the enthusiasm in the name. Mikki's ex had finally gotten fired for throwing one too many parties in the vacant rooms, but from what Lark saw across the concrete lots behind the Travel Stop, there were still plenty of parties here.

She just didn't get invited anymore.

Lark still hadn't slept when she pulled in, midmorning, but she'd showered, blown out her shoulder-length hair, and changed into her nicest jeans and a fitted black button-down. She'd polished her engagement ring with toothpaste (a trick Nini had taught her), layered her favorite silver necklaces, and zipped on high-heeled boots that meant business. She would not be written off as travel-stop trash. There'd be no better time for this task: Dove was at school, and Nini was distracting herself with a sudden zest for home organization. Lark herself was a stress cleaner, so she knew when to step aside. When she'd left, Nini had been engrossed in the upended contents of their junk drawer, sorting the mess of expired coupons and old mail.

As usual, there were only a few cars parked beneath the crooked sign with YES, PLEASE! scrawled in a retro script, and it was easy to spot Chris's at the far end. His Toyota sedan was a far cry from the convertible that had turned Mikki's head years ago, but it was still the only vehicle in the lot that didn't look ready to fall apart. The building was a concrete slab divided into two floors, each with ten exterior guest room doors. Every door was painted red, which Lark had always heard was bad luck.

Lark took a guess Chris would've requested a second-floor walkup, where it was marginally quieter and the bugs had higher to climb. She was halfway to the stairs at the end of the row when another car pulled up behind her.

Not just any car. Heath's cruiser.

She froze, but she was too exhausted to muster much surprise. So much for not needing permission.

He exited the car looking equally unshocked but didn't remove his hat the way he usually did when he approached her. That's when she realized how strange it was for him to be wearing it during the day.

"You look nice," he observed.

"Why are you on duty?" she deflected.

"Rummel covered my shift last night, so I'm on my way to do his."

"I thought Rummel was on afternoons."

Heath shrugged. "I said I was on my way, not in a rush. Had a hunch I wanted to follow up on first." He raised an eyebrow. "Has anyone ever told you that you're a terrible liar?"

She felt her face redden.

"When I asked you not to come here, it was written all over your face that you found my opinion adorable yet negligible."

She relaxed a little, seeing he wasn't truly mad.

"I don't know if I'm a *terrible* liar," she said. "It's not my fault you've been trained as a human polygraph."

"Yeah? Well, so have those deputies, FYI."

She didn't know what made her more uneasy: that he was right, or that he found it necessary to point this out. "I'm sorry," she began, but Heath buzzed like she'd answered wrong on a game show.

"My polygraph must be sensitive today. Don't say you're sorry when you're not."

She sighed. "Fine. The truth is, I do not have it in me to sit back and do nothing. I understand your concerns—I do—but when I got home this morning . . ." She trailed off.

"Nini?" he guessed, and she nodded. "I wondered if I should have gone home with you. Did she not take the news well?"

"She got disoriented. It's not unusual when Mikki comes up, but it always throws me, you know? She's been doing so well. We can't afford to have all this stress derail her progress."

Heath frowned. "There was that thing at the hair stylist last week too."

"Anyone could forget their purse," Lark said defensively, trying to reassure herself Nini had been more embarrassed than upset that day. When the stylist had handed Nini the salon phone to call Lark to bring her wallet, Nini hadn't been able to recall Lark's number. Nini insisted she'd just been frazzled. *That woman was staring me down like I'd master-minded the theft of this second-rate beauty school hack job.* She'd scowled. *Like I was a waste of her Aqua Net. Can you imagine?* And Nini *had* seemed completely fine by the time Lark got there. But still.

Now, as he had then, Heath let it drop. "Well," he said, "it's under-standable she'd need a minute. This has been a shock for everyone."

"That's just it. For a second, she was talking about Mikki like we could call her up. Like she was going to have something to say about this too."

He bit his lip. "Okay. I don't think I can escalate my shift change until Stush is retired, but I could start asking around about nighttime childcare. We could afford it if—"

Lark stopped him there. "I don't want to reduce my concerns about Nini to childcare. You know she and I deal with our feelings about

Mikki very differently, but . . . It's not good for her to let this drag on any longer than necessary. Not for me either."

"What are my chances of talking you out of going up there?"

"Zero."

He nodded, like he'd expected as much. Up to the last few surreal hours, he'd never done anything but accept her complicated feelings about this whole tragic mess. In fact, he was the only one, besides Dove, who'd never questioned or judged her role in it all. She owed it to Heath to show him the same respect, to try to understand that his feelings on Mikki would be complicated too—more so by the minute, now that it wasn't all in the past.

"I assume you've looked up Redmond online?" he asked.

"I tried." It was the logical step, now that they had his name. But browsing all the search results had been weirdly deflating. "There's so much stuff about the Redmond business, it was hard to tell if anything was relevant without going down the rabbit hole. I got the sense I knew his type, though. Entitled."

"I saw enough to know they're not squeaky clean. They've admitted wrongdoing and paid settlements, so it's a good bet they've gotten away with stuff too. Then again, hard to say how much of that comes with the territory of an investment firm that big."

"Do you think you could look into that more?" she ventured. "Make sure you don't spot anything the deputies might miss? My mind is in a million places. I can't sit in front of a computer and read."

"That I can do," Heath said. "What I can't do is go up these stairs with you and knock on that man's door. The last thing we need is me on anyone's shitlist for overstepping."

"Not a problem," she assured him.

"Yes, it is. Because I can't let you go alone either."

"I'll be fine."

"If something goes wrong, I won't be. You of all people know what that's like." He pointed to his cruiser. "I'm staying where he can't miss me. With my eyes on that door and my hand on my radio."

Lark fidgeted with the ends of her hair. "That's not overstepping? Being here in uniform, in a patrol car, giving the impression you're on duty?"

"I can't control other people's impressions. Only way I let the woman I love go in there is with an obvious police escort putting Redmond on notice. Non-negotiable." It was *the woman I love* bit that was still just shiny and new enough to get her, and he knew it.

"Thanks," she said. "Now that I'm here, I'm . . ." She looked up at the rusty steps she was about to climb. They looked like no one had checked them for structural damage in years. "I'm glad I'm not alone," she finished.

〜〜

When Chris opened his motel room door, he already had an apology in his eyes. Unlike Lark, he hadn't showered. The bed behind him was as rumpled as the T-shirt and joggers he wore, but he looked weary as his eyes flitted past her to Heath's cruiser. She could tell it had the intended effect.

But he'd already been on notice from the second his eyes met hers.

"You're not surprised to see me," she said.

"No." He made no move to open the door further, but his knuckles whitened as he tightened his grip on the frame. "Listen. There's no way to say this without sounding like a dick. But I just got off the phone with my lawyer."

She laughed, bitterly. "You're right," she said. "There's not."

"I didn't want to call him, but that's what you do when you've spent half the night with the county sheriff."

"That's what *you* do," she corrected him. "Some of us can't afford to pay professionals to make our excuses."

"That's not what's happening here. He just doesn't think it's a good idea for me to speculate with you about anything that might've happened after Mikki and I said goodbye. At least until the deputies finish their inquiry. I don't want to be a hard-ass. I just don't want to be dumb either."

"Lucky for you, the role of dumb has already been filled. I've been playing it for years."

"That's not fair."

"You're right," she said coolly. "It isn't."

He hung his head, a damned-if-you-do, damned-if-you-don't gesture, and she almost felt sorry for him. He might still be realizing what he'd gotten into, but to his credit, he hadn't turned tail and run, not even to a more suitable hotel someplace a little harder to reach.

"Mikki told me you were tough," he said. "I should have expected you were this good at standing your ground."

"I had no choice but to learn," she said.

An awkward silence rose around them, the long exterior walkway stretching away from Lark, the tiny room beckoning Chris back into the dim. Neon numbers flashed on the faux wood alarm clock on the nightstand behind him, begging for someone to reset the time.

"I get why you can't speculate," she said, more softly. "But your lawyer didn't say not to talk to me at all, right? Bet you could tell me plenty of other things that might shed some light."

His eyes flicked to Heath's cruiser again, then back to hers. Then he stepped aside and gestured at the little round table with two chairs squeezed between the door and the TV stand.

She dipped past him before he could change his mind, hooking her purse over her chair as she dropped into it. He pulled the curtains open, making the room feel mercifully less intimate, before perching across from her. In the cramped quarters, every breath was too loud, every second an invasion of personal space. Lark wished she'd brought some peace offering—decent coffees, muffins. She hadn't come with peace on her mind.

But maybe she should have.

"I'm guessing you're a mom now?" he asked. For some reason, this was the last thing she'd expected. "Mikki talked about you a lot," he added.

"About how I was ruining her life by getting knocked up by someone who already has a family?"

"You can't really believe that's how she saw it." His expression turned sad. "I guess this whole situation would make you second-guess everything."

"Welcome to the club," she said. He worried the chipped edge of the tabletop with his fingertips. "Why was Mikki using my name?" The question burst out of her unplanned, but it was as good a place as any to start.

"I think she wanted a vacation from being herself. But also a name she'd answer to. It was obvious your friendship meant a lot to her. Everything we did, she kept saying she wished you could see it." Lark's eyes began to tear. She did not need this man, of all people, to validate her friendship with Mikki. So why did she want to beg him to say it again?

"You can see why the cops would think that's shady," she pointed out. "I didn't like the way they looked at me."

"I can set them straight on that," he said. "If anything, it was an homage."

Lark scowled. "Let's not get carried away. Mikki wanted a lot of things, but never to be me."

"Not you," he agreed. "But more like you. You don't think she envied your ability to make lemonade out of lemons? And actually be happy drinking it?"

Lark's eyes narrowed. It wasn't really a compliment, was it, that Mikki had wished her standards could be so low? But why were they talking about Lark, anyway?

"Tell me about the wedding," she said. "I never even knew where it was."

"The Topaz Amelia Island." Lark was pretty sure Topaz resorts were in the same luxury class as the Ritz or Omni, but Chris didn't say it with any kind of air. He tugged at the collar of his T-shirt like it was choking him. "It's not a weekend anyone in my family likes to replay. We'd been through a lot, losing my parents, and we were about to go through a lot more. At the time, we thought that weekend marked a new start, but looking back, it was more of an intermission."

"Who was getting married?"

"My sister."

Lark did a double take. "You brought a stranger to your own sister's wedding?"

"I know. But . . . is it weird to say Mikki never felt like a stranger?"

Something about the way he said it made her look closer. "Did you two, I mean . . ."

He ran a hand through his hair. "I only meant I've never met anyone like her."

"And what about her? Did she have fun?"

It sounded flimsy and overeager, like she was picking Dove up from one of her playdates. *Did she have fun?* After all this time, *that's* what she wanted to know?

Strangely, it was. It had been so long since she'd had any reason at all to be happy for her friend. Pure joy on Mikki's behalf had always been one of the best feelings. Selfless. Real.

Rare.

Chris smiled. "She did. She was admirably unfazed by my family's baggage. We hadn't been there five minutes before she told me it was all worth it. The long drive, the uncertainty of doing this crazy thing . . ."

He stopped abruptly, realizing what he'd said. This time, Lark couldn't blink back the tears. They trailed down her cheeks in hot lines. *Worth it.* Sure.

But just because it had seemed worth it at first didn't mean it had stayed that way.

"The deputies said she *came into some money*," she said. "What are they talking about?"

Chris's face flushed. "That will veer us into speculation territory. I'm sorry."

Lark toed the dirty carpet with her boot. If she hadn't taken time to dress for this meeting, if she hadn't lingered to make sure Nini was engrossed in her puttering, if she hadn't been confronted by Heath in the parking lot, maybe she'd have arrived ahead of the phone call with the lawyer and Chris would have told her everything.

She hated this feeling, this overpowering, hopeless need to rewind and do things over. She used to live inside it. Only recently, giving herself over to love with Heath and contentment with Nini and a joy in parenthood, had she finally let it go.

"But the cops wouldn't explain," she said. "They told me to ask you."

"Sorry," he said again. "I ignore my lawyer whenever possible, but I can't on this. Let's just give it time."

"Do you not think," she said with a calm fueled by quiet fury, "I have waited long enough?"

Chris didn't have an answer for that. He stood and went to the window. Lark imagined Heath's eyes on him from below, and it made her feel stronger. Reinforced.

"They didn't explain much to me either," he said. "How hard did they look for me, before?"

"Not very."

"That's unfortunate. I wish they'd found me. It seems kind of hopeless now."

This was the last thing she wanted to hear from the person who had restored her hope for the first time in years. The authorities might not have looked for Chris, but Lark had never stopped. She had looked for him in every face she saw: at the Travel Stop, on the street, behind the wheel of every vehicle she passed. She had looked for him in grainy surveillance video of customers and shiny Instagram photos of strangers, in reports of rapes and kidnappings on the news, in the stands behind home plate during televised baseball games. She'd looked for him scattershot, without direction, because she'd never known where or how to start.

Now here he was, and she *still* didn't know which way to turn before taking her next step. Was it possible the deputies were right, that this wasn't much of a lead at all? And that Heath was right, too, that this could upheave her life again for nothing?

"Nobody who mattered would believe me that anything was wrong," she said carefully. "Maybe they'll believe you."

"Maybe," he said, and for the first time, Lark considered that she might have found in Chris an unlikely ally. That working together, unappealing as it was, might be the smartest way to resolve their mutual problems. Lark wouldn't like it, but she could do it. When it came to Mikki, the old rules still applied: say yes as much as possible. Heath would hate it, though.

"About the deputies," Chris said. "They seemed confused on the issue of Mikki not having her phone."

Lark's palms went clammy beneath the table. "What about it?"

"They said you didn't discover her phone until you went home. That you'd have tried harder to stop her leaving if you'd known she didn't have it."

She wiped her palms against her jeans. "So?"

"So, you knew she didn't have it. You argued about it before we left. In front of me."

Lark's face burned, remembering. How she'd followed Mikki to the parking lot. How Chris had been inside his car, face obscured by the glare of the lights on the windshield, overhearing the whole thing. The scene had been embarrassing, but had no bearing on anything.

At least, not until she'd kind of, sort of, not quite accidentally lied about it later.

"How am I in the hot seat here?" she exploded. "Nini was right: you have a lot of nerve." She got to her feet. She never should have sat down. She never should have come at all.

"For the record," he said, "I would've waited if she wanted to go get her phone. Or lent her mine or bought her one of those prepaid mobiles. She was never a hostage."

Lark gripped the back of the chair she'd been sitting in. It teetered flimsily. "You were just such the perfect gentleman, weren't you? You did everything a woman could possibly want, except for making sure she got home safe. Details."

She could tell it stung, but he didn't go on the defensive. Understanding dawned in his eyes. "You were trying to save face," he said. "When they blamed you. It sounded better to say you didn't realize she had no device pinging her location."

"Don't tell me what I was trying to do." Lark headed for the door. Her hand was on the knob when he called after her.

"Might look shady, but you had your reasons, right?" She hesitated, leaving an opening just big enough for him to slip through. "Well, so did I," he went on. "You can wait and see what the police turn up, or you can believe me now: they're not going to catch me in any kind of lie. You and I, we're not the ones with anything important to hide."

Lark squeezed her eyes shut, hating how he grouped them together. There would never be a *you and I* between them. Besides, lots of liars believed they were too smart to get caught.

"Mikki would have hated how this turned out for you," he said.

At that, she turned to face him. It was irritating, how he acted like he'd known Mikki so well when allegedly they'd spent only a few days together.

It was even more irritating that so far, everything he'd said was true.

She pulled a slip of paper from her pocket, where she'd written her name and cell phone number before she came, and tossed it on the table.

"Call me when you're ready to speculate."

14

Mikki

Mikki stood on the balcony, looking down at the coastline sparkling in the late-afternoon sun. Twelve stories up, she felt removed from it in a way she hadn't when she could feel it beneath her toes, but her view was all-encompassing here, the scene even more impossibly beautiful.

Chris had given her the room key at check-in, staying behind to see to the valet and luggage. The convertible's tiny trunk had been packed like a clown car—a roller suitcase, garment bags, golf clubs, gifts wrapped in shiny silver paper, a box of enough liquor, wine, and mixers to set up his own bar cart, a cooler filled with seltzer and beer. Whereas Mikki, with all her purchases jammed into the duffel bag she'd bought, looked like she was heading for the gym instead of checking in. Not that she'd been the only one. The Topaz boasted tennis courts, racquetball, golf, and other sports you could look very put together while playing.

Mikki had never seen such a resort, much less imagined herself at one. Tiers of infinity pools, polished fountains running alongside footpaths, canvas umbrellas, and cabanas arranged artfully around the grounds, uniformed staff carrying trays of drinks garnished with fruit slices, palms casting delicate lines of shade over lush flowering gardens—all of it was the stuff of private islands whose names she couldn't pronounce, where world languages mingled and anybody glamorous enough to come must be somebody special. It was hard to fathom this was the northern Florida coast, where anyone could drive on up, line chairs on the sand, and say, "I do."

Mikki felt like an actress in a movie surveying it all. She'd left the french doors open at her back so she'd hear Chris come in, gauzy curtains billowing in the breeze. He'd been right about the layout of the suite: the pullout couch was no consolation prize. In fact, she might sleep on one of the plush loungers out here. She wondered if there were mosquitos this high, or lizards. It seemed a hotel this ritzy would have found a way to have complete control over its environment, removing even the smallest of uninvited guests.

Mikki was still waiting for the catch.

It was one thing to finally get a lucky break. It was another to let that convince you everything you knew about the world was suddenly less true.

From inside, she heard the door click open and Chris's polite chat with the bellman over the shuffling of bags and boxes being unloaded. She lingered, sliding down to peer over the far end of the wraparound railing, giving him a moment to settle things. From this vantage, she could see the full perimeter of the pool closest to the beach access. She couldn't believe how few people were enjoying the amenity. She could count the number of swimmers on one hand, and none were actually swimming, but rather standing at the edge with a book or lounging in pairs.

"Chris!" At the squeal behind her, Mikki instinctively took a step farther out of the sightline from the room. "I told them to text me the instant you arrived," the voice gushed. "I was starting to think you might not come after all."

Mikki peered through the sheer, billowing curtains and saw a woman throwing her arms around Chris. She was a brunette, with the broad shoulders and athletic build of a competitive swimmer, maybe, or a tennis pro, and shockingly tall, stretching several inches above Chris's six-foot frame with her Barbie heels on. A one-shouldered black linen number showed off a modest amount of perfectly tanned skin.

He pulled back to give her an affectionate, if hesitant, look. "You were not. You know I wouldn't miss my big sister's wedding for the world."

Mikki didn't know why she'd been expecting a different sort of sister. A platinum blonde, size zero in a take-no-prisoners pantsuit. This woman seemed more warm, more real, more complex than the hyperdriven businesswoman Chris had painted a picture of. She was smiling wistfully at her brother with tears in her eyes.

"It's hard to know anything anymore. You've missed every other invite I've sent you the past six months," she said quietly. "Plus ninety-five percent of my calls and ninety-two percent of my emails."

"But who's counting," Chris joked, but Mikki could see Kim wouldn't let him off so easy. "Sorry," he said more quietly. "I kept telling you I wasn't ready to talk about rebuilding."

"And I kept telling *you* with a little time, you'd come around."

"And when I agreed to *take* time, I meant more than a day without my phone ringing."

"And when I agreed to *give you* time, I didn't know I'd be managing a PR nightmare with no one but Cooper to help." Mikki's whole body cringed, and she wondered if they were about to launch into a year's worth of repressed arguments right there. But then Kim clapped her hands once, as if pressing a reset button, and the moisture cleared from her eyes. Her smile returned.

"Well, we're both here now. We have the whole weekend. I know Cooper teased you about coming alone, but I'm glad you did." Chris's eyes flicked to the balcony, and Mikki didn't move fast enough. They found hers and brightened. "Because we really do need—"

"I didn't actually," Chris cut in. He slung an arm around Kim and started leading her outside. "Come meet Lark."

The name caught Mikki off guard. She'd already forgotten and wished she could take the decision back and stick with her own name, one familiar thing in this beyond-her-comfort-zone place. But it was too late to play it off—or to make a better impression on the bride. Mikki regretted not having stepped directly into the shower to avoid any chance of this scenario.

"Oh." Kim was smooth. Only her eyes betrayed a hint of displeasure at Mikki's service-worker-chic outfit. Or maybe at Mikki's presence in general. "Lovely to meet you, Lark. Chris, you should've told me. I'll have the seating charts adjusted. And a welcome bag sent up for your guest." She pulled out her phone to fire off a text message, glancing up to wink at her brother. "Sorry, but they're just for the women. You'll have to get your own samples from the spa."

"Brought my own," Chris deadpanned. "Never leave home without them."

Kim's polite smile stayed in place as she looked Mikki up and down curiously. Mikki felt stale and frumpy from the long car ride, feet gritty with sand inside her socks, tacky footing next to the perfectly manicured, perfectly pedicured woman. Worse, she felt rude and uncouth, the sort of wedding guest who arrived without a thought that seating charts would need to be adjusted, favors bagged and delivered, even though the oversight was not hers. Chris could have sent a note ahead that he was bringing a plus-one after all. Kim's eyes fell on the gym bag Mikki had tossed on the couch. Though she'd torn the Target price tag from the handle, she'd missed the bright yellow clearance sticker on the side panel.

It could not have been more obvious she didn't belong here.

"He talked me into coming last minute," Mikki stammered. Remembering something, she decided to take a chance. "Apparently you inspired him to be more spontaneous? And he inspired me. But I might have packed a little *too* spontaneously." She rolled her eyes at her own bag, as if she might have reached for her Chanel tote in a dark closet and silly her, not noticed that she'd come up with last season's off-brand vinyl.

But Kim was nudging Chris playfully. "Wonders never cease. You occasionally listen to me after all."

Chris moaned. "Lark, you weren't supposed to tell her. This'll go straight to her head." He kept saying Mikki's assumed name as if to remind them both. *You're Lark. What a lark. Isn't this a fun, larky, larky, larky lark.*

Kim didn't miss a beat. "It's good to see you're capable of making a decision without overthinking it to death. I can't wait to see what others are in store." Before Chris could deflect the jab, Kim turned to Mikki. "You'll see lots of girl time on tomorrow's agenda. Bachelorette-style stuff. You're welcome to join anything you'd like. You're my brother's date after all."

Mikki felt panicked at the idea of attending any part of this without Chris. She'd known she'd be a fish out of water here, but he was the one who'd plucked her out in his net, and they'd established some trust between them. In fact, in this environment, she trusted him more than she trusted herself to know what was right, what was expected.

Besides, she didn't need an agenda beyond walking along the water or perching here on this stunning balcony, alone. What she really wanted was to keep as much of this experience as possible for herself. To experience a different kind of independence for a change, one that she sought out instead of having it foisted upon her like a burden.

Then again, she'd told herself there could be opportunities here, and she wouldn't find them alone.

"That's so nice of you to include me," Mikki purred. "But I do have to steal some hours to keep up with work while I'm here. It was the only way I could get away on short notice. Chris promised he'd be so busy with the wedding party it wouldn't be rude for me to hang back in the downtime."

"Of course," Kim said easily. "Been there. *Live* there. Where do you work?"

Mikki could not look this force-to-be-reckoned-with squarely in the eye and feed her some glib line about imports and exports. Kim wasn't merely no-nonsense but formidable.

"Actually," Chris said, "Lark is looking for a new job. In case you know of any leads. Her hours are terrible. Bringing her laptop along to the beach is nothing compared with all the sleep she's been losing."

He gave her a conspiratorial look, looking proud of his slick wording, but Mikki squirmed. Was she . . . feeling *defensive*? Of the job she hated, of all things?

"I envy anyone who's hiring these days," Kim said breezily. "My hands have been tied for almost a year. Speaking of." She pivoted expertly to Chris, whose proud expression quickly fell. "Since your date has to squeeze in some work, I'm sure you can find time for a quick conference with Cooper and me. We've got this deadline with the end of the fiscal year, and optics to manage. It's time."

Chris's face darkened further, and Mikki realized too late she'd set him up for this.

"We're here to celebrate you, Kim," he said. "For once, let's give the work stuff a rest."

"Sure, I'll give it a rest. As soon as I have your signature on some papers we need out of the way. They're in my room. If we do it now, I'm officially off duty. Best wedding gift ever."

"If they're the papers I think they are, I'm afraid I'm not prepared to sign them in the next four days."

His line sounded as rehearsed as Kim's had, like they were putting on a stage play for Mikki's benefit. She hoped she was interpreting this conversation wrong. That she was not in a front-row seat to an actual come-to-Jesus about the fate of the Redmond estate.

"I've made every effort to get this taken care of before this weekend," Kim countered. "So if you don't want to deal with it here, that's on you. We can afford no more delays. As far as I know, you haven't actually put together your own proposal . . . have you?" Chris remained silent. "Right. Well, you were the only one who was interested in pursuing alternative build locations or plans to sell. And since you didn't pursue them, here we are. Fortunately, Cooper and I have done the work, and I guarantee you won't find one advisor who'd look at our numbers and call it a bad plan. All we have to do is say go. And I intend to say it before I leave for my honeymoon."

"I can find plenty of advisors who'd call it bad karma."

"If you'd taken my calls, you'd know this is what our clients want. Letting them down is far worse karma than rebuilding on property you think has bad juju."

"It's the grounds of a very real lawsuit, Kim. Not a haunted ancient burial ground."

"Exactly. One tragic incident does not overshadow generations of our family's legacy on that land. If we sell it off, tragedy *becomes* the legacy."

Mikki found it a convincing argument. But Chris didn't bend. "More like, if we don't sell it off, you save a buck by rebuilding on land that would sell well below market."

"I'm not the only one in favor of this."

"And which part of the work did Cooper do, exactly?"

Kim fixed him with a stony glare. "The part where he didn't waste everyone's time. Come on, Chris. Lark says you're being more spontaneous. Come look at the paperwork. We've laid out a couple options; just choose and we can put this behind us. I give you my word, whether you take your starting spot back on the field or claim your cushy spectator seats in the owner's box, I promise I'll understand. As long as you're off the sidelines, because no offense, but we need those benches for our players and coaches. I imagine you're free now."

Both siblings looked at Mikki, then away, back to the reality that they'd been having a very familiar argument in very unfamiliar company.

When Kim first walked in, Mikki had honestly thought she just wanted to make things right with her brother before the weekend's ceremonies. But Kim was not only forcing him to talk business but also using her own wedding as an ultimatum to solidify the future of the company—with or without Chris. No wonder he hadn't wanted to bring a date, and no wonder he hadn't wanted to come alone.

Feeling trapped by obligations; *that* Mikki understood.

"Actually, Chris," Mikki said, "the front desk called. There's some kind of valet issue. They requested you come back down. At your 'earliest possible convenience,' they said."

Kim frowned, and Chris straightened. They both recognized a lifeline when they saw it.

Mikki had the uncomfortable feeling they recognized a lie when they saw it too.

"I'd better go," Chris told Kim, risking a grateful nod at Mikki. "Let me walk you out."

After they'd gone, the empty nice-to-meet-yous and reminders of this evening's cocktail hour echoed in the empty room. Mikki closed her eyes and let the exhaustion wash over her, waiting for the strained voices to fade until all she could hear was the distant pounding of the waves through the open balcony door. Then she went for her duffel.

She wouldn't risk anyone else coming to the door before she'd had a chance to freshen up. She wouldn't underestimate anything about this trip anymore. She had to stay focused, for a change, on herself.

15

Lark

Lark felt as if she was living in one of those multiverses.

In the universe she knew, the unstoppable linear progression of one day into the next, her life was grounded in the ever-changing *now*, as only a parent's can be: the banter with other moms at school pickup, Dove's familiar calls to *Look at me!* and *Watch this!* at the playground on the way home, the snuggles and giggles in front of the TV as Nini called out wrong guesses to *Family Feud*.

But some parallel reality seemed to exist in Lark's peripheral vision, only to disappear each time she turned to face it head-on. And that universe felt too much like a time warp back to the aftermath of Mikki's disappearance, those endless days when a tense undercurrent followed Lark through town. The whispering behind Lark's back she pretended not to hear, the sideways looks she pretended not to see.

This time, Lark didn't need to be told that everyone was talking about how the driver who'd taken Mikki had resurfaced. Even in a town with actual news, this would make a splash, and in Becksville, it was a cannonball of gossip. *Waltzing in like he did nothing wrong,* they'd be saying by now. *But if he didn't,* they'd inevitably wonder, *then who did?*

She already knew how this would go: the squirmy discomfort of all eyes on her, all ears, all hands, too, pressing into the crook of her elbow, falling onto her shoulder, squeezing her hand—all the falsely intimate ways she hated to be touched. *We're here if you need anything,* they'd say, hoping to find out some new tidbit the rest of them had yet to hear. And when she caught them talking, they wouldn't have the decency to be embarrassed.

It didn't take long for her suspicions to be confirmed. Only until dinnertime, when Dove wanted cheesy macaroni and Lark had to run out for milk—and caught the cashier, Cindy, dishing with Darla, who ran the bargain haircut place next door.

"I've never understood how the grandmother could forgive her," Darla was saying. When she looked up and saw Lark, she merely pivoted.

"How *is* Nini these days, honey?"

Darla was one to talk about forgiveness. The one time she'd ever cut Mikki's hair, Mikki cried for days about how misshapen it was.

"Still a cranky old bat," Lark told them, and they laughed and laughed: *Good ole Nini.* Lark plunked her dollar bills onto the belt and didn't wait around for her change.

There was no fighting it, so she wouldn't. She'd play along, the gullible doormat who'd once had potential. And that potential's name had been Mikki. They could have their fill of Lark; she knew how to bear it. But she only knew how to bear it alone. She didn't know what she'd do if Heath felt this same heat burning the back of his neck. She didn't know how to stop it from singeing their relationship. Worse, the whole powder keg would explode if anyone so much as breathed a word about this within earshot of Dove.

Fortunately, Heath's uniform commanded respect, and even that paled next to Dove's cherubic face, which radiated an innocence that inspired best behavior from friends and strangers alike. Postures would straighten, smiles would brighten, cigarettes would extinguish beneath the soles of shoes, curse words would turn to *gosh dang.* Even Nini, despite the nerve-racking day, had stopped her anxious puttering through the house once Dove got home, an unspoken agreement not to let on that anything was amiss until they had real news. Lark didn't know whether to carry Dove around like a shield or to keep her hidden away.

It doesn't matter that everyone knows, Lark told herself. *It changes nothing.*

Funny, how the prospect of nothing changing could be both comfort and cause for panic.

~~~

Pete offered Lark the night off work, knowing she hadn't slept, but staying home felt like conceding that she had reason not to show her face. All night, she'd watched Nini for recurring signs of confusion, but Nini was on to her, speaking and moving with unnatural precision. When Lark told Dove it was bedtime, Nini retrieved Dove's reading log without reminding, shooting Lark a look that said, *We're fine. Don't make this worse by second-guessing me.*

So Lark pinned on her name tag and went through the regular bedtime routine with her daughter. When Dove asked, "What's our dream tonight, Mama?" Lark was ready.

"We're floating in a big hot-air balloon, just you and me," she said.

"Like Dorothy and Toto?" Dove asked.

"Just like. Only this balloon is even prettier, with flowers all over it in every color of the rainbow. And we're floating over town, so high that all the houses and cars and streets below us look like tiny miniature figures. Like a toy model, like the people inside can't even be real."

"Way up in the air, where no one can touch us," Dove said, yawning her approval.

"Where no one can touch us," Lark echoed, hugging her close.

When she walked into work a short time later, Sergio's eyebrows disappeared into his hairline. "Sure you're okay to be here, boss?"

She nodded. "If anyone asks for me tonight," she tried to joke, "get their mug shot first, will you?" She ducked into the back office and was shrugging off her coat when she caught sight of a white letter-size envelope tossed on the desk. *Lark* was printed on the front in nondescript handwriting, and the flap was sealed. Thinking it odd, she tore it open right away.

Inside was a single piece of paper. She recognized the black-and-white photo from her high school yearbook: a candid shot of her and Chad after one of his football games. He was holding his helmet, sweaty and smiling in his muddy uniform, and she was wearing his letterman's jacket, resting her head on his shoulder pad and gazing adoringly up at him. Whether it'd been photocopied from the yearbook or printed from somewhere online, she couldn't tell; the photo saw a lot of mileage in their class reunion groups whenever the chat turned to the glory days of Chad and their winning record. No one ever commented on who he was with.

This paper did, though. In the same handwriting from the envelope, someone had scrawled one short sentence:

If you stir up the past, other people might too.

It took her a minute to register why it sounded so much like a threat.

Because it was.

But a threat to do what, exactly? To tell Chad he was Dove's dad? To tell *Becksville* Chad was Dove's dad? To tell Chad's parents or his wife? To tell Dove?

Lark read it again and again, and each time the words stung her more—and alarmed her less. What purpose could this letter possibly have, other than being randomly cruel? Such overt basking in the drama of her misfortune was a new low, but it wasn't new. Why else would anyone care whether Lark "stirred up the past" looking for Mikki? What else was she supposed to do after Chris strolled back in asking for her? Look the other way?

Unless . . . Chris himself had left the letter? He was the only one she could think of who'd want Lark to back off and keep her mouth shut. But how would he possibly know about Chad?

She stomped out to the counter, jamming the letter back inside the envelope so Sergio couldn't see what it said. Lark never had headed off any rumors about who Dove's father was, and as a consequence, she assumed it was something of an open secret, easy to guess that it was Chad. But for better or worse, the rumors orbiting Mikki's disappearance had relegated Dove's paternity to a footnote on the juicier gossip. Lark didn't care to know what people thought, and so she didn't.

"Where did this come from?" she demanded, waving the envelope.

Sergio looked at her blankly. "Dunno, boss. What is it? Where was it?"

"On my desk. Did Pete mention it earlier?"

"I don't think anyone's been back there. Pete had car trouble today."

"Was the office unlocked when you came in?"

"Yep. The door was open and the light was on."

Great. Virtually anyone could have ducked into the employee hallway unnoticed, and it was certainly no secret that Lark worked here. Concern must have shown on her face, because Sergio said, "There's a trooper here fueling up now . . . Want me to ask if Heath is around?"

"No!" Lark shook her head. "No, it's no big deal," she said, forcing nonchalance into her voice. Heath already had reservations about her having gone to see Chris, which she had every intention of doing again. If Heath knew about the odd tone of this letter, she didn't know how he might react, but he wasn't likely to let it go.

Lark had always appreciated that Heath was a pretty black-and-white person. After living too many years inside the gray area where she didn't know anything for certain, she'd welcomed the move to Heath's world of right and wrong, yes or no, rules are rules. But she hadn't counted on the grayest thing in her life tinting everything again. Especially not now, when she and Heath were in the process of melding the contrasts of their lives into a pattern that pleased them both.

Which meant for now, at least, she'd have to deal—or not deal—with this herself.

Backtracking to the office, she logged in to view the day's surveillance footage and found the system had been turned off overnight, presumably when the deputies had requested a copy of last night's video, which was still open on the screen in the download confirmation window. But there was no recording from today. An inconvenient oversight in the chaos.

Inconvenient for Lark anyway. There was no way to replay who'd put the envelope in the office now. Convenient for the culprit, though.

Toggling the system back online, Lark ignored her inbox and instead returned to last night's surveillance video, forcing herself to rewatch it all: Chris lingering by the coffee and her awkward approach with her body on guard, like an animal unsure whether to flee or pounce.

When the police replayed this, what would they be looking for? What would they think they saw? Would they zoom in on Chris for his reaction, or would they be watching Lark, same as everyone else seemed to be?

She thought back to Chris's parting words in his motel room. *You and I, we're not the ones with anything important to hide. They're not going to catch me in any kind of lie.*

The emphasis seemed purposeful. Not *I didn't lie,* but *They're not going to catch me.*

Or maybe there had been a smidge of inflection: *They're not going to catch me.*

Maybe she was being too quick to dismiss the possibility that Chris was behind this stupid envelope. But it seemed like a pretty big risk for him to have skulked back in here after the scene they'd made last night. Especially knowing the cameras were there.

No. This letter was no more than a waste of valuable space in her brain.

It probably really was nothing but someone's idea of a sick joke. And even if it was something, there was no reason to presume Chris was behind it. Or to read more deeply into his posturing about which of them would more likely be caught in a lie. Besides, not disclosing Chad's paternity wasn't lying . . . was it? For all the bluntness on display in Becksville, no one had ever once asked her directly.

At least, not anyone she owed the truth to.

Not about that.

In the panic of losing Mikki, Lark had never intended to be anything but a hundred percent honest with law enforcement. And she would have been if the deputy taking her statement had not filled in the blanks as he walked her through the timeline.

"And when you got home that night," he'd prompted. "Or should I say that morning. That's when you saw her phone on the table and realized she'd left it?"

She looked in his eyes, about to correct him, but what she saw there made her pause.

He'd clearly thought she'd done a foolish thing in watching her friend walk out that door without doing everything in her power to stop her. He already pitied her. He knew how unlikely it was that anyone would be able to help, not today, not tomorrow, not ever. And he knew when things turned hopeless, people would blame Lark. At the very least, they'd want some explanation as to how she could be so cavalier.

He was assuming she had one.

The truth was, Lark had chased Mikki to the parking lot as soon as she'd remembered, tripping over her own feet to catch her friend in time. As she'd thrown open the door, she'd been so certain this would change things, stop Mikki from going, she'd had the audacity to feel prematurely relieved.

"Mikki!" she'd called. Mikki had her hand on the roof of the BMW, about to open the door, looking starry-eyed, flushed, and determined. "Your phone. Remember?" Lark had smacked her own forehead for effect. "At the very least, you have to stop home for it."

She'd chosen her words poorly.

"*Have* to?" Mikki's free hand found its way to her hip.

"It's not safe to go without it." Lark was stating the obvious, wasn't she? Mikki hesitated, as if for one honest instant, she was about to agree. "That's the problem with cell phones." She'd scowled. "Everyone acts like we can't live without being at the world's beck and call 24-7. Pretty sure no one would have gone for that sales pitch out the gate."

Lark checked herself. Did she feel so strongly about the phone because she truly felt Mikki needed it? Or because *she* would feel better if Mikki had it?

Well, so what if both were true. Was that so bad?

"But this is when they make sense," she insisted. "When you're about to do something like, oh, I don't know, get in a car with some stranger."

Lark hadn't cared if Chris overheard. She only cared about protecting her friend. But the way Mikki looked at her then . . . It didn't just shut her up, it followed her home. It haunted her still. Like she was disappointed in Lark for caring about all the wrong things.

Like she was disappointed in Lark, period.

"When I said earlier that I didn't want to hear from anyone but you, I meant it," Mikki said, unbending. "Tell everyone I'm too sick to talk. I never call in sick—even from a terrible liar like you, they'll buy it. Look, I'll still check in, okay? Hotels have phones. I'll be fine." She'd opened the car door then, closing the discussion. "Catch you later."

Lark couldn't deny she could've forced her own phone on Mikki right then, insisted they switch for a few days. Or thrown herself onto the hood, threatening that no one was going anywhere until Mikki had a phone in her pocket. She could have protested louder, launched every argument she could think of until Mikki relented.

As stubborn and unpredictable as Mikki could be, Lark didn't think Mikki would have actually gone through with leaving if Lark had doubled down on her objection. If Lark had tearfully told the truth: that she was too scared to let her go, that she needed her too much to risk any chance this trip would not have a happy ending. If Lark had not always ascribed to the idea that if you loved something, you had to let it go.

Days later, when the uniformed deputy turned that pitying gaze on Lark, somehow, she saw all that guilt and shame reflected back at her. All the ways things could have been different.

"Ma'am?" he'd repeated. "When you got home from your shift, that's when you realized she didn't have her phone with her?"

Lark had blinked away tears. She didn't need to hear anyone else's judgment to know that Mikki may have done a stupid thing, but Lark was the truly stupid one. And Lark was going to pay.

"Yes," she heard herself say. "That's when I realized."

She told herself it was no big deal. An insignificant detail. And wasn't it better to stay focused on the real issue at hand? Wasn't it easier and smarter and even healthier not to get mired in could-have-would-have-should-have details that were a distraction from finding Mikki?

But on some level, she'd recognized it for what it was: a lie she'd missed the opportunity to correct.

One that would stick with her from that point forward.

When Nini finally decided to set aside her grudge against Lark.

When Dove needed her to reinforce the difference between right and wrong.

When the man she wanted to spend her life with, a man in a different law enforcement uniform, told her that he could see her lies coming a mile away.

When Chris Redmond returned and said, *You were trying to save face.* Far be it for him to remember one single useful thing to help them find Mikki, but naturally he could clearly recall her whole argument with Lark unfolding right in front of him.

If the police knew she had lied about something so stupid, how would it look for the investigation? How would it look for the rumor mill? How would it look for Nini, Mikki's only family, whom Lark had tried so hard to make her own? How would it look for Lark's sweet, dependent daughter? For her trusting, devoted fiancé?

The answer would look the same for them all.

Like Lark was not to be believed.

Chris had said the police seemed "confused on the issue" of Lark not knowing that Mikki was leaving without her phone. He'd implied he hadn't corrected them—yet—out of sympathy for Lark. But they'd surely question him again, and what if he contradicted Lark's statement then? What if they asked her about it again? Lark would have only two choices: to double down on a lie she never meant to tell or to fess up to having lied in the first place.

Either way, her credibility would be shattered. And not only with the men in uniform.

She didn't realize until after, people still said, like that was Lark's only defense, her only justification for her actions that night—or lack thereof.

No matter what Chris Redmond thought he'd heard or seen, no matter what he said about her, only Lark knew that when it came to excuses, the truth was, she had none.

The best thing she could do for the investigation, and for herself, was find something else to go on.

She couldn't speak for Chris Redmond. But he was right about this: she was not the one with something to hide.

She keyed in the home page for the Topaz Amelia Island and stared as a slideshow filled the laptop screen with high-resolution beauty where the grainy surveillance footage had been.

The contrast was jarring. Familiar fluorescent lighting replaced by foreign sun and sea. Stacks of paper coffee cups replaced by daiquiris in elegant glasses. Lark let the photos transport her to this different world, just as Mikki had allegedly been transported.

A world where elegant couples enjoyed candlelit dinners on a marble terrace overlooking the sea.

Where hammocks piled high with throw pillows swung invitingly from stands.

Where champagne chilled on ice at the edge of a private Jacuzzi, where embroidered robes and slippers awaited at the spa.

ESCAPE, the ad campaign promised. RELAX. UNWIND. CELEBRATE. INDULGE.

This was it, the place where her best friend had spent the last few days they could account for. It was so strange to look at photos of a venue Lark had only ever imagined, a place she'd felt *foolish* imagining, a place she'd doubted was even real. She scrutinized each image as if she might spot some clue Mikki had left behind, some confirmation that *Mikki was here.* She imagined Mikki strolling those manicured paths, swimming those glimmering waters, sipping Dom Pérignon from the monogrammed crystal, mingling with those beautiful, untouchable people. Dressing up, shaking hands, swaying to a band under the stars.

Introducing herself as Lark.

It all looked so out of reach, she might as well have been imagining a mission to Mars. In her aimless search for Mikki, Lark had never once envisioned getting past the front desk of a place like the Topaz Amelia Island.

She didn't belong there.

But if Mikki had managed to feel like she did, even for one night? A voice inside her head couldn't help but say it.

No wonder.

If Chris's story was true, all Mikki had done to get there was *say yes.* To accept a ride out. If Mikki had done that once, who's to say she couldn't do it again? And again and again?

No wonder she hadn't retreated, when she could taste what the rest of the world might hold. No wonder she hadn't come back. Not even for Lark.

Either Mikki had been taken in by this place or Lark should feel a foreboding when she looked at these photos, all manufactured smiles and magnified sunshine. Scrolling through the endless, curated loop, Lark didn't feel it. No sense of impending doom. No agony of waiting for the other shoe to drop. But no comfort, either, that Mikki had found herself someplace too beautiful for anyone to be entirely unhappy there. No relief that Mikki had almost certainly had moments where she hadn't regretted her choice to go, regardless of how things turned out in the end. Lark closed her eyes and tried to channel the Mikki of 2016, the one she'd said goodbye to, and felt nothing at all.

When she switched back to 2024 Lark, though, that wasn't entirely true.

Because something unexpected was rising, turning, balling itself up somewhere in the center of her chest.

Anger.

Lark would keep on waiting for the police to get back to her. She'd follow the process, the rules, that would supposedly lead to justice. She had gotten good at waiting, after all.

But she would not *only* wait. While she was at it, she would make a plan B.

She had gotten good at that too.

16

Mikki

2016

"Don't take this the wrong way," Chris said from the balcony doorway, "but you look beautiful."

Mikki was stretched on one of the heavenly chaise lounges, her black maxi dress splayed around her legs. When she'd gotten out of the shower, the bedroom door had been closed, but Chris had scrawled a note: *Taking a power nap. Take your time getting ready.* On the doorknob hung the welcome bag Kim had promised, and inside, the agenda listed the night's "welcome cocktails" attire as "evening seaside casual." Mikki had no idea what that meant, but black seemed safe, and she took her time curling waves into her hair and doing a full face glow-up before bringing the bag and agenda out to the balcony to peruse with a view.

She smiled back at Chris, who looked pretty beautiful himself. "What would be the wrong way to take that compliment, exactly?" she asked, and his smile widened. The shower and shave masked his exhaustion, his face had taken on nice color from their beachy afternoon, and he looked every bit as comfortable in a sport coat as he had dressed down for the drive.

Chris dropped into the chaise next to her, folding his hands behind his head, no less at ease with her in the aftermath of Kim's awkward visit. If he wasn't going to bring it up, neither was she. "You don't have to come this far to get a view like this, you know," he told her. "Parts of Lake Michigan are gorgeous too."

"I went to Lake Erie once," she told him. "With Lark and some guys who invited us camping. It wasn't quite what I'd envisioned."

He nodded sagely. "Was it the toxic algae that got you, or the smokestacks?"

She burst out laughing. "Both. They did have seagulls, though, which was cool, except we felt sorry for them. *This isn't the sea,* Lark kept yelling. Poor geographically challenged birds."

"Come up to Michigan sometime. The Upper Peninsula is a hike, but there are nice coastal towns closer to you—South Haven, Saugatuck. It's no ocean, but I can almost guarantee you won't feel sorry for the seagulls."

"They should put that on a bumper sticker," Mikki joked. Lark's name must be rubbing off; she was talking like her now. "Michigan: where you won't feel sorry for the seagulls."

He laughed. "How was Lake Erie besides all that? The camping part, I mean?"

She told him how she and Lark had rented bikes and pedaled along the lakeshore, how they'd sneaked into the pool at the lodge, swimming for hours before they got busted for not having the requisite guest wristbands, how they'd followed the boardwalks into the marsh too close to sunset and been swarmed by mosquitos and mayflies, how the fireworks on the campground beach had been fun until the guys started shooting them at each other.

How they never truly regretted their rule to say yes, though there was usually a point when they'd look at each other, thinking, *This might be the time we should've said no.* That weekend, the point had come while sleeping in their car. But it had still been an adventure.

"You two sound closer than sisters," Chris observed. "Without the sibling rivalry."

A tide of guilt was rising in her, but Mikki tamped it down.

"You weren't kidding about your sister being type A," she ventured.

"No one kids about my sister," he agreed. "Thanks for coming to the rescue, by the way."

"No problem. Should I . . . carry my life preserver all weekend?"

He hesitated, gazing at the water. Mikki liked how the waves could fill the silence. How if you were looking out at the ocean with someone, the energy between you felt companionable, both of you plugged into the rhythm of this same kinetic thing.

"You know how you worried I might not like you?" he asked finally.

Mikki nodded. "You're worried I might not like your family?"

"No. I'm sure you won't like them."

She thought about saying that he wouldn't like hers either. Or that it didn't matter, that everyone had family stuff and weddings were heady times, and that their suite was a judgment-free zone. But it was all too loaded or too flippant or too . . . something.

So instead, she said, "I'm just happy to be here." He looked over at her, like he was about to make some other excuse, and she could see the way he stopped in his tracks, understanding that she wasn't bullshitting.

"I'm going to channel that," he said, glancing at his watch.

It must be time to go. She could feel it in the air, smell it in the whiff of tiki torches, see it in the lights twinkling below: The whole night, waiting. The whole world, waiting.

"Just happy to be here," he repeated.

Smoothing her dress over her curves, Mikki gave a little twirl as she made her way over to offer him a hand up. "Shouldn't be hard in a place like this," she said, pulling him to his feet.

"No," he agreed. "It shouldn't be."

The last hotel party Mikki had attended was at the Yes, Please! Motel, where no one ever stopped making jokes about the name, even though no one laughed at them anymore. There'd been dancing on tables, jumping on beds, and filling bathtubs with ice to chill cans of cheap beer.

Here, there was champagne. Top-shelf liquor in sweating crystal glasses. Floating paper lanterns, elegantly strung white lights, vases of flowers on every table, even though the gardens around them were so fragrant and colorful no one would have missed the centerpieces. Flameless candles flickered on high-tops offering hors d'oeuvres and a welcome station where guests could write well wishes in the guestbook.

Mikki and Chris had barely stepped onto the terrace before an affable man clapped Chris on the back. "Chris-sy!" he said. "What's good?" Chris returned his embrace with the most enthusiasm Mikki had seen from him since they'd arrived.

"Lark," Chris said, breaking free and smiling back at her, "meet Al."

Al thrust out a hand to shake hers warmly, then said, "To hell with it!" and pulled her into a rambunctious hug. "Pleasure to meet you, Lark. I'm either Chris's favorite cousin or his favorite uncle, depending on who you ask."

He guffawed. After the transactional exchange with Kim earlier, this wholesome reception was not what she'd expected from another relative. Al looked like a gussied-up Southern Mister Rogers, complete with a cardigan. She guessed him at maybe ten or fifteen years older than Chris, so he really did look like he could be either his youngest uncle or his oldest cousin. She found herself laughing too.

"Oh, boy," she said gamely. "Sounds like there's a story there."

"Always a story with this guy," Al said affectionately, and Chris picked up the cue.

"When I first started working for my dad, he sent me down to Texas to vet a prospective client who wanted to expand into Michigan. I had no idea how close their office was to Al's house, or I'd have called him myself. But we'd only talked at weddings and reunions and funerals; I wasn't used to hearing his name out of context."

"His dad tipped me off, though," Al chimed in, "so I drop by this office to see about taking him to lunch. The receptionist buzzes him and says, 'Alister Williams is here to see you.' And you'll never guess what Chris-sy here says."

Chris squeezed his eyes shut in embarrassment. "I said, 'Who the hell is Alister Williams?'"

Mikki burst out laughing. "That's not even the good part," Al said. "The receptionist looks at me, all suspicious now, and she goes, 'He *says* he's your cousin.'"

"As soon as I heard Al laughing, I knew I was on speaker and was never going to live it down. All I could think of was to say, 'You're kidding. I always thought he was my uncle.'"

Both men cackled. "Hey," Chris added. "In my defense, I assumed Al was short for Albert or Alfred. Never heard anyone call him Alister, before or since."

"Guess I was feeling fancy that day," Al said. "Speaking of which, I hear that's your Bimmer in the parking lot. Did you know that was my first car? Not a convertible, though, you dog. Promise me a spin while we're here. I'm feeling nostalgic."

"Sure," Chris said, "or I'll hand over the keys, and you can take her yourself. Say when."

"Don't tempt me, I might drive all the way home, leave Cathy to board the plane alone."

"Make him an offer," Mikki suggested, and Al guffawed again. "Seriously," she nudged, winking at Chris. "He could be talked into trading up."

"Where's this spontaneous side of you been hiding?" he asked, jostling Chris's shoulder. "One minute you splash out with a new car, the next minute you're willing to sell, the *last* minute you bring a surprise wedding date. I'm into it." He grinned at Mikki. "Easy to be spontaneous about that with a girl like you next door, I'm sure."

"Al," Chris groaned. "Leave the woman alone. We're good friends, and I could use more of those. Let's not chase her off."

Mikki's mind tripped over the words. She'd been expecting him to say, *We're just friends. We're good friends* was something different. And he'd sounded sincere.

Al raised his hands. "Forgive me. I get all lusty when I start talking Bimmers, is all."

They excused themselves to get drinks, but not before Al lowered his voice to get a last word in. "Find me anytime you get stuck with no one to talk to," he told Mikki. "I've mastered the art of having a good time in spite of all these bastards."

Mikki had the feeling that at a party surrounded by friends, having a guy like Al latch on could be a nightmare. But where she didn't know a soul, Al could be her new best friend.

"He's not wrong," Chris murmured. "I've spent many a family function happily cornered by him in some buffet line."

"But who the hell is he?" she quipped, and they both laughed.

They started toward the bar but couldn't move more than a few feet before someone else would put out a hand to stop Chris. A few nervous men who Mikki presumed were clients addressed Chris as if he was a boss they were overdue in reporting to, promising "those projections for next year" and "news on that expansion soon." One unsubtly implied that he hoped Chris, not Kim, would review his next proposal, but Chris proved adept at remaining noncommittal. The real test came from the fussy older women tutting about how much his parents would have loved the party.

"So sad, Kimberly not having her father to walk her down the aisle, but she must take such comfort in having a brother on each arm," said a woman draped in silk scarves.

"I appreciate the sentiment," Chris said. "But you've met Kim, right? She's going to walk herself down the aisle. Cooper and I will be admiring her from the sidelines like everyone else."

As Mikki realized just how big the guest list was—more couples arriving every minute—she felt the pressure ease. These people had come to celebrate the wedding of their friend, or their cousin or their niece or their spouse's old dear classmate, not to gawk at who the bride's brother had brought as his plus-one.

Beneath their designer handbags, fresh manicures, and polite laughs, these people didn't seem so different from anyone she knew: they were wrapped up in themselves and only marginally interested in anyone else. Nobody here wanted anything from Mikki. And while plenty of them did want something from Chris, that didn't mean they'd be interested in anything she had to say. For the first time in her life, all she had to do was strive to be dull.

"Look what the cat dragged in," a voice drawled behind her, and Mikki turned to see a guy who looked a little like Chris grinning wildly but without mirth.

Even as she gathered that this was probably Cooper, she wished for Chris's sake that it weren't. You'd never know the party was just getting started by the looks of him, as if he'd time-traveled from the other end of the night: shirt untucked and splattered with something wet, tie loosened, gait sloppy enough to tumble into a bed and stay there. His energy was all wrong, and it wasn't just the inebriation. Where Chris seemed at ease with himself—even when Kim had put him on the spot—Cooper was the opposite, his posture shaped by resentment and self-loathing.

"I could say the same about you," Chris said. "What happened to your suit, man? Was there an actual cat involved?"

"A she-cat, maybe," Cooper answered devilishly, though this seemed unlikely. His eyes slid toward Mikki, appraising her. He didn't seem to be waiting for an introduction: No, he seemed to know exactly who she was and was none too happy about it.

Chris cleared his throat. "Cooper, this is Lark. Lark, meet my brother."

Mikki put out her hand, and Cooper shook it. "Look at me, going on about cats when you brought yourself a bird." The smell of whiskey enveloped Mikki as he addressed her. "What's the story with you two? Heard you were in such a rush to come along you didn't even get the tags off your bags."

Mikki stepped back, caught off balance by the remark, and one of her platform heels buckled, sending a warning jolt through her ankle. *Great,* she thought. *So it's not my imagination. Kim clocked everything about me. And repeated it.*

"Rude," Chris said, the word carrying the unmistakable tone of parental disproval disguised in brotherly shorthand. *Rude.* Mikki could see from Cooper's face that he registered the reprimand exactly the way she did. And appreciated it much less.

"I'm not the one who has our sister diagramming new seating charts like a general in a war room, but sure, I'm the rude one." Cooper smiled tightly at Mikki. This time, she kept her heels firmly planted, though his words stung more sharply than her twisted ankle had. "I don't know how he suckered you into this, but I hope you're milking it for all it's worth."

Cooper was clearly looking for any excuse to take issue with Chris, and he'd found one in Mikki. She could almost see him warming to the idea that if this wasn't an appropriate venue for outward hostility toward his brother, he'd simply redirect it at his brother's date.

She told herself Cooper deserved the benefit of the doubt. The emotion rolling off him might not be sibling rivalry or even self-loathing, but grief. She had an impulse to offer condolences, but it seemed crass to bring it up and equally crass not to.

Fortunately, someone clanged a spoon against a glass, and Mikki turned to see Kim and her husband-to-be strolling in, hand in hand. Both were dressed head to toe in crisp white, and everyone burst into applause—hoots, cheers, whistles. The two beamed at each other as if they were just as eager to walk down the aisle as they were to sneak off to a dark corner. Watching them together made Mikki like Kim better somehow.

She leaned close to Chris's ear. "Do you have to give a toast?"

"That's all Cooper," he said, loud enough for his brother to hear. "His idea, not Kim's."

"Didn't hear you volunteering." Cooper snorted.

"Nope," Chris agreed. "You ready?"

"I have two versions." The chatter around them was picking back up now, almost enough to disguise the slur in his voice. "The one I might have to give, and the one I want to give."

"What's the difference?" Chris asked.

"You." Cooper threw back a swig and shook the ice in his glass impatiently, eyes darting around in search of a refill. "Kim was hoping we'd have something more to toast. Like the future of the family name. You know she's keeping it, right?"

"I've known she was keeping it since the day she was born," Chris said. "And I don't think whether I sign those papers should have any bearing on her wedding toast."

"If you'd talked to her much these past few weeks, you would. You might think I don't carry my weight around here, but at least I've been showing up. We can't all be lost in our feelings, contemplating our next moves like we're off on some gap year."

"A gap year was exactly what I thought we needed. Not my fault you couldn't sit tight."

"Hello? Here on Planet Earth, if you tell your clients you're checking out for a year, you'll have no clients to come back to. But people still think I'm the goof-off. Goes to show you never can shake a label." He laughed. "Guess you knew that, since you've been dodging so many new labels this year. No toxic work environments when you're around— because you're not around. Sign me up for that." With that, Cooper stomped off to the bar. Kim had praised him earlier, how he hadn't slowed the rest of the family down. But watching him go, Mikki wasn't so sure he wasn't in his own kind of hurry.

Meeting Chris's siblings kept reminding her there was more than one side to every story. But in this case, it was irrelevant. She was on Chris's. She was his guest after all.

"Sorry," Chris muttered. Mikki saw Kim catch his eye across the crowd, and he raised a glass in her direction, but up close, his discomfort was palpable. "Believe it or not, Cooper used to be the fun one. What's backward is he seems to think he's more fun now."

"Don't be sorry." Mikki slipped her hand into his. She did it without thinking, but feeling his fingers curl around hers, gratefully squeezing back, she wondered if the weight of this occasion would be too heavy for two strangers to ever keep things light between them.

But she couldn't wish away this beautiful place.

And for reasons she didn't want to think too hard about, she didn't like to picture Chris here alone.

17

Lark

2024

Lark was busy with a new project: listing every question she was determined to ask Chris before she let him out of her sight again.

The pocket-size notebook she'd designated for this task was more than a needed distraction; it was a place to convert her newfound anger into fuel, ready for action. Her body might be stuck going through the motions—walking Dove to the school bus, filling Nini's prescriptions, assuring Heath she was holding up *fine, thanks, really*—but her mind was traveling every new possible avenue, looking for turnoffs she hadn't considered before while revisiting the ones she'd already been down with new eyes.

That dumbstruck night in her office—was it only thirty-six hours ago?—caught between dingy surveillance footage, stylized images of the Topaz, and the baffling, quasi-threatening letter jammed out of sight in her purse, she'd made up her mind: she needed to know everything Chris Redmond knew. The next time they came face-to-face, whether the police were done with him or not, she intended to force him to fork over *everything* he knew about Mikki. To hell with his lawyer's warning to avoid speculation.

She'd been doing nothing *but* speculating for going on eight years. She sure as hell wasn't about to stop now when the answers might finally be within reach. This was too important to rely on anyone else to get them for her—not the deputies, and certainly not Heath, who was being wary enough for them both. No one, no matter their training, was better equipped than Lark to comb through Chris's responses for hints of what might have swayed Mikki to stay gone.

She recorded every panicked possibility that sprang to mind, trying to calm her brain by getting the chaos onto paper. Her list was the only thing tethering her to some future day when her sanity would return, and she kept it with her at all times, filling page after page, not caring whether her questions were phrased carefully or even if some were more accusations than questions at all.

What you did after the wedding.

Where you went if not home. And what next. And how you decided to keep going without looking back or checking in or following up.

Why you stayed gone.

She crossed it all out and tried again: *Where have you been?*

Why did you never try to reach out until now, if you truly had such a nice time together?

Why just show up? Did you really not exchange a phone number or address or email?

Who else connected with Mikki that weekend?

Who was friendly enough to her that they might have a more specific memory of her?

It was a little unhinged, maybe, but at least she felt like she was doing something. Heath was always talking about how the troopers intercepted more illegal activity *because* they were proactive, as opposed to the reactive deputies. Well, this was proactive waiting. She could only hope it would have the same effect.

So after another failed morning of obsessing when she should've been sleeping, she sat cross-legged on her unmade bed, phone and notebook in hand, and decided to expand her approach.

"Denny Dean on the line. What can we help you find?"

Lark's palms went slick, and she verged on ending the call before it started. She'd long since written off her foray with this private investigator as a waste of money; she was unprepared for the way his voice took her back. The last time she'd heard it, he'd let her down ungently, having drained most of her crowdsourced #FindMikki fund: *Sorry, kiddo. I got nada.*

"Um. Hi, Denny," she managed now, unsure where to start. Dramatic music vibrated through the floor from downstairs, the crescendo of Nini's daytime soaps. "You probably don't remember me, but I engaged your services briefly years ago, looking for a friend—a coworker who got in a customer's car and never returned?"

She wasn't sure if she was imagining the awkward pause that followed, or even if there was a real pause at all. Maybe it felt awkward because she was already anxious, or because of the muffled TV soundtrack coming from downstairs. Maybe it felt long because she was holding her breath.

"Name?" Denny asked without a hint of recognition, as if people called about this very scenario every day.

"Lark Nichols. My friend was—is—Mikki Jensen. This would have been late 2016."

"I remember." She definitely wasn't imagining the awkwardness now. Denny Dean sounded unquestionably displeased to hear from her. Then again, maybe he just felt bad about how little he'd turned up. As he should. "What can I do for you?" he asked, all business.

"Well, there's been a . . . development."

"Oh?"

"I'm not sure how much you remember about the case . . ."

"I'm not sure there *was* much to remember about the case."

"Right." Lark had known this call would be another waste of time. Still, she'd resolved to try everything she could think of, and if that left her grasping at straws, so be it. She cleared her throat. "I'm not calling about rehiring you or anything like that. But I'm touching base because the driver who Mikki left with has resurfaced. I have his name, I know where they went, and the police are on it. But in the meantime, I wondered if it was worth running the new info by you on the off chance it shines new light on anything at all you remember from before."

"Look," he said, though his tone said, *Whoa, take it easy.* "I'm glad you have more to go on now. But I can't help you; 2016 was a long time ago, and even if I did keep my files that long, this one would be virtually empty. Like I said, nothing to shine new light on."

Lark tapped her pen on her notebook, eyes narrowing at the blank page. "You're not the slightest bit curious? You're not even going to ask who or where or why? Call me crazy, but that's not the best endorsement for your services."

"I'm not trying to endorse my services. You said you didn't intend to rehire me."

"Well, not yet."

"Well, the answer is no, I'm not curious. And not interested. Sorry I can't be of help."

This didn't make sense. Lark was increasingly certain she could do much better than Denny Dean if she ever did hire investigative help again. But he was a rough-around-the-edges bouncer type, not some suave undercover suit swimming in income. Hadn't she been easy money? All he'd had to do was check all the nearby surveillance cameras he could find for some glimpse of the car and flash Mikki's picture around southbound travel stops to see if anyone recognized her. Why act as if Lark was some problem client?

"Can I ask why you're so uninterested?"

"I have enough clients, okay? I don't need any trouble."

"What trouble?"

Denny paused again, longer this time. Finally, he said, "Guess enough time has passed, so it don't matter. First time I took this on, I got . . . correspondence. Warning me off it."

Lark's breath caught. "What do you mean, correspondence?"

"Nasty emails. I ignored them at first because, well, you'd posted about hiring me online for all to see, so I figured some troll from your hashtag was having fun at my expense." He said this as if it were Lark's fault. "That kind of unwanted attention comes with the territory, to a point, at least in the comments when stuff goes viral. But these emails got more strongly worded. Saying if I knew what was good for me, I'd tell you I struck out and call it a day."

"Are you telling me someone threatened you not to look for Mikki and you didn't think that was worth conveying to your paying client? Worse, you listened to them?"

"No," Denny said evenly. "I'm telling you I did my honest best on your case, but while I did, I got nagged and harassed, and I don't need that in my life."

Lark was incredulous. Her mind couldn't help but go to the envelope she'd found on her desk. "I don't need it in mine either. Which is why it would've been nice for you to *warn* me."

"It would've been mean of me to *scare* you. Poor pregnant girl taking all that heat. Far as I could tell, no one was looking to give you trouble—I was the buffer. Like I said, I didn't put much stock in it, and you shouldn't either. But if you're in the market for a new buffer, I ain't interested."

"Do you still have those emails? Did you get an IP address or—"

"No. I'm no hacker, and I don't employ them to hunt trolls. Good luck, honey, okay?"

Before she could answer, he hung up, leaving Lark alone with her spinning thoughts.

She raged. How dare he think he knew what was best for her, then or now? She was tempted to call Denny back and scream at him that she'd never needed his pity, she'd needed his honesty. And by the way, he didn't get to fail her spectacularly and call her *honey*.

Then again, hard as it was to admit, maybe she had needed his pity.

Say she'd known about the emails then. They'd have spooked her, but would they have convinced her of anything? Or would they only have turned her inside out again, for nothing?

Worst case scenario, if the threats were legit, they signaled that not only had something bad happened to Mikki but the responsible party knew Lark was looking for her—and didn't like it. The possibility felt chilling, dangerous for Lark and maybe even for the people close to her.

But she couldn't disagree with Denny's take that this was a *huge* if. Then or now, the police wouldn't be easily persuaded that some anonymous emails were evidence of foul play. Far more likely, they'd have discounted the so-called threats as quickly as Denny had, and the same went for the media. Denny was right: Lark had shared too much personal information publicly. Where she worked, what investigator she'd hired, how to reach them. She'd had no choice.

If Denny's story was worth anything, maybe it was this: a reminder that she had every reason to be more careful now. Dove, most of all. *That kind of unwanted attention comes with the territory,* he'd said. She'd already seen that with the envelope in her office. *Duly noted.*

Still, it bothered her. If Denny had really discounted the threats, why practically hang up on Lark now? Was he merely downplaying them to mask the fact that he'd chickened out and ripped her off in the process? And was it a coincidence that as soon as Chris showed back up, she started finding out she wasn't the only one who'd been paying attention to this case all along?

She began graphing it all in her notebook, making the world's sparsest, most depressing timeline. *Did you threaten my PI to back off?* she wrote under Chris's name. *Did you threaten me?* Then she scribbled it all out, feeling silly.

Because another possibility was dawning on Lark. The first one, in fact, that she could make real sense of.

The messages to Denny Dean could have been from Mikki herself, trying to spare Lark's feelings by not telling her directly to back the hell off.

Lark couldn't bear for anyone else to point this out. Not the deputies. Not Nini. And especially not Heath. What did it say about her that the more she learned, the less she wanted to share? Better yet, what did it matter? She wasn't obligated to report anything to anyone. They'd all ordered her to just sit tight anyway.

They couldn't fault her for doing just that.

~~~

Lark woke to the feeling of an uncomfortable weight where there shouldn't be one. Something foreign, angular, rough-edged.

Literally. On her face.

Groggily, she batted it away and felt the unmistakable flutter of paper against her cheek.

Her notebook. She must have drifted off obsessing over her notes. Again.

She squinted into the afternoon sun, orienting herself to the clock. It was almost time to pick up Dove from school. *How* had she lost another day?

Everything was starting to blur together: her visit to Chris's motel, her call with Denny Dean, Heath stopping by for an almost luxuriously mundane talk about utility bills. By now, it had been nearly seventy-two hours of waiting for the police to follow up about their findings. Three days since she'd tasted food or breathed without telling herself to or listened to the entirety of a conversation or looked anyone in the eye without worrying that they could see how not fine she was. Heath, especially. Three days since she'd slept in anything but worried fits.

The exhaustion had been bound to catch up with her. Maybe it was even working in her favor. If her emotions weren't numbed by sleep deprivation, she might be curled up in a ball, crying. Or running to the sheriff's office, screaming.

She opened her notebook to the page where she'd left off. Admittedly, her endless list of questions was starting to look a little . . . rambling.

Lark had resorted to thinking that if details from Chris could put her—and not just her name—there in that moment with Mikki, maybe *something* would make sense.

What songs did you dance to?
What dress did she wear?
What did she say when she first saw the ocean?
What else did she say about me?

She'd thought that if she couldn't have Mikki back, understanding as much as she could about Mikki's time with Chris had to be the next best thing. But seeing it with fresh eyes, she had to wonder whether, deep down, she was already preparing herself for the possibility that none of this would lead to anything. It didn't help that she'd asterisked every line, which had the effect of making nothing stand out except that she might be losing it.

Downstairs, she found Nini brewing a fresh pot of coffee for her. A kind gesture, even if her words didn't match.

"You have ink on your face," Nini observed. "Would that be from your manifesto?"

"Hey," Lark said, checking her reflection in the microwave door. "At least someone's taking notes on this case."

"Sure, Detective. And I'm the crazy one." Nini moved aside so Lark could fill her mug. "Anyway, I'm glad you're up. Have you seen my checkbook?"

"You mean the checkbook the doctors told me to keep safe for you?"

"It's hilarious you all think I'm going to get swindled out of money when I don't have any. I just want to know how much we paid last year for the damn septic. Millie called to see if she's being taken for a ride. They're trying to act like they ain't raising rates on shit. On actual shit."

"Just write down the guy's name, and Heath will look into it. He's got all our other bills to compare with his own before he moves in. I told him how tight things are, and he thinks if we consolidate sooner than later—"

"Don't change the subject," Nini cut in. "This isn't about anyone handling things, it's about principle. It's about me having a conversation with a friend. Nobody said I wasn't allowed to *see* the checkbook anymore. Where is it?"

"I don't see why . . ." Lark trailed off. Nini was tearing up. Unheard of.

"Can't a woman maintain some autonomy?" Nini sniffed, dabbing her eyes with a napkin. "We talked about this yesterday, Mikki."

Lark froze. "Lark," she said, gently. "I'm Lark."

"Well, you sound like Mikki," Nini snapped, "bossing me around. Stressing me out. Monitoring me is one thing, but somehow I'm the only one around here who's not allowed to make an innocent mistake. Ever. About anything. Even if it doesn't matter."

Lark was chagrined. So it wasn't just her at a breaking point. Even if they had managed not to discuss it in front of Dove, the stress of *not knowing* had moved into their house with the energy and presence of a physical being, almost as if some version of Mikki herself had returned. Of course, it was taking its toll. It wasn't fair to single Nini out.

Even if her slips *were* concerning.

"Sorry," she said. "You're right. I just can't believe the police haven't called yet." Lark scalded her tongue on the coffee, but she didn't even care. She needed caffeine.

"Oh, they did call," Nini said, opening the refrigerator and rifling through the shelf on the door. "Is there any more creamer?"

Lark's heart quickened. "What do you mean, they did call? When?"

Nini gave up and pulled the milk off the shelf, letting the fridge door fall closed. "Of course they'd call when you were finally sleeping. Those men are so good at bad timing, it's like they do it on purpose."

Lark plucked her phone from the counter, sure she hadn't slept through a call. Her heart sank at the DO NOT DISTURB icon. The pre-programmed weekday sleep schedule was a godsend for anyone working night shift, but she'd meant to disable it. Sure enough, as soon as she toggled off the setting, a missed call from the county sheriff's line appeared, plus two more from Heath.

The police must have called the landline when they couldn't reach her. And reached Nini in rare form instead.

"Well," she asked, trying to keep her voice level, "what did they have to say?"

"What did *they* have to say?" Nini *tsk*ed. "How about what *I* had to say?"

Lark could only stare.

"Don't look at me like that. For years I've stewed on everything I wish we'd had the guts to say to those smug, condescending officers. You think I'm not taking my opportunity once I finally get it? They're lucky I waited for *them* to call *me*."

Lark was fully awake now, every alarm bell in her body ringing. She'd warned the deputies not to put stock in conversations with Nini, but the last thing Team Mikki needed was another strike against them. They needed law enforcement firmly on their side.

"Okay," Lark said. "What did *you* have to say?"

"Plenty. I told them they picked a fine time to start looking for Mikki, right when someone finally told them exactly where she'd gone. How above and beyond of them. I told them I was writing up their nomination letters for the Congressional Medal of Honor."

"You didn't," Lark groaned.

Nini waved her hand. "Please. I'm under no delusions they care what some old lady thinks, and you shouldn't be either. It felt good to say it. They deserve to know how hurtful they've been, acting like if something bad *had* happened to Mikki, she'd had it coming."

This did not seem the time to point out Nini had acted the same way, casting indiscriminate blame on Mikki and Lark both. Nini preferred to get what she called *mad on principle*. It wasn't about who was right or wrong; it was about who had a right to an opinion. That list was short and only occasionally included Lark.

"I know you probably told them I'm going demented and they shouldn't pay any attention to me," Nini went on. "And if you didn't, someone else did. So what do you care what I told them?"

Lark thought better of answering. Nini seemed content to have both sides of this conversation on her own.

"Anyway. I think they've finally decided to leave us alone," Nini assured her. She splashed some milk into her mug and gave it a stir.

"Leave us . . . I'm sorry, what?"

"They're more trouble than they're worth anyway. Good riddance."

Lark's chest tightened. Whatever had happened, she hoped it was fixable. She'd warned them about Nini after all.

It was just that, well, they'd never listened to her before.

"What, exactly, did they say?" Lark asked.

"They asked for you. They implied I should wake you, which, I told them, if they had any idea what they'd been putting you through, they wouldn't ask."

Lark rubbed her temples. "After all that." She gestured impatiently. "What did they *say*?"

"I wrote it down, like you always say to." Nini pulled a pad out of the newly organized junk drawer and handed it over. *Will not be opening an investigation,* she'd written. Lark stared at the words as they blurred and came back into focus, then looked up at Nini.

"That's it?" she asked. "Did they say anything about Chris? Whether he's free to go?"

"I assume since there's no investigation, he's free to take a flying leap. I hope he will."

Lark clenched her fists. At first, she'd been baffled at Nini's utter lack of interest in finding out what Chris Redmond had to say. But after three days of having her own mind torn apart by unknowable hypotheticals, she was starting to understand. This was simply more than any healthy, fully functioning brain should ever have to process. To Nini, it was too much. It made sense to shut it down.

But Lark had prepared for this moment, and it wasn't meant to go like this. Not this time.

Chris Redmond might have money and power and even, perhaps, an alibi, but he wasn't getting off the hook. If the police weren't going to pursue this, if they had determined he really didn't know what happened to Mikki, that didn't change what mattered:

He owed it to Lark to help her find out.

Lark grabbed her keys off the counter and flung open the door. She nearly crashed into Heath.

"Whoa," he said. He wore his most buttoned-up street clothes, dark jeans and a polo shirt, his expression tight with concern.

"Hi," she said, feeling caught. She didn't have time to hash this out if she wanted to intercept Chris before he left town and get to school to pick up Dove on time. "Sorry, I was . . ."

"DeLue called me. He thought you might rather not be alone when you come in."

"I'm supposed to come in?" She opened the door wider and turned back toward Nini, who sat at the table, cradling her coffee mug and blinking very fast. "You didn't write that down," Lark said accusingly.

Nini scowled. "I wrote down the part that wasn't preposterous."

"I believe your exact words were that they'd 'decided to leave us alone.'"

"Well, I told him that's what *I'd* decided they should do, and I believe *his* exact words were that he 'didn't disagree.'"

Lark looked at Heath in despair. "I can see how that would send mixed messages," he said good-naturedly, but his eyes were serious when they met Lark's. "Did you listen to the voicemail he left you?"

"Not yet," she admitted, instinctively moving her hands behind her back. Not that she had anything to hide. But she did happen to be holding her phone. And the notebook Nini had dubbed her *manifesto.* "They want to fill me in face-to-face?" she guessed.

"Not exactly." Heath's weight shifted, uncharacteristically unsteady. "They don't want you to come in to be briefed. They want you to come in to answer some questions."

18

Mikki

First thing in the morning, Mikki slipped downstairs and across the courtyard, following signs for the business center. All around her, groundskeepers moved between the buildings, some meticulously hand-trimming the landscaping, others taking paintbrushes to invisible blemishes on the crisp white exterior walls and gazebos. Mikki's mind was too busy to be impressed by the maintenance standards. She saw only one thing: service jobs, and lots of them.

With so many employees visible, untold more must be behind the scenes: catering staff, bartenders, housekeepers, laundry, customer care, all applying the same skills she and Lark had mastered, only in an infinitely better setting. It was impossible not to fantasize about trading up.

"Excuse me," she asked a uniformed attendant hurrying past with a cart of rolled navy-and-white-striped pool towels. "Do you know the starting hourly wage here? Ballpark?"

The woman looked at her strangely, then mumbled something unintelligible and rushed off, as if a guest had never asked about employment before. Which, Mikki realized too late, probably none had. She resisted the urge to chase after her and explain. One thing at a time.

Swiping her key card, Mikki let herself into the business center—empty at this early hour—and breathed in the quiet as the door closed behind her. No traffic noise, no guest chatter, not even the sound of waves here. Just a curated silence for travelers with important things to do. She popped a pod into the single-serve coffee maker and surveyed her surroundings.

She hadn't expected to spend her limited time here seeking out a computer, of all things. But as she'd lain awake last night on the pullout, with the balcony door cracked open to let the waves drown out the unfamiliar sounds of Chris's soft snoring from the adjoining room, she'd realized this was not the ordinary wedding-where-she-didn't-know-anybody. For one thing, she didn't even *really* know the man she was sharing a suite with, which might have been more awkward if they weren't both so tired. For another, it was obvious even the other plus-ones here knew more about the Redmonds than she did. You could tell from the hushed tones, the reverent looks, the self-conscious way they smoothed their hair when Kim or Chris or even sloppy Cooper breezed past.

Mikki had to play catch-up. She needed context, the kind she wouldn't get from Chris.

He'd joined the other groomsmen for an early tee time, so he'd be none the wiser. By the time he or anyone else in the wedding party returned, she'd be cooling off in the pool, jogging the beach, or finding an out-of-the-way spot to stretch out on the sand. The rehearsal and subsequent dinner were tonight, and as a reluctant guest of a reluctant attendant, she'd need good energy to put her best face forward—and at tomorrow's ceremony and reception too. She intended to keep as much of the day for herself as possible.

But she had homework to do before she could play.

Mikki took her coffee to one of the monitors partitioned with privacy dividers. A rack of real estate pamphlets was mounted to the wall. Seaside vacation homes with rooftop decks beckoned: OWN A PIECE

OF PARADISE. She grazed her fingers across them and landed on the Island Apartment Rentals guide hidden in the back—the lone newsprint weekly in a sea of glossy covers.

Was there any harm in looking? Was it so far-fetched to think she might return home to Lark with some actual leads on relocating? This one resort sustained more gainful employment than their entire town, blissfully far from the father who didn't know about Lark's baby and didn't want to. True, the cost of living was surely higher here, and it'd be tricky to manage childcare in a place where they knew no one, but they had no plan for managing it in Becksville either. Maybe she and Lark could each work two gigs and stagger shifts. It'd be tough, but at least they'd be working toward something, and when they did have time off, they'd be *here*. In paradise.

And what about Nini? Florida had a booming population of seniors; was it crazy to think there might also be better resources for her here?

But as Mikki flipped through the classifieds, she could see the answer to all her questions was a resounding *yes*. Yes, it was far-fetched to think of moving here. Yes, it was crazy. And yes, there was harm in looking. Because even for the worst apartment she found listed, the one with all the code words renters knew to avoid—"cozy basement" and "a little TLC" and "shared amenities"—the rent wasn't just high, it was eye popping. She could only imagine how far inland they'd have to go to afford a place, and she and Lark had one unreliable car between them. In this light, the hotel staff seemed downright heroic if not foolish. Did they live ten to a room? How did anyone do it? Chris had checked on public transit before leaving Mikki carless this morning and told her the only option was a tourist shuttle with two stops: the marina on the Intracoastal side and the historic district of Fernandina Beach. Hardly working class.

Sighing, she tucked the newspaper back on the shelf, resisting the urge to flip through the spreads of vacation homes instead. She hadn't come here to torture herself.

She'd come for insight. She took a steadying sip of espresso—wow, was it good—opened the web browser, and started searching.

Evidently, news of the Redmond family had been everywhere, for decades; if anything, Chris had underplayed the scope of their wealth, business, and reputation. But in his defense, maybe he'd never had to brief anyone before. Redmond was a household name beyond Michigan, through much of the Midwest. Even in Ohio, they'd made the *Columbus Dispatch* and Cleveland's *Plain Dealer*. They didn't have the glamour of the Kennedys, the political sway of the Bushes, the glitz of the Vanderbilts, but they were prominent enough for their circles to overlap in Venn diagrams of polite society. Mikki was, apparently, the last to know, and yet the first to hop in the passenger seat, none the wiser.

The family estate—the one lost in the fire—was not merely a big house surrounded by woods. Reports couldn't even speculate about the property values because the Redmonds had owned it so long and their renovations had been not remodels but "expansions." Their investment firm hadn't been operated from home offices, or even a new wing, as Chris had implied, but an additional building on the opposite end of the property. It all created the effect of something kept intentionally close to home yet scaled up to be consequential. Plenty of employees, but only Redmonds at the top. Plenty of growth, but only with purpose and heart. Cover stories called them "the pride of Michigan," and local leaders praised their commitment to helping small businesses thrive: restaurant franchises and watersports providers and lakefront inns and golf courses and marinas with award-winning charters. Their investment strategy honored their roots, keeping much of their money in the state when they might have gone national or even global. She'd sympathized when Chris called the job boring, but now, seeing all the people they'd worked with . . . Surely his parents could've found a role that would have made him happy?

Maybe that was Chris's point: maybe they hadn't cared to.

Still, Mikki could see the Redmond firm was something special and began to feel torn between Kim's stance on rebuilding and Chris's aversion to it. Kim's name was in all the coverage too—the most-quoted source behind deal reports, the smiling headshot in *movers and shakers*. Mentions of Chris were harder to parse, as his father had also been a Christopher. Most references seemed to be to the elder Redmond, though it was hard to tell without reading through everything, which no one could possibly do.

With a guilty look over her shoulder to make sure her screen wasn't visible from the hall, she narrowed her search terms to the wildfire tragedy. It was all there, and all real: the lives lost, the acres consumed in hours, and the long, bitter mess still waiting to be cleaned up.

Mikki sorted chronologically from the date of the fire. The coverage started with a collective sense of shock and heartbreak, a tone of paying tribute to one of Michigan's most upstanding families. There were Chris and his siblings, walking into church dressed in black for the funeral. There were the staffers and investors and families their foundation had employed or funded or touched, lining up to pay respects. There were photos showing how enviable the estate had been, the before and after of the private residence and executive quarters alongside aerial shots of the devastation, charred tree trunks, piles of ashy brick, and paved drives that no longer led anywhere at all.

But it didn't take long for the headlines to turn judgmental, then salacious. INVESTMENT MOGULS WERE WARNED TO EVACUATE. TRAPPED STAFF AT THE REDMOND ESTATE MADE FRANTIC CALLS TO THEIR FAMILIES. Even when the lawsuit was settled, when "official statements" from Kim said all the right things, the tone of the coverage didn't change.

Anyone could see the Redmonds had not been at fault for the worst of it, really. Mother Nature was to blame. They might have heeded all the warnings and still not made it out in time: some experts hypothesized that resistance would have been futile. The problem was that they *hadn't* erred on the side of caution, and the outgoing texts and voicemails that survived the tragedy were damning. Everyone trapped in the estate had lived just long enough to suffer fear and regret, to realize the end was closing in, to know they "needed a miracle," as their marketing director had wept in the last message she left for her husband, who would never hear her voice again. And once the world stopped viewing them through rose-colored glasses . . . Well, it was going to take some doing to shine up their reputation again. New Questions About Michigan's Oldest Family Business. Allegations Build as Redmond Investments Remain on Hiatus. The headlines reserved judgment, but the comments . . . not so much.

"The Redmonds might not be obscenely rich, but they're close," one commenter had written. "Anyone who thinks this lawsuit will hurt them is dreaming."

Mikki was starting to understand why the wedding festivities weren't happening in Michigan. And also, she had to admit, why Kim was frustrated with Chris for sitting on the sidelines. Even though Mikki sympathized that he'd never wanted to play in the first place.

Maybe everything about it should have made Mikki hate them. She couldn't imagine growing up the way Chris and Kim and Cooper had, that certainty that your needs would always be met, that your life would be fulfilling and good, that success and happiness and respect were already yours, and all you had to do was *not* squander them. But she knew what it was like to have the rug pulled out from under you. To have to atone for your parents' sins. For everyone to know your tragedy and judge you by it.

Mikki's glimpse into the family dynamics yesterday wasn't eye opening after all. Anyone who'd followed the Redmonds even distantly would know that Kim called the shots, and you could read Chris's reluctance between the lines. Cooper was the most debatable; depending on the day, he might seem like the wild card, the black sheep, or even the antagonist. He appeared at the outer edge of photos, looking sullen, lost, and a little envious. His expression hadn't changed from photos taken before the tragedy, but it had intensified, as if he'd given up any attempt to hide his true feelings. Or maybe they'd been dulled by whatever he was using to get through the day. And the more Mikki read the comments calling their workplace "toxic," the less she was sure whether they were referring to Kim's high standards or Cooper's lack thereof. People talked about them passing over the truly struggling entrepreneurs for the "safe bets," of having a "savior complex" that stood in laughable contrast to their bad judgment the day of the fire, but that meant they were still seen as saviors, right? Respect for the family name seemed to be winning out—salvageable, but only just.

As clearly as Mikki could see why Kim couldn't leave the Redmond legacy behind her, she could see why Chris needed to. Why they had different stances on karma. Even why Cooper was in such a sorry state and hiding it so poorly. Mikki had only meant to better understand what she'd gotten into, but she'd seen enough. She couldn't stomach how the voyeurs gawked at their loss and the way she'd become one of them simply by sneaking away to this room.

Suddenly, she missed Lark. Or maybe she just missed having someone, anyone familiar, within reach. Closing the browser, she decided to check her email to see if Lark had written back. Maybe Mikki would write again, let Lark know she'd made it to paradise. She wished she had a way of snapping photos to send and caption, *Get a load of this place.*

And something else too. Something she wished she'd said last time, even if she had been in a random Target store.

Wish you were here.

But when she keyed in her username and password, the browser window merely vibrated. Account locked for your protection. Too many log-in attempts. Check two-factor authentication device for instructions.

Oh, no. No, no, no. This was Mikki's first log-in attempt since the Target. And her two-factor authentication device was at home, with the very person she was trying to reach.

The Target. She *knew* she never should have logged in from that display computer with open Wi-Fi.

She groaned, realizing the depth of her error. She'd be lucky if this lock on her email was the extent of it, if her account hadn't been hacked or worse, someone following the trails of every message in her inbox. Not that she had much money in her bank account, but logging in to check from yet another public computer was no way to set her mind at ease. Besides, without either her phone or Lark's help, she couldn't resolve this now even if she wanted to. She'd only give Lark a chance to point out how dumb she'd been. Not what she needed to hear right now.

For once, she wished she were on social media. In Becksville, people didn't have the usual mindless scrolling addiction—their cell reception was so bad, you had to be on Wi-Fi. Most people only had accounts to keep tabs on friends who'd gotten the hell out anyway. Mikki had deleted hers when she realized she spent all her online time burning with jealousy. Lark, too, had stopped posting years ago, logging on only in weak moments of self-loathing.

Mikki pushed back from the desk, resisting the urge to reach for the courtesy phone instead. She'd take this as a sign to stop using Lark as a crutch every time the big bad world spooked her. Maybe Mikki hadn't been as independent as she'd always thought. Soon, Lark would be supporting someone else. Mikki wouldn't be any help to her if she didn't stop being so needy.

It was time to start now.

19

Lark

"Your grandmother is quite a character," Deputy DeLue said by way of greeting. He gestured for Lark and Heath to join him at the same long rectangular table where they'd met him and his partner several nights ago, but Deputy Rodgers was nowhere to be seen now.

Lark felt foolish thinking of how the last time she'd walked in this room, she'd dared to hope it signified a new beginning for Mikki's case, a second chance to get things right. Now, she couldn't even wish for a do-over because she had no clue how things had gone wrong *again*.

"Sorry about Nini," Lark said quickly, sliding into a chair and wincing as it scraped the linoleum. "She's not my grandmother," she reminded him. "She's Mikki's." She'd meant only to distance herself from Nini's antics, but it came out sounding like she'd corrected his grammar.

"Right," he said, clearing his throat. "Well, she *sounded* like your grandmother."

Deputy DeLue didn't know the half of it. When Heath had chided Nini for not immediately telling Lark the sheriff wanted her to come in, she'd lashed out.

Lark has been through enough, she'd snapped. *We both know those deputies don't have serious questions for her. They're wasting everyone's time so they can shame her just for show. We're not interested in going through the motions to help them look effective.*

Lark had never seen this fiercely loyal side of Nini before, not even when Nini had been left to grapple with her only daughter hanging Mikki out to dry so unforgivably. It was hard not to feel a little flattered, though of course she couldn't show it.

Nini, she'd said. *That was not for you to decide.*

Nini had doubled down. *Like hell it's not. I'm the missing person's next of kin.* Nini had jabbed a finger at her own chest for emphasis, leaving red blotches above her puff-painted blouse. *No diagnosis can change that. Besides, at every one of my assessments, I pass the test that I still know right from wrong. And those deputies have been nothing but wrong since the day Mikki left.*

When Nini's tirade was over, Lark had waited for Heath to reassure them that being called in to the station was routine. That the concern on his face didn't mean they should worry about the deputies having questions for Lark. That Heath could never doubt her.

But he didn't. He merely suggested that Lark call the school and instruct Dove to ride the bus home—something he knew Lark hated to do, because the ride to their fringe of the school district was a full hour long—so they could go to the station without further delay. Then when Lark said she'd prefer to drive herself, he'd insisted on following, like an awkward police escort.

What she needed was Fiancé Heath. Not Trooper Heath. But she was starting to think he couldn't separate the two, a revelation that caused more anxiety than it probably should have.

What about Chris Redmond? Lark wanted to protest. *If he's free to go, we have to stop him.* It's what she'd been on her way to do, and for Heath of all people to be the one to intercept her felt especially unjust. His demeanor stopped her from protesting. She had the feeling he knew something she didn't.

Something that may or may not have anything to do with Chris at all.

The whole way to the sheriff's office, she'd clutched her purse, wedged on her lap beneath the steering wheel, so she could feel the outline of the notebook inside. Her questions for Chris still felt like the only ammunition she had. If she showed her list to Heath, might he agree to detour to Chris's motel first? Or would he question why she hadn't brought more of this to him before now? She just couldn't guess which way it would go.

Which meant she couldn't risk it.

If she kept her notebook to herself, Heath couldn't stop her from using it. If she didn't tell him her plans, he couldn't ask her to change them. Her best bet was to get this done in a hurry.

Fortunately, Deputy DeLue seemed to agree.

"I'll try not to take too much of your time," he said now. "I know you've been waiting a few days for an update while we've followed up on this unusual situation. We do appreciate your patience, so how about I bring you up to speed before we get to tying up loose ends?"

Lark nodded, relaxing a little. Being here to tie up loose ends sounded less intimidating than the hot seat she'd imagined.

Methodically, Deputy DeLue began to relay everything his team had done with the tone of a man recounting personal favors he'd gone out of his way to do.

They'd verified the wedding's relevant details, the where and when and who and how.

They'd spoken with members of the wedding party, as well as the resort's private events coordinator, though she'd left Florida years ago to manage a property in Savannah.

They'd conducted cursory interviews with select wedding guests who recalled Mikki's presence and verified that housekeeping staff had not reported anything unusual left behind in Chris's suite after checkout.

They'd checked with the agency where Chris had rented a vehicle in Mikki's name, but like many companies, their records didn't go that far back. Chris dug up an old credit card statement that showed his prepayment of the nonrefundable rate, but they couldn't verify whether the car had ever been picked up or where it had been returned, only that his card hadn't been billed further. The police could determine with greater certainty Mikki hadn't boarded any outbound flight at the nearest airports. They reconfirmed no movement on Mikki's old bank account, even as they pointed out this was unlikely an issue for someone newly flush with cash. Most grimly, they'd checked again for Jane Does brought into hospitals or morgues between Florida and Ohio in the months after Mikki was last seen.

More than once, he reminded her he'd "overlooked limits" and "stretched resources" to do all this without "sufficient cause." When he finished his recap, Lark had the distinct impression they hadn't done it for her. Or for Mikki. Or even as a favor to Heath. They'd done it for Chris Redmond. They'd focused on clearing his important name so he could get on with his important life.

The message was plain: finding "someone like Mikki" was not the sort of thing their agency spent taxpayer dollars on without an indisputable reason. And that reason was apparently something Lark would never be able to give, no matter who walked through the Travel Stop door.

"What about the BMW?" Heath asked. "Redmond had an explanation for the skipped title, the fact that his name was never even on it?"

Deputy DeLue nodded. "He did. And we located the Bimmer right where he said it'd be."

"What about forensics on the vehicle? I know it's been a long time, but . . ." Heath's face looked pained, like he knew he was reaching but felt obligated to, even if it meant compromising himself. Watching this good, reliable man take up her own long, feckless protest drained the fight out of Lark. Almost like she'd needed to see it from the outside to finally accept how futile it was. Maybe Heath knew this. Nini spoke of the police going through the motions "for show," as if it were an act of cruelty, but maybe it was kindness. Lark felt a surge of love for her fiancé.

Deputy DeLue was less charmed. "You know we don't have cause for that."

"You have cause to *try*," Heath persisted.

"I disagree." The deputy turned to Lark. "I know you'd hoped to learn more, but take comfort that we didn't find reason for concern. Maybe now it will be easier, in time, to accept your friend made her choices and the outcome was one you couldn't have prevented. When you let her get into Mr. Redmond's car, you weren't being conned or complacent. He was who he said he was. They went where he said they were going and did what he said they'd be doing—all things she agreed to. None of this was your fault, no matter what happened next. Sometimes, that has to be enough to leave it go."

Lark let the words sink in, and she tried—really tried—to consider that he was right. Maybe that was the key: to make peace with all the grief and anger inside her by making peace with herself. She almost asked if he'd mind repeating that last bit so she could get it on record and play it back on demand.

None of this was your fault.

Even if he had betrayed his own theory by using those same old words.

When you let her.

You let her.

You.

Fault.

"I'm not sure I buy Redmond's whole perfect-wedding-date act," Lark said. "Considering how it ended up. You don't think it sounds a little too easy?"

"Nobody said he was the perfect date," Deputy DeLue said. "Even Redmond admitted he wasn't."

"What did he admit to?" she scoffed. "His hair being out of place in a photo?"

He crossed his arms. "I doubt any two strangers on a long road trip would have a *perfect* time. So if you're planning to independently verify all of this, I can save you the trouble. He fessed up to getting in a bit of a yelling match with Mikki at the reception, which some guests we interviewed mentioned as well. I gather the open bar didn't help matters."

Lark and Heath exchanged a look. "That's not a red flag?" Lark asked.

The deputy shook his head. "There's a consensus they kissed and made up, so to speak. Festivities continued the next day, and they were getting on fine. Plus, we have copies of the itinerary his sister distributed for the entire four days. Helps to have a guideline to jog memories, and Chris has an ironclad alibi for almost the entire trip."

"Almost?" Heath prodded him.

"All except the last night, when he slept alone on a boat, allegedly to let Mikki have the room to herself. While that's tough to verify, we do have the vessel bill of sale confirming he took possession that day, and a receipt of dockage fees paid to the marina."

Lark recoiled from the image this immediately conjured: her friend slipping overboard, disappearing into the depths. "And *that's* not a red flag?" she demanded.

"No, it's not. Kim Redmond swears up and down she not only saw Mikki in the lobby the next morning but also spoke with her. We've examined photos posted by guests who said their goodbyes at checkout and identified a woman we believe to be Mikki visible in the background. Her back is turned, but her build and a distinctive duffel bag are consistent. Which deems Chris Redmond's whereabouts the night before irrelevant. The window we're interested in is *after* Mikki was last accounted for. During which Chris was with family, handling a private matter."

"What kind of private matter?"

"Very private." He crossed his arms, case closed.

"And the money Mikki supposedly came into—"

"I think you agree we've been forthcoming with our findings. In case new information should come to light regarding this *potentially* missing person, we won't be discussing specifics of the money."

"So that's it?" Lark asked. "Chris goes back to wherever he came from, like nothing happened? And we all keep pretending nothing did, like he has been for the past eight years?"

"He's been a decent sport if you ask me. He's free to go back, or stay, or fly off in a rocket to Mars. And he's free to do it without a trooper hanging around, watching his every move."

Heath stared down at the floor, but not before Lark caught the look in his eyes. Not before she had time to wonder just how much of the last three days he'd spent staked out at the Yes, Please! Motel, ostensibly looking out for her while she'd gone down her own rabbit hole of obsessive worrying, not so subtly shutting him out. He looked, in this fleeting moment of being chided by a patronizing deputy, like a man who should have known to stay in his lane in a town this small. Like he *had* known better, but he'd crossed the line anyway.

She was the only reason he'd ever find himself in this position. And they both knew it.

"I haven't mentioned that bit about you taking such interest in Redmond to any of my colleagues," DeLue told Heath now. "Or to yours, because frankly, in your shoes, I'd have done the same. But if you overstep again, I'll do more than mention it. We clear?"

Heath looked from Lark to Deputy DeLue and back again, but his expression didn't soften. A part of him still seemed to be in that motel parking lot, standing guard over her last hope. Maybe it was inevitable he'd feel this conflicted. Maybe she should have given him more credit and shown him the damn notebook full of questions to ask Chris. Maybe if she had, they'd be questioning Chris themselves right now instead of sitting here, enduring this.

Or maybe the opposite was true. Maybe if Heath had her notebook, he'd be demanding to know about the notes on her PI and why she hadn't told him the instant she'd hung up the phone with Denny. And how it was best, or at least safest, to accept defeat and move on.

"I can't speak for Lark," Heath said, "but given the challenges of investigating anything so far after the fact, three days doesn't seem very long to spend digging back eight years."

This time when Deputy DeLue spoke, the warning tone was unmistakable. "Between you and me and your fiancée and the wall here, I'm going to stop you there. If we spend longer than three days, I don't know if you'll like what we find. Which is the other reason we asked you both to come in." Lark stiffened as the deputy's eyes slid back to her. "We didn't find discrepancies in Redmond's story. But that doesn't mean we didn't find discrepancies."

Her mouth went dry. *Not the phone,* she pleaded silently. *Please don't ask me again about Mikki stupidly leaving her stupid phone. It was a stupid lie, and I was stupid for telling it, but it's just as stupid that this matters.*

"What discrepancies?" Heath demanded.

"Nothing of consequence, on the surface." He coughed. "On the surface," he repeated. "Now, Ms. Nichols, Deputy Rogers wants me to ask you some questions today. He only has one mode, and it's . . . young. Personally, I'd rather not spend more time on this, because as I said, we haven't found *real* cause for concern. Assuming we're on the same page that we can leave this here."

Lark was caught up on that emphasis on the word "real." And on the way she could feel Heath looking at her, even as the detective's gaze held hers.

"If I were in your shoes, Ms. Nichols," Deputy DeLue went on, "I might be asking myself if I shouldn't be careful what I wish for. I might be wondering, for example, if I hadn't started rolling a snowball downhill years ago that I'm no longer prepared to chase after. If I might have omitted or misconstrued any details, maybe even by mistake. If there were any money transfers that I might not be able to explain if someone looked at my banking statements. Or any long calls from area codes where I claim not to know anyone on my phone records."

Lark shook her head in disbelief, face blazing. Chris had warned her that he could cast doubt on her credibility by contradicting her, but only about the phone. Only about the night Lark watched Mikki go. Whereas DeLue seemed to be implying . . . what? That she was getting kickbacks from whatever money Mikki had "come into"? That they'd been in cahoots, staging her disappearance from the beginning? That *she* was the reason they refused to explain how Mikki's financial situation had changed, "in case new information should come to light"? What motive would she possibly have to do that, let alone keep up the facade this long? Not only had she mourned Mikki for years, and taken custody of her grandmother, she'd apprehended Chris and dragged him here for questioning, thrusting herself into the center of scrutiny yet again.

She opened her mouth to say this was ridiculous—no, it was *offensive*—but as her blood pounded in her ears, she realized her outrage might be mistaken for guilt. Because Deputy DeLue appeared self-satisfied, even sympathetic. Maybe he was bluffing, throwing out theories he had no evidence behind. But it hardly mattered: He'd gotten himself off the hook, hadn't he?

All he'd had to do was make it clear pushing for an investigation would be self-defeating. Because she'd have no control over the scope, and she probably wasn't going to like it.

His approach was working. Heath was looking at her in a way he never had before.

Like he didn't know what to believe.

Like it had just occurred to him that he might not know the woman he loved at all.

The woman he'd been sticking out his own neck for.

Lark wished with all her might Chris Redmond hadn't reappeared. That she'd never recognized him. That all the surveillance cameras had been on the fritz, that he hadn't asked for her. Because all he'd done was make everything worse, and what did she have to show for it?

If I were in your shoes, the deputy had said, *I might be asking myself if I shouldn't be careful what I wish for.*

But if he were Lark, he'd know she hadn't dared to wish for anything for a long time. All the good things that had finally come together in her life—Nini and Dove and Heath—had happened not because she'd wished for them but despite the fact that she hadn't dared to.

"This is outrageous," she said. "Nini was right: there was no reason to come here. You have nothing, and through some mental gymnastics, somehow that's on me." She got to her feet. "If that's all, I'd like to leave, please. My daughter will be getting home."

"Of course." He stood. Heath was the last to get to his feet, slow and uncertain. If Lark looked at him, she'd lose her composure, and she *would not cry* anywhere near this meeting. She would not let them hold that against her too. She turned for the door.

"A lot of people think it's nice," Deputy DeLue called after her, "what you're doing for Mikki's grandmother. Taking care of her like that. Not that there's nothing in it for you—I mean, you get to live in her house, right?"

Lark glared at him. What kind of opportunist did this man take her for?

"Dementia is a terrible disease," he said. "Especially hard on the caregivers. Plenty of people would go to great lengths to avoid having to take on that kind of responsibility."

Not until later would she process what he was implying about Mikki. But she had her usual defense at the ready. "It's mild cognitive impairment," she said icily. "We're doing all we can to keep it from progressing to dementia. We're both doing our best."

He nodded. "I do believe most people are."

~~~

They were in the parking lot before Heath spoke, catching up to Lark in the vacant space between their cars. His arm felt so gentle on hers, she wanted to lean into it, bury her face in his shoulder, and cry this infuriating day away.

But it wasn't over yet.

"Lark?" he asked quietly. "What was he talking about?"

She swallowed the rising emotion, no longer sure this was a safe space to share it. Which only intensified her despair. Maybe she should have kept Heath closer these past few days, instead of pretending she was fine and pushing him away. After Mikki, it had taken a long time to let anyone in again, but against all odds, Heath had become her person. She was still learning what that meant, because Mikki had always loomed so large in her life that the top slot would never have been open. Lark was beginning to understand she should have come clean with him about the mistake she'd made, her little white lie eight years ago, and all the strangeness she'd tried to dismiss this week too. By now, she may have missed her chance.

But even if she'd done everything right, she still wouldn't have an answer for this.

"I have no idea what he's talking about," she said, but her voice was barely a whisper.

Deputy DeLue had backed them into a corner, and all three of them knew it. She would never be able to explain DeLue's line of questioning, and Heath would always wonder where it had come from and why. He'd always have a nagging doubt that he'd put his reputation on the line for her when maybe he shouldn't have.

"I didn't walk out of there because I'm afraid of what they'll find if they investigate me," she said. "I walked because they made it clear they have no intention of trying to find out what happened to Mikki. So what's the point?"

Heath ran a hand through his hair. Out of uniform, he looked more vulnerable. "I'm as frustrated as you are. I'm going to see what I—I'm going to . . ." His voice trailed off. When he spoke again, he sounded less sure.

"I need you to look me in the eye and tell me you've never been less than one hundred percent honest with the police. I'm not talking ninety-nine; I mean one hundred."

Instinctively, Lark ducked the request, sticking to the truth. "I don't know what he's getting at," she said. "I don't know anything about bank statements or phone calls. Do you really need to ask about my bank statements? I'm barely getting by."

"That's not what I asked," he said. "Lark, look at me."

She wanted to. She did. She just . . . couldn't. It was too much, all at once. All her last hopes about Mikki slipping away, and Chris maybe already on his way home, and now this. Tears stung her eyes, and the pavement beneath their feet blurred. "I'm so sorry, Heath. I hate that you're messed up in this. Your job means so much to you, and I don't want to be the one . . ."

"Forget that for a second," he said. "*Look* at me."

"I just want to go home to Dove. You can go. I'm fine. I just need some time. Alone."

"But I can—"

"I don't want you to do anything," she cried. "It doesn't matter that what he said was bullshit. It's pointless to argue with him, and especially with each other. Let's just drop it."

She did look up this time. It was Heath who couldn't meet her eye now.

She really was a terrible liar.

"If that's what you want," he said finally. As if DeLue had left her any choice. "Call me when you're ready. I'm here."

He was here, saying the right things, yet he was not the same man who'd parked his cruiser outside Chris's motel because he loved her too much not to. He was a man who wanted her to assure him of something that wasn't entirely true. And maybe she could have—if she hadn't sensed he really might not be able to move on unless she did. If she hadn't been so hurt that this, of all things, was his first and only question for her after *that* meeting with DeLue.

Watching him drive away, she wondered if it was too late to salvage what she and Heath had. If, as the deputy had said *Just between you and me and your fiancée and the wall*, the damage had already been done.

When she'd stood alone in the parking lot long enough to be sure Heath wasn't coming back, Lark got behind the wheel, hands trembling, wiped the tears from her cheeks, and drove straight to the Yes, Please! Motel. Just as she should have from the start. Deputy DeLue could have waited. Heath might have protested, but she hadn't saved herself any trouble by putting everyone else's needs before her own. When would she learn? She had no one to blame but herself.

She didn't see Chris's car in the lot, but she ran up the stairs anyway, heart in her throat, notebook in her hand, flying to the window where he'd left the curtains open.

Housekeeping had already come to make the bed and tidy the empty room.

Chris Redmond had swept in long enough to ruin everything.

Yet still, she was devastated to find him gone.

20

Mikki

2016

Mikki had staked her claim on a wide hammock stretched invitingly in a circle of palms between the buildings. She was about to tear into the boxed lunch she'd snagged from the grab-and-go table marked "Redmond/Winscott Wedding Guests" when she heard Chris coming, humming Jimmy Buffett. Even before he broke into a loose, wide grin, she could tell he'd come back from the golf course with more than the scorecard he twirled in his hand.

He'd acquired a buzz too.

"There you are," he said, gesturing like a game show host. "Did you have an amazing morning?"

"I did," she said. "Those foam floats for the pool are divine." She didn't mention that she'd kicked the day off with a marathon internet search into his family's tragedy, but her conscience twinged at the thought.

"Good!" Without preamble, he flopped into the hammock, which swayed and shifted until he was *right* beside her, hip to hip, knee to knee. Mikki laughed. His languid body language was so obviously well meaning, nothing like the bitter, mean drunk his brother seemed to be.

"And did you enjoy any golf with your mimosas?" she teased.

Chris groaned. "Cooper kept tipping his flask into my sweet tea without asking." He wasn't slurring exactly, but the words strung together like beads on a chain. "In other news, I may have been too optimistic about you and I not needing more of a story."

"The groomsmen were asking about me?"

"Relentlessly. Who are you, where did you come from, where is this going . . . You have captured their imaginations as a woman of mystery."

Mikki blushed. She didn't take it as a compliment; attention was the last thing she wanted. She just wasn't used to anyone giving her a second thought. Ever.

"On the plus side," Chris added, "it gave them something to badger me about besides Kim and the Great Redmond Rebuild. Which they badgered me about plenty too. Say," he said, tapping the box on her lap. "How attached are you to that lunch?"

"Not at all. Want to share?" She popped open the lid, and they both peered inside to see a giant sandwich cut into halves wrapped in wax paper. Pasta salad, fruit, chips, cookies.

"Perfect." He swung his legs to the ground and offered her a hand up. "Bring it. We'll eat in the shuttle."

Mikki looked down at the wrap skirt she'd tied over her wet swimsuit. "Shuttle to where?"

Chris grinned. "You'll see."

~~~

Mikki clung to the railing of the dolphin watch charter, joining in the squeals of delight every time a dorsal fin surfaced in the boat's wake. Kim and her bridesmaids huddled nearby with their phones pointed toward the spray, recording the spectacle. Chris had found a great equalizer for Mikki's childlike wonder with the ocean: dolphins. No one could resist them.

Still, she was grateful for Chris's solid form beside her as she struggled to acclimate to the bucking of the speeding boat beneath her. It was a sleek white vessel with tinted windows, and from a distance she'd have taken it for a private yacht. She suspected this wasn't the typical tourist cruise, just like the Topaz wasn't the typical tourist resort. Still, she couldn't believe these people weren't wearing the life jackets stacked on the metal bins behind them. Gratefully, Chris was the only one who seemed to notice her discomfort. He'd promised this boat did dozens of these trips every week, and if it was going to go down, it wouldn't be on a sunny day like this.

"What do you think?" he asked, lips inches from her ear so she could hear.

"Amazing," she shouted. "They're so playful." They watched as a mother and her calf jumped out of the water in unison, making picture-perfect arcs against the rolling blue. The boat pitched into the air, and her knuckles went whiter, trying to hold herself steady. This really *was* amazing. She wasn't going to ruin it by letting on that it was equally terrifying.

"It's a little choppy," he observed, biting back a smile. The sandwich had sobered him up, or maybe it just seemed that way because Mikki was a little tipsy herself. The crew had offered champagne flutes as they boarded, and she'd already downed two to calm her nerves.

"A smidge choppy," she agreed.

"Want a break? Bet the captain won't mind if we pop up and see what his view's like."

"Really?" Mikki squinted at the dark, angled windows a level above them. Surely it must be more stable up there.

"Come with me."

The captain looked commanding in his formal uniform, complete with the crisp white cap, and he didn't merely tolerate their presence, he greeted Chris like an old friend. Away from the whipping wind and spray, in the temperature-controlled cabin appointed with white leather and polished brass, Mikki could catch her breath. She dropped into an armchair anchored to the floor while Chris launched amicably into questions about the differences between boating Lake Michigan and the Atlantic. She should have guessed he'd be an experienced sailor; Chris seemed to have tried everything at least once. He and the captain conversed in an unfamiliar language, bearings and flanks and knots and the virtues of forty feet versus thirty-five.

"You'd have fun learning the ropes," the captain said. "You should try it." He turned to Mikki. "I can always spot a first timer. Anything I can do to enhance your time aboard?"

Mikki pointed at the coastline in the distance. It was surreal, gazing back at it from here, a reversal from how she'd spent the morning. "What am I looking at?" she asked. "Is this still Amelia Island?"

The captain waved her over and pointed out the silhouettes of the Topaz, the more remote southern tip of the island, and the nature preserve across the sound. "They call this concrete bridge connecting them the pier," he explained, "but it's a misnomer. More pedestrians and bikes than fishermen. If you ask me, a proper pier is wooden, leads nowhere, and looks like it's one hurricane away from disintegrating. The state park has one there."

"That looks walkable from the Topaz," she said. "Funny I didn't notice it."

"It's the way the island curves," he told her. "Cool trick, huh? It's a different perspective out on the water." He turned to grin at Chris. "You never took her out on Lake Michigan even once, huh? What kind of date are you?"

Chris met Mikki's eyes, and she gave a slight nod. They had no need to keep up the facade here, away from the rest of the wedding party. He flashed the captain a devilish grin. "Don't tell anyone, but I kind of met her on the way down here. Stopping for coffee."

The captain burst out laughing. "Thought I'd heard it all," he said.

"Don't blow my cover," Mikki teased. "I'm trying to keep him out of trouble with the bride."

The captain linked his hands behind his back, nodding appreciatively. "You know," he said, "if this were one of those rom-coms, you wouldn't be up here with me. The unsuspecting bride would separate you from Chris and pull you into all the antics with the bridesmaids."

Mikki smiled. "True. I'd be a fish out of water, and they'd all hate me."

"Until you win them over with your heart of gold," Chris chimed in.

"Eventually," Mikki agreed. "But first it would come to a head at the reception. Someone would snub me, and you'd grab the mic and give an impassioned speech or . . . no. You'd sing a song with the band."

"Serenade or duet? What if you join me onstage for 'Islands in the Stream'?"

Mikki almost dropped the thread, hearing him randomly name her karaoke song with Lark. But she recovered quickly. "Excellent choice. By the end of the weekend I'd have inspired Kim to transform your family business into a charitable foundation to fund scholarships for girls whose wayward parents drained their college savings. You'd propose and appoint me your community ambassador who understands the people you're trying to help."

"I'd watch that movie," the captain said. "Almost too bad this isn't a rom-com." He winked at Chris when he said it, and Mikki's face flushed.

"Huh. I was reading this as more of a legal thriller," Chris said, and they laughed.

"It could be," Mikki teased. "They're probably all down there right now, convinced I'm thwarting your sister's plans to swindle you out of your share of the company."

Chris snapped his fingers. "You were planted in that Travel Stop by a competitor, and you're here to ruin the Redmond name, once and for all."

She grinned. "I'd watch that too."

"We are high concept," he declared, putting his arm around her.

"I'm just glad no one mentioned *Titanic*," the captain joked. "I'm always having to pull people back from crawling out on the bow."

Back at the marina, Chris hung back to shake the captain's hand, and Mikki filed off behind Kim and her entourage toward the resort shuttle. She leaped gratefully to the dock, anticipating the relief of solid ground, and her eyes went wide when she lurched off-balance instead. *Sea legs,* she thought, and smiled to herself, marveling at how quickly her footing in the world had been altered. Although *possibly* they were champagne legs. The bottles had come out again as they'd glided back down the calmer Intracoastal.

"I recognize that look," she heard Kim say. "A woman in her happy place. This is more your speed than Michigan, huh?"

Mikki took a second to register that Kim had stopped on the dock ahead of her and was waiting for Mikki to answer. *Right. Mikki was supposed to be from Michigan, not Ohio.* "Palm trees and dolphins are way more my speed," Mikki admitted, recovering quickly. "Excellent choice for your wedding."

"Why thank you." Kim giggled in a way that struck Mikki as un-Kim-like. Maybe they'd both lost count of their drink refills. "Jeff and I have talked about relocating," Kim said, "but our business ties are too strong back home. How about you, though?"

"Oh, I'd love to move here if it were that simple. But yeah, my job and . . . you know."

Mikki glanced back toward the boat, willing Chris to save her from this conversation. But he and the captain had their heads bent together over Chris's phone, laughing at something.

"Do you travel much for work?" Kim asked, and Mikki shook her head.

"I work with a lot of people who do, though," she said, risking a glimmer of honesty.

"Well. There's more to life than a job. I mean, so I've been told."

Mikki laughed. "True, there is more to it. My roommate . . ." She faltered. Was she supposed to have a roommate? Too late now; she'd already said it. "My best friend," she clarified, "is having a baby, and she doesn't have any support. So I'm signing up."

"Wow. That's big of you." For maybe the first time, Kim looked sincere, not patronizing, even a little. "What's the deal with the father?"

"No deal. Not in the picture." Mikki allowed herself the smallest eye roll, and man, did it feel good to let it out. Guilty, but good. Besides, it didn't count as spilling secrets if she'd never see this person again. "It's her old high school boyfriend," Mikki added. "Chad."

Kim wrinkled her nose. "Oh, no. I've never liked a Chad."

"You wouldn't start with this one." Kim laughed, and at last, Mikki spied Chris heading toward them. "Didn't mean to overshare," she added. "Champagne must be going to my head."

"Overshare away," Kim said, loud enough for Chris to hear. "You'll make up for this one never telling me anything."

Chris nudged Mikki's shoulder, pretending he hadn't heard. "Want to skip the shuttle and walk back? You'll get your land legs faster that way."

"You read my mind."

"Sure," Kim joked. "Keep going off, just the two of you. It's not giving the rest of us a complex or anything."

Chris was unmoved. "It's not far. We'll see you back there." But as he led Mikki past the waiting shuttle to the footpath, she felt a twinge of remorse. Kim was making an effort to be friendly. "Don't worry about her," Chris assured her. "At least we came along at all. Cooper had a sudden urge to learn to kitesurf instead. From the looks of the instructor, I'm guessing he was just hoping to score some weed."

The pedestrian shortcut across the narrow slip of island to the Topaz was shaded by a canopy of live oak trees draped in Spanish moss. Aside from some golfers far ahead of them, no one else was around, and Mikki felt herself relax.

"Well, Cooper missed out," she said. "Thanks for taking me. I'll never forget it."

"Glad you liked it," Chris said. Then he heaved a sigh. "I wish we could go again. I'm happiest out on the water. I'm not ready to go back."

"Then let's walk slower." Mikki dropped from a stride to a stroll, and he scuffed along beside her, giving a little laugh.

"I didn't even realize I was walking so fast."

She hummed the chorus of Simon & Garfunkel's "Feelin' Groovy," and he took her hand and swung it lazily between them.

"I always think of . . ." she started, then felt self-conscious. She'd already shared enough of herself today—with the captain, even with Kim—and she was supposed to be someone else here. Someone less vulnerable. Wasn't that what she wanted? "Never mind. It's silly."

"Come on. Try me."

Mikki didn't really need persuading. Not with Chris anyway.

"Well, when my graduation trip got canceled," she told him, "and everything was falling to pieces, I woke on the day we'd been scheduled to leave, not knowing what to do with myself. So I went to Lark's. Her mom was never home, and that day we raided the pantry and Lark made the most perfectly crisped waffles. We lined the whole counter with toppings—chocolate chips, butter, whipped cream, strawberries from her garden. We sat down to eat, and I looked at her and said, 'Well, I'm supposed to be in the car right now, headed south.' And without missing a beat, she goes, 'Yeah, you'd have been gridlocked in Cincinnati's morning rush hour. And instead, you're eating waffles.'"

He smiled slowly. "In a moment-to-moment comparison, you were actually better off."

"Moment for moment. Lark has always been good at missing the point on purpose." He laughed. "But it was kind of profound, right? It's become a shorthand for us. When we have to do something or be somewhere we'd rather not, we remind each other to eat the waffles."

"That's the first piece of helpful advice anyone has given me about this entire weekend," he said. "Count me in. If you catch me wallowing at the rehearsal later, you have my permission to waffle me." Mikki grinned at him, and he tugged her hand closer, so their shoulders were almost touching as they walked. "You're big on making up rules to live by, aren't you?"

Mikki shrugged. "If you can get a friend in on it, it's not a bad survival hack. I'm kind of an expert at wishing I was someplace else."

"Do you wish that right now?"

"Definitely not." Mikki knew better than to wish one second of this day away. Especially the imperfect bits, when she'd been feeling insecure and trying not to let it show—because those were how she knew it was real.

This place was here all along. And all I had to do was get in the car.

She looked over at him again, and he reached out a hand and caught the ends of the windblown hair that had snagged in her neckline, pulling them loose. Their feet seemed to stop moving at the same time, and they stared at each other, grinning with a new shyness.

And then he was kissing her, tentatively, softly.

Chastely.

She let out a giggle at the exact same time he did.

He pulled back, the spell broken. "Why is this weird?" he asked, laughing. "I mean, assuming *you* think it's weird . . ."

"It's weird," she agreed.

"Have we bonded *too much*?" A look of horror crossed his face. "Have I been too *brotherly*? At my *sister's* wedding? Is this some Freudian thing?"

Her smile went crooked. "I think it's more like we've both been honest about what we have going on. Maybe we're just clear that neither of us is in a good place for this?"

"That would be very mature of us." Tentatively this time, purposefully, he took her hand again and rubbed his fingertips over the palm. It wasn't unpleasant, the nearness of him, the touch. In fact, it was undeniably nice. But not *electric*.

Chris was attractive, kind, rich, and totally out of her league. On paper, she should've been all over him. But that was just it. Mikki had no interest in fooling herself. She could accept she'd never belong with a guy like Chris without getting down about it. She could enjoy his company without indulging feelings that would overcomplicate things. Maybe it was self-preservation, so she wouldn't get hurt. Or maybe his lifestyle seemed just alien enough to short-circuit whatever chemistry they might have had.

"We do have a connection," he said. "We get each other. Wouldn't you say?"

"I would," she agreed. "Maybe we shouldn't think of this failed kissing thing as weird. We should think of it as an achievement. We respect each other, and if we take it off the table . . ."

"It's a good thing we got it out of the way?"

"No drunken making out, no tearful outbursts or jealousy, just good friends. That's what you told your cousin-uncle, after all."

He dropped her hand. "Oh, crud. My cousin-uncle. I'm supposed to take him for a test drive. I think he's calling your bluff about the car. Although I can't really sell it here. Can I?" He glanced at his watch and started walking again. She kept up. "I'm going to have to tell him we don't have time anyway. I'll be cutting it really close before the rehearsal."

"I can take him," she offered. "It doesn't matter if I'm late, as long as I make the dinner."

"But I need to show him how the air was kicking off, how to take the top down . . ."

"I paid attention."

He looked tempted. "This is your only free time, though."

"So I'll spend an hour of it riding along the beach in a convertible. Woe is me."

"Really? Thank you." They walked on, falling back into an easy rhythm together. "Now all I have to do is forget you said the words *failed kissing thing*."

Mikki laughed. "Sorry. Failed kissing *achievement*." He jostled her arm, and she briefly leaned her head on his shoulder as they walked on.

Never mind that all her favorite quotes about failure had to do with trying again, failing better. She wouldn't think about that now.

Chris was a little like the ocean: she knew she was out of her depth. She'd be no match for it until she had time to get comfortable, to temper her trepidation. Which was to say, not yet.

But you never knew. Maybe one day.

21

Lark

2024

Dove came running, launching herself off the porch steps and into Lark's arms.

Lark squeezed her tight, grounding herself in the moment that was always the best part of her day, good or bad or in between. She'd wanted so badly to give her daughter a life with Heath. After today, she didn't know if that was still possible. If she drove to his house and spilled every single thing she'd withheld from him, maybe he'd forgive her. And if he said he was sorry for letting the deputies cast doubt—if he promised he trusted her judgment even when he didn't agree with it—maybe she'd forgive him. But even that didn't guarantee she and Heath could put this behind them and move on. She knew too well how the tension of all the *what ifs* about Mikki never went away, how they piled between people, like a wedge. She breathed in her daughter's sugary smell, and all she could think was, *It's me and you and that's always been enough. That will keep being enough, no matter what.*

"Was the bus okay?" Lark asked, and Dove nodded.

"Where were you?" Dove chattered. "Did the man find you?"

"What man?"

"With the pretty pictures of Aunt Mikki."

Lark sank onto the top step and pulled her daughter down next to her. "Someone was looking for me? A man who showed you pictures?"

"He showed them to Nini, but I saw. Aunt Mikki and him all dressed up by the ocean. Can we go to the ocean too? Not just in our dream, but for real? I want to build sandcastles."

Lark put her hand on Dove's shoulder. "When was this? What else did he say?"

The storm door creaked open. "I told him to buzz off," Nini grumbled. "Why would we want pictures of the trip Mikki never should have taken? But no one listens to me." She crossed her arms, but her stance seemed off. Like her heart wasn't in it. "He's around back, waiting for you. Says he wants to buy you dinner."

～～

"Thanks for agreeing to this," Chris said. He and Lark sat at a back table at the Neon Moon, where she'd brought him not because the food was good but because Heath wouldn't be there—bad look for a trooper to be in a bar before his shift. The place was empty this early in the evening except for a couple of burnouts throwing darts and some loudmouths who bet on sports all day camped out at the bar. Lark gripped her pint glass and stared at the untouched burger platters on the dirty high-top between them. She hadn't come to eat.

"I thought you'd left," she said. This was strange, feeling both relieved and guarded at the same time.

"I wouldn't have done that to you," Chris said.

She raised a skeptical eyebrow and took a long sip of her beer, though it did little to calm her nerves. Chris had ordered them, but his sat frothy and untouched. "What about that letter on my desk?" she asked, watching closely for his reaction. "Or the emails to that two-faced Denny Dean. Would you have done *that* to me?"

"Huh?" Chris looked genuinely clueless. He leaned in. "I don't know what you mean. But I don't blame you for having the wrong impression of me. It's been surreal, scrolling through the #FindMikki hashtags and reliving everything I missed, play by play. How you crowd-funded to hire a PI. How you made those CATCH YOU LATER bumper stickers. You still have them in the Travel Stop, don't you, near the counter?" Lark nodded. "You know what's crazy? I think I've seen one or two on the road before. I just never knew what they meant."

"Mikki would know," she said, automatically. "If she ever came across one."

"She would," he agreed. "While everyone else thinks it's about leaving other drivers in your dust. That's why it's brilliant."

He looked pensively around the bar, and she wondered if he was picturing Mikki there. Maybe he was just biding his time until he could clear his conscience and go. "It hardly seems possible that the whole time, I had no clue about any of it," he said. "I can't imagine what it's been like for you. All those comments, the haters . . ."

Lark frowned, unable to stop ruminating on everything the deputies had told her about Chris. Arguing with Mikki at the reception. Choosing that of all days to buy a boat. Leaving Mikki alone in the hotel lobby that last morning to say her goodbyes to the bride. Leaning on a vague alibi of dealing with a "private family matter" in the days after. Lark wanted to hear him out, but she didn't trust him. If he wanted to relive everything she'd been through, good on him for getting a clue, but she hardly needed to be reminded about any of it.

"Well," she said, "if you're here to talk me out of doing a public push all over again, you'll be happy to hear I don't have it in me. I have too many other things to consider now. A daughter, a fiancé, Nini. So you can tell your lawyer not to worry about me, okay?"

"Screw my lawyer," Chris said.

Lark stared at him.

"He has my best interests at heart, but zero interest in the big picture. I'm a decent human, Lark. I cared about Mikki. And I know

Mikki cared about you." He nudged her basket of food toward her. "Please," he said. "Eat. Least I can do."

She nibbled a french fry to appease him and raised her pint glass. "To being decent humans," she said. Though if she'd learned anything working at the Travel Stop, it was that everyone saw themselves as the hero of their own journey. If Mikki was off living a new life right now, she probably thought she was the hero of hers too.

He took the world's smallest sip of his beer. "I don't drink much anymore," he admitted. "My brother put me off it."

"Don't worry," she said. "The taps here are watered down beyond recognition."

"Right. Well. So. You're probably wondering about the money they're making such a big deal about Mikki coming into."

Lark tapped the notebook next to her on the table. She hadn't cracked it open yet. "Probably," she agreed. "Any idea where she got it?"

"I gave it to her."

Here, at last, was new information. "Why?"

"The short answer? That money meant a lot more to her than to me. And this might sound strange, but I owed her. Before I met Mikki, nothing had been going my way, and suddenly everything was."

"To be honest," Lark said, "that doesn't sound like Mikki."

"I know. She felt like some harbinger of bad luck. But Mikki ended up helping me see how I'd been stuck, in a way no one else could. She had this perspective that made things seem simpler. Like I could just let go, and as soon as I did, other things fell into place." He bit his lip. "Mikki and I made a pact that our road trip would have a happy ending, and I was trying to make it happen. I wanted that money to make a difference for her. All this time, I've imagined her starting over with you, finally out of the trap of living paycheck to paycheck. I was way off. Obviously."

A happy ending? Lark wanted to cry. "Maybe that is what she's doing," she said numbly. "Just not with me."

He shook his head, like there had to be more to it, and Lark had a bizarre urge to thank him, anyway, for trying. Even if he had led the police to suspect *her* in the process.

"Were you and Nini always close?" he asked. "Or did Mikki's leaving bond you?"

Lark decided to level with him. "Neither," she said. "We were never close, and when Mikki left, Nini blamed me. Didn't say a word to me for nearly a year."

He put his glass down. "Seriously?"

"Seriously."

"What changed?"

Lark hesitated. This wasn't a story she liked to tell, and so it wasn't one she had told. Not to anyone but Heath. But she couldn't see what she had to gain by withholding it now.

"I don't really know what changed," she said, truthfully. "Dove was a month old. I'd barely left my apartment since I'd brought her home. It was all a blur. Mikki had promised to be there when I became a mom, and when she wasn't, I guess that's when it sank in that she was really gone. When I stopped waiting and started grieving." Chris nodded like this made sense, but how could she really explain? Lark knew all young mothers with newborns could get sucked into a vortex of sleep deprivation and depression. But hers had been so all-consuming and lonely, after a few weeks she could no longer see a way out. Emotionally *or* logistically. How to dig out from being months behind on rent now that she was responsible for twice as much of it? "I didn't even know if it was day or night half the time," she went on. "All I did was sleep, nurse the baby, and cry. But I had to go back to work. I couldn't afford not to, and I had no clue how I'd manage any of it. I just kept thinking, *This was a mistake; I can't do this alone. I can't do this at all.*"

"So you went to see Nini?"

"I wouldn't have dared. The looks she'd given me . . . No. But one day, someone knocked on my door—which never happened. Everyone had either written me off or forgotten about me by then." She shrugged.

"It was Nini. She looked me up and down with disapproval and stared for a long time at the baby. Then she sighed and said, 'Guess you'd better move in, then.'"

Chris half laughed, incredulous. "She led with *that*?"

"She led and finished with that. Told me to pack and she'd be back for us the next day. I wasn't sure about the state of her decline by then—I thought maybe she was confused, thinking I was Mikki or even forgetting Mikki was gone. But it was such a relief to have someone tell me what to do for a change that I did it. I started packing. And wouldn't you know, she was there the next day with a couple guys she'd talked into loading up our cars. That was that."

Of course, that hadn't really been that. Nini's resentment toward Lark had permeated the house long before she'd moved in, as if a dog had been skunked or a roast left in the crock pot far past the point of done. The window to deal with the origin of the problem had passed, leaving nothing to do but ignore the lingering unpleasantness and hope it would fade or become buried underneath fresh, new scents, better memories in the making.

It had been a long and arduous process. And though it was mostly behind them now—only the occasional whiff catching her off guard these days—Lark could never forget the way those early years had felt and tasted and smelled. She knew Nini wouldn't either.

"What about Dove's father? Does he even know about her?"

Lark searched his eyes for any sign that he knew damn well about Chad. That he'd written his own caption to that old yearbook photo of them just days ago. But she saw none.

"You know, I used to worry about him finding out until I realized he doesn't want to know. He's seen her around. He's never asked. I'm more relieved than surprised."

Chris proved perceptive enough to change the subject. "I love that she has a bird name too. How did you come up with Dove?"

"Did you know larks are one of the few birds that sing as they fly?"

"I didn't."

"Mikki taught me that. It's where the expression 'happy as a lark' comes from. When my baby turned out to be a girl, I thought about calling her Robin or Wren. But what I really wanted in my life at that moment was peace. So, Dove."

He was fidgeting with his beer glass again, turning circles of condensation onto the greasy tabletop. "You still don't have peace, though, do you?"

She had no good answer for that. Chris pushed his platter to the edge of the table, giving up the guise that either of them could muster an appetite.

He should have been an easy target for all her frustrations. And maybe he would have been if he weren't so damn *respectful*. Despite all her reservations and resentments, it was hard to begrudge the police for finding him credible.

Then again, maybe he was just skilled at disarming people. Specifically, lost, lonely women from Becksville.

"I've been carrying around this notebook full of questions to ask you," Lark told him. "But maybe it's pointless. Maybe the cops are right: you *don't* have any of the answers."

"I wish I did," he said.

Lark nodded. "Still. Some people might say you owe it to me to help find them."

"I agree. I wouldn't blame you for thinking I owe you a lot more than that."

She opened her mouth to argue, then realized what he'd said.

"I know how it must look," he went on, "but Mikki and I sort of romanticized this idea of being in each other's lives for this finite period of time and then going our separate ways. When we said goodbye, we meant *goodbye for good*. But if I'd changed my mind and checked in with her after she left, if I'd realized back then something wasn't right . . ."

He didn't need to finish the sentence. Everything could have been different. For Lark, for Nini, for half of Becksville. Hell, Mikki could have been here right now.

Lark took a deep breath. "I heard you two were arguing at the reception. What about?"

He shook his head. "Nothing. Everything. It felt kind of inevitable, tensions were so high—and not just between us. We were so different, though. This might sound trite, but the argument brought us closer. I don't think Mikki wasted energy on anyone unless she cared." He wasn't wrong. "It makes me sick, thinking how much more you and I could've done if I'd known," he said. "Starting with getting the police to take her disappearance seriously. And not having to beg strangers on the internet for money. I cannot express to you how sorry I am."

"You really never tried to contact her?"

"I thought about her a lot. But no, I never did. It wasn't just that we'd agreed not to. My family . . . What you said, about how all-consuming grief could be? We lost a lot in a very short time. After the wedding it was clear none of us were coping well. So I focused on that."

"While sailing your new boat?"

"Yeah. I needed a clean break. Staying gone might sound selfish, but the rest of my family was happier that way too. We do better with some distance. That's something Mikki and I talked about too—she felt weird, knowing you hadn't wanted her to go with me, but she was also seeing that a little headspace could actually be good." He winced. "Temporarily. I hope you know what I mean. It was important to her that you two stay close."

It had been a long time since anyone had told Lark a Mikki story she hadn't heard. Mixed up in all her complicated feelings about Chris— and the idea of him discussing her with Mikki—she felt a new, sort of preemptive sadness that they couldn't have done this on better terms.

"Look," Chris said. "What you said about not having it in you to do this publicly all over again . . ." He cleared his throat. "If you're open to it, I have a different idea."

Lark didn't have the faintest clue what she was open to. "What do you suggest?"

"I'll fund a new PI if that's what you want. But before we decide about reopening that can of worms, might you want to just . . . go down there? I could take you, show you. Give you a chance to see how you feel about things once you've walked in Mikki's footsteps a little?"

Surely she must be misunderstanding. "You want me to drop everything and go to Florida with you? Because that worked out *so well* for my friend last time?"

"No." Chris looked appropriately horrified. "God, that *is* how it sounded. It doesn't have to be *with* me." He began tripping over his words, babbling in a very un-Redmond-like way. "But I'd like to send you, along with Dove and Nini. I'll get plane tickets, or you could drive if you'd rather. Did you ever think it might be meaningful to follow the exact path she took?"

He'd done an impressive job of not putting his foot in his mouth until this exact moment.

"I might have," she said, through gritted teeth, "if I'd *known* which path she took."

"But that's what I mean. You said I owed it to you to help find her, and I can't help feeling I owe you this too. It might be good for you to go, even if only to get out of Becksville and process this without the whole town watching for once."

Lark paused, considering. It was a kind, insightful offer.

And too good to be true.

A road she'd stared down before. Even if she hadn't been the one to take it.

Chris kept talking. "It's a beautiful resort . . . Seeing it in person might be like putting a name to a face. I could come along as a sort of tour guide to Mikki's time there, or I could just leave you to it. Up to you."

Lark tried on this vision of herself as a sort of Nancy Drew, audacious enough to take matters into her own hands. She wasn't deluded that she could do a better job of investigating, popping out of stairwells to ask unsuspecting hotel maids if they worked there eight years ago.

Short of that, wouldn't she be taking advantage of Chris's generosity, using his guilt to her advantage? Even if it *was* his idea?

"Say I did go," she said. "Then what?"

"Even if all you do is walk the same shoreline, sit under the same palm trees, breathe it all in, it might finally bring some sense of peace or closure. Or maybe it reenergizes you for whatever comes next. I know I can't make this right, but if I can do the next best thing—whatever that is—I will."

Lark felt almost as if she owed Mikki an apology for all the times she'd cursed Mikki's poor judgment, because now, Lark had every reason to judge Chris as a human red flag, yet she *still* had a hard time resisting. In fact, she was actively picturing herself and Dove and Nini stepping right into that glossy resort slideshow and building sandcastles, like Dove had asked to. Under any other circumstances, she wouldn't believe her luck.

And under these circumstances?

She didn't believe it either.

No way would Heath be okay with her going. She already knew what he'd say, how incredulous he'd be. She couldn't help channeling it now.

"You want to make it up to us with . . . a *vacation*?"

"A trip," he corrected her. "I'm not saying it'll be all pina coladas by the pool. I know this is emotional. But if even one second of it feels like a vacation, even for Dove, I think Mikki would want that." He offered her a weak smile. "If you won't let me do it for you, let me do it for her. I've never seen anyone appreciate the ocean so much. Honestly, she changed the way I see it. For good. She'd want you to see it too."

Lark recognized the look on his face. The struggle. The hope. The doubt.

All these years, she'd known there was another side to this story, known she couldn't ever truly understand what had happened without Mikki telling her the other half. But she hadn't fully considered that there weren't two crucial sides after all.

There were three.

22

Mikki

This was what convertibles were made for. Mikki tamed her hair into a haphazard ponytail as Al steered them over the A1A bridge, rolling ocean to the left, glimmering Intracoastal to the right.

"Who cares if the damn AC is broken in a convertible?" Al called over the rush of the air, the Beach Boys singing about Kokomo cranked to full volume on the radio.

"That's what I said!" Mikki called back.

"Only one thing could make this drive better." Al pulled into the tiny lot of a tiki hut with a hand-painted sign that read MILKSHAKE SHACK.

When they both had chocolate shakes with extra whipped cream in hand, Mikki perched on the rear bumper while Al circled the car appraisingly.

"You know," he said, "I've splurged on a few cars over the years. But hand to God, I haven't regretted a one." He chuckled softly, though it seemed more for his own benefit than for hers, like he was reminding himself of his own story. "Funny thing, though. Of all those cars, the ones I lusted over the longest were the ones to let me down. The ones I never really planned on, never tried to think through—those were the best surprises."

He sighed, running his finger over the paint. If he hadn't been examining every detail, Mikki might have wondered if he were really talking about cars at all.

"I don't know how I'd sell Cathy on this," he said. "But damn, I wish I could."

Mikki took a pull of her milkshake, which was just the right thickness, rich and sweet. Suddenly she didn't just want to see Chris move on from this car. She wanted to see it transferred to someone who'd appreciate it—all of it. Someone who'd told her from the jump how much he loved a good story.

"Is your wife a romantic?" Mikki asked.

He raised an eyebrow. "She likes those novels, if that's what you mean."

"You might try telling her the real story of why Chris doesn't want to keep driving this car."

Al grinned back. "Any relation to the real story of how Chris came to be here with you?"

He shot her such an affable look, she was tempted to tell him everything. He'd painted himself as an outlier, and Chris would spend a lot of the next three days tied up with family obligations. She could use an ally, or at least a friend. But was it really her call to tell him the truth, without clearing it with Chris first?

Maybe. It had never been Chris's idea to tell this lie in the first place. So he could hardly get upset with her for *untelling* it. Besides, he'd been eager enough to tell the ship captain earlier. "What makes you think there's more to that story?" she asked, and Al kept on grinning.

"There's always more to the story with Chris. He's a more-to-the-story kind of person."

23

Lark

2024

Lark surveyed the task of what it would take to pack up Nini to spend any length of time away from home. The puzzles and brainteasers that made up her daily mental workout. The checklists, calendars, and reminder notes. The meal trackers to confirm she met her daily dietary recommendations. The herbal supplements—lord, the herbal supplements—enough to require their own carry-on: omega-3 fatty acids, mega-boosts of B vitamins, vitamins D and E soft gels, ginkgo biloba, coconut oil. Some of them studies had shown to improve cognition or slow the decline in responsive thinking. Others were more of a *just in case this helps* or a safeguard against a deficiency that could exacerbate things. But none of them were expendable in Lark's mind. Not even for a few days.

"Leave the coconut oil," Nini suggested. "I'll drink it from the trees."

It was a rare boost of optimism from the woman, but Lark pulled a face. "Maybe this is too much, Nini. If it's better you stay here, I could arrange for someone to check in . . ."

Nini rolled her eyes. "If it's too much, I'll die in a better place. Either way, I win."

Lark shook her head in exasperation, but Nini was smiling. *Actually* smiling. She'd been a surprisingly easy sell on the trip. Lark couldn't tell whether Nini was really this enthusiastic to see firsthand where Mikki had run off to, or whether she just wanted to milk Chris for a luxury resort stay. She knew better than to ask. Nini would only scoff, *What does it matter?*

"You need me to help look after Dove, anyway," Nini said. "Safety in numbers. Even if we've decided to take this Redmond character at his word, we have to keep our guards up."

Lark had thought about this, too, of course, wondering if she were crazy to take Dove along at all. But leaving her here was out of the question, for many reasons. And it did seem far safer for three generations of women to go than for Lark to venture there alone. Dove and Nini had their own ways of attracting all kinds of attention. They couldn't *all* disappear with no one noticing. Plus, they'd opted to fly, more public and traceable that way, though Lark felt anxious about her first foray into air travel.

"Besides," Nini added, eyes gleaming, "won't you and Heath want a little time on your own? Once Dove is asleep for the night, I will be, too, and you can go back out. You'd waste those nights in the room otherwise."

Lark busied herself rearranging the toiletry bag, so Nini couldn't see her face. "Heath *is* coming, isn't he?" Nini pressed. "What did he say about all this?"

"I haven't told him," Lark admitted.

"Yet? You haven't told him yet?" When Lark didn't answer, Nini started right in. "Oh, no. No, no, no. You can't just *go*. He'll be beside himself with worry."

"He'll try to talk me out of it."

Nini raised an eyebrow. "So? You tried to talk Mikki out of it, too, but would it have been better if she'd just up and left? You, of all people, know how that feels."

Lark's first thought was that this was unfair—but then again, maybe not. Maybe Lark, of all people, did know. Maybe Lark, of all people, wanted to be the one running away for a change.

"Plus," Nini added, "Heath is on your side."

"Heath is on both sides," Lark corrected her. "That much was clear at the sheriff's station. That's why I can't put him in this position again. They're already accusing him of overstepping, and he hasn't even spoken to Chris directly. I'm pretty sure accepting a paid trip to Florida from the guy they just interrogated is out of the question. But Heath won't want me to go alone either. It's lose-lose."

"The only way you lose is if you shut out your fiancé. There's no conflict of interest about that."

"You didn't see the way he was looking at me. He tried to stand up for me, and it backfired. He might not like those deputies, but he trusts them. Maybe more than he trusts me at the moment."

"Those deputies let you down, not the other way around. I can't believe Heath would side with them. It might've felt that way, but all those men with badges had you outnumbered. You and Heath just need to talk this out."

"What's gotten into you?" Lark tried to tease. "Giving me grand-motherly advice? Having faith that love is enough? Are you *sure* you're okay to travel?"

Nini bit back. "What's gotten into *you*? Ever since this Redman reappeared, dredging up things that were best left alone, you've been acting like it's your burden to carry alone. Like no one else could possibly relate. We all know you didn't ask for any of this. But if you let it come between you and Heath, that *is* on you. That's the one thing you can control."

Lark knew it was a valid point, but it didn't escape her that Nini had every reason to want Lark and Heath to work things out. And not all of them were selfless.

"No matter what I do or don't say to Heath," Lark said, "he's still not going to want me to go to Florida with Chris."

"Then invite him along. Let him be the one to say no."

"It's not that simple. I'm not letting him stick his neck out for me again. And even if he could get his commander's approval, he doesn't have the time off. He barely has enough for our wedding and the move. It's better I go alone. Ask forgiveness later."

Nini looked at her hard. "But what if you don't get it?"

Lark wanted to cry. The idea of handing Heath back his ring was so unthinkable, she wanted to kick and scream and throw herself at his feet, begging for mercy.

But not following through with Chris wasn't an option either.

"If Heath won't forgive me, then I guess I don't deserve him. Or he doesn't deserve me. Anyway, you're changing the subject. We were discussing whether it made sense for *you* to travel. Not Heath."

Nini gestured toward the high-maintenance pile Lark had been gathering. "Is this even necessary? Who cares if I miss some of my . . . my . . . oh, the do-se-whats-its."

Nini blinked at the array of bottles in concentration, clearly bothered that she couldn't conjure the word.

"Supplements?" Lark said gently. *I forget words too,* she told herself. But she knew it was more than that.

"Supplements. Yes." Nini blinked rapidly. "We're going down there to honor Mikki. Why can't we just let all this slide for a few days?"

Lark didn't know how to tell her that honoring Mikki *was* the reason they couldn't let it slide. More than ever, she needed Nini's memory intact. She needed Nini to remember Mikki the way she'd really been. Before. Because no one else seemed to—or ever would again.

"I'll tell you what," Nini said. "I'll come, and I'll do everything your way down there. You call all the shots, and I won't make a fuss about any of it—provided you go tell Heath to his face what's going on. That's my condition. Otherwise, you're on your own, I'll stay here, and *I'll* be the one to tell him."

"Nini," she protested. "Come on."

"Sorry, doll." Nini did actually look sorry. It wasn't a look Lark was used to seeing, and it stopped her short. "I might not have always done right by you. But I've seen you try to do right by everyone else. And I can't let you sabotage this and tell yourself it's for Mikki's sake."

Lark knew when she'd lost an argument. Fine. She'd go to Heath's. Even if only to lose another one.

24

Mikki

2016

The wedding rehearsal was staged in a tasteful courtyard, with a flower-strewn altar, center aisle, and rows of white chairs arranged in a scaled-down approximation of the setup for the ceremony on the beach the next day. Mikki had slipped into a seat on the far left, hoping to go unnoticed on the fringe.

Not that it was working. Chris kept looking conspicuously her way, and every time he did, a few other curious heads turned too. She didn't know whether to be flattered or to mouth to him to please cut it out.

"You're all familiar with the traditional lighting of the unity candle," the officiant said, "but we're going to put a special spin on the tradition. Would the Redmond brothers step forward?"

Chris and Cooper each took an obedient half step toward the officiant. The brothers moved alike, or at least they did when Cooper was somewhat sober. The officiant, on the other hand, seemed almost inhumanly polished, as if he'd come with the resort. With his gelled hair, bespoke bow tie, and smooth, slender fingers, he looked even more salon-fresh than the bridesmaids, who'd literally come from the on-site salon.

"Now typically," he went on, gesturing to the white candles arranged inside a wide glass hurricane to shield the wind, "the bride's parents light her candle, the groom's light his, and then the bride and groom hold those flames to the center wick, symbolizing their union. Kim has beautifully requested we modify this ritual to honor her parents' memory, to symbolize them watching over this joyous celebration with their heavenly blessing."

Cooper coughed, and Kim shot him a dirty look.

"Chris, Cooper, these two additional candles signify your mother and father. We'd like you to lead us off by lighting these first, then holding them together to light Kim's. There won't be a dry eye in the house."

Cooper barked out an incredulous laugh. "Because we're using fire?" he asked. "Isn't this symbolism a little on the nose?"

Mikki gasped audibly before she could catch herself. But she wasn't the only one. Everyone in the courtyard recoiled. Kim stood stoic, beautiful in a white off-the-shoulder cocktail dress, but from her half-open mouth came a whimper, and Jeff slid an arm protectively around her waist.

The officiant cleared his throat. "Let's break for a few minutes, regroup, and take it from the top," he suggested. "Then we'll get you all off to the best rehearsal dinner of your lives. Our chef has outdone himself—you're in for a treat."

The maid of honor scurried to Kim's side with a champagne glass and a plate of sliced fruit, chattering about *natural sugar* and *nerves*. Kim didn't look nervous so much as furious, and she whispered to her friend furtively, who said something to Chris, who picked up the whole hurricane of candles and walked off without as much as a glance in Cooper's direction.

"Too soon, huh?" Cooper said loudly to no one in particular. "That was my point."

The air shifted, and Mikki turned to see one of the bridesmaids plunk down a few chairs over. Mikki had noticed her during the run-through because her body language looked exaggeratedly impatient. She wore a wine-colored sheath dress, her hair in a sleek twist, and if she was here with a date, he'd gotten a pass on this obligation.

"That was a shit show," the bridesmaid grumbled. "I don't see why we have to run through it again. At our age, it's not like we don't know the drill."

Mikki wondered what the woman supposed *our age* to be, as she looked at least ten years older than Mikki, but she kept on talking. "You're here with Chris, right? Lark, is it?" She didn't wait for an answer. Clearly, she knew. "*Please* tell me he's talked to Kim by now."

Mikki gestured toward the altar, where he had yet to reappear. "I mean, yeah. I think he's helping her right now."

"Right. I guess they're swapping the candles for vases of sand. If the wind picks up and someone gets a scratched cornea from *unity sand*, I hope it's Cooper." She rolled her eyes. "But I'm not talking about Chris being a helpful errand boy. I'm talking about him sitting down with her. Last I heard, he'd been giving her the slip all day."

No way was Mikki getting pulled into their family drama. "I think Chris respects this might not be the place for business negotiations," she said, hoping this woman would take the hint that it wasn't the place to grill Mikki either.

"That's not respect." She huffed. "Do you realize he's got us nearly at a standstill? Do you know how many of our clients are here, counting on us to quit stalling? Kim doesn't have the luxury of a purely personal wedding—not with this guest list."

Mikki frowned. "You work for the Redmonds?"

"Came on as marketing director last year. I'm Olivia, by the way. Kim and I are old friends, and she called me after my predecessor was caught in the . . ." She cleared her throat, and Mikki paled, remembering how the original marketing director's voicemails during the fire had made headlines. If her cries for a miracle had been answered, would she have been the one at this wedding, sitting here in Olivia's place?

Of course not. Without the tragedy, the wedding would've surely happened in Michigan. Chris would never have come through the

Travel Stop, and Mikki wouldn't be here either. "That must have been hard," Mikki managed, "stepping into a job under those circumstances."

"Wouldn't have done it for anyone but Kim. She really doesn't take no." Olivia slid closer. "Look, Chris clearly cares what you think. We've all seen him looking over here. Like he's suddenly more comfortable around you than with anyone he's known half his life."

Mikki opened her mouth. That couldn't be true. She was categorically out of place here.

"I'll tell you my take, and pretty much everyone else's," Olivia went on as if Mikki had asked. "If Chris wants no part of the rebuild, we get it. I think their parents would even have understood, given all that's happened." She shook her head. "But holding everything up while he makes up his mind isn't fair. Especially not to Kim, who's been hustling her ass off to save face. With the current structure, all three of them need to agree for any investments over a certain amount to move ahead. Chris isn't voting no, he's refusing to vote at all, which might as well be no for the people stuck waiting on a yes."

She must have clocked Mikki's discomfort, because she added, "I wouldn't mention it if I didn't see this taking such a toll. He's like a dead weight hanging off the edge of the family ship, about to tip it. He needs to either climb on or let go."

Mikki bit her lip. This was not quite how Chris had explained things, but it didn't contradict what he'd said either. Maybe it was the least biased version of the truth she'd hear.

Still, Kim wasn't the only one it was unfair to.

"You sure Cooper isn't hanging over the side too?" Mikki asked. "Maybe the captain needs to slow the ship down a little."

"Nope. Cooper is on board, sunning himself on the pool deck." Olivia nodded at the altar, where Cooper and Kim were hugging now. "Honestly, even if he isn't the best at reading the room, he makes good points." Mikki watched as Kim dabbed her eyes with a tissue so her makeup wouldn't run. Sure enough, it was Chris who was standing aside, looking awkward.

Looking, as it were, straight at Mikki.

"So?" Olivia asked. "Can you talk to him?"

Mikki wondered what Olivia would do if she turned to her right now and confessed that Chris might not be open to business advice from a woman whose job entailed taping "out of order" signs on slushie machines. But she'd used up her remaining allotment of radical honesty on Al during their test drive.

"I'm Chris's guest," Mikki said carefully. "I'm here for the wedding, not any drama. And I'm going to dance with the one who brought me."

"No such thing as a wedding without drama," Olivia scoffed. She stood to go. "Look, Chris is a good guy. I'm sure he's told himself he's just being thoughtful about where they go from here. But he's being selfish. This might not seem like the place, but it's time to make things right one way or another. If he isn't ready to make any big decisions, all he needs to do is either bow out or defer to Kim and Cooper until he's ready to step back in. It's not like she's pressuring him to sign his life away. He has options." Mikki remembered Kim telling Chris he'd be *pleasantly surprised* by the options. This must be what she meant. "It's bad enough what's happened to them, and between him and Cooper barely keeping his shit together, they're making it worse." The wedding party was lining up to restart the rehearsal. Olivia moved to join them.

"Think about nudging him, please," she called over her shoulder. "Otherwise, we're all here on borrowed time. Even you."

~~~

Mikki looked around the rehearsal dinner for Al, hoping for a friendly face, but he must not have made the cut. She'd expected a scaled-back version of tomorrow's reception, in the wide open-air ballroom that was the jewel of the resort, but instead their group had been escorted to an intimate, out-of-the-way restaurant in an outcrop of the southernmost building. The space was, impossibly, even more upscale than the rest of the Topaz, a minimalist room enclosed in glass, with doors opened to a cascade of terraces extending like an enormous ornamental fan poised above the dunes. You could almost forget you were still in the resort at all; the view was all watercolor sky, sea oats silhouetted against the pink and yellow sunset.

"So?" Chris asked cheerfully, appearing with two cocktails. Mikki took one gratefully. "Did you close the deal on my dream car? Sell Al some Florida swampland while you were at it? Rumor has it, he's swinging by later with some prized cigars. How'd you leave things?"

"He was tempted but said his wife's a hard sell. Even if she didn't object to the car in theory, I gather she won't be keen to fly home alone or ditch the ticket to drive."

"And I don't suppose you fancy a detour to Texas?"

Mikki didn't want to tempt herself by asking how that might work. "When the clock strikes midnight at the end of this ball, one of us has to make rent."

They were interrupted by an announcement to find their seats, and Mikki trailed behind Chris in the ensuing shuffle. She was relieved to find Chris and Cooper had not been seated together, though it did seem out of step with tradition. Maybe it was just logistics. Cooper sat at a table of singles, and Mikki and Chris were paired with couples, cousins from the groom's side and their spouses. Only the groom's brothers sat with Jeff and Kim, along with Kim's future in-laws.

As their server came around for their orders from the prix fixe menu—filet mignon, swordfish, a Mediterranean vegetarian dish Mikki couldn't pronounce—Chris leaned to her ear.

"If one more person I barely know tells me what my parents would have wanted," he whispered, "I'll scream. All thanks to that stunt with the unity candles. None of these people have the first clue what they would've wanted. Kim and Cooper and I can't even agree on it."

Before she could respond, Kim called over—"Siblings photo! Both sides!"—and he was whooshed away. On her own yet again, Mikki slipped away to the opulent ladies' room and stared at herself in the mirror.

She didn't want to dwell on the uncomfortable exchange with Olivia, or what she'd meant about them all being here on borrowed time. But Mikki couldn't stop thinking about how she'd said Chris thought he was doing the reasonable thing but was blind to his own selfishness. Wasn't that how Mikki had felt about Lark sometimes, so sure her friend's wait-and-see approach was holding them both back?

Now that Mikki had some distance, she had to accept that Lark hadn't backed them into this corner by herself. Yes, Lark had shown poor judgment around her ex, and yes, she'd embraced her pregnancy without a plan for how she'd manage it . . . But none of that would've been possible if Mikki had gotten them out of Becksville a long time ago. If Mikki had ever said, *Lark, I'm going, with or without you*, Lark might not have liked it, but she'd have gone. And even if she hadn't? Then it would've been up to Mikki to do the hard thing and move on without her.

Now it was too late. Mikki was the one who'd have to go along, like it or not. Who'd have to stay behind, knowing it could have gone some other way. She'd told Chris she was secretly mad at Lark, but the truth was, she was mad at herself. And this was why.

If Olivia was right about Chris—if he was never going to feel good about taking his seat at the Redmond table, and if he just didn't know how to admit, even to himself, he'd never want the same thing Kim and Cooper did—would he realize too late that he wasn't just tripping up their plans but hamstringing his own options too?

Maybe Mikki owed it to him, as possibly the lone person here with no stake in the game, to try to help him see that perspective. On paper, Mikki was the one who needed help, who was maybe even desperate for this weekend to be transformational in *any* positive way. But realistically, the outcome of her trip was predetermined. At the end of the weekend she'd turn around and go home, whereas Chris had alternatives. He'd said it himself—*untaken roads*—and now he was at a convergence of them. He might not even realize he kept going round and round the traffic circle, watching them all pass him by.

Back at the table, he was waiting for her, forcing a smile. Wire baskets of warm, rustic bread had appeared at every seat, smelling of fresh rosemary and glistening with a dusting of sea salt. Each came with a dish of butter and roasted garlic cloves soft enough to spread with a knife.

Mikki took a bite, then another. She looked him in the eye and knew just what to say. "This may be the best bread I've ever tasted. Next best thing to *waffles*."

He took another bite, and the smile stretched slowly across his face. "You're right," he said. "I almost forgot to notice."

~~~

It was hours before Mikki had another moment to herself. Several drinks in, Chris was having more fun, pulled into some line dance that everyone but Mikki seemed to know. She seized the break to drift out to the terrace closest to the ocean. The moon was a sliver in the sky, but the stars were bright, and a plane blinked high overhead, heading north. She looked quickly away, so as not to be reminded of the way home.

A lone bartender manned a station at the far end of the terrace, away from the crowd. She looked about Mikki's age, with short hair slicked into a tight ponytail, counting the empty wine bottles in the crate at her feet. Already Mikki was pleasantly buzzing, floating above her inhibitions, shaking loose her lingering worries about Olivia or Cooper or what anyone else thought of her. She didn't need another drink, but when the bartender gestured to the framed menu, she ordered a champagne. *Why not.*

"Cheers," the bartender said, sliding the flute across to Mikki, and she lingered, taking a decadent sip. Before this trip, she'd never known champagne could be anything but bitter.

"Mind if I ask," Mikki ventured, "if it's as great as it seems, working here?"

The bartender glanced toward the dance floor, a moving square of glitz. "There are worse places to clock in every day," she said.

Mikki stared toward the dark ocean. Without a sight line beyond the whitecaps frothing onto the deserted beach, it filled her other senses, the sounds of the sea growing fuller, the vibrations in the wind stronger.

"It's different in the dark, isn't it?" Mikki didn't know she'd said it aloud until the bartender answered.

"It is. It's different every day too. People say they'd get bored living someplace without four seasons, but it's not as much the same here as they think."

"How so?" Mikki slid onto a stool.

The bartender turned toward the sea, considering. "Do you know we could be standing on a shipwreck right now? They get uncovered sometimes, after storms. Even in touristy areas, you never know what's been there all along. Sometimes they just leave it and let it get buried again."

"They don't even excavate for buried treasure?"

She shrugged. "Treasure is in the eye of the beholder. Point is, the ocean is changing all the time, if you're paying attention. And changing everything around it too."

Mikki nodded, and the women paused together for a moment, looking out at the dark. Wasn't this the definition of faith, knowing something was there that you couldn't see?

The bartender picked up the case of empty bottles. "If anyone asks, I'll be back."

Mikki nodded, in no hurry to leave this spot now that she'd found it. She undid the strap of one sandal, then the other, and stood barefoot on the pavers, still warm from the day's sun. She'd never grasped that something as big as the Atlantic could never just be in front of you, like a projection on a movie screen. It was all around, placing her at the precipice of something too big to comprehend.

"Hello, Lark." Mikki knew it was Kim without turning to face her. She glanced around, hoping for someone else trailing behind the bride, but they were alone. Again.

"Bartender just stepped away," she said dutifully. "If you'd rather try another bar."

"I'll help myself." Kim reached over the counter and filled a clean champagne flute to the brim. "Good idea," Kim added, gesturing at Mikki's sandals, and she stepped out of her heels to stand barefoot beside her, sipping her drink in silence.

Waffles, Mikki told herself. *Waffles, waffles, waffles.*

"I miss my mom," Kim said quietly. Mikki looked over at her, caught by surprise, and she saw that Kim's eyes were wet, fixated on the sky.

"I miss mine too," she said softly. Mikki never admitted it to herself, certainly never said it aloud, and she was surprised by how true it was. She and her mom never had a conventional parent-child bond, but they'd had an understanding, a mutually beneficial partnership of sorts. And when her mom failed to keep up her part, Mikki found it easier to be angry than sad.

"Is your mom alive?" Kim asked. Something complicated flickered behind her eyes.

"I don't know," she answered. "Long story."

Sometimes she fantasized about her mom resurfacing. In some of the fantasies, her mom was clean, begging for Mikki's forgiveness, and in others she was strung-out and gaunt, knowing her days were numbered. But Mikki always imagined responding the same way, with a facade of steel, unleashing a torrent of *How dare you show your face* and *I never want to see you again.*

The point of the fantasy wasn't to have her mom back; it was to have the last word. Now, for the first time, she let herself imagine running into her somewhere as beautiful as this, where old resentments would seem petty. Where her mom wouldn't say anything at all, but they'd link arms, grateful to be alive, and she'd just *know* her mom was wishing she could take it all back somehow. *Give* it all back somehow.

"I think the real reason people like being by the water is that we can see the sky better," Mikki said. "You can't help but wonder if they're up there looking down, you know?"

She saw immediately it was the wrong thing to say. Kim blinked a few times, fast, and her eyes went dry. The moment had passed, and Mikki was left wondering why. What she'd said wrong. Or maybe no response would've been right.

"I try not to wonder," Kim said, downing her glass. "Because I sure hope they're not."

25

Lark

"You can't be seriously considering this," Heath said. Lark sat in the middle of his grandfather's saggy plaid couch, surrounded by boxes of old books and records Heath had been diligently sorting to donate. Surrounded, in other words, by reminders that Heath was a good man who took his time doing the right thing. He'd listened quietly while she told him about Chris's invitation, and how he'd already booked them into the Topaz Amelia Island. A whole suite for her family. Oceanfront, with a breakfast buffet credit. She couldn't stop babbling all the details, and now Heath was pacing as if his strides might talk some sense into her.

"I'm not considering it," she said. "I'm going." She stopped short of telling him she'd already started packing her bags for the first flight out tomorrow.

Heath dropped onto the couch beside her. "Do you remember when you asked me to look into the Redmonds online?" Lark nodded. Was it really less than a week ago they'd strategized to divide and conquer, wait and see? All the wrong things had changed since then. "Well," he said, "I found out there's more to this. I just didn't want to dredge it all up unless I had to."

Lark didn't like the implication that she was on a need-to-know basis. Even if she'd had Heath on one too—that was different. This was *her* mystery. Her Mikki. Her mistakes. "Dredge all *what* up?"

"After we talked with DeLue, I was curious about Redmond's alibi for after Mikki left the resort. Turns out that 'private family matter' wasn't too private to make headlines. It usually does when a dead body washes up on a beach."

Lark could only stare. Surely DeLue would have mentioned *that*. "What body?"

"Another Redmond—his brother."

"He drowned?"

Heath nodded. "Their family had taken some big blows—they lost their parents and their whole estate in a fire, there was a lawsuit—and by all accounts the brother wasn't taking it well. Developed a drinking problem, depression, started popping pills. Based on where he was last seen, local police surmised he'd jumped off a pier during a storm the night before. Of course, that's circumstantial. All they know for sure is he drowned hours before he washed up."

Lark could scarcely breathe. Her whole body had gone rigid, fight-or-flight in overdrive. "A pier?" she managed to ask. "Not a boat? Because Chris spent the night at a marina—"

"No mention of a boat. Odd coincidence that he'd just bought one, though. Odd coincidence, too, that a woman also went missing the next day."

"Can you tell how closely they looked at alternatives before ruling it a suicide?"

"Not too closely. Apparently a hell of a suicide note was found in his room. Or what they took to be a suicide note anyway. I guess it was written like a toast he'd spared everyone the embarrassment of actually giving at the wedding. Made it sound like he'd been biding his time so he wouldn't ruin his sister's day."

"But he was okay with ruining her honeymoon?" Even as Lark tried to process this, she was replaying her conversation with Chris at the Neon Moon. The way he'd ordered a beer and not touched it, explaining he didn't drink because of his brother. The way he'd empathized with her grief over Mikki, the closest thing she'd had to a sister.

Chris had lost his actual brother at the same time. No wonder he hadn't had the bandwidth to track down his spontaneous wedding date to check in on her trip home. That gave Chris more than an alibi: It gave him a damn good excuse.

"But they saw Mikki after that," she said, trying to reassure herself. "She was on camera in the lobby."

"Someone who *looked* like her was on camera. I don't know what happened at that resort, but this is not a situation where you want a closer look. Certainly not by yourself on the same beach with Redmond. I take it he didn't mention any of this?"

Heath clearly meant the question rhetorically, but Lark wasn't sure the answer was so simple. Chris hadn't necessarily concealed his brother's death—maybe he'd assumed Lark knew. Heath said himself it was in the news. And the same deputies had briefed them both.

"I won't be by myself with him," Lark said. "I'll be with Nini and Dove. If you'd feel better about coming along, that's fine too."

"It's *fine*? Do you know how that would look for me? You heard those deputies. You can imagine the racket at the trooper post. Do you know how it looks for *you*, even if I don't go?"

Of course, she knew. But she'd let Nini convince her to come here, so she had to see it through. "I don't think it looks any way," she said weakly. "DeLue said himself they are 'not the be all and end all.' I've done my own investigation before; it won't be any surprise to them if I do it again."

This was it. Her window to tell him about calling Denny Dean and learning her own PI had sold her out, scared off her case by some stupid spam emails. She reached for her purse, where the envelope left in her office was still tucked out of sight. As if she could forget what it said: *If you stir up the past, other people might too.*

Maybe this was the worst time to show Heath the cruel, ambiguous threat, when she was trying to convince him it was safe for her to travel with Chris. But there would be no better time. If Heath was ever going to understand why she couldn't just let this go, leaving herself indefinitely vulnerable to any rando who felt like messing with her, it was now.

"Oh, please, Lark," Heath said. "You've 'done your own investigation before'? You made a hashtag and some bumper stickers. You hired the cheapest PI you could find. You did not zoom off into the eye of the hurricane like some storm chaser. Don't act like this is more of the same."

Lark's hand froze on her purse strap, retracting slowly. Tears stung her eyes, hearing all her work, all her hope, reduced to such dismissive terms. *Oh, please, Lark.* Was this what he'd thought of her all along? That she'd done little more than put on a pathetic show?

"Wow," she said, swallowing the lump in her throat. She tried to tell herself Heath was speaking from hurt. She had to own her role in this. If she'd been a hundred percent truthful with law enforcement *and* with Heath from the jump, this would not be happening now. Not like this.

But she'd also believed, apparently foolishly, that it would take more than a few days in the hot seat to shake his faith in her.

"I did everything I could for Mikki at the time," she said. "Just as I intend to now."

"Even though they made it clear that if you give them a reason to keep investigating, they'll focus on you? Like if you, I don't know, jet off with the original suspect?"

Lark crossed her arms. She wouldn't dignify his question with a response.

"It doesn't matter what I say, right? Can you see how that gives the impression that Mikki is still the most important adult relationship in your life?"

"That's not fair. Mikki's disappearance *defined* my adult life. I never asked it to."

"No, but you let it. Which was one thing when you had no choice, but now you do."

"Do I?" The rebuttal was out of her mouth before she thought it through. "Is that what you see when you look at my life? Choices?"

"At this moment? That's exactly what I see. You're choosing the woman who abandoned you over me."

"Chris really doesn't think she willfully abandoned me. If he did, I wouldn't be going."

"So Redmond is *Chris* now. Got it."

Unfortunately, Chris pulled into the driveway at that very moment, slowing to a stop behind Heath's cruiser. He had the windows down, the radio up, and they heard him before they saw him through the open blinds. Heath flew out the door before Lark could stop him, but she was on his heels, catching the screen door midslam.

"You shouldn't be here," Heath barked from the porch. Chris was already making for the front walk. "Not one step closer." Lark leaned against the doorway, watching.

Chris raised his arms as if Heath had pulled out a weapon. He held a manila envelope in one hand, his car keys in the other. "Sorry," he started. "I know it might not be appropriate . . ."

"It's highly inappropriate. If you'd ever stooped so low as to live in the same neighborhood as a cop, you'd know everyone watches every little thing I do."

"I'm not here to make trouble," Chris said. "I'm just here to give you this." He waved the envelope. "Flight voucher, in case you change your mind about joining Lark down there. That's all. I know you're between a rock and a hard place. But I don't want you to think there's anything underhanded going on here."

Heath didn't move. "And you think showing up at my home to personally deliver a travel voucher is on the up-and-up?"

Lark pushed past him and down the stairs. "For heaven's sake, Heath, he's trying to do the right thing." She took the envelope and hugged it to her chest.

Chris jammed his empty hands in his pockets. "I recognize there *is* no right thing at this point."

Lark looked pointedly at Heath. "Since I feel I have no *choice* but to go, and Heath feels he has no *choice* but to stay, we appreciate that. See you tomorrow, okay?"

When he was gone and they were back inside, Lark tossed the voucher onto the coffee table.

"You know," Heath said, "I used to think the only good thing that came out of the whole Mikki mess was that in a roundabout way, it brought you and me together. I always wished I'd been there for you when it all went down. It's backward to let that same history tear us apart."

Lark knew what he meant. She'd softened to Heath because of his job in the first place. The staties had been the kindest, come the closest to offering help. "Maybe we're finding out it's better that you weren't the one there," she said. "That we've always been separate from all that."

"Or maybe we're finding out nothing will ever be separate from it." He sighed. "Say for argument's sake the guy means well. It's still unlikely you'll bring home answers. More likely you'll need eight more years to get back to a good place with all this."

She shrugged, afraid he was right. "When it comes to Mikki, I have to take those odds. Anything above zero, I'll *always* take those odds. It's the only way I know how to live with myself."

Heath opened his arms, and she stepped into a hug, but it felt wrong. Stiff. They weren't themselves. Or maybe they were, and they didn't fit the way they used to.

Lark was blinking away tears when he pulled back.

"I'm not saying I don't get where you're coming from," Heath said. "But if you get on that plane, I'm not sure where we stand."

Lark smiled at him sadly. "That makes two of us."

26

Mikki

2016

The morning of the wedding, Mikki awoke before dawn. She'd slept in fits and starts, the champagne headache setting in early, and as she peered through the balcony door at the lightening sky, her thoughts remained restless.

She'd fallen asleep with all her clothes on, waiting for her turn in the bathroom. When she woke later, she found Chris had unbuckled her shoes, draped a blanket over her, and shut himself in the bedroom, the "perfect gentleman" as promised.

She kept replaying the emotionally charged beats from the night before. Olivia's plea that Mikki help talk sense into Chris. Chris's embarrassment as he'd stared at the unity candles, next to Cooper's satisfied smirk. Kim's polished facade faltering, alone with Mikki at the terrace bar. What had Kim meant when she said she hoped their parents *weren't* watching over them? Had she only meant that they wouldn't want to have to see their kids dealing with the fallout of the tragedy, or was there more to it?

In that moment, Mikki had surprised herself by wanting the opposite. For the first time since her mom's betrayal, she'd wanted her. She'd wanted her to see that Mikki was okay—still standing—but also that she was not okay, that standing wasn't enough. If Mikki had found anything here, it was clarity: She needed forward motion in her life. But she wouldn't get it by being swept into the Redmonds' current.

Today was a new day. And as she watched the horizon brighten, she knew how to start it.

She made it to the water's edge before sunrise. A few early risers jogged in the distance, but here in front of the resort, she had the whole beach to herself. She waded ankle deep in the water and stared into the east until the sun appeared, sliver by sliver, becoming a fiery sphere. It was amazing how fast a day could be upon you, whether you were ready for it or not. Mikki was ready. Today and tomorrow would be her last days here, and then she'd be back in the passenger seat pointing toward home, where nobody bothered to watch the sun come up. Where she'd spent years preferring the night, if only as an excuse to sleep the day away. Lark had big changes ahead of her, and maybe it was time Mikki did too.

Maybe she could start now.

She waded farther out until the tide swirled over her knees, sending a chill up her body in the damp morning air. Someone last night had said they'd seen dolphins out here, and she scanned the rolling surface of the water for some welcome early-morning company. She ventured farther still, bending to trail her fingertips in the water, not caring when her shorts got wet. She embraced the moment of calm, pushing hip deep, watching the next set come in.

She was going to do it. She was going to dive into the next wave, let it wash over her. She was going to greet the day like a dolphin, like a mermaid, like a woman who trusted her own footing in a new, enticing depth.

Then she swore she heard it, a woman's voice calling through the wind. "Mikki!" She whirled around, surprised, but saw no one. She strained to hear the voice again, but no—she must have imagined it. Even if someone had called to her, she wasn't Mikki here. She was Lark.

She turned back a second too late. The wave met her head on, sweeping her feet out from under her with startling efficiency, sending her roiling into the rough, shifting sand below. Mikki tried to scream, but she was still under, flailing her arms, bicycling her legs to no avail. She tumbled in zero gravity, at its mercy, until the wave deposited her in the froth, leaving her coughing and spitting in water so shallow she was baffled at how she'd been knocked sideways at all.

She scrambled backward in an awkward crabwalk. Her mind spiraled—*What if it had sucked her out, instead of tossing her back? What had she been thinking, with no one here to see?*—but she clapped back at the fear, shaking it off. *I'm okay,* she told herself, getting to her feet and wiping at her face with the wet fabric of her T-shirt. *Ocean one, Mikki zero. Duly noted.*

That's when she heard it: not a whisper on the wind, not an echo, but a solid voice this time. Masculine. Laughter. Low and slow. Then: a few claps of sarcastic applause.

She turned, ready to laugh it off—*So much for my mermaid moment*—but stopped short when she saw her audience of one. Cooper shimmied down a clapboard lifeguard platform in his rumpled clothes from the night before. She could smell him from some distance away, whiskey and cigar smoke and something sour. She crossed her arms in front of her wet T-shirt self-consciously, not knowing which of them should be more embarrassed.

But as he dropped to the sand and staggered sideways, something in his eyes gave her pause. Not his usual look of amused disdain, but something less sure of itself. Almost suspicious.

Surely not of her?

"Here I thought I was the only one who'd rather hurl myself into the ocean than sit through this wedding," he drawled. A black dress shoe lay half-buried in the sand, with a sock a few feet away. He turned in a distracted circle, looking for their matches.

"I'm fine, thanks for asking," Mikki said, face burning as she wrung water from her hair. She spotted his other shoe at the base of a dune and jogged to retrieve it, if only to have something to do besides meet his eye. The more she learned about the Redmonds, the more sympathetic she became to Kim's position, and Chris's too. But Cooper wasn't doing himself any favors, sneering at everyone else's bad judgment calls while making plenty of his own.

Mikki handed over the shoe, but he didn't say thanks. "I knew you were fine," he said instead. "That was quite the panicked display, though. Can you not swim?"

"Not well." For some reason, she immediately wished she could take the admission back.

"Where's my brother?" She didn't like the way he said it—or the way he looked at her, like it was she and Cooper, not she and Chris, who were in this together, outcast and misunderstood.

"Still asleep. In a bed." As far as she could tell, the whole family gave Cooper carte blanche to take his rage and despair out on them because he was the one who'd witnessed the tragedy. But they might draw the line at him waking up in public, halfway wasted, on the day he was supposed to be delivering toasts at his only sister's wedding.

"He really gave you a key to his room, huh?" He looked so vulnerable, standing there holding his footwear, that it took a Mikki a beat to realize what he was implying.

"Why wouldn't he?" She hated how her voice turned up, guiltily, like she maybe did require supervision. She had an impulse to hold her head high and just walk away.

The way his eyes narrowed at her, what she really wanted was to run.

Cooper plucked his remaining sock from the sand. "My brother is usually more particular about things. And about people who have access to his personal effects." Seeing her expression, he began to laugh again. "I see. Chris sucked you in with his whole down-to-earth-rich-boy routine, did he?" He rolled his eyes. "Don't be fooled. He's a snob, no different from the rest of us."

"No, he's not." Mikki didn't know why she bothered. She had the feeling she could have told him Chris had galloped up on a horse and rescued a hundred orphans from a tower, and he'd scoff at the idea of Chris on a horse.

Cooper did scoff, on cue. "Just because he picked you up practically off the side of the highway, you think he doesn't believe he's better than you? Or me? Or pretty much everyone?"

She froze, feeling wet and pathetic, her hair dripping water in rivulets down her shoulders. Chris had *told* him? Confided her secret in Cooper, of all people? For a mortified instant, the ocean beckoned her back, beneath the surface, out of sight.

"Who told you that?" she snapped. It wasn't an admission. She could still deny—

"Oh, did Chris promise not to tell?" Cooper *tsk*ed. "That's no surprise. All he cares about is appearances anyway. Good ole Al never shuts the hell up, though."

Mikki's heart dropped. She didn't have a right to feel this betrayed by Al, thinking they were what, friends? Then it plummeted through the floor, remembering how she'd never really blended in at the rehearsal dinner last night. How Olivia had remarked that Mikki seemed disproportionately close to Chris. How most everyone else had talked around Mikki, like she wasn't there, looking away when she met their eye.

All night, Mikki let herself believe that it was Chris, not her, who drew the attention. That it was flattering, the way he kept turning toward her like a compass pulled north. Now, she wondered if the unwanted attention had been gossipy and mean-spirited all along. If everyone had been openly gawking at the random girl who'd had so little going for her she'd dropped everything for a stranger. Or who'd somehow tricked him into bringing her. Had Cooper told Kim too? Had Kim been sizing her up last night, deciding whether to say anything?

He really gave you a key to his room, huh? My brother is usually more particular about people who have access to his personal effects.

"A little friendly advice," Cooper said, though there was nothing friendly about it. "If you think the fact that he brought you as his date proves he's not a snob, think again. The only thing that proves is how much he loves getting under our sister's skin."

Why had Mikki told Al the truth? At the time, the story had seemed to make Al like her more, not less. He'd even told her about how he'd failed out of college and his parents had cut him off. How he'd had years of barely making rent, how he couldn't stand being around his elitist family during that time, but how he'd come to think being cast out was the best thing to ever happen to him. She'd related, confessing it wasn't the lifestyle that appealed, but the luxury of not having to worry about basics like health care, especially given the shape her grandmother was in.

But letting her guard down had been stupid, careless. Chris hadn't cared about people knowing before, but now telling the truth meant admitting to a lie.

"Look," she said. "I don't know what Al told you. But Chris and I, we're friends. Maybe it was impulsive, him bringing me, and easier to tell everyone I'm his neighbor. But neither of us is out to prove anything. He said he thought we'd have fun, and we are—when someone isn't trying to get something from him. As far as I can tell, I'm the only one who's not." Cooper's jaw set, and Mikki knew she had to tread carefully. "I know this can't be easy for any of you," she said, "with what you've all been through. I hope Kim and Jeff have the day they deserve today."

"The day they deserve," he repeated numbly. "You know it's all about image with them, too, right? Sure, Kim has ambitions, but she wants Chris to sign those papers for *appearances*. She can't have people saying she ran off to have some destination wedding because she was too ashamed to do it in Michigan. She needs a new headline to overshadow it. To spin this as celebrating a new chapter for the business while rebuilding gets underway back home, involving plenty of Michigan expansion with Jeff's properties conveniently at the center.

She's probably banging down your suite door right now, begging Chris for this one teensy wedding gift. Because she's starting her new life today, and the business is her life, and blah blah blah."

Mikki tugged at the wet clothes clinging to her skin. She hoped Kim *was* at the room right now. Then this could all be resolved and she wouldn't have to hear about it anymore. Maybe there *were* some benefits to a dead-end job. Like not confusing it with your actual *life*.

"And what do you want?" Mikki asked Cooper.

Cooper flashed a lopsided grin. "I want a drink."

Was he ever a mess. Mikki scanned the sand around the lifeguard chair. "Do you have everything you had with you last night? Cell phone, room key? Are you okay for me to go?"

"I don't need help from you." At the emphasis on *you*, Mikki backed away. So that was what Cooper was hiding beneath all his *poor me* posturing. He was the biggest elitist of them all. He patted his pockets, his frown deepening. "Shit. I might not have my room key."

This was rich. Hadn't he'd just been questioning whether Mikki could be trusted with one? And what was that about, anyway? She knew her mom's history made her oversensitive to any implication that she was a thief. But what else could he have been implying?

"Why don't I let you through the gate," she said, "and you can go request a new one at the front desk before people start coming down." *Before someone sees you*, was what she meant. He huffed but followed behind her, not speaking until she held the gate for him.

"My family will always remember this day," he said, looking awfully smug for someone who'd awoken in a lifeguard chair. "Including who was here to share it. We might not be on the best terms right now, but we look out for each other. So watch your back. I know a fire hazard when I see one. And I'm not going to watch my family get burned again."

Her skin crawled. How dare he put her on notice? She'd done nothing but accept an invitation to come here—she hadn't wormed her way into anything. In fact, they were making it hard to stay out of it. Yet all she could think of was Olivia saying Cooper made good points, even when he'd embarrassed the bride at her rehearsal.

As if Mikki needed any reminder of how vulnerable she was here. She couldn't even wake up to greet the sun without being instantly knocked down.

"The only one who's been making a mockery of this wedding," she said, "is you."

She was good at getting back on her feet. Even if she never did make much progress from there.

~~~

Mikki's first thought, as she squished down the hallway to Chris's suite, was that Cooper had been right. She could hear Kim inside, just as he'd predicted. Her second thought was that he'd been wrong. Because Mikki didn't hear fighting. Only crying.

"Nothing is how I pictured it," Kim said, sniffling loudly. Chris murmured consolingly, and Mikki halted outside the door, debating. She shouldn't eavesdrop. But if she backtracked, she'd risk running right back into Cooper. Plus, she was sopping wet.

"I don't mean to sound ungrateful," Kim cried. "I know it's going to be beautiful. It's nothing to do with Jeff or anyone here. It's who isn't here, and everything that still isn't settled."

She could only be talking about the wedding. Mikki didn't dare move.

"Hey," Chris said. "Look, it's been driving me nuts how everyone keeps saying what Mom and Dad would have thought. But I'm going to get annoying and do the same thing."

Kim laughed a little and blew her nose. They must be just inside the door, maybe in the club chairs by the bar. From the sounds of it, she'd been crying a while before Mikki got here.

"The truth is," Chris went on, "Mom and Dad would've been sad this couldn't happen in their garden, same as us. But they'd also agree what matters is that you and Jeff are happy together. You've found the perfect match, so this day can't not be perfect. That's the rule."

"The rule, huh?" She said it teasingly, but Mikki could tell Chris had said the right thing.

"A little trick a friend taught me: make one rule you can rely on when things get overwhelming. Like a mantra. It really does help." Mikki flushed with pleasure. So what if Chris hadn't named her? He'd actually liked her idea. Enough to share it.

"Meaning Jeff and I are the right decision, so this day can't not be the right decision?" Kim asked.

"Gotta love that double negative."

"It's very positive."

They laughed, and Mikki looked around for some stairwell or alcove to duck into. There was none. If Kim came busting out, they'd come face-to-face.

"I'm sorry I've contributed to your stress," Chris said. "I like being here for you better."

"Me too." Kim's voice broke again, and the room descended into silence. "It's not just you," she sniffed finally. "I didn't want to admit it and deter you even more, but Cooper . . . well, the whole truth is, he's been a lot. Especially one-on-one."

She doesn't take no, Olivia had told Mikki, almost lovingly. Cooper had been more cynical: *She can't have people saying she ran off . . . She needs a new headline to overshadow it.* But it sounded like Kim was only turning to Chris for comfort. As far as Mikki knew, Kim hadn't brought the papers up again since the day they arrived. And now Chris was doing the stand-up thing and alluding to them himself.

Either everyone else had the wrong idea, or Kim was playing Chris with expert skill. "I don't doubt that it's all been a lot," he told her now. "I know you said it was too late for a truce, but can we call one? Just one more day?"

"I'd like that," Kim replied. Then, after a beat, "I'd like a meeting more, though," and Chris laughed genuinely this time.

"Tomorrow," he promised. "If you still want. But Jeff might prefer you in honeymoon mode." The door opened and both siblings emerged into the hall, smiling but red-faced, holding wads of tissues. To Kim's credit, her smile didn't falter when she saw Mikki.

"Is it true you're a barista?" Kim asked pleasantly. "Who made Chris coffee on his drive here?"

Mikki's mouth fell open in surprise. It was closer to the truth, yet still a gussied-up version. Her eyes darted to Chris's, but he was already putting his arm around her, in that easy way she was getting used to—though this was only Day Three. Two more to go.

"I couldn't leave her behind," he explained. "It was the best coffee run I've ever had."

27

Lark

2024

Lark tried not to feel self-conscious as she stood on the beach with Chris, taking in the enormity of the scene before her. Dove skipping and whooping in delight where the surf met sand. Nini, awestruck into a rare near silence, managing only to repeat the same sentence every thirty seconds or so. "Well, I'll be damned," she said again now. "I'll be damned."

And Chris, keeping a respectful distance, looking so obviously like he just wanted her to be glad she'd come, to affirm that he'd done the right thing, bringing them here.

But she couldn't.

She'd expected to feel overcome, to wish with all her heart that she and Mikki could have experienced this side by side and not separately, eight years apart. But that wasn't it at all. The emotion was choking her.

"What do you think?" he asked finally.

Lark shook her head, and the tears spilled over.

Chris came closer and wrapped an arm around her shoulder, squeezing awkwardly. "You okay?"

The words burst out of her on the crest of a sob. "I didn't look for her!" She began to cry, hearing the truth of it amid the calling of gulls above and the foaming of the waves at their feet.

"Of course you looked for her—" he began, but Lark ducked out of his grip.

"I did not!" She'd been fooling herself all along. Only now that she'd followed Mikki's trail so far from home could she appreciate the difference. Heath's hurtful words that had sounded unduly harsh yesterday now rang true.

Please, Lark. You made a hashtag and some bumper stickers.

"I never came here!" she sobbed. "I 'looked' for Mikki without ever leaving Becksville. What a joke!" Lark hadn't done a single thing right. Even her investigator hadn't looked. This had always been a needle-in-a-haystack situation, but now, seeing for herself one of the infinite alien places her best friend had actually been, she absorbed the futility of it all. She had nothing to gain here, not anymore. She was way too late.

And coming might have already cost her everything.

She looked into Chris's sad eyes and wished that he were Heath. That she had done whatever it took to set things right with him instead of being so damn single-minded. If she were with Heath it would be okay: they could face the hopelessness of failing Mikki together and resign themselves once again to never knowing. With Heath she could still be happy, maybe even happier than she'd ever been before, once an unthinkable thought. But without Heath . . .

She didn't want to think about a future without Heath. Even if they were further apart than ever, in every way. She wanted to beg him to forgive her for letting this happen to them, and yet . . .

She still did not want to go home.

She wiped the tears away before Dove could see. Even though she'd so obviously botched everything, she wasn't sorry they'd come. How could she be? Never before had she left a place that was still cold and dead from winter and only hours later emerged into warmth, into sun, into paradise. It felt like a magic trick: she might not trust it, but she couldn't look away. Where else had Dove ever played so joyfully, as if one of their dreams had come true? As for Nini, she'd literally waited her whole life for this. Even Chris was trying so hard, though it would have been infinitely easier for him to run away.

Lark needed to try harder too.

The truth was, she'd always been more sad than hurt that Mikki didn't come back.

Maybe now she could finally find it in her heart to be happy for her.

28

Mikki

Mikki had never seen such a wedding, beautiful down to the last coordinated detail. The lead-up had seemed like too much fuss, but seeing it all come together, she could only sit in awe. If your wedding day didn't deserve all this pomp and circumstance, then what did? She was moved, too, thinking back to the rule Chris had given Kim: *You've found the perfect match, so this day can't not be perfect.* And Kim's rephrasing: *This day can't not be the right decision.* Mikki found herself dabbing tears along with the other guests as she sat feeling grateful that she'd followed her own rule to say yes. Even if it did make her itch for something else to say yes *to*.

After tomorrow, she'd be back to hearing *no*. But she didn't want to think about that yet. It was the reason she hadn't called Lark, the reason she hadn't ventured back to the business center or borrowed Chris's tablet or even turned on the TV to check in with the outside world. The Redmonds' drama aside, being here was still fantasy. Why spoil it by letting reality in?

A platform had been erected for the elegant beachfront ceremony, and the ocean provided "something blue" as a stunning backdrop. Kim and Jeff were glowing, both Redmond brothers were passably sober, and no unity sand blew in anyone's eye. Mikki didn't overhear a single snide remark about the family, though for the first time she felt self-conscious about her appearance next to the off-the-charts ensembles surrounding her: hand-sewn beads and satin wraps, fascinators and couture hats, diamonds and pearls and woven strands of gold. Her lace-overlayed dress and costume jewelry felt like just that: a costume. But the larger crowd was filled with new faces, and without Chris at her side, no one paid her any attention.

After the ceremony, an army of photographers ushered the wedding party away, while catering staff circulated pink drinks in slender glasses described as "the wedding signature." Mikki had skipped lunch: her encounter with Cooper had been enough to keep her lying low after Chris left to get ready with the other groomsmen, and the first sip of the sweet cocktail went straight to her head.

"Lark." Al appeared with one of his affable claps on the back. "This is my wife, Cathy."

Mikki stiffened, nodding formally. Cathy wasn't what she'd expected. While many wives here appeared notably younger than their husbands, Cathy looked marginally older than Al, and she'd dared to wear white, which made her Texan tan look even deeper. She beamed at Mikki as if she'd heard *so* much about her from Al.

Then again, so had Cooper, and that hadn't been good.

"Lovely to meet you," Mikki said, sipping her drink and looking around furtively for Chris. She spied him standing on the beach with a few bridesmaids while Kim posed with Jeff's family, so maybe it wouldn't be terribly rude to head over. "Excuse me," she said, swiping a second drink from a passing tray. "I was about to take this to Chris, but I'll catch you later."

Cathy turned and melded into the crowd, but Al lingered, undeterred. "We just meant to offer that we've got a table if you'd like to sit with us until the reception begins. I'm guessing Chris will be tied up a while."

"I don't mind standing, but thanks." She turned to head in Chris's direction, hoping he might spot her and wave her over, but all the people milling about were blocking her view.

"You sure?" Al called after her. "Kim can get—" Mikki glanced back, irritated, and he stopped short. "Everything okay? You seem upset."

He really wasn't going to let her go. Mikki turned to face him. "I'm not upset," she lied. She *wanted* it to be true. "I just . . . Can you just . . . tell me how many other people you've told?" She didn't know why it mattered—a game of telephone had already commenced, turning her into a barista and who knew what else. But Al looked baffled.

"Told what?"

"What we talked about at the Milkshake Shack. The real story about me and Chris."

"Zero people." Mikki stirred her drink, fixing him with her best cut-the-crap stare. He held up his hands. "I haven't even told Cathy. As soon as I said the letters BMW, she cut me off. She said, *Al, let me get through the dang wedding before you start fussing over the trip home.*"

Mikki glanced around for Cathy, but she was gone, probably holding the table Al had mentioned. "Well, Cooper knows," she said flatly, "and says he heard from you."

"Maybe Cooper can't see straight enough to know who's who, but I didn't say a word." He held up a finger. "Except to Chris. He slipped out to join me for a cigar after dinner last night, and I mentioned you'd told me and I thought the story was great. Wasn't trying to stir up any kind of trouble."

"Cooper wasn't there?"

"He never showed, so I gave Chris a Cuban to take back to him."

Mikki frowned, trying to remember exactly what Cooper had said. *Al never shuts the hell up.* Was it possible Chris had been irked about Al knowing the truth, and vented about it to Cooper? Or drunkenly let it slip?

The idea of Chris being responsible for Cooper's disdain toward her hurt way worse than the idea of Al gossiping had. She had no relationship with Al. She certainly didn't have to drive all the way up the coast with him just to get home.

"Hey," Al said, more gently. "You might want to take it easy on that drink. They're stronger than they taste." Mikki looked down at her glass and was surprised to see it empty. She discarded it on a nearby ledge and started in on the one she'd intended for Chris. Al raised an eyebrow. "I doubt anyone here will think less of you, for what it's worth," he said. "I mean, who will care? Look at this perfect day."

Why was everyone suddenly so obsessed with perfection? When Chris first told Kim this day couldn't *not* be perfect, Mikki had been on board, but now it was giving her a complex. The whole morning flooded back: Kim calling her a barista, Chris readily accepting that version of the truth before Mikki did. *I couldn't leave her behind. It was the best coffee run I've ever had.* Mikki had taken it as a compliment, but now she wondered if he'd meant it the way people said they couldn't let a good babysitter or housecleaner go . . . like good help was hard to find.

Chris had barely asked anything of Mikki the whole time they'd been here. Or had he? She'd volunteered to take Al on the test drive. And before that, she'd been the one to give him an out when Kim got on his case. And to laugh off his drunken attempt at a kiss too. She'd only tried to be a good date the way any friend would.

Or maybe she'd done exactly what he'd played her to do, every step of the way.

~~~

By the time the reception got going, her head was floating. She had not, in fact, taken it easy on the drinks. This late in the fall, evening arrived early, and the extended twilight sped up and lost focus, like fast-forwarding an old VHS tape in bursts in search of the parts worth watching.

In one flash, Chris was bringing her more of that delicious bread they'd had the night before, and it was effectively sopping up the bad feelings she'd sucked down. The wedding party was seated together at a long, banquet-style table with their plus-ones included, and Mikki sat at the end across from Olivia, who kept up such progressive running commentary as, *Tell me she's not throwing the bouquet, because the real prize is* not *having to marry someone.* "What?" Olivia kept saying, every time someone raised an eyebrow. "Everyone was thinking it." Each time, Chris gave Mikki's hand a reassuring squeeze under the table, and it was almost reason enough to stop second-guessing him.

But in the next flash came the wine pairings for each course, and the etiquette started getting fuzzy. Was it rude not to drink the wine when it was built into the most decadent meal of your life? Even if you knew it was too much to handle in polite company? Even if you skipped on half the food because you couldn't identify what it was?

Cooper delivered a vanilla but passable toast to the newly betrothed and was promptly upstaged by a gushy speech from the maid of honor. Only as Chris led Mikki onto the dance floor for the first slow dance did she appreciate how many eyes were drawn in her direction. She tried to tell herself the dim lighting would mask the dullness of her hair next to all the salon highlights, the blisters from her synthetic shoes, the bra strap that wouldn't stay tucked. If it seemed like people were watching, whispering, if Cooper seemed to sneer every time she whirled by . . . Well, soon Kim and Jeff would cut the cake. If the drinks didn't make all this bearable, maybe dessert would. Even when she caught a cluster of women *pointing* at her, she did what any self-respecting woman would do: she ducked into the ladies' room. But instead of a quiet reprieve, she immediately heard Olivia's commentary continuing from a stall.

"He just better not bail on the meeting he promised you tomorrow," she said. "He is the king of bailing."

"I'm not holding my breath," came the response from the adjoining stall. Kim. "As if planning the wedding hasn't driven me crazy enough, my stupid brother is going to finish the job. The only reason he agreed to meet was because he didn't want to ruin my special day." She said these last words in a mocking tone Mikki might have expected from anyone *but* the bride.

"Hey," Olivia said. "If he can make a random barista's dreams come true, then why not yours?" In the burst of ensuing laughter, Mikki slipped out, humiliated.

But before her self-consciousness could take over, Chris was waving at her from the dessert table, eyes wide with delight. (He hadn't skipped any of the wine either.) Beside him, actual waffles had appeared, topped with perfect dollops of whipped cream drizzled with chocolate. "We manifested it!" he called, and she broke into a smile.

It was a well-timed reminder. Besides, only fools chose bathroom gossip over waffles.

She could have gotten on fine like that all night, ignoring the bad turns to focus on the good ones.

She almost did.

Later, Mikki couldn't pinpoint how things got out of hand. The dance floor was in full swing, the sunset faded to darkness, and they were in the drunken thick of it, jumping and laughing, the crowd moving as one. Then Chris's goofy frat-boy dancing inexplicably turned into a shoving match with Cooper, first jokey, then less so.

"Don't you dare!" Chris yelled. A few heads turned, but they could still pass it off as horsing around if they stopped now. Only Mikki could see in their eyes that they were much too serious to walk away from this fight. They already had their coats off, sleeves up, collars loosened, and the moment found them eager, like they'd been waiting for an excuse.

"C'mon," she said, tugging Chris off the dance floor, toward the calm darkness of the beach. "Take a minute . . ."

But Cooper was right there with them, springing ahead. "This is the hill you're going to die on?" he said, wheeling at Chris. "Defending *her*?"

"Don't say it like that," Chris seethed. "Mikki and I are way more alike than you could guess."

Cooper blinked. "Who's Mikki?"

Embarrassment crept up Mikki's neck, as she and Chris both realized his mistake too late. Cooper swiveled his head from Chris to her and back again, then let out a laugh. "Oh my God. You didn't even use her real name?"

Chris's face flushed with anger. "Stop being a prick, Coop. This is exactly why I didn't tell you."

"How *down to earth* of you, to save all your disdain for me. But I don't trust her. And apparently, while you're under her influence, I can't trust you either. Which is a valid concern as long as you're holding a third of our business assets hostage."

"You're one to talk about being under the influence," Chris growled. "When were you going to mention the Grandison group is walking because you showed up drunk to their board meeting? I had to hear it secondhand. Does Kim even know? But sure, worry about my date."

The crowd craned their necks to see what all the shouting was about. Worse, Chris and Cooper were looking at her now, as if Mikki was supposed to say something.

But she'd come on this trip to reach for something better, not to defend everything she already was. And everything she wasn't.

Mikki locked eyes with Chris. "We're not alike," she said. "Not at all. And the fact that you can't see that—well, that's half your problem."

"I didn't realize I had a problem," he said quietly.

"Exactly," Mikki shot back.

She needed space. Distance. No good would come of this. Maybe walking off would defuse the situation, allow everyone to cool down. She wobbled down the stairs to the platforms left on the sand from the ceremony, but as soon as the sea wind caught her hair, something came over her, and the next thing she knew, she was running.

So was Chris. She could hear him behind her, breathing hard. Her feet hit sand and she slowed long enough to kick off her shoes. That's when he caught her arm.

"Let me go," she cried, twisting free. Cooper was scrambling several paces behind him and tripped over his own feet, pitching forward and kicking up a spray of sand. The reception ground to a halt, the guests looking down on them over the dunes now, though the music still blared. Mikki burned under their collective gaze, every fear she'd had since she'd arrived coming true.

"What's with you?" Chris demanded. "I stood up for you, and you threw me under the bus!"

She was crying now. "You wouldn't have had to stand up for me in the first place if you hadn't run your mouth about me to Cooper."

"What? All I told Cooper was that you and I were *alike*."

"Stop saying that. We're not."

"We are," he insisted. "I knew it from the second you told me *exactly* how long it would take to get so many places you've never been."

"Oh, please," she cut him off. "In case you haven't noticed, I have actual reasons I'm stuck where I am. What's your excuse? Plenty of people want a different life, but you're in a rare position where you have the means to go get one, and you're squandering it!" Mikki wasn't trying to be mean. She wasn't even mad. But the idea that he could be so blind was baffling, and now that she'd opened the floodgates, all her unvoiced thoughts burst out of her. "Don't use relating to *me* as an excuse to justify *your* inaction. Your family is fed up with you holding them back. My family is holding me back and doesn't care enough to feel fed up. See the difference?"

"I told you." Chris looked wounded. "My family expects things of me that I don't want."

"Bullshit. Your parents might not have given you options, but guess what, they're not here anymore. Are you afraid if you walk away, it'll look like you're taking advantage, like you're happy they're gone? Because Kim is giving you a chance to choose exactly what you supposedly always wanted, and you're still not taking it."

"A choice between the lesser of two evils isn't much of a choice."

"We all do it. What's so special about you that you shouldn't have to?" Cooper was back on his feet now, encroaching like he wanted in on the action. Fine. Mikki pointed at him. "You're both so used to privilege you don't even know you're taking it for granted. You're spitting in the face of everyone who gets by with way, way, way less." With each *way*, Mikki's voice rose, and at last the DJ cut the music.

"You can't even stop bitching about your beautiful, luxurious car!" Mikki yelled into the sudden silence. "Do you know how many people would *kill* for a car like that?"

The stunned wedding guests jostled for a better look, backlit incongruously by twinkling lights. *Well, let them.*

"You knew I'd make a fool of myself here," she told Chris. "But I'm not supposed to care. I'm only here to remind *you* of how great you have it. Next time you go slumming to feel better about yourself, be a little more self-aware. I have the kind of problems someone like you could actually fix, but by all means, let's spend every minute *pining* over yours."

Chris's chest was heaving, his face stricken, but he didn't yell back. He didn't respond at all, only stood frozen. Here was another lesson learned the hard way: judging a man by the company he keeps wasn't just an asset, it was a survival skill. One that kept college savings untouched and night-shift employees safe and married ex-boyfriends faithful and plans for a better future intact. If Chris had been so sure everyone here would be awful to Mikki, that should have been a glaring indicator he wasn't such a good guy after all.

Two employees had started down the beach toward them. She could already see that Chris and Cooper would live to regret this whole scene. But not as much as she would.

29

Lark

Lark slid onto a stool at the poolside bar, keeping one eye on Dove and Nini playing shuffleboard on the deck beyond the table seating. Chris had made polite excuses to give them family time, then sidled off toward the racquet club. Nini looked weary from the long travel day, but Lark wasn't taking any chances leaving her in the room. Not until she could observe how Nini coped with a new environment.

"What can I get you?" the bartender asked, sliding a leather-bound drink menu in front of Lark. She flipped it open, and her eyes widened at the prices. Chris had told her to charge whatever she wanted to the room, but she wasn't sure she could bring herself to do it.

"Anything on special?" Lark asked.

The bartender started to shake her head, then caught herself. "Actually, a party sent back a nice rosé earlier, stuff we don't sell by the glass. Nothing wrong with it, just not to their taste. I can do a six-ounce pour for the cost of the house white."

"Sold," Lark said. She didn't drink rosé, but it sounded right for a warm, breezy afternoon. She was alone at the bar, and the bartender took her time decanting the bottle with a flourish. It looked like the white zinfandel she and Mikki used to drink from a box, but it tasted infinitely better. She nodded her thanks. The bartender seemed about Lark's age. Her hair was slicked back into a tight ponytail, revealing rows of delicate cuff earrings, and she wore a bold mauve lipstick Lark couldn't have pulled off.

"How long have you worked here?" Lark asked, sneaking another glance toward the shuffleboard. Dove was chasing the pucks with her cue, awarding herself points for every number she passed.

"Seven plus eight plus ten!" Dove announced. "What's that add to?"

"You tell me," Nini responded, catching Lark's eye and flashing a thumbs-up. Lark wouldn't let herself wonder if Nini was creating a teachable moment or could no longer do the math herself.

"I've been here almost ten years now," the bartender said, bringing Lark's attention back.

"Ten years?" Hope rose in Lark's chest, but she tamped it down. This bartender wouldn't remember Mikki, even if she had worked that wedding. And if Lark started peppering her with overzealous, oddly specific questions, the conversation would end fast. "I've gotta ask," Lark said. "Is your gig as great as it seems?" Too late, she wondered if even that was off-putting. "Sorry," she added. "I bet people are always asking you that."

"Nope," she said, matter-of-factly. Then, smiling a little: "There are worse places to clock in every day."

"Tell me about it," Lark agreed. "I've been clocking in at one of them." The bartender laughed appreciatively. "Seriously, though. Do people move here for these kinds of jobs and make it work? Or is the cost of living too high unless you're already local?"

The bartender shrugged. "You have to get lucky. Most people aren't on the ten-year track. But I happen to like living with my roommates— we've been friends for years, and I don't take up much space. Plus, Topaz guests are generous tippers." She looked instantly horrified. "Oh, I didn't mean that to sound like I'm fishing for a tip. I shouldn't have said that."

"It's okay," Lark said, flashing her a mischievous grin. "I'm not the one paying."

They both laughed. "In that case, I'm Tina. Find me anytime you need a refreshment." Lark laughed too—genuinely. They were good. This was good. Lark decided to risk it.

"I'm Lark," she said, "And I will." She took another long sip of rosé. Why not. What did she have to lose? "This is far-fetched, but I have a friend who attended a wedding here years ago. You don't happen to remember the Redmond wedding? Kim Redmond and Jeff Winscott."

"Everyone remembers *that* wedding," Tina said. "Or at least, everyone who's still here."

"You mean because of the . . . ?" Lark held her breath, not wanting to say it.

Tina looked around to make sure no one was listening. "Suicide," she mouthed.

"So sad," Lark said. "I always wondered . . . Did you ever question what really happened?"

Tina shook her head, though she didn't seem surprised Lark asked. How many people had sat right here on these barstools in the days after, gossiping about this very thing?

"I mean," she said, "I guess it's possible he was messed up enough that he thought he could swim to shore? But otherwise, no. Anyone could see that man was on a dangerous trajectory. Too bad no one intervened." Her eyes snapped back to Lark's face. "Why? Did your friend think something different?"

"Nope," Lark said quickly. "Same as you. Guess I just hate to think of anyone making that choice." It was now or never. And Lark already had more than her share of *never*. "This is silly," she said, "but I don't suppose you remember my friend?" She pulled up Mikki's picture and tilted her phone across the bar. Tina looked at the screen for several seconds, then smiled.

"Believe it or not, I do," she said. "She gave me her duffel bag. I still use it for the gym."

"She gave you her duffel bag?" Lark tried not to let her voice jump, but she sounded like a human bagpipe, the tone and tremor making no secret of her nerves.

"Actually," Tina said, "she switched me. Hers was brand new, barely touched, and she saw me walking with my gym bag at the end of my shift and asked if we could trade."

"At the end of your shift—at night? Why'd she do that?"

"You'll have to ask her," Tina said, laughing it off. "My bag was the opposite of new. I was constantly dragging it back and forth to my boyfriend's, and nothing came out of his apartment unscathed." She smiled wryly. "Not even me. Cheating bastard."

"Well, what did she say when she asked you?" Lark worried she was being obnoxious, but she couldn't help it. Was this reality? Had she really just started playing private eye and uncovered real information the police didn't have?

"Um, she was packing for early checkout, I guess? And she said she didn't like the bag." Tina wrinkled her forehead, thinking. "No, she said her date didn't. He'd made fun of the big brand logo, and she wanted something nondescript so she didn't have to hear it again."

The big, cheesy logo. The easily recognizable duffel. Lark was getting a bad feeling.

That was how the cops had described Mikki's presence in the background of a photo the morning she allegedly walked out of here and vanished with no trace. The morning after Chris's brother had drowned, but before he'd washed up. The morning after Chris had bought the boat.

The morning after Mikki had given the duffel away.

Lark appraised Tina with a new eye. She didn't look like Mikki, not head-on. But she was a similar height and build. Ponytails could be nondescript. Same with her pay grade, her clothes.

She might look like Mikki from the side or the back.

"Were you here the morning the body was found?" Lark asked. She wasn't sure she wanted to know. But even before Tina nodded, part of her already did.

"Unfortunately. I wasn't supposed to be, but I got called in. I had to come straight from my boyfriend's and borrow a clean uniform here."

Lark told herself not to panic. Just because Mikki hadn't been the one with the duffel didn't mean Mikki hadn't been here. Chris's sister swore she'd spoken with her that morning. But memories were funny. Sometimes even on important days, time had a way of filling in the blanks. Embellishing. Supposing.

Sometimes it was the people everyone assumed would forget who remembered everything exactly right.

30

Mikki

By the time Mikki stalked back to the room, she was shaking. She was sobering up. And she was sorry. Not that Chris could know that. He hadn't followed her.

She didn't blame him.

How had she lost her cool? She'd embarrassed them both, made a scene, and over what? His *brother* being a dick over something Chris may or may not have told him? Something that was one hundred percent true? Mikki had been way overserved—everyone had. How much of what got her so upset had been all in her own insecurities, and all in her head?

She barely made it to the toilet in time for everything she'd eaten to come back up, serving her right. Then she flopped onto the couch and buried her face in the pillow, hot tears of shame streaming onto the high-thread-count fabric.

She didn't know how she'd ever face Chris again, let alone Kim and Jeff or Cooper or Al and Cathy or Olivia and the rest of the polished wedding party. She had no excuse for letting her emotions get the better of her in front of his family and friends. She'd achieved nothing by hurling insensitive truth bombs in his face on this of all days, even if Chris did need to hear *some* of it from someone who cared enough about him to be honest. All she'd done was put them both under even more scrutiny, making everything worse.

If she could have gotten herself home, she would have packed her stupid duffel bag right then. But this was a problem she couldn't run away from. Chris deserved an apology, and he deserved it immediately. Kim had orchestrated a whole menu of after-wedding activities for the next day, treating guests to their choice of guided excursions to "make the most of their time on the island": a historic homes tour and boutique-shopping trolley, a deep-sea fishing charter, or a club package of tennis or golf. Afterward, everyone would convene for a bon voyage beach party with a steel drum band. Nobody would miss Mikki if Chris went alone. When he got back tonight, they'd make up in the half-hearted way of people who have no other choice. Then she'd make herself scarce and hope some genuine good feelings would return before the awkwardly long drive home.

She could fix this. Chris wasn't the only one who needed to get out of his own damn way.

Which was only another reminder that he'd been right about that too: they did have more in common than anyone else could guess. It should have felt good to hear him articulate the connection she'd felt. Why had she thrown it back in his face instead? Did it have to do with who was watching? Because if so, she wasn't any better than she'd accused him of being.

She lay there, letting the room spin as she played through all the things she'd say, all the lame excuses she'd give, all the promises she'd make when he came back.

But she didn't need them. Because he never did.

31

Lark

Lark was trying not to panic.

She didn't know anything anymore.

If there was no way to verify Mikki had been in the lobby that last morning, preparing to walk out of the resort of her own volition, then she couldn't be certain Mikki had even survived her last night here. She couldn't prove Mikki hadn't gone with Chris to his boat. Or even that she hadn't ended up in the water with his brother and never washed up.

There was no way to tell whether it was safe for Lark to be here with Chris now. Or for Nini.

Or for Dove.

The decision to come here was never as hard for her as Heath had wanted it to be; her curiosity about Mikki would always outweigh her fear, just as it had the day Chris walked back into the Travel Stop. She'd been afraid of him then, but not afraid enough to stay away. And she'd talked herself out of every other new fear that had been unlocked since he'd arrived.

Until now.

The police had said hardly anyone from 2016 still worked at Topaz. Yet Mikki had found someone right away. Someone with a crucial bit of info, in fact, who hadn't said, *How strange, I got a call from a cop the other day asking about the same wedding.* Someone who'd inadvertently told Lark everything she needed to know about just how hard the authorities had been trying to get to the bottom of this.

What she didn't know was what on earth she was supposed to do now.

If Chris had anything to do with what happened to Mikki, he would never have come to Becksville, she tried to assure herself. *He certainly wouldn't have brought me here if there was anything incriminating to find.* Unless he was one of those overconfident criminals, a charming sociopath who got off on leading her on, heightening the danger for them both.

Or unless whatever happened, Mikki *had* been in on it, maybe as more of an unwitting sidekick than a victim. There were plenty of unsavory reasons someone might want a plain old dirty duffel bag that would go unnoticed. To transport money or evidence or stolen goods or . . .

For goodness' sake, this was Mikki she was talking about. Mikki was no Goody Two-shoes, but she was no criminal, and ever since her mom's downward spiral, she'd taken extra care not to associate with any. Lark was overreacting, succumbing to all the worries Heath had planted in her head when he'd begged her not to come. It had been a long day, everything new, her senses overstimulated to the max.

She didn't trust anyone, Chris included.

Not even the deputies.

If she called to tell them about her conversation with Tina, there was no telling whether they'd deem the detail about the duffel bag a hot tip or something else entirely. For starters, they'd want to know what the hell Lark was doing at the Topaz on Redmond's dime. They wouldn't know what to make of things, but they hadn't exactly been looking for new reasons to take Lark's suspicions seriously. In fact, they'd warned her that their own suspicions involved her.

And what about Heath? If she called and told him, he'd want her on the first flight home.

"What's with you?" Nini demanded when they were back in the room, feet up on the oceanfront balcony as sunset approached. Dove had collapsed in front of the TV, tuckered out from the sun and sand. "You're not yourself. Did something happen?"

"No," Lark said automatically. She wasn't about to unload any more stress on Nini. Especially not now—if something was amiss here, she needed Nini to be at her sharpest.

"Well, snap out of it," Nini groused. "Mikki was right about this place. I mean, just to have something this nice to look at . . . You do remember our view at home, right? No one ever brags that their house is 'dumpster front.'"

Lark would have laughed at that, if not for the bit about Mikki.

"What do you mean she was right about it, Nini? She never told us about it."

"Well, she didn't have to, did she. Now that we're here and can see for ourselves . . ." She gestured to the ocean. "Can you blame her?"

Dove padded out sleepily and climbed into Lark's lap, curling her bare feet up beneath her, sprinkling sand across Lark's legs.

"This is where Aunt Mikki came, right, Mama? Is she still here?"

"No, baby. She couldn't stay. But we thought a nice way to honor her memory would be for us to come and think a lot of happy thoughts about her. If we're lucky, maybe the ocean breeze can pick them up and carry them to her."

"That is nice," Dove said. "What happy thoughts are you thinking?"

"That I miss her very much."

"That's not happy."

"Oh, but it is. Because it reminds me how lucky I was to have a true-blue, once-in-a-lifetime friend like your Aunt Mikki. The kind of friend some people never find."

"Nini says she's always watching over us." Dove yawned.

"Does she?" Nini was always more sentimental with Dove than she'd dare be with Lark. Worry and gratitude tugged at opposite sides of Lark's heart, as they always did when she thought about the special, softer bond between Nini and Dove. Only this time, it felt different.

This time, it reminded her why she'd come here.

A text pinged into her phone. Seeing Chris's name, any serenity she'd felt evaporated. Would you like me to make us all a dinner reservation?

She looked from Dove to Nini, who was nodding off in her chair. The youngster and oldster are about to crash, she typed. Do they do carryout here?

The reply came instantly. There's room service. Menu by the desk.

Then, a second text: What about the middle-ster? Would she like to go to dinner?

What Lark would like to do had become irrelevant a long time ago. I can't leave them, she replied.

I can make the reservation for later if you want to wait until they're asleep? Like you do at home?

Absolutely nothing here was like at home. She couldn't stand the thought of Nini or Dove waking up, disoriented, and looking for her.

Then again, they both looked due to sleep more soundly than they had in years.

Lark had two choices when it came to Chris. She could cut and run, or she could follow the adage to keep her friends close and her enemies closer. Besides, he was suggesting dinner in a public place, not inviting her to his suite or luring her to a dark beach.

"You hungry?" she asked Dove, snuggling her closer. "Or just ready for bed?"

"Bed." Dove slipped her hand into Lark's and squeezed it as they went inside.

"What's our dream?" Lark asked, and Dove looked up at her with wide eyes and a big smile.

"We're already here."

～～

"Everything okay?" Chris asked. They had a two-top on the bar and grill's unfussy patio. In the corner, a white-haired man strummed an acoustic guitar. Flameless candles glowed on all the tables. And apparently none of it was enough to calm the tension.

Lark had been so busy getting Dove and Nini settled, she hadn't found the headspace to think through what she'd share—or not—with Chris. Might as well just come out with it.

"You know how Kim turned over that photo from the morning she supposedly left, with Mikki in the background?" He nodded. "That wasn't Mikki."

"What do you mean?"

She didn't feel secure telling him about Tina, but how else would she find out if these details meant anything to him? If Chris might be the one who could help her piece things together after all, he wasn't merely her best option, he was her only option.

So she recounted her conversation with the bartender as briefly as she could, feeling increasingly anxious as his concern appeared to grow.

Because it was sinking in that she hadn't told anyone *but* Chris.

A reckless oversight. Careless. A bit, you might say, like Mikki.

"I forwarded her info to Deputy DeLue," she added hastily. Could Chris tell she was lying, the way everyone else always seemed to? "And to Heath, of course."

"Of course," Chris echoed. "No one looked familiar behind the bar, but tomorrow I—"

"No," Lark cut in, realizing too late that even if she hadn't made herself a target, she'd made Tina one. "Let's not draw attention to ourselves. I didn't tell her why I was asking."

"I was just going to suggest we ask her who else worked here back then."

"Oh. Right."

Again, she reassured herself: *Why would he be trying to help if he had something to hide?*

Lark hadn't come here to collect more worst-case scenarios. She'd come here to make peace, one way or another. With Mikki's fate, with herself, and even with Chris.

"Will you tell me about the boat?" she asked, trying to smile. "There has to be a story to how on earth you came to a wedding in a car and left in a boat."

He gave a little laugh. "I didn't buy it to leave on it," he said. "I bought it to *live* on it."

"Just like that?"

"Yep. I thought if I went home to actually plan for it, I'd lose my nerve. So I hired a crew to pack my stuff into storage, had my lawyer sell my condo. I was lucky to be able to delegate." He looked out toward the water, as if he wished he were still on it. He probably did.

"But I never would have done any of that," he said, "if it weren't for Mikki."

32

Mikki

2016

Mikki's eyes flew open in the darkness. A hand was on her shoulder, jostling her. She yelped and tried to squirm away, but the hand gripped tighter.

"Mikki, it's me." She blinked up at the dark figure sitting on the mattress beside her. Chris. She shivered and groped around for a blanket to pull over her, curling reflexively into a ball as the dread from the disastrous end to the evening rushed back. She was still in her dress, her cheeks sticky with tear-streaked makeup and hairspray. How late must it be?

"You scared me," she whimpered. Then: "You came back."

"Where else would I go?" Her eyes found the horizon through the sliding glass door, just visible in the lightening sky. So it wasn't late; it was early. Maybe he'd waited until an acceptable hour to ask her to get the hell out.

But as Chris came into focus, she realized he was still dressed from the wedding too. He didn't look mad—and not drunk anymore, either, though his eyes still had that look of being lit from within. He looked *excited*. "I want to show you something," he said.

She tried to sit up. Her feet were sore from dancing in heels, her eyes swollen from crying. "Okay," she said, her tongue thick in her cotton mouth. She needed water. An aspirin. A shower. "What? Where?"

"Not here," he said. "You'll have to come with me."

She looked down at herself, picturing the walk of shame. Maybe the party was still going downstairs. Maybe this was a trick, a trap. She was too tired to think, too embarrassed to care.

"Should we change first?" she asked.

He looked down in surprise, as if he'd forgotten his tux. He yanked at the buttons like a kid leaving church. "Oh, that's better," he said. "Yes, please."

Ten minutes later, she followed him silently down the walkway they'd taken back from the marina after the dolphin cruise days before. She felt a little better, having washed her face and slipped into a T-shirt, sweats, and her old trainers, but her stomach churned with nerves and a fierce hangover. She couldn't imagine how Chris was functioning on no sleep at all, but his strides were long and purposeful. He still hadn't said where they were going as the resort lights faded behind them. Beneath the canopy of dense live oaks, the night lingered where the light from the pre-sunrise sky had yet to reach, and she questioned the wisdom of following him blindly. Yet they were both too tired for the silence between them to feel entirely unnatural.

Mikki had always found intimacy in walking with someone in the dark. She and Lark used to do it as teenagers, slipping out their bedroom windows and meeting in the middle when neither could sleep. Sometimes they'd walk and talk all night; other times they'd simply fall into quiet step together. The world was different in the dark, with an edge of danger that intensified the closeness between them, an awareness that the night beyond could encroach on their circle of safety at any time. In hindsight, those were the moments that had made working night shift seem like a good idea in the first place. Back when it was supposed to be temporary.

Here, with Chris, there *was* no circle of safety. But the edge of danger remained.

Still, he'd seemed so sure she would come, no questions asked, that she wasn't about to be the one to break the silence. Even if the waiting was slowly killing her.

Was he still angry about last night? Or had he already moved on to . . . whatever this was?

After a few more minutes, the path opened to the marina, straight ahead. She stopped to stare down the expanse of road toward the undeveloped southern tip of the island, where buoys marking the inlet blinked in the distance. It looked so empty and calm. She'd meant to venture down there, to see the state park and the pier.

She'd meant to do a lot of things differently.

Chris nodded across the street, toward the docks. "Come on," he said. "Almost there."

All was quiet except for their footsteps, which echoed as they started down the wooden planks. Nearly every slip in the dock was filled by boats of all kinds, from pontoons to sailboats to yachts. Somewhere, a fish splashed. Seagulls called. The animal world was waking now, but Mikki didn't see another human as Chris led her past a row of fishing vessels to the one tied at the far end—smaller and less flashy than the others. He hopped into the open bay in the back, offering her a hand. She hesitated.

"It's okay," he said. "I have the owner's permission. This is what I wanted to show you." It must have been obvious she didn't relish the idea of leaving solid ground, because he added, "We won't leave the dock."

She took his hand and hopped unsteadily over the threshold, feeling it sway beneath her feet, and when he indicated she should sit opposite him on the cushioned benches, she did.

He looked to the sky, taking in the glow of the sunrise they were on the wrong side of the island to watch. *Let him talk first,* she ordered herself, squirming. *You've said too much already.*

"I know I owe Kim an apology." The words fell out of her anyway. "I owe you one too."

He popped open a cooler at his feet and took out two electrolyte waters, offering one. The bottle was cool to the touch, and the ravenous thirst she'd been ignoring overcame her. "I have already groveled at Kim's feet," he said, twisting his bottle open and taking a sip. She couldn't read his expression, but she did the same, coming back to life as the liquid cooled her throat. "I owed the apology," he added, "not you."

This only made her feel worse. Of course, he'd felt responsible, as the one who'd brought her. They'd had a deal, and she'd broken it—Kim and Jeff would be angry with them both. The difference was, Mikki would never see them again, whereas Chris might never live it down. "It wasn't okay, what I did," she said. "Every insecurity I've had since I got here must have piled up, and then with all that liquor and Cooper pushing my buttons—I was way out of line."

"It took me a while to piece together what you must have thought. And what must have really happened." He propped up his feet. If he was holding a grudge, he hid it well. "Turns out Cooper overheard me talking about you with Al. We were saying only good things, but I have no doubt he twisted it otherwise."

Mikki tried to poke holes in his explanation, but it did gel with Cooper saying Al had a big mouth, while Al swore he hadn't breathed a word. She moaned, remembering how self-righteous she'd been. "I shouldn't have hurled accusations at you."

"I should've anticipated better what this wedding would be like for you. I only thought of the advantages. And if it came across as selfish, that's only because from the moment I met you, I thought . . ." He trailed off, and she wanted to let him drop it. But that was the coward's way out.

"You thought what?" she asked, voice trembling. "That if I had nothing, I'd be up for anything?" Tears pricked her eyes. Regardless of whether Chris had thought about her that way, it had been true—in all the worst ways and the best ones too. But now he'd only remember her as the crazy bad-idea date who'd screamed at him in front of everyone that he was a spoiled brat, that people would kill for his stupid car.

"I don't know what I thought," he said. "I just liked you. You seemed surer of yourself than I'd ever be. Like you knew who you were, and maybe no one else did, but you were okay with that."

"I don't know who I am, though," she said. "I know less every day. And it's not okay."

"But I still like you." He looked right at her then. "Also, everything you said was right."

"Everything I said was completely inappropriate. Nobody needed to hear all that."

"Maybe nobody else did," he agreed. "But I did. When you pointed out how I finally have options with the business but won't take them . . . That hurt like only the truth can."

"Obviously I'm the least qualified person to give life advice. Or business advice."

"The least likely, maybe," he said, "But who's qualified, anyway? It's not about the business, and you saw that. The only thing stopping me from stepping aside and making *everyone* happier—myself included—really has been my own hang-up on my dad's stubborn mandates. Even though, like you pointed out, if he'd survived that wildfire it's safe to say his priorities would've changed." He cleared his throat. "Also, you were the first person who didn't try to sugarcoat things for me. And who didn't have any stake in the game to bias you."

Mikki forced herself to meet his eye. "You don't hate me?"

"Far from it." He held her gaze with a steadiness that pulled her endless night of shame-spiraling to a stop. "I'm scared to ask you the same, though."

"Of course not," she managed. "I've regretted everything I said from the second I stomped away. I didn't mean to—"

"Oh, yes, you did," he cut in, laughing. "And I'm glad. I don't care what those people think. I only care that I'm finally close to figuring my own stuff out. And I care what happens to you. I care what you think."

Tears of relief spilled down Mikki's cheeks. She never cried. What was getting into her? "I think meeting you is one of the luckiest things that's happened to me," she said. "Even if I did make a mess of it."

"Glad to hear you say that," he said. "Because I need to apologize for the trouble I'm about to cause you."

He got to his feet, and Mikki noted the excitement on his face again. The cooler at his feet. The way he was strutting around like he owned the place. And the keys dangling from his hand as he eyed the door to the cabin with the eagerness of a kid hopping off the bus on the last day of school.

"Does it have to do with this boat?" she guessed.

Chris smiled. "Now we're getting to the good part."

33

Lark

Dove was up with the sun, bouncing on Lark's bed. "Mama," she insisted. "We have to go looking for seashells *right now*."

Lark opened one eye. "Why now?"

She expected some generally impatient response, but Dove's answer was surprisingly scientific. "Because the beach is bigger now, which means the tide is low, which means more seashells have washed up."

Lark sat up on her elbows. "How did you know that?"

"Because I'm a smarty-pants." With that perfect impersonation of a miniature Nini, Dove bounced to the floor, yanking Lark's arm. "Also, I asked a girl with a bucket full of good ones yesterday, and she told me. So come on, already."

Lark couldn't argue, especially once she saw the sky—dark, streaky clouds in the distance threatening to rain out the later morning. Better to get beach time now while they could. Even if she was exhausted from lying awake half the night, trying to make sense of the sunny picture Chris had painted of his last day with Mikki. If everything had truly fallen into place for them both, would Mikki really have not come home even to say goodbye?

Something was off. Lark had come all this way without getting closer to figuring out what. Maybe the best thing she could do was simply leave the unanswered questions here and help her daughter collect mementos of this beautiful place to take home with them instead.

She got dressed quickly but when she poked her head out to the balcony to urge Nini to get ready, Nini only looked up at her from her chair and shook her head.

"My dogs are barking from yesterday. I'm fine here. Besides," Nini said, swiping at the speckled bare skin of her legs, "nobody talks about how sand sticks to everything. *Everything.* It ain't all it's cracked up to be." Lark wavered, hiding a smile. Of course, Nini's sunny disposition yesterday had been too good to stay. She didn't want to drag the woman around against her will, nor did she feel comfortable leaving her. "Please," Nini said, gesturing toward the ocean. "I'm impaired, not deranged. Do you think I'm going to forget where I am? What could I possibly confuse this with?"

It was tough to argue when she put it like that.

Dove and Lark walked the beach all morning, marveling over the seashells and other treasures they found washed up in the sand: dried sand dollars, driftwood, starfish, even sharks' teeth. Dove scooped up everything that caught her eye, collecting them in a broken bucket they'd found discarded in a dune. A surf fisherman waved them over to see a sea trout he'd reeled in. A jogger pointed out a jellyfish tumbling in the shallows. A group of kids caught a ghost crab and welcomed them to their circle watching his sideways scramble. Lark relaxed into the vibe: everyone seemed happy, eager to share their finds with strangers, unhurried and unstressed far from the obligations of home. She'd never quite experienced anything like it, and it felt like a gift to be able to give this morning to Dove. She didn't want it to end. For once, the universe cooperated, and the rain blurring the sky in the distance never approached.

By the time they finally headed back to the room, the smell of the oceanside grill prepping lunch made Lark's stomach rumble. Nini was probably wondering what had taken them so long. Lark could already hear her: *Didn't you two leave any shells* on *the beach?*

But Nini wasn't in the room. Not on the balcony, where her coffee mug sat half-full, and not in the living room or bedroom or bathroom. Lark repeated her lap of the suite, panic rising as she threw open the closet and checked behind the doors, as if Nini might be playing a twisted game of hide-and-seek. "Nini?" she called, Dove echoing behind her in her tiny voice. "Nini?" Lark ran to the railing of the balcony and looked to the ground a dizzying six stories below, terrified that Nini had somehow fallen.

But she saw nothing but the beautifully landscaped paths and gardens.

Nini was gone.

34

Mikki

Mikki and Chris pulled into the bank parking lot to wait for Al. He'd called in a favor before leaving the Topaz and stopped for a cousin with a Florida notary license to sign over the BMW's title to him. Someone who knew Al and Chris well enough to trust they'd come by the car legally, and who was willing to overlook the fact that Chris's name had never been on the title in exchange for a couple of Al's Cuban cigars.

"You're really doing this," Mikki said, grinning at Chris from the passenger's seat. It was sinking in that this was the last time she'd sit beside him in this car—or any car. That Chris wouldn't be hitting the road tomorrow but hitting the water instead. While Mikki drove home by herself.

"I'm really doing it," he agreed. "Trading my nightmare car for my dream boat."

Mikki had to laugh. As far as she could tell, the boat's new leather seat covers were its only luxury feature. Chris had given her a tour of the tiny cabin, which was more of a well-loved man cave. But unbeknownst to Mikki, the dolphin charter captain had taken Chris's number and introduced him to a #boatlife aficionado named Jim, who was trading up and feeling nostalgic about "rehoming" his old vessel. Jim was from the Great Lakes, too, and he was headed with friends down the coast toward Miami. He invited Chris to caravan with them, learn the ropes. The way Chris told it, everything clicked then. Having seen the Atlantic anew through Mikki's eyes, this chance looked and sounded like freedom, like cutting loose and drifting off to find himself in a way he'd never been allowed. *The men in my family do not drift,* he'd told her the night they met. *They establish themselves. They pick a direction and stay the course.*

"What kind of boat is it, anyway?" she asked.

"A cruiser," he said joyfully, then thought again. "Or is it technically a trawler? Anyway, it's from a great manufacturer."

You would never know he hadn't slept in over twenty-four hours. He was floating on the kind of weightlessness that came from unloading big, heavy decisions, and now that he'd made them, he was determined to see them through before he could rest. She was happy for him. But she wasn't above teasing. "You don't think you should learn more about boats before buying one?"

He humored her with an exaggerated shrug. "After this car fiasco, maybe there's something to be said for caring less about the specs. It floats. And I was in the right place at the right time to get it for a steal. Barely more than my share of the BMW money." He started collecting his things from the console—phone charger, sunglasses, straw wrappers—and jamming them into the pockets of his khaki shorts.

"What do you mean your share? Don't you get all of the BMW money?"

Chris had offered Al an aggressively generous deal on the car first thing this morning, hoping to sway him, and Al had countered with a higher, fairer price. As it turned out, after Mikki and Chris's blow-up at the reception the night before, Al told his wife the real story of how they wound up here together, and Mikki had guessed right: Cathy was indeed taken with the BMW's improbable, semiromantic/semitragic history. What's more, she'd said Mikki had "moxie."

"Well, I've got to pay the woman who brokered the sale," Chris said now. Mikki tilted her head. He couldn't mean . . . "Yes, you," he said.

"I can't accept that," Mikki said quickly, embarrassed. "You're paying for my rental car home. That's plenty."

"No, it isn't." He looked straight at her. "Al made clear it wasn't me who sold him *or* Cathy on the car. Plus, if it weren't for you, I'd be wasting another day of my life avoiding Kim and Cooper. Do you know how floored they're going to be when I sign over my stake? If you'd told me a week ago that I could feel this at peace with my choice, I wouldn't have believed you. Maybe I would've gotten here on my own eventually, but who knows who else I might have lost along the way. I can't repay what you've done for me. But let me try."

Mikki let herself imagine what it would mean to accept the kind of gift he was alluding to. When you lived paycheck to paycheck, when all it took was a stroke of bad luck to set you way back, even a small boon could be enough to break the cycle—if you used it wisely. But she'd told him from the outset she wasn't a charity case.

"You repay kindness with more kindness, not money," she told him. "And you've been nothing but kind to me since the moment we met. So we're even. Promise." She felt a twinge of disappointment as she waved him off, but it passed. As twinges did when you were doing the right thing.

"Let me worry about how I want to repay kindness," he said. "Come in with me and fill in your account number for a transfer. Or your full legal name if a cashier's check would be better. It's still Michael, right?"

She winced at the reminder that she had a mess of passwords to reset and accounts to recheck when she got home. "It's still no," she told him, popping open her car door. "But the fact that you'd offer means a lot." A white Audi with rental car plates pulled in, and she spotted Al in the passenger seat. "Here they are," she said. "Game on."

Cathy lowered her window and called out to Mikki, pointing to a coffee shop a few lots down. "Want to grab an iced coffee and ride back to the Topaz with me, like *regular* people on vacation? Or do you prefer bank meetings and title transfers, like these two loons?"

Al threw up his hands. "I'm buying a convertible, for God's sake. He's buying a boat. We're practically bringing the vacation home with us."

Mikki could tell Chris wasn't thrilled by the abrupt end to their conversation, but when she ran for the Audi, he waved and said they'd catch up later.

"On a scale of one to ten," she asked Cathy as they pulled away, "how embarrassed should I be to show my face back at the Topaz?"

"You and Chris are good now, right?" Cathy's hospitable Texan drawl was reassuring.

"Yeah. But I wouldn't blame anyone else for not being good with the scene we made."

Cathy steered into the drive-thru line. "Sugar, there are two occasions that make emotions run excusably high: weddings and funerals. The Redmonds have had plenty of both lately, and you and Chris are hardly the first to tussle. Bet it's already forgotten."

"You think?"

"I think. Are you doing one of the island tours this afternoon?" Mikki shook her head. They'd all sounded sort of wonderful, but she had something else in mind. "Well then, the only other thing is tonight's beach barbecue, and that'll be the most laid-back you've seen this crowd. I just have one question."

"What's that?"

"Do I call you Lark or Mikki from now on?"

Mikki had to laugh. "I've lost track," she admitted. "But it's Mikki. And sorry if I was rude when Al introduced us yesterday. I thought he'd done something that it turned out he didn't do. Something that meant he didn't have the best opinion of me."

"It's a new day," Cathy said breezily. A truck idled at the window in front of them, the bed full of serious fishing gear, rods and reels and tackle.

"Did you know there's a fishing pier around the bend from the Topaz?" Mikki asked. Just because she had plans in mind didn't mean she had to go alone.

Cathy grinned at her. "Sounds like the perfect place to drink these coffees."

~~~

The pier was longer than it had looked from the dolphin cruise. As Mikki turned to look back at the island, the ocean below her was mesmerizingly deep, and the waves formed a pattern of whitecaps rippling on their slow, rolling approach to shore.

"Good thing it's so pretty out here, isn't it?" Cathy trilled. "Fishing is intensely boring."

Mikki found Cathy easy company. It was in her confidence, how she'd wended her way between the staggered fishermen, as if she and Mikki had just as much of a right to be here, even though they were spectators. These were not the khaki-clad tourists who'd boarded charters with fancy rods at the marina, but locals who reminded Mikki of the truckers back home. They all communicated in wordless nods and looked like they could use a soft bed and a hot shower.

"I can't decide if I hope we see something big get reeled in," Mikki admitted. "I'm not sure I'll swim again if I have a look at what's in there."

"You will not," Cathy confirmed. She rested her iced coffee on the railing. "So," she said. "We're both heading home alone."

"I don't mind," Mikki said. "I never get time alone. It'll be good for me."

Cathy nodded. "Time alone is important. Especially for us women. We're programmed to put other people's needs first. If we're never alone, we never stop and consider what we want."

Mikki thought about that. Even her mom had been that way before she'd abandoned her long list of obligations in a spectacular flare-out.

Maybe if she'd made space for her own desires, the addiction would have had less pull over her as an escape from her endless day-to-day.

Chris had shown Mikki that no matter how much money she saved, no matter how many breaks went her way, simply wanting things to be different would never be enough. You had to say yes to yourself, whatever that looked like: A sturdy old boat for sale, and an offer to tag along on someone else's adventure. An escape from a job you felt trapped in. A peace offering to a sister, even if it meant giving in before you were ready.

Mikki had always had the right idea with her rules. But it was time to get more selective about the next ride she accepted, to figure out what direction she wanted to go. And most of all, to stop waiting around for someone else to ask the question in the first place.

"You're right," she told Cathy. "Being alone will force me to take my turn in the driver's seat." She turned until the Atlantic was all she could see. By now, Chris was probably at the title office, handing over the BMW money to the boat seller with a handshake, a smile, and visions of this sparkling open water, ready for whatever awaited him beyond the horizon.

"You know," Cathy said, "Al really wouldn't have bought that car if not for you. He said he sees it as a good reminder of the kind of person he wants to be. More spontaneous, but also more generous. Happy to help a cousin who got suckered into a raw deal. And not so focused on where he's going that he doesn't pick up a good story on the way."

"Al is already that type of person," Mikki said. "Also, now I feel like I should apologize again about the car."

Cathy let out a big Texas laugh. "Well, you catch my drift."

"I do, thanks. Actually, do you mind if I walk back? Chris is heading into a meeting with Kim—I might as well take the scenic route. And I want to hit the gift shops to pick out something for my roommate."

"Go right ahead," Cathy said. "I'd walk, too, if the sand weren't so hard on my knees."

Mikki bought a disposable camera at the tackle shop and took her time walking back, stopping to capture all the little things she wanted to remember. The clusters of palm trees rustling in the breeze, the pelicans swooping low in twos and threes, the water swirling around her bare toes. An Amelia Island koozie tumbled in the shallows, and she scooped it up and wrung it out, sticking it in her pocket. Every time she used it back home, she'd think of this. A walk to soak everything in. A walk to say goodbye.

Do you realize Chad finally gave me something I wanted? Lark had asked, glowing with expectation that last night in the Travel Stop. Mikki hadn't seen it that way. But now, Chris had given Mikki something she wanted, too, even if only a glimpse. And she understood what it meant to be grateful to a man and want nothing more from him at the same time. To be ready to accept the gift and move on.

Back at the Topaz, she rinsed her feet, strapped her sandals on, and headed for the cluster of curated on-site shops: no tacky souvenir huts here. She browsed a few boutiques before finding one stocked with baby sun hats and onesies. Mikki was trying to decide between sets with tiny blue dolphins and iridescent sea turtles when she felt the unmistakable sensation of being watched. She turned and locked on to frosty eyes narrowed at her from across the store.

Mikki had hoped not to see Kim again until Chris was with her. When they could both properly apologize for their argument and Kim could see for herself that Chris had forgiven her. But Chris and Kim must be done with their meeting already. Mikki looked around for some other familiar face, hoping for a last-ditch rescue, but Kim was already heading for her.

"Hi," Kim said, eyeing the onesie the way an expert saleswoman might. "Gift for your pregnant roommate?"

Mikki nodded, remembering how days ago she and Kim had laughed over disliking guys named Chad. It already seemed like a distant memory. The space from Lark really had done her good. Before, mention of the pregnancy had spiked Mikki's blood pressure.

Now, she felt nothing but happy for her oldest, dearest friend. This trip had taught her that things could always change for the better. Without notice. Which gave her hope for them both. For lots of things.

"About last night," Mikki began. "I'm probably the last person you wanted to run into."

"Not at all. I hear I have you to thank for my brother's about-face today."

Mikki had expected Kim to seem happier. Instead, she looked almost suspicious.

"I had nothing to do with it," Mikki demurred. "That's just Chris being gracious about me having too many drinks and putting my foot in my mouth. For which I am very sorry."

"Very modest. I suppose you're going to turn down his little donation to your cause too."

Mikki frowned. "I'm unsure what you mean. He's paying for me to get home—that's it."

"Mmm." Kim smiled tightly, the way Nini did when she was sure someone else was dead wrong. "Well, it's not the outcome I was hoping for, to tell the truth. I've always liked working with Chris—I never dreamed of buying him out. But anything is better than a standstill, so beggars can't be choosers, I guess."

Unsure what else to say, Mikki held up the baby sets. "Dolphins or turtles?"

Kim shrugged. "Everyone loves sea turtles, but honestly? They're dumb enough to mistake a porch light for the moon and get themselves killed. I respect animals with a better sense of direction. And people, for that matter."

Mikki returned the turtle set to the rack. "Dolphins it is."

The boutique door opened, and a cluster of women called out to Kim. "Married lady!"

Kim slid her eyes back to Mikki. "See you tonight."

Shrinking away, Mikki added to the onesie set a box of saltwater taffy for Nini and a dolphin bumper sticker for Lark that said LIVE LIFE WITH PORPOISE. She hurried through checkout, suddenly eager to get back to the room. As soon as she stepped off the elevator, she could hear Chris's music blaring down the hall through the closed door. The song made her smile: the Rolling Stones' "I'm Free."

Inside, she found him popping the tops off two bottles of beer.

"Are you celebrating?" she asked, tossing her shopping bag onto a chair. "Doing what you want any old time?"

"We're both celebrating!" Chris handed her a beer and danced her around, planting a sloppy kiss on top of her head.

"I'm happy for you," she said, laughing.

"I'm happy for you too," he said. "I even packed your bag."

He spun her toward the couch, and Mikki saw that her bed had been folded in, the space returned to its living room form, her duffel neatly zipped up on the center cushion. She tried not to let her smile fall. Did he mean for her to drive back tonight—to skip the last party after all? No wonder Kim had singled her out downstairs; she'd been saying goodbye.

"Oh," she said. "Okay. What do I do? Just take my license to the rental car desk?"

"I'll handle that. Good call, though; I do need your license." He was grinning devilishly, and that's when she realized he was packed, too, his suitcases stacked in the bedroom doorway.

"I'm breaking in my new bed on the boat tonight," he said. "Don't want to leave her lonely now that she's mine. Which gives you the run of the suite. Housekeeping already changed the sheets in the bedroom for you."

"Seriously?" He nodded. Not that she'd minded sharing, but the idea of having the suite to herself for the last night filled her with some of his giddiness too. "Hey, thanks."

"You're welcome. I'll arrange the car and bring your license back to you at dinner. Then you'll just pick up the keys from the concierge desk in the morning. Whenever you're ready. We'll say our goodbyes after the party tonight, I guess."

"Guess so."

She was still staring at the duffel. None of this explained why it was packed. "Go ahead," he said. "Open it." He rubbed his hands together so excitedly that she laughed. Obediently, she coaxed open the zipper of the bag and gasped.

She could hardly believe what she was seeing. Bundles and bundles of bills. Twenties. Fifties. Hundreds. She vacillated between a *Price Is Right*–level ecstasy and total horror.

"I can't—" she started.

"You're not," he said calmly. "I am. Mikki, I tried to tell you before. I always told myself life was about the journey, not the destination, but you made me realize I wasn't even on a journey. I hadn't thought enough about what it really took to get anywhere . . . not until you got in my car. This money is a small hit to my balance that will make a big difference to you. Just like you have made a big difference to me. I want you to take it."

"I don't want people thinking I came here because I wanted anything from you."

"Who cares what people think? No one even has to know."

Mikki shook her head. Where to start? For one thing, Kim obviously already knew. *That's* what her comment had meant downstairs. Chris was oversimplifying, and it had never been more simultaneously maddening and endearing.

He put his hands on his hips. "Ask me how many hours it takes to sail down the coast to Saint Augustine."

She blinked at him. "What?"

"Ask me."

"Uh . . . how many hours?"

"Probably around three, with four small no wake zones. Ask how far to the closest Bahamian island from Florida."

"Is it . . . a hundred miles?"

"Only fifty, believe it or not. And once I'm in Fort Lauderdale, I can start looking into the Keys, if the Bahamas aren't my thing. Because of you, I'm not just going to have my own party trick of memorizing mileage on a map: I'm going to have my own adventure." He grasped her hands. "I won't let you say no. This money is the difference between you staying in Becksville and moving somewhere with real opportunities. It's the difference between staying in a job you hate and getting a certification or whatever you need to do something you actually enjoy for a living. It's the difference between resenting Lark's new phase of her life and making it work for both of you. It's the difference between letting your grandmother rely on you and letting her bankrupt you through no fault of her own. The fact that you're even trying to turn this down . . ." He shook his head. "These are your waffles, Mikki. All you have to do is eat them."

A nervous laugh escaped her. "In *cash*?"

He shrugged. "You wouldn't give me your banking info, so this was my only choice. It's bad form to refuse a gift. Don't make me follow you around, finding ways to sneak it to you."

Mikki wavered, staring at the money. Could she really do this?

"You can do this," he said.

He stepped closer, so close she thought he might try to kiss her again—and she might let him. If she could, she'd do this whole weekend again. Maybe not differently, but definitely again.

"Let's make a new pact," he said. "Since, I must say, we nailed the old one. Promise you'll take the same advice you gave me. No reverting to how things were. Don't use the money as a safety net—use it as a lifeline. You don't have to go back to Becksville at all if you don't want to."

Mikki's mind was racing. But her head nodded on its own.

"I do have to go back," she said. "But not to the way things were. I promise." He swept her into a hug, laughing, and she didn't pull away. She'd never been fuller of unexpected joy.

She'd never been more determined.

Finally, things would be different. The idea of returning to Becksville only to get the *good* things she'd left behind . . .

It was the most excited she'd ever been to go home.

"I promise," she repeated into his shoulder. "I don't know how to thank you."

"Good," he whispered back. "Thank me by keeping it."

35

Lark

"Where is Nini, Mama?" Dove chirped, more annoyed than concerned. "I'm hungry. I thought we were bringing her to lunch."

Lark shook her head, phone to her ear. Chris answered on the first ring.

"Have you seen Mikki's grandmother? Anytime this morning?"

"No," he said, picking up on her frantic tone. "What's wrong?"

"I took Dove beachcombing. We came back and Nini's gone."

"Maybe she got restless in the room and wanted to explore?"

Lark thought of how she'd left Nini and Dove alone last night—and knew she'd never do it again. What if Nini had decided to wander off *with* Dove? Lark would never forgive herself.

"She promised not to leave," she stammered. "She knows she isn't . . . She might not . . . She gets confused."

"Maybe she forgot she promised?"

"Very funny."

"I'm serious."

"Can you hang on a second?" Lark turned the TV to the Disney Channel and handed Dove a bag of gummy bears left over from the airport. Might as well add stellar parenting to her morning of stellar elder neglect. Dove zoned out to the animation on screen, and Lark slipped into the bedroom to continue the conversation.

"She knows how worried I'd get," she told Chris. "We have a system at home. I didn't know if it would work here, but I let her talk me into it. This is exactly what I was afraid of. What if something happens to her? She could be anywhere."

Lark tried not to think of Nini lost and afraid. What if she were snowballing deeper into confusion? Or what if she'd been found by authorities and admitted to some hospital or care center? Lark would never be able to pay the bill.

"Why don't you stay there in case she comes back, and I'll have a look around." Chris's voice was calm, more reassuring than it should have been. "I bet she went down for lunch and figured she'd run into you. She might not have realized there's more than one beach access. Or more than one restaurant for that matter."

As soon as they hung up, Lark began dialing the extensions on the resort directory. She couldn't just sit here. She rang the front desk, then the spa, then the racquet club, asking about a woman meeting Nini's description. With each no, her anger at herself only grew.

Lark had let Nini convince her she was perfectly fine—the sarcastic jabs about how she could possibly be confused by the ocean, the half-hearted pleas to leave her supplements at home, her rare intonation of deceptively youthful joy. Lark had bought it all, even though she'd *known* how much Nini had come to rely on constant reminders and familiar surroundings and daily-routine cues. Lark had taken meticulous note of all Nini's little slipups, and yet. Just like with Heath, she'd let what *she* wanted cloud her judgment about what was best for someone else.

This was all her fault. Again.

She dangled her legs over the end of the unmade bed, blinking back tears. There was only one person she wanted to talk to—and she realized with a start that it wasn't Mikki. Not anymore. It was the man she'd left back in Ohio with disappointment in her written all over him.

Never before had she needed so badly to see his face, to hear his voice, even if only for him to say, *I told you what a bad idea this was.*

She heard a muffled knock on the door. *Chris.* Maybe he'd found Nini. Or maybe a staffer had and figured out which room she belonged to. Lark burst into the living room, where Dove remained zonked into the TV, and flung open the door to the hall.

It wasn't Chris. Not Nini, either, and for a split second, Lark forgot to wish it was.

"I've never been so glad to see you," she gasped. "Even though I know you're really mad at me right now."

Heath opened his arms as Lark rushed in. "I'm glad to see you too."

36

Mikki

Mikki's last hours with Chris went by in a blur of happiness.

Cathy had been right about the beach barbecue being more laid-back. Instead of champagne and fancy entrees, guests enjoyed bottles of beer, grilled sliders, and herb-sprinkled french fries. A pleasant chill blew in off the sea, and most of the women donned cardigans or wraps, with a few gift shop hoodies in the mix for those who'd packed light. Chris wore an eggplant-colored sport coat that would have looked utterly ridiculous on any man Mikki knew back home. She'd miss his effortless, adaptable style, his easy company. She had a lot to unpack from this experience, besides the Target haul and the contents of her clearance duffel.

She planned to dust off some old dreams, too, and try some new ones on for size.

Chris didn't leave her side, making it easier than she'd feared to face the gawking crowd from the night before. Unlike all the other wedding festivities, when he'd been called away for photos and consultations and whatever else, Chris's obligations were behind him now, and Mikki didn't have to navigate tables full of strangers alone. They spent the evening laughing together, giddy with the possibilities of what lay ahead.

But it wasn't going to be a late night for anyone. Too soon, the band was winding down, the wind blowing harder now, clouds blocking out the sunset. People shifted to the fringes in clusters, saying goodbyes.

"Should we exchange numbers?" Chris asked her. "Stay in touch?"

"I don't know," Mikki said honestly. "Should we? Or is this the perfect place to leave things?"

Mikki was pretty sure they both knew the answer, though neither wanted to be the one to say it. The truth was, maybe they cared too much what happened to each other. It was easy to envision how things could get weird if they attempted to stay connected once they'd left this bubble and retreated to very different worlds: Chris checking up on what she'd done with his *little donation*, as Kim had called it, and Mikki trying not to ask how long he could afford to keep on drifting without having to drop anchor. Maybe those worries were unfounded, but even so, Mikki wasn't sure their story could be improved upon. She was still a little haunted by his observation that *all* of Mikki's stories seemed to take a sad turn.

He'd said earlier that they'd "nailed" the pact they'd made at the outset for this trip to have a better ending, but Mikki was keenly aware this story wasn't over yet. Not until she got home to Lark, walked back into the Travel Stop, and reality resumed around her.

"I'll never forget you," Chris said, his voice low. "You have changed my life."

Their eyes locked, and Mikki wondered whether she was the only one thinking this was it: the last chance for one of them to suggest Chris come back to the room after all and leave the couch folded this time. She had the distinct feeling that if he did kiss her again, the chemistry wouldn't be weird anymore. Time hadn't worn down anything between them, exactly, but a lot had changed. *They* had changed.

He leaned closer—or was she imagining it? She wavered, uncertain whether she was verging on one last delicious glimpse of *what if* or one colossal mistake.

Until Cooper sauntered loudly over, his uneven steps suggesting his sauntering would soon turn to staggering. Mikki and Chris stepped reflexively apart, and as quickly as it came, the moment passed. Mikki shook off the confusing wave of disappointment.

It was probably for the best. This wasn't about that.

The fact that it almost, maybe, could've been . . . That was enough.

"Hey, hey," Cooper said, clamping a hand on Chris's shoulder and shooting Mikki a sideways look that conveyed in no uncertain terms, *What the hell are you still doing here?* "I hear it's official. Kind of crazy that all it takes is a few signatures to sign over your life's work, isn't it?"

"It actually is," Chris agreed, pretending not to notice Cooper's put-off tone. Or maybe he really didn't notice it. "Almost seemed like it should be harder. But I'm glad it wasn't."

"Guess you didn't think to wait until I could be around for the big moment?"

"Considering you'd presigned the paperwork, I thought you'd be happy we didn't wait."

"There are just so many of us siblings to keep track of. I know it's always been hard for you and Kim to remember to count to three. Word is, you *two* are meeting after this little shindig for one last touching Redmond family toast. Is that true?"

Chris sighed. "Kim asked me to stay after. I assumed she invited you too. I think she wants to make sure the last thing we do together is a little warmer than shaking hands and cutting ties."

"I'm sure that's how it always goes," Cooper said, swaying slightly. "You assume she invited me, she assumes you invited me. These things happen. Funny they never happen in a way that leaves either of you out, but still."

"Cooper," Chris said, levelly, "have you considered Kim didn't invite you to have another drink because you've already had too many? Not because she doesn't care, but because she does?"

Cooper took this in for a few seconds, then burst out laughing.

"Damn, you really are good at making it look like you're always on the high road. If I bought a boat to piss around aimlessly, that would be irresponsible, but when you do it, it's noble, it's *good for you, take some time, find yourself.* If I brought a girl I met on a bathroom break to my sister's wedding, that would be trashy, but when you do it, it's charming. It even works on me half the time. I can hardly be mad that everyone thinks the sun shines out your ass."

Cooper hadn't dressed for the changing weather, and he shivered in his short-sleeved polo, sniffing loudly as his nose began to run. He pulled a tissue out of his pocket and a smattering of little white pills came out with it, bouncing onto the patio pavers. Chris eyed them with a mixture of fascination and horror, and Mikki looked away, embarrassed for them both.

She wasn't the only one who'd have some hard things to sort through after this. But with Chris out of the business picture, surely Kim would embrace Cooper as more of an equal partner. Things would rebalance after far too long hanging in limbo.

"You know what, Cooper?" Chris exhaled slowly, shaking his head. "You're right. Tomorrow, I'll be out of here, Kim is finally putting her out-of-office on, and you'll be holding down the fort back in Michigan. That's big for all three of us. But let's make the ceremonial drink coffee. None of us needs another hangover anyway."

"Sure, coffee," Cooper said drily. "I'll bring some Irish cream then, but you do you."

He started to stomp off, but tripped and caught himself on a vacated table, which went crashing to the ground, shattering dishes and glasses. Heads turned, and Chris started to help his brother up, but Cooper shook off his arm and kept on stomping.

Cathy had been right. Last night's scene was already forgotten, replaced by a new one. But Mikki felt sorry for Cooper, even if he had just called her *trashy*.

"Aaaaand the weekend ends not a moment too soon," Chris said, watching him go. "Sorry. Again."

"I guess relinquishing your role didn't instantly fix everything," Mikki said.

"Not instantly," he agreed. "But I still think it eventually will. Even the way he just told me off . . . He had a little more swagger in his step, don't you think?"

Mikki tried to smile. "I'm not sure. I was blinded by the sun shining out your ass."

He laughed. "This is Cooper's chance to rise to a challenge he's always said he wanted."

"And if he doesn't rise to it?"

"There's nothing Kim can't handle. If the last year made me sure of anything, it's that."

Mikki nodded. She'd always envied that kind of certainty. Now it was time to see if she could muster it for herself.

"Looks like it might storm later," she said. "You sure you really want to sleep on the boat?" Her cheeks warmed, and she was grateful for the chilly breeze to hide her blush.

"Nah," he said. "You enjoy a night of peace. Besides, I'd rather find out now if the boat leaks. If I come knocking in the middle of the night, that means it does."

"I'll hope for the best but prepare for the worst," Mikki said.

"I know you will," Chris said, hugging her tighter and tighter, until she was sure they weren't just talking about the room anymore.

~~~

Mikki was stepping into the shower, fantasizing about watching the storm roll in, snuggled in her pajamas—blissfully alone with the bottle of wine Chris had left chilling in the ice bucket—when it hit her: she'd forgotten to get her driver's license back from him at dinner. It must have slipped his mind, too, but this couldn't wait. Her plan was to get up early, grab her keys from the concierge, and get a head start on the long drive, with several hours of cushion before she had to clock in at work. The nearest rental car agency was a thirty-minute drive from Becksville, but remarkably, they were going to drop her off at home just like on the TV commercials. She'd never rented a car before, and she intended to enjoy every last moment until she got to see Lark and tell her in person that they were finally going places.

But she wouldn't get anywhere without her license.

Hastily, she shut off the water, stepped back into the dress and shoes she'd just taken off, and rushed for the elevator. With any luck, Chris was still toasting to the Redmond future with Kim and Cooper down on the beach. She didn't want to have to run all the way to the marina alone after dark.

Back outside, the sky was losing light, though how much was from nightfall and how much from the threatening clouds Mikki couldn't say. She skimmed all the tables but saw no sign of Chris or his siblings. Stepping out of her sandals, she walked out onto the sand and strained to see farther into the dusk.

There. Relief flooded her as she spotted two figures heading down the water line away from her, toward the sharp bend that hid the south tip of the island from view. She recognized Kim's statuesque form and the broad purple back of Chris's jacket. She didn't see Cooper, but knowing him, he'd begged an invitation just for the satisfaction of blowing it off.

At least Chris wasn't gone—she just had to catch up with him.

Mikki started after them, but they were farther ahead than they looked, and her legs were tired from the long walk down this same stretch of beach earlier that day. The wind was picking up, blowing her back with every step. She called out to them futilely—"Chris!

Kim!"—but the words were drowned out by the roar of the ocean, which foamed with anger at her feet, warning her back to shelter.

She couldn't go back. Not without her license. Mikki had made a promise to return tomorrow night, and she intended to keep it. Mikki was homesick for Lark. Lark *was* her home; Mikki saw that now, and it didn't matter if anyone else understood. She was already envisioning how they'd joyfully quit their jobs and start applying elsewhere. *Way* elsewhere. They'd build a life they wouldn't want to run away from, and they'd start by agreeing to stop settling. They would accept nothing less than full benefits and good schools and safe streets and faithful men and love and laughter and beauty and all the other things Lark's baby deserved. The things *they* deserved. The anticipation kept Mikki moving forward against the wind. Amazing, how good it felt to stop thinking of the long drive home alone tomorrow as the end, to start thinking of it as the beginning.

Ahead of her, the figures disappeared around the bend, and she broke into a jog, zigzagging to make more headway against the force of nature. As she rounded the sharp curve across the state park boundary, she could see the heart of the storm across the channel. It was still miles off—she had time—but it looked like a doozy.

For a few seconds, she thought she'd lost Kim and Chris, but there they were on the pier, halfway to the end. The fishermen had all packed up, as any sensible person would do. *Why* were these bullheaded Redmonds still out here? Mikki scanned the sky for lightning, fear tightening its grip on her. Maybe there was more to this ritual of one last celebratory drink. Maybe they had ashes to scatter, or unity sand, or whatever else made braving the elements worth it.

"Chris!" she yelled again, as loud as she could. "Chris!" But he didn't seem to hear, so she started down the pier after them.

They'd reached the end now, turned to face each other, and she could see that they weren't celebrating after all. They were arguing. Chris hung his head in frustration, his jacket flapping in the wind, while Kim gestured animatedly with her hands. The sky opened and heavy rain began dotting the wooden planks around Mikki's feet, pelting her. Still, the siblings seemed too wrapped up in the heated exchange to notice. The drops came down harder, faster, slicking Mikki's hair to her face, and she hugged her cardigan and started jogging again, alarmed now, needing to pull these two out of their bubble before something bad happened.

A pair of empty Styrofoam cups rolled in the wind, whipping around her feet, and she nearly tripped trying to dodge them, steadying herself on the railing as a whirl of empty fast-food wrappers zipped by her.

She looked up just in time to see Kim hurl her body toward her brother in a dizzying rush of aggression. It caught Chris off-balance, off guard, and Mikki stood agog as they struggled, Chris thrashing to get away while Kim held on, screeching words that Mikki couldn't make out above the roar of the sky and the sea. Kim sprung back like a slingshot as the purple jacket came loose in her arms, and she dropped it to the ground and rushed at her brother again, arms outstretched, throwing all her weight into him in one hard push. Everything happened so fast: One minute, Chris was there, upright, defiant. The next, he caught the railing at his waist and tumbled, head over feet, into the ocean below.

For an instant, Mikki couldn't breathe. Couldn't move. Then the force of her horror propelled her into a run. The waves churned beneath and all around her in an infinite abyss, and frantically she scanned the water, looking for signs of life breaking the surface. None.

"No!" she screamed. "Chris!"

Kim heard her that time. She turned, eyes blazing through the driving rain. When they met Mikki's, it was like looking into the eye of the storm: all the noise and the chaos parted, calmly revealing the true depths of Mikki's mistake.

Nobody knew she was there.

Nobody knew what she'd seen.

And Kim had every reason to keep it that way.

37

Lark

2024

"Nini's gone." Lark gripped Heath by the shoulders, half-in, half-out of the room, keeping her voice low. "She convinced me it would be okay for me to take Dove to the beach, just the two of us, but when we got back she wasn't here. Chris is out looking for her, and I'm trying not to freak Dove out, but I'm so scared, Heath. I really messed up."

"How long has she been gone?" There was no judgment in the question. Only the unmistakable tone of Heath switching into trooper mode. Just like she needed him to.

"I don't know," Lark admitted. "It could be hours. We got caught up; I was just trying to be a good mom but . . . I was so careless. You were right: this was a terrible idea. And now I'm going to get you in trouble for coming after me too."

"No, you're not. Look, even if it has been a while, she couldn't have gotten far."

"But what if she's in the water or—"

"Nini hates water. I doubt any level of cognitive impairment will change that."

"Heath!" Lark turned to see her daughter bounding off the couch, running for her signature high-five greeting with Heath: up high, down low, too slow. "It's so cool you're here. Want to go to lunch with us, right next to the pool? They have a kids' menu with four choices, and I'm going to be here long enough to try them all."

Heath snatched his hands away just in time, and Dove giggled. The lump in Lark's throat thickened, watching the two of them together. "Do they have chicken fingers?" he asked.

"And fish fingers. Fish don't even have fingers. But I guess chickens don't either?"

"Yum. Wonder if *I* can order off the kids' menu?"

She giggled again. "Nini wondered that, too, but it's only for under twelve. And you know what else? My food comes on a Frisbee, but you're stuck with a regular plate."

"That is so unfair. In a place this nice I'd expect nothing less than a Frisbee." He ruffled her hair. "Actually, I saw a kids' party starting in the lobby right now. They have beach balls and water balloons and face paint and pizza."

Dove tugged Lark's hand. "Mama, can I go? I'm so, so, so hungry."

Heath met her eyes. "I stopped and asked—it's a drop-off thing in a separate kid zone that looks well staffed and safe. Twenty dollars, charged to the room, and they assured me they stay out of the water. Might give us time to sort what's what."

Lark vacillated. She didn't like the idea of letting Dove out of her sight. But she felt reassured knowing Heath had already asked every question about the program that she would have. It made twenty dollars sound like a deal.

Because whether sorting *what's what* had to do with Nini or with the two of them, Heath was right. They could use the time.

Lark nodded at Heath over Dove's head, and he took Dove by the hand. "Let's go sign you up! If we hurry, we can catch them."

Lark handed him her key card, wondering how long she could go without it if Chris called. "I'll come right back," he assured her. "I'll give them your cell number and mine."

She knelt to hug Dove tight. "Be good. Be careful, okay?"

She didn't want to let go. Something was shifting, something beyond her control. But she'd wished for Heath, and he was here.

She had to trust that not everything unexpected would turn out to be bad.

~~~

When Heath returned, she was waiting on the balcony, eyes on the water, ears tuned for the door or the room phone. He walked to the railing, taking it all in.

"You were right not to turn down the chance to see this."

"No, I wasn't," she said. "If I'd turned it down, Nini wouldn't be gone."

"We don't even know that she is," he said. "We do know you're very good at putting other people first. Nini. Dove. Mikki. Me. Once in a while, you have to do what's right for you. I shouldn't have made you feel like you needed permission. But there's something else you were wrong about. And that's the reason I'm here."

Lark waited. *Don't cry,* she told herself. She appreciated the sentiment from Heath, especially the part about not needing permission. But when it came to putting other people first—well, Dove would always come first. Dove needed her to keep it together.

"You act like what happened with Mikki is this part of your life that's totally separate from me because I didn't come along until later. Like I'm never going to get it. Like I'm expecting you to get over it and take down all your pictures when I move in."

He stepped closer, putting his hands on her arms, giving her no choice but to look right at him. "That might be how other people see our story, but not me. I was there, on those slow nights at the Travel

Stop when you were still so lonely without Mikki. I found excuses to stay with you. On your breaks, when you used to skip dinner at home to eat old hot dogs and soft pretzels from under the heat lamp because they were free, I brought my own dinners in to trade you. When Nini had to switch specialists and Medicare tried to deny her coverage, I rode with you to meet the doctor when you were so nervous—for Mikki's grandmother, Lark. Mikki's."

Tears streamed down her face, but he didn't let go. "You know what else? I wasn't there when Dove was born, either, but that doesn't mean I can't be her dad. You all are my family, and that doesn't just mean now. That means everything that came before and everything that happens next. So don't you dare tell me I'm not part of what happened with Mikki, that I missed it, and you don't expect me to understand. Of course I was a part of it because you were a part of it, and I'm going to keep being part of it, damn it. I'm not going to let you minimize what we've been to each other every time this comes back up. Do you know how much I hate that I haven't been able to do more? I'm the one in uniform, and I feel like everyone's looking to me. Because it's not like my hands are totally tied, but . . . I only have so much rope."

"I'm trying to let you off the hook," Lark sniffed. "I'm not trying to hurt you."

"I know. You've been punishing yourself all these years, and I won't let you keep on doing it by sabotaging us."

She had to tell him. No way around it anymore.

"That's just it," she said. "I might have sabotaged us before I even met you. I wasn't a hundred percent honest when Mikki disappeared. I let everyone think I didn't know she left without her phone, but the truth was, I did know. We fought about it, and I let her win. That might seem like a little fib to double down on, but it made a big difference. To everyone. It was my only defense, and it wasn't even true. Later, you tried to warn me to set the record straight, but it was too late. I'd already set up the deputies to think I'm a liar, and now they're using it against me. And against you. Which is the last thing I ever wanted."

Heath took his time responding. "Why didn't you tell me this before?"

She threw up her hands. "I wanted to tell Fiancé Heath. But I was not so sure how Trooper Heath McKenney would react. He can be kind of a stickler, and the more he tried to help, the more I worried that he wouldn't separate Lark, the woman from Lark, the witness."

Again, he paused, but he didn't argue. "I think that's something we can both work on," he said. "Trusting each other to put our relationship first. Showing each other grace. The truth is, the instant Redmond showed back up, I think part of me got scared I was going to lose you. You've always made it clear that when you had Mikki, you didn't need anyone else, and of course, I want her back for you, but contending with her ghost . . . That's something else. You were putting out all these signals that you needed space, so I tried to tread carefully. But I shouldn't have left any question in your mind that I'd be there no matter what. I should have packed a bag and moved in right then, whether you wanted me to or not."

Lark opened her mouth to answer, but she started crying harder instead. She'd been putting on a brave face for so long. She couldn't do it anymore.

Or maybe she just finally knew in her heart that she didn't have to.

"Hey," Heath said. "These past few days, I've been heartsick. Not for me, but for you. Once I got past the whole mess at the station and our stupid arguments, I kept coming back to the same thing: you've suffered enough. It's time for you to let it go. Not of Mikki—I'm not saying that—but of the guilt. The resentment. The fear. It's enough. And if coming here was a way of trying to get that closure, I shouldn't have tried to stop you."

"I think that's exactly why I came," she cried. "But I'm sorry I didn't explain it better. I was scared of losing you too. I was scared of everything."

"I know," he said. "I realized that once I stopped being such a hothead."

He stepped closer, and she leaned into him, letting the tears fall until they ran out. He felt soft and familiar, like the home she'd never really had. "Does your commander know you're here?" she squeaked out finally. "Will you get in trouble for using Chris's flight voucher?"

"Let me worry about all that. I can take a little heat. You've taken more than your share."

She took a deep breath, then another. "You're really not mad?"

"No one's mad." He slid his arm around her shoulders, and they faced the sea. Lark was still beside herself with worry, but having Heath here—not just at her side, but *on* her side, despite everything—made her feel less alone.

"I've been thinking since I first laid eyes on this place," she told him, "about all the times I've felt so sure Mikki was still out there, looking up at the same moon, remembering all the same old stories. Even if she is, she must think about me less than she used to. That's what time does."

Heath was quiet for a minute. "Maybe the best you can hope for is that she remembers you with as much love as you still feel for her. Quality, not quantity, right?"

Lark smiled up at him. For the first time since this whole ordeal had restarted, she felt as happy and grateful as she had on the day Heath had proposed. She'd managed to be close to fine before—better than fine. And she would be again.

No. *They* would be again.

"I don't know what I've done to deserve you," she told him.

"I'd say you've deserved better for a long time." He sank onto one of the balcony chairs and pulled her into the one beside him.

"I have more to tell you," she admitted. She didn't want any secrets between them anymore, no matter how small. Heath could have made her feel better about the stupid note on her desk and the maddening call with Denny Dean, too, if she'd given him a chance. She wasn't going to assume the worst anymore. Not about people she loved. "But it can wait," she said. "The clock is ticking on Nini."

Heath nodded. "Give me the highlights. What did I miss?"

She recapped the trip, starting with her chance meeting with the bartender. She was about to suggest they call Chris and make a new search plan when Heath turned serious again.

"Listen," he said. "About Nini . . ."

They were interrupted by a loud knock. Lark leaped to her feet, Heath on her heels as she beelined for the suite door and flung it open.

Chris stood alone in the hall. Lark caught the anxiety on his face straightaway. He started to say something and stopped short when he saw Heath. The last time they'd seen each other, things hadn't exactly gone smoothly.

Heath cleared his throat. "I was just about to come find you," he said by way of greeting. "See if I could help." Chris gave a brusque nod, seeming to understand this was a peace offering. But the anxious look in his eyes didn't fade.

"Have you found her?" Lark asked, breathless, glancing past him down the empty hall.

To her relief, Chris nodded. His expression, however, didn't change. "She refused to come with me," he said.

"What do you mean, she refused?" Lark slung her cross-body purse around her neck and grabbed her phone and room key.

"Nini wants you to come to her. She wouldn't say why. I tried. But we have to go now—I'm meeting my sister soon. I called her last night to ask whether she could've somehow mistaken that bartender for Mikki the last morning in the lobby. And since it's my hundredth phone call this week, she just booked a flight to see if she can help piece together the timeline in person, once and for all. So it's a good thing. But better to get Nini back where she belongs first."

Lark looked to Heath. He was still standing there, sizing Chris up.

"Where is she?" Heath asked, clearly trying not to sound like a cop and failing miserably.

"She hasn't left the resort. She's just in a spot that's kind of . . . out of the way."

"Great." Heath's face broke into a bright smile. "Then you won't mind if I come too."

38

Mikki

2016

"What did you do?" Mikki cried, running past Kim to the railing where Chris had gone over. Mikki was hyperaware of the dangerous woman steps away, but she couldn't be intimidated, couldn't cower. If Chris wasn't already dead, it was up to her to save him—not that she had the first clue what she could do. But someone had to try.

She planted her feet, ready for Kim to rush at her any minute, just as she had at her brother—*at her own brother*. Mikki desperately looked down at the waves, her heart sinking further with each swell. In the fading light, there was nothing, no one, the churning ocean no longer blue but verging on a sinister black. The pier vibrated beneath her, sapping the last of her hope as she clocked the true force of the water battering the wooden beams below.

"Chris!" she screamed into the waves. "Chris! I can't see you!"

She'd been only hip deep earlier when the waves swept her feet out from under her in a calmer, friendlier undertow. Even if she were a stronger swimmer, even if Chris were an Olympian, the waves simply did not look survivable. If she jumped in she'd be smashed into the pier supports with bone-crushing force, tossed like a toy caught in the spin cycle, sputtering for air until her body gave out. Was it happening to Chris right now? She turned toward the beach behind her, hoping he might have started swimming for shore, but she could barely even make it out through the blinding sheets of rain. Her eyes stung, her skin burned under the cold torrent.

It was useless. Useless without help.

She wheeled on Kim, who stood stock still, water pouring off her as if she were a stone statue in the middle of a fountain.

"I tried to stop him," Kim said, eerily calm. "He meant to go over."

"Liar!" Mikki recoiled, more aware of the threat with each passing second. If Kim managed to wrest her over the edge, she wouldn't stand a chance. She waited for Kim to double down on her story, to dial 9-1-1 and report a terrible accident—surely she had a phone on her—but still Kim didn't move. "We have to get help." Mikki persisted, scanning the waves on either side of them again. Nothing. The pier's tackle shop was closed, the windows dark, but maybe there was an emergency phone for after hours.

"I reached for him." Kim's words sounded measured, no hint of panic. Just the quiet command of a woman painting a different picture of what Mikki *knew* she'd seen.

Mikki hugged the railing. She might be powerless to do much more than watch and cry, but if he surfaced—a head, a hand—at least she'd know he had a fighting chance, against the odds. They'd met against the odds, after all. Against the odds was their thing. He couldn't just leave her to do it alone.

"Chris!" she screamed again, uselessly. "Chris, please!"

Kim looked down at his purple coat, trancelike, and bent slowly to pick it up.

"He had too much to drink," Kim said. "I don't think he's slept in days. He was belligerent, not making a word of sense."

"So that's it?" Mikki gaped at her. "He could be underneath, hanging on . . . We have to get help. Hasn't your family lost enough?"

"It's too late." An edge crept into Kim's voice. "Something like this was bound to happen. Ever since our parents . . . He couldn't deal."

Mikki shook her head hard. "That's not true. Maybe before, but—he's ready to carry on. He's not depressed, he's *excited*. He's happy." She refused to speak of Chris in past tense. He'd been standing right here a moment before.

Kim hugged Chris's coat, running her fingers over the fabric as if it were already some treasured memento. "A lot of people feel peace once they've decided to end things. It might look like happiness, but it's relief. I guess when he said he couldn't bear to watch me rebuild, he meant it. Even if he wasn't involved anymore—I guess it wasn't enough."

No. She was wrong. Mikki bristled. "You won't gaslight me into believing Chris killed himself. I know what I saw."

"I know what *I* saw," Kim countered, unfazed. "Who will people believe? His sister, or some random girl he picked up on the road?"

"They'll believe the truth," Mikki shot back, though she wondered if it were true. "What are you going to do, throw me over too?"

Kim just looked at her. "I don't need to. You're the outsider here, not me. I'll say you're the one who pushed him. You tricked him into selling his car. You have a stack of his cash in your room, after all."

"I didn't trick him into anything. Al will back me up." She tried to keep the fear out of her voice, but her whole body shook with it.

"Will he? You've been here under an assumed name. Everyone saw your huge fight at the wedding he so generously brought you to. Everyone heard you say—What was it?—that people would *kill* for his car. And now it's gone, and somehow, the money is with you. You wanted a taste of the good life, and he gave it to you, but a taste wasn't enough. You got greedy."

Mikki's tears mixed with the rain. In her mounting panic, she couldn't work through the logistics, couldn't think of any defense, couldn't deny it looked bad. Even Al could end up looking like a sucker here. Chris was the only person to vouch for her, and Chris was gone.

"Go ahead, try and frame me," she cried. "Plenty of people know about you pressuring Chris to sign those papers. I'm not the one coercing him. I'll take my chances. There's not much difference between my town and prison anyway. I don't even care."

A switch flipped in Kim then. "What about the real Lark?" she snapped. "Does she care about her life? Does she think it's a prison? You've been using her name—maybe she's involved in this too. Pregnant and desperate and . . . well. You two just do everything together, don't you?"

No. She couldn't possibly know how to find Lark. Mikki had mentioned her, but only by her first name—and she hadn't had any contact with Lark since she got here, which meant no call history to trace. "Leave Lark out of this," she demanded. "It's nothing to do with her."

Kim extracted her hand from the fabric of Chris's coat, looking oddly triumphant as she held out the smooth plastic rectangle grasped in her fingers.

Mikki's breath caught, realizing what Kim held. It was her driver's license. The one she'd come for.

The one with her full name and address. *Lark's* address.

Kim began to recite it aloud, slowly, enunciating every digit of the house number.

Mikki had been so close to everything she wanted. She should have known it was too good to be true.

"Give me that." Mikki stepped toward her, but Kim snatched it away, tucking it out of sight into the folds of her dress.

"You didn't think I was going to have you here at *my* wedding with *my* brother using *your* roommate's name and not look you both up, did you? She doesn't update her profiles much, but she's easy enough to find online. Not much harder in person, I'd imagine." Kim loomed closer, daring Mikki to come for her, to grab for it, to give her any reason at all to defend herself. "Single mothers lead such a fragile existence, hanging on by a thread. Seems it would be easy to come along and cut it. Shame for anyone to lose their mother, as you know. Chris told me how yours sold you out, how he wanted to make up for it. But no one can, can they?"

Kim sneered, and Mikki saw more of a resemblance to Cooper than she had before. This was his fault too. If only he'd shown up, this never would have happened. Mikki looked down the pier toward the shore, as if he might have been lurking there all along. And what if? Would he help Kim justify what she'd done? Dive in after his brother?

It was moot. Because he hadn't come. And if he had it out for anyone, it was Mikki.

"Are you threatening Lark?" Mikki's voice shook. "Are you insane?"

"I'm quite sensible," Kim purred. "You leave me out of this; I'll leave her out of this. That's how collateral works. And our little deal doesn't expire. Anyone starts asking questions about me, today, tomorrow, ten years from now, I'll know where to send them."

All Mikki could do was shake her head. This wasn't happening. It couldn't be.

"If you know what's good for you, you'll take your tacky little duffel bag full of my brother's cash, keep your mouth shut, and become very hard to find. Become someone else. That's what you've always wanted, isn't it? Of course, I'll always know where to find Lark, but if I never see or hear your name again, I'll never need to find her."

Mikki began slowly backing away. She'd watched her own mother destroyed by an accusation, then become exactly the person she'd been accused of being. Thief. Junkie. Deadbeat. Kim's accusations would be far worse. What if Kim had second thoughts about letting Mikki, the only witness to her crime, walk away? It would never be safe to go back home—to any address in tiny Becksville; it'd never be safe to go by her name. It all felt so far-fetched, but Mikki had seen it with her own eyes.

Kim was a murderer.

What else might she be capable of? What lengths would she go to protect the life she'd built? Her wealth, the legacy of the family name, the business Chris had just stepped away from, the marriage they'd gathered here to celebrate?

For Kim, everything was at stake.

Just like that, the same was true for Mikki. But Mikki had far less. Which made it so much easier to wipe away.

"Don't do this," Mikki begged. "You're not a bad person. One mistake doesn't mean we need to go down this road and make more."

"Who said anything about a mistake?" Kim's eyes were steely, confident. If Mikki ever dared go toe-to-toe with her, Mikki would lose. Kim had resources, legal teams, the reputation and trust of her family and countless associates. With the year the Redmonds had had, it would indeed be simple to frame Chris's death as a suicide and get away with it. Simpler, in fact, than the truth.

How long did they have until Chris's body washed ashore? The authorities would come looking for Mikki when it did. They'd have questions about how she'd come to be with him. Why should they believe she'd fed everyone else a fabrication but was being honest with them?

She was disgusted with herself for this switch into self-preservation mode. The idea of Kim walking away from a crime of passion made her skin crawl. But Mikki had no choice; she couldn't report this. Nor could she think of a single way back to Lark. She could stay up all night trying, and she would, plus many nights to follow. But the most important thing was for Lark and the baby to stay safe. If any discrepancies in Kim's story *didn't* add up, Kim would see to it that a girl from Becksville would take the fall. And it didn't matter to Kim which one.

The last of Mikki's dreams of the life Chris had put within reach evaporated as she absorbed the impact of what she had to do.

There would be no new start with Lark. No returning home the triumphant road-trip hero. No blissful last night alone in her hotel suite. She couldn't so much as pick up her rental car under the reservation Chris had made. It would be too easy for Kim to track her, or to claim that even now Mikki was bilking Chris for every cent she could.

She bent over and retched right there in the middle of the pier, hugging her stomach, stars swimming in her vision. A new noise sounded above the chaos in her brain, and she lifted her eyes to see Kim's face twisted in a mocking laugh.

"Your Travel Stop doesn't seem so bad now, does it?" she asked. "Still. I know you can do better. You might even want to look me up and thank me one day. But I wouldn't if I were you."

Mikki had to get control of her thoughts. She couldn't do anything about the fact that Kim had her license. But she could shed every other recognizable, traceable trait easily enough. Starting with the duffel Kim had eyed closely enough to mock.

Her feet were already sliding backward, the ground shifting under her, the entire world as she knew it swept into the raging storm.

It wouldn't be hard for Mikki to become nobody; she already was. She just had to be a different sort of nobody. So much easier than if she'd ever been somebody to anybody.

To anybody, that is, besides Lark.

"You'd better get going," Kim said, "before I change my mind."

Mikki took another step back. "Forgive me," she whispered, in case Chris's soul remained close enough to hear.

Then she turned her back on it all. Once she began to run, there was only one thing to do.

Keep on running.

39

Lark

2024

Lark had always thought there should be some sign from the universe when your whole life was about to change—some energy shift that was perceptible only to you. It was wishful thinking, of course. Everyone knew there was no such thing. And Lark knew better than most.

The night Mikki left, Lark had been worried for her friend and more than a little annoyed at having to cover for her, but she hadn't dreamed she wouldn't lay eyes on Mikki again. And nine months later, when Nini had come to offer a lifeline when Lark was drowning in grief and exhaustion with her new infant, Lark almost didn't even answer her knock. She never in a million years would have guessed a solution stood on her doorstep, just waiting for her to let it in. In fact, Lark couldn't even say for sure which of the endless nights at the Travel Stop she'd first met Heath, though he claimed to know down to the second, down to the pencil she'd had tucked behind her ear. The night Chris Redmond resurfaced in Becksville had caught her just as unaware, preoccupied this time—at last—by her own happiness.

Every life-changing moment Lark had ever experienced had started out feeling extraordinarily ordinary. No tingling sixth sense, no hint of pressure change, no hair standing up on the back of her neck.

On this overcast Florida afternoon, as she followed Chris through the resort lobby and out to the grounds, as he led the way toward the spot where he'd left Nini waiting, Lark was thinking only of her daughter, off eating pizza and playing games without a care that she didn't know a soul. So much braver than Lark had ever been.

So much more like Mikki.

Kids weren't supposed to learn so many hard truths about life. Kids were supposed to think of adults as solid providers, not fragile individuals. Kids were supposed to be blissfully unaware their mothers were lonely women whose lives looked very different with and without a partner. And that friends could vanish without explanation. And that surrogate grandmothers had to be checked up on and reevaluated as capable of independent living.

Every day, Dove proved her resilience, accepting the simplest explanations for the most complicated things. That they lived with an old friend's grandmother because nobody knew where the friend was. That her mom had a shiny ring from a nice guy with a cool uniform. That her dad lived far away with another family. That if you dreamed a lovely dream, someone else could dream it too.

And every day, Lark wished Dove didn't have to believe any of these things. Especially here. If this trip became the thing to finally push Nini over the threshold of her cognitive decline, it was Dove who'd have the hardest time understanding what had changed. And it was Lark who should have protected them all better, tried harder, made different judgment calls.

Heath's phone chimed, and he dropped back a few steps. "Gotta take this," he said. "Don't wait on me. I'll catch up."

"Hey," Chris said softly, making space for Lark to fall into step beside him. "I'm glad Heath decided to come."

"I'll bet," Lark teased. Chris had to be less than thrilled by the presence of the state trooper who'd been watching his every move back in Becksville.

"I'm serious," he said. "I sensed you were genuinely happy together before I stirred up all this." He gestured indiscriminately around them, not at the resort but at the memories.

"We were," she said, then corrected herself. "We are."

"Good." They were weaving between the Topaz's southernmost buildings. Two boardwalks led into the dunes ahead of her, forking and zigzagging between the mounds of tall grasses like a maze, connecting to the state park somewhere on the other side.

"Nini is way out here?" she asked, doubtfully, and he pointed farther ahead.

"There are overlooks," he said. "Picnic areas. There's more to it than the walk."

"I'm just worried about her staying put," she said, quickening her step.

"Don't do that," he said. She glanced over, taken aback. "I'm serious. Don't hurry on to the next thing on your list to worry about. Nini's exact words were that she'd be 'just hunky-dory.' But even if she isn't, let me and Heath help. My sister is another set of hands too. Okay?"

Lark blinked back tears for at least the third time that day as they started up the stairs to the first boardwalk. It was peaceful there. A large, slender white bird sat perched on a post, and at the sound of their footsteps ascended into graceful flight. "I owe it to Mikki . . ." she started, and again Chris shook his head.

"You don't owe her more worrying. Mikki would not want that for you. She'd want you to enjoy the waffles. Live in the moment, right?"

Lark's mouth fell open. "How did you know about the waffles?"

"I wouldn't forget the best pep talk anyone's ever given me. Changed my outlook on life. The way I see it, you had as much to do with that as Mikki did."

Lark's voice failed her, but she nodded, grateful. They walked on in silence until a wide platform came into view ahead of them. Nini was there, looking anticlimactic: simply sitting on a bench, looking out at the sea. She really did appear hunky-dory, and Lark's heart leaped in relief. "Sorry," Heath said, breathless as he jogged up behind her. "Work thing." At the sound of his voice, Nini turned, spotting the three of them, and wobbled to her feet.

"Let's get one thing straight," Nini said. "You aren't allowed to get upset with me."

"Since when do you care who's mad at you?" Lark joked, but Nini didn't laugh. She waved a finger horizontally to indicate Chris and Heath on either side of Lark.

"That goes for all three of you," she said. "Keep your heads on."

The men looked at Lark, equally bewildered. "Okay," Heath said slowly, though he was clearly more comfortable giving orders than taking them. "What's this about?"

"It's about time," Nini said meaningfully, cryptically, and as Lark felt that familiar concern rising in her chest, she silently replayed Chris's words from a few moments earlier. *Let me and Heath help. Mikki would not want that for you. Live in the moment, right?*

Lark looked out at the Atlantic, which she'd never known could hold so many shades of blue. She breathed in the salty air and let the gentle breeze calm her pulse. It was time to stop holding on to all the wrong things about Mikki and to start remembering the right ones.

When she looked back, Nini was beckoning toward an opening in the railing, where steep stairs led to the beach. A woman came into view, ascending toward them. She must have been sitting there, out of sight, but now, Lark was sure she was seeing things—or conjuring them. This woman's hair color was all wrong, bright and brassy. She had sunspots on her bare arms and creases around her mouth and eyes, the weathered look of a Floridian who spent enough time outdoors to age ahead of schedule.

But her face was unmistakably Mikki.

So was the way she stood when she reached the landing: broad and ready, daring the world to pick a fight. And the way she bit her lip, eyes averted, the way Mikki used to when she was trying not to cry.

Lark heard Chris suck in a sharp breath at her side. At her opposite shoulder, Heath snapped to attention, his training kicking into gear.

Lark looked back to Nini in disbelief. Nini looked satisfied, not surprised. Nini, who never did quite have her story straight on the subject of Mikki. Nini, who hadn't once wavered in her insistence that she accompany Lark on this trip. Nini, who'd shown up at Lark's old apartment door seven years ago and begrudgingly taken her in, looking like a child whose parent was making her do it.

Or, maybe, like a grandmother whose granddaughter was forcing her hand.

Lark opened her mouth to say something, anything, to Mikki—but after all this time, she didn't know how. She didn't know if she could run to her friend and hug her with relief. She didn't know if she could scream at her either. She felt an odd urge to laugh, that after all this time, she didn't even know if she wanted this to be real.

She turned to Nini instead, and her voice came out raspy. More disbelieving than accusing. "You've known where she was? All along?"

"Not hardly," Nini replied.

"But you knew she was okay?"

Nini grunted. "Nobody's okay. I knew she was in trouble."

The word tumbled in Lark's mind. Trouble. That summed it all up, didn't it? The feeling she'd had in her gut for too many years. That she'd done wrong, that she'd been wronged, that eventually the other shoe would drop and someone—or everyone—would pay.

She pivoted to Heath. "The kids' program . . . The phone call . . . Were you in on this?"

He held up his hands. "Nobody tells me anything."

Lark's eyes snapped back to Mikki, trying to get used to the idea of her. But Mikki was barely looking at her—or at Nini. She was looking at Chris, the color draining from her face.

As if she'd seen a ghost.

40

Mikki inched forward until she was close enough to place a trembling hand on Chris's forearm. Beneath the soft cotton of his shirt, she could feel his warmth, solid and real. He placed his other hand atop hers as if he were doing the same, testing this was not a dream: they were both here, standing a breath apart.

It wasn't possible.

She'd been there, the night Chris tumbled into the dark ocean and never resurfaced. She'd checked the news incessantly, hoping for a miracle, until she'd seen the headlines she'd dreaded, confirming his body washed ashore. TOPAZ BEACH CLOSED AFTER DESTINATION WEDDING DROWNING. DROWNING LATEST IN STRING OF TRAGEDIES FOR PROMINENT MICHIGAN FAMILY. She'd skimmed the lead paragraphs, eyes landing on the details she didn't want to find—Christopher Redmond . . . sister's wedding . . . found the morning after a band of strong storms. Why torture herself by reading further? She'd seen it happen with her own eyes.

Chris was dead.

Indisputable fact.

Indisputable, that is, until a week ago, when Nini had called the number Mikki gave her strictly in case of emergency to relay that a man who appeared to be Chris had resurfaced in Becksville, of all places, looking for Mikki, of all people. Mikki had known this couldn't be true, but she'd also known it couldn't be good. Relying on Nini had always been an imperfect plan, born of necessity, and all Mikki's fears came to a head. Was Nini losing touch with reality, or was Cooper or some other Redmond pawn posing as Chris, and why? How dare Kim Redmond mess with her after all this time? Mikki had kept her end of the deal. She'd kept it even when it was tearing her apart. For a year, then two, then five, when the self-imposed deadline finally arrived when she'd deemed it safe to risk venturing back, after enough years had passed that surely she could at least explain herself to Lark. At which point . . . Nini had convinced her not to.

She's happy now, Mikki. Finally. The best thing you can do for Lark is let her be.

Nini had never seemed more lucid, or more impassioned. She'd even risked sending a photo of Lark with her beau and her daughter, smiling so brightly that Mikki didn't know whether her heart was leaping with joy or sorrow. Maybe a small part of Mikki had been relieved to hear it. The part that didn't know how she'd ever begin to atone for everything that had gone wrong. So reluctantly, she'd left well enough alone—until that phone call. And the next. Then there were too many calls, too many risks, when she and Nini had taken pains to never get this sloppy.

Mikki couldn't make sense of a thing Nini said. That Lark had identified the man as the same driver Mikki had left the Travel Stop with nearly eight years ago. Nini claimed the police were taking things more seriously this time. She even used the deputies' names, and Mikki verified online that they did, in fact, exist.

I'm not a good messenger anymore, Mikki, Nini had said. The admission broke Mikki's heart with all the things it didn't say. Nini sounded tired. This wasn't Nini leaning on her diagnosis as a crutch, the way she often did to cover for Mikki—to cover for both of their inevitable slip-ups. This was Nini admitting her mind couldn't hold this weight much longer. *You need to see for yourself,* Nini said. *Who is doing this, and why.*

Even after Mikki had relented, she'd played over the endless possibilities, wondering what she'd find here if their plan managed to work, and whether she wanted to find it. Because she, too, had a new life now. As close to happy as she could get, considering. Happy adjacent.

But all that worrying had been needless, aimless.

This really was Chris, looking gobsmacked and overjoyed at the same time. He pulled back from Mikki to take her in. Nothing about him looked menacing or calculating—and of course not; it never had. He was *smiling* at her. Wary, yet relieved.

Speechless, she looked to Lark, steeling herself to meet her old best friend's eyes for the first time. She'd known facing Lark would be infinitely harder. Facing Lark meant facing years of wholly consuming mind-body-spirit guilt. Facing Lark meant facing everything she was ashamed of, everything she was beholden to. Mikki had tried to look out for her friend the only way she could, as best she could, but it had never been enough. She didn't expect Lark to forgive her. The best she could hope for was that Lark would understand.

But Lark didn't look understanding now as she searched Mikki's face, disbelieving.

She looked split into two: one half-relieved, the other gravely wounded.

As Mikki watched, Lark took a step backward. Away from her, toward the man at her side, presumably her fiancé. He put a protective arm around Lark's shoulders, and Mikki was glad. Lark would need him.

All Mikki could do was sort things with Chris first and trust the rest would follow.

"How?" she gasped, tears coming to her eyes. "I was there. The night you drowned."

Chris's whole body tensed. "The night—? With Cooper? You were there?"

"Not Cooper. You." Mikki shook her head in confusion. She'd never shaken the nightmare of Chris in profile in the driving rain, struggling with Kim. From a distance, she'd never had a clear look at his face, but she'd never had a doubt either.

Now she wondered. *Could* it have been Cooper? The brothers stood alike, moved alike, and maybe if they weren't facing you . . . But no. She hadn't let Kim gaslight her back then, and she wouldn't let Chris do it now.

"You were wearing that purple coat," she insisted. "I followed you all the way down the beach. I had to; my license was in the pocket. We forgot to do the handoff at dinner."

Chris went pale. "Oh," he said softly. "Oh, Mikki. I lent Cooper my coat. He was shivering so hard. At the time, I thought from cold, but we know from the coroner's report it was the combo of alcohol and uppers. It causes tremors, palpitations, masks more obvious signs of inebriation. It can make you think jumping off a pier is the answer to everything."

"That's not what happened." Mikki's heart crumpled at how gently he was trying to frame this for her, for all of them. She thought back to what Kim had said, in the heat of the moment, about Chris being drunk, messed up, sleep deprived. It had all been bullshit. Unless . . .

Kim hadn't been talking about Chris. She'd been talking about Cooper. Mikki had drawn her own conclusions when she saw the coat. Kim just hadn't corrected her.

"Back up," she said. "The articles all said Christopher Redmond."

Chris nodded. "Every Redmond man is named Christopher. My dad, grandfather, me; I'm a rare Chris, though. Most go by nicknames or middle names. Like Cooper."

Mikki tried again to reconcile this with the picture she'd held for so long. "But Cooper didn't show that night," she said.

"He showed. I was the one who left. I'd never seen him so antagonistic and jittery. I couldn't pretend to celebrate with him like that. I gave him my coat and went back to the boat. It wasn't going to end well for any of us if I stayed, and I was bent on ending things on a good note. We'd promised each other, remember?" He cringed. "Hindsight's a bastard. Maybe if I'd sucked it up and stayed, he'd have ended up back in his room, sleeping it off. Maybe things would have looked brighter for him in the morning."

How could she be the one to tell him the truth? Chris might indeed have saved Cooper's life if he'd stuck around that night, but not for the reasons he thought. *No wonder* Kim had had to get rid of Mikki, to make every threat she could think of to convince her to disappear. If Mikki had realized Chris was alive, Kim's story never would have stuck.

If Mikki had known Chris was alive, Kim wouldn't have gotten away with murder.

Chris cocked his head at Mikki. "This whole time, you really thought I was the one who killed myself? Why would you think I'd do that?"

She'd known he wouldn't. What she hadn't understood was why she was the only one who grasped that. Why no one else questioned the easy explanation. "I was so sure it was you," she stammered. "I followed you and Kim—Cooper and Kim—all the way to the pier."

He frowned. "Kim was with him on the pier? She never told me that."

"Did I hear my name?"

Kim emerged from the boardwalk, and Mikki's blood ran cold, her legs turning to mush. Her mind told her to run, but she couldn't even if she wanted to. There was no telling how long Kim had been standing out of sight behind the tall dune grass, listening. Calculating. There was no escape now. Mikki's eyes landed on the steely face she'd spent the last seven and a half years determined to never see again. Kim returned her stare with warning daggers.

"Kim," Chris greeted her. "You made good time from the airport."

"Who is *she*?" Nini demanded, eyes wide with something Mikki had never seen there before. Fear. A mirror of Mikki's own. She'd never told Nini what happened at the wedding, only that something had. Something terrible and irreversible, something with inescapable consequences. But Nini remained sharper than she got credit for.

"My sister," Chris said, seemingly oblivious to the tension. "We've been in touch a lot this week, since the cops called her to verify my story. Once I told her we were all here and still not satisfied that they'd investigated this thoroughly, she offered to help try to set Lark's mind at ease. I told her it wasn't necessary to come all this way, but . . ." His voice trailed off. Mikki could see it on his face, the instant he began to wonder why Kim was *really* here.

Mikki had to talk fast. To get out ahead of whatever this was.

But what was it? What was she doing? She'd left this all behind. She'd made a choice and stuck with it. And at the end of all these hard-fought years, she had a job she actually liked, a husband she adored, and a stepdaughter she loved like her own, who she often marveled was nearly the same age as Lark's baby now. Was Mikki really going to risk it all just so Chris would know the truth? She'd never stopped believing Kim would make good on her threats. And Kim was right here, looking like she still intended to.

But Chris was here too. And Nini. And Lark. People who'd cared enough to continue looking for her. People she'd only wanted to protect—but let down in the process. People she couldn't lie to anymore. No matter what it cost her.

"Kim wasn't just on the pier with Cooper," she told Chris. "They were fighting. I only wanted to get my ID from you. I wasn't trying to *witness* anything. But there was a struggle."

His expression turned ashen, his eyes darting sideways to his sister. "You were trying to stop him? From jumping?"

Chris didn't wait for an answer, and it didn't come. He turned back to Mikki, his voice rising an octave in denial. "She was trying to stop him?"

Mikki's face burned under Kim's fiery stare. But for the first time, she was one step ahead of Kim and her lies. Because Mikki now knew the truth was on her side. So what if she was nobody next to Kim? She was done being intimidated. She looked to Chris and shook her head no.

"It was an accident?" Chris guessed again, sounding crushingly hopeful.

"I'm so sorry, Chris." Mikki took a deep breath and faced Kim. "You have no power over me anymore," she said, her voice low and clear. "You can't frame me for the murder of a man who's alive. And all those things you threatened to use against me—the money from the BMW and my real name—all those things you said looked bad not just for me, but for Lark? They don't apply to Cooper. What motive would I possibly have for wanting to hurt Cooper?"

"Please," Kim spat back. "He was terrible to you."

"Sure he was. But it only made me feel sorry for him."

"Kim?" Chris asked. "What's Mikki saying? Framing her for murder? *Cooper's* murder?"

"She's lying." Kim put her hands on her hips, though her voice shook. "She's desperate to justify what she's done, running out on her family and friends." Kim gestured to Lark, then Nini. "It's not my fault she sold you out for a duffel bag full of cash."

Chris ran his hands through his hair, a nervous gesture Mikki still remembered from the time they'd spent together here. She remembered everything. She always would.

"Mikki," he said. "Are you saying you saw Kim push Cooper?" He didn't need to hear her say it. She could see that he knew. "I don't understand," he said. "Why would you leave?"

"I thought it was you," Mikki pleaded. "All the news coverage said your name. I'd hoped against hope you'd survived somehow. But you didn't—he didn't. And I was terrified. She had my ID from your coat pocket, my name, my address. Which was Lark's address, and she knew Lark was pregnant. Kim had a roster of things to use against me: You and I had that ugly fight in front of everyone, and she was twisting what I'd said to sound incriminating. You'd cut me in on the car sale in cash, and she threatened to go after Lark. She was going to make it out like I'd been scamming you all along and Lark was in on it since I was using her name. Without you, there was no one to vouch I wasn't a con woman, a blackmailer, a murderess. I felt trapped and terrified and so, so sad you were gone."

"Ridiculous," Kim snapped. "There's no proof of any of this."

Mikki turned to Chris. "Not exactly. But I had a disposable camera on me, bought that last day. Once I ran back to the beach, I snapped some pictures. They're not good—there's water damage—but you can make her out in the distance, leaving the pier in the rain. You can tell she was there. They're time-stamped the next day, when I had them developed at a one-hour place."

He turned to face Kim, suspicion dark in his eyes. "You let her think I was dead?"

"I had to," Kim snapped. "If I hadn't, she'd have . . ." The words faded out as she realized what she'd admitted to.

"She'd have known your threats were bullshit," Lark finished for her. "She'd have known you didn't have her cornered without a single person in the world on her side." Lark sounded so much older than the last time Mikki had seen her. So much more self-assured. And yet, in spite of everything, loyal as always.

Chris was locked on his sister now, as if Lark hadn't even spoken, as if Mikki were no longer there. "All these years, you knew I blamed myself about Cooper. You let me."

Kim deflated at the words. This was obviously the thing she'd come here to prevent, and she hadn't arrived in time. What was the plan now? There was nothing she *could* do.

"I don't get it," Chris said. "Once I'd stepped away from the business, wasn't everything going to work itself out? You and Cooper wanted the same thing." He stopped cold, hearing himself. Then, slowly, he repeated it. "You wanted the same thing."

"I didn't plan it." The words came out of Kim in a rush. "I hit a breaking point with him, and in the heat of the moment . . . He looked so miserable. He *was* so miserable. He didn't want to be here. He wasn't happy for me, he wasn't happy for you, and he sure as hell wasn't happy for himself. He was going to self-destruct. How could I succeed in a fifty-fifty partnership with that? I'd worked around the clock to get things on track, and he couldn't even get his shit together for a hot minute the entire time he was here. He chased away clients who'd waited patiently in the wings *all year*. He ridiculed me in front of my guests. He heckled you, harassed your date. He thought it was a laugh riot to be an embarrassment. If anything, I saved him from himself. Put him out of his misery."

Chris recoiled. "You sat with me that morning while everyone looked for him. In the lobby, making calls, asking hotel staff to do a welfare check on his room. And the whole time, you knew he was dead. Because you'd ki—" He shook his head, unable to say the word. "He was your brother. There were a million ways you could have *actually* saved him."

"While you sailed off without a care in the world?"

Chris's jaw twitched. "That's why you let me blame myself. Because you blame me. You shoved him and left him to drown, but that's my fault, too, isn't it, for daring to want something different than you two did? And Mikki's fault for seeing you for what you were. Even if you're deluded enough to rationalize losing your cool with Cooper, how can you not care how many people you've hurt in the process? It's all worth it as long as you get what you want?"

"If I didn't care, I wouldn't be here."

"Why *are* you here? Certainly not to help me. To cover your own ass? Or did you have some other sick plan?"

Kim was turning paler by the second. "No, I—I don't even know. With everything dredged back up, and you back here, I just had this terrible feeling she wouldn't be far behind. I thought if I could head her off somehow, take a different approach, offer her some money to keep quiet . . . But I was too late." She wasn't looking at Mikki. Her eyes were locked on Chris's, growing more desperate for him to understand. "You know me. You know I'm not a bad person," she pleaded. "Just because I did a ba—" Her voice caught. "A thing," she said weakly.

Mikki couldn't take it anymore. Tears streamed down her cheeks.

"I'm so sorry, Chris," Mikki cried. "If I'd ever imagined it wasn't you, of course I would have stayed. I wouldn't have let you think . . . I wouldn't have done that." She turned to Lark. "And if it had been just about me, I would have taken my chances. But Kim threatened to drag you down with me or instead of me, as long as anyone but her took the fall. She even threatened Dove, talking about how sad it would be for her to grow up without a mother. She swore the only way for me to protect you was to never see you again. If I'd made contact with you, she'd have assumed I'd told you everything I'd witnessed. She'd have seen us both as liabilities."

Lark turned coolly to Kim, her face a mask of confusion and anger. "Are *you* the one who threatened my PI?" she demanded. "Way back at the beginning of all this? And what about the letter in my office after Chris showed back up? That was a low blow." Mikki's blood turned to ice. After everything she'd sacrificed, Kim *still* hadn't left Lark the hell alone?

Heath made a noise of disbelief, his head snapping toward his fian-cée. "The *what?*"

But Lark didn't so much as wince. "I told you I had more to tell you," she answered, holding steady. "In my defense, you just got here. And I never needed rescuing." Kim was looking at the ground in defeat, and when she still didn't acknowledge Lark's questions, that seemed answer enough. Lark turned to Mikki, unblinking. "You know my daughter's name?"

Mikki's tears fell faster. Out of everything Lark could have said, this was the thing that undid her. They should never have had to reunite like this. It should have been on their own terms, with both their daughters along, laughing, talking. Not rehashing a past they might never rebound from. "I wanted to call you, every day. But I didn't want to put you or Dove at risk. I didn't want you to have to lie about me."

"Ah, yes." Lark's face clouded. "Because I'm such a terrible liar. So you'd rather let me think you were dead."

"If it was the only way to keep you safe, then yes. I knew I'd have to find other ways to look out for you."

"What other ways?" Lark demanded.

"We don't need to rehash *all* the details right now," Nini cut in, eyeing Kim sharply. "Certainly not in front of *her*. Are we done here, ladies? Chris?"

Kim snapped out of it at last, stepping toward her brother. "Surely we can work this out privately," she said. "It's a family matter."

Mikki's stomach lurched at the idea of Kim just boarding a plane home. Chris letting it go, deciding enough damage had been done. If that happened, would she ever feel safe?

But Chris couldn't even look at his sister. The disgust was plain on his face as he caught Mikki's eye. "All this time, Mikki," he said, "I thought I'd given you a new start, when the reality was . . . I can't bear to think of how different your life would have been if you'd never gotten caught up in all this. It's inexcusable. It's unforgivable."

A lump of emotion lodged in Mikki's throat. But she forced herself to swallow it.

"You did give me a new start," she said. "Both things can be true—for me and for you. Have you ever honestly wished you stayed with the business, went back to Michigan? Would you have been happy that way?" Chris looked at her like she must be kidding. He'd just found out his sister was a murderer. But that didn't negate everything else he'd been through.

"Hey," Mikki said. "I've had plenty of time to obsess over that map we were both so fond of. All those untaken roads?" She waited for him to nod, to show that he was really listening. "So I can tell you, it doesn't lead anywhere. It's fun to look at sometimes, but when it stops being fun, when it becomes agony to trace those routes instead? That's when it's better that we stop."

Chris tried to smile, but it went sideways. She'd missed this lopsided connection of theirs, and she could tell he was thinking the same.

She could see Lark absorbing it too. Mikki wanted to pull Chris into one of his good, long hugs, but this wasn't the time.

She could only hope they'd have more of it now. Even if things between them were irreparably different.

Heath cleared his throat. "Kim Redmond," he said, "I didn't get a chance to introduce myself. I'm the real Lark's fiancé. Heath McKenney, Ohio State Highway Patrol."

Kim's eyes narrowed. "You are way out of your jurisdiction."

"True," he said. "Thing is, I'm moving in with Lark and her family soon, and Mikki's grandmother here let me go ahead and add my name to the utility bills. You know, to get a jump on helping out. So when all this came up with your brother, I put through a request for our house phone records, and strangest thing: Nini had made multiple calls to a random Florida area code. I did some digging and—well, I won't bore you with details. But I had a hunch this trip might need the proper jurisdiction. So I gave a heads-up to a buddy who used to work with me in Ohio."

"Right," Kim drawled, calling his bluff. "Because people in Ohio up and move to Florida all the time."

Mikki spotted the glow of the cruiser lights, flashing blue and red over the dunes. The pair of officers approaching on the sand.

"Actually," Mikki told her, "they do."

41

Dove couldn't decide between chicken fingers and fish fingers, so Heath ordered both. "Don't worry if you can't eat it all," he told her. "I just want my own Frisbee." Nini threw back her head and laughed. The sky behind her was a sunset lavender haze, and Lark felt grateful, despite everything, to be sitting here haloed by strands of white lights, her family gathered around her.

Mikki had texted Lark an invitation to meet later for a walk after dark. Like they used to.

Lark hadn't decided yet whether to go through with it. Maybe, in a backward way, that was progress. Mikki always did used to say that Lark was too quick to forgive people who'd done her wrong. Her parents, for checking out. Chad, for checking in. Then again, Lark had spent years countering all that by refusing to forgive herself.

"Where's Mr. Chris?" Dove asked. "Doesn't he want dinner too?"

Lark and Heath exchanged looks. Kim had gone with the police willingly: even she wasn't underhanded enough to deny an entire confessional conversation in the presence of law enforcement. They'd all given statements at the scene; then Chris had gone along to the station, looking so distraught Lark felt awful for him. Mikki had also been taken in, sobbing in terror that she'd be charged with failure to report the felony. But the kind officers on the scene reassured her Kim's threats of retaliation were likely to warrant leniency, even an exception.

All that had been hours and hours ago.

"I think Mr. Chris has plans with his sister tonight," Nini told Dove, and Lark kicked her gently beneath the table. "What?" Nini asked innocently. "I didn't say they were fun plans. It's the truth."

"Ah, truth. What a refreshing change," Lark said, rolling her eyes.

"I'm an open book now that I'm not under duress," Nini said. "Ask me anything."

"What's duress?" Dove chirped.

"It's when you really want to do the right thing," Heath cut in, "but someone else is trying to force you not to. And maybe they have a good reason, too, and it's hard to figure out what the right thing is anymore." He might have acted unconcerned about his commander earlier, but Heath had been under a kind of duress of his own. Undoubtedly things were going to be a lot easier for him now that this case was solved. No conflict of interest, no harm, no foul.

Dove thought about his explanation. "That sounds complicated," she said finally.

"It is," Heath agreed.

"So when I want to stay up late to see the moon over the waves, but Mom says I'll be too tired the next day if I do, I'm going to bed under duress?"

When everyone started to laugh, Lark couldn't help but join in. "The young always go to bed under duress," Nini told Dove. "When you get old like me, going to bed becomes the easy part. It's waking up that's hard."

"Then how come you're up every morning before I am?" Dove wanted to know.

"My body wakes up against my will, though I have nowhere to be. That's the duress."

Dove pushed back from the table. "Can I feed my leftover fruit to the seagulls before the beach gets too dark?"

"Stay where I can see you," Lark told her, and they all watched the little girl bound down the boardwalk to the sand. Then they fell into a semiawkward silence. Lark was reticent to break it. But Nini *had* said to ask her anything.

"How long was it until you heard from her the first time?" Lark asked, finally.

"It felt like eternity," Nini answered. Then: "Couple days before I came to your door."

Lark watched her. She'd expected Nini to look healthier now that her secret was out, but the opposite was true. More like Nini was crumpling in relief that she didn't have to keep it together anymore. "So you really were holding a grudge against me? That wasn't just for show?"

"I don't fake grudges," Nini said.

"Me neither," Lark said, crossing her arms. The truth was, she was angrier than she wanted to let on. But she wasn't sure quite who she was angry with. Everyone? No one in particular? "What did Mikki say, exactly, when she called?" she asked.

"She said I'd have to trust her that it wasn't safe to come back, and it wasn't safe for anyone to know I'd heard from her either. Especially not you. I said, 'Mikki, can't that rich boy who picked you up help you out of this?' She got hysterical, said he was gone. The way she said it, I knew it was bad. She said she wouldn't leave us high and dry, she would look out for me as best she could on the condition that I looked out for you. Much to my chagrin."

Lark shook her head. "I should've known," she muttered.

It was an attempt at a joke, but Nini shrugged. "Maybe you should have. I remember the last thing Mikki's mom ever said to me. It was about you two. She said all anyone really needs in this world is one true friend. She was glad you two had found each other so early in life."

"Yeah, well," Lark said. "We lost each other."

"No, you didn't," Nini said. "You just thought you had."

Lark scowled at her, in no mood. "You remember an awful lot all of a sudden."

Heath leaned toward Nini, folding his hands on the table. "This is how you've been affording your bills, isn't it?" he asked. "When I was trying to help Lark with some of that Medicare mess, nothing added up."

"Well, I'm not allowed unsupervised access to my bank accounts—Lark has to help with that. So Mikki getting us money was easier said than done. Sometimes she'd call my doctors and put money down before they could bill us. That sort of thing. She figured no one can make sense out of those invoices anyway. They always say, *This is not a bill*."

"That time you supposedly won all that money for our transmission repair on a scratch-off?" Lark asked.

Nini nodded.

"The chicken soup delivered by accident? The perfect Christmas gifts for Dove?" Again Nini nodded, and Lark's stomach dropped. "Oh, God. That's why the cops thought I knew more than I was letting on, isn't it? They really did see some strange transactions . . ."

Nini pulled a face. "She never could leave well enough alone."

Lark shook her head in frustration. "I didn't want any of that. I only wanted her."

"You think she didn't feel that way too? You think I didn't?" Nini grunted. "Do you know what kind of pressure I've been under, knowing my brain might not let me keep this secret much longer? And then what? But after enough time had passed, I convinced myself everything would be okay. Because it already is. As hard as it might be to say aloud, you've built a fine life without her, and as hard as it might be to hear, she has almost everything she's ever wanted. She has far more than she probably would've if she'd never gotten in that car. And I'm not talking about material things. Life is a journey, and like she said earlier, about that map? We're still on it."

Heath looked annoyingly impressed. Lark wagged her finger at Nini. "Mikki warned me a long time ago not to take advice from you."

"Well, I'm not giving you advice. Everyone knows I'm just a rambling old shrew. Now that we have her back, we can either spoil it with hurt feelings or we can move forward. Besides, the *what-if* game goes both ways. We're always going to wish Mikki had come straight home to us. But if she had, you might not have Heath now. And I might not have Dove. We can't really know what we'd have been open to or where any of us would be."

Heath met Lark's eyes, and a startling moment of clarity passed between them. Not just clarity but gratitude.

"I won't tell you what to do," Nini finished. "I for one feel lucky to have the choice. Plus, this state has lots of resources for elder care. Maybe we should check them out."

Lark was just beginning to grasp the scope by which things could be different now—if she wanted them to. How funny that she wasn't sure if she did.

Then again, that had always been the biggest difference between her and Mikki.

The dinner crowd was transitioning into lines at the bar for drinks, and the bartender turned up the music. A Rolling Stones song was playing: "You Can't Always Get What You Want." Lark thought of her favorite trucker, who always came in serenading her with his best Mick Jagger. Who seemed content driving the same old route every night to the same old songs. She reached over and squeezed Heath's hand.

"Maybe we should," she agreed.

~~~

It was darker than Lark had expected on the beach. She could barely make out Mikki's face as they fell into stride next to each other, not speaking. She didn't mind; it made her feel like she could hide behind the darkness too. Everything between them was different now, along with everything around them: their bare feet in the sand, the roar of the waves. But there was nostalgia in it, easy to slip back into. Because wasn't this always what they'd been walking toward?

On hundreds of nighttime walks together since they were kids sneaking out back in Becksville, each had been doing her part to help the other one escape.

"So," Lark said. "I'm guessing your name isn't Mikki anymore."

"Technically, I changed it to Michaela."

Lark nodded approvingly. "As your parents should have in the first place."

"Guess I had to set something right while I was doing everything else wrong." She cleared her throat. "Also, I hoped if we got back in touch, I could still be Mikki to all of you."

Lark didn't know what to say to that. "What else?" she asked. "I guess Nini has kept you posted on my life, but I don't know anything about yours."

"Do you want the play-by-play?" Mikki asked. "How I became someone else? How I felt guilty every time something went my way?"

Lark wasn't ready to make Mikki feel better about any of it. Not yet.

"How about you skip to the good stuff," Lark said. Not that she didn't want the play-by-play. But eight years' worth would take some time. If they wanted to let it.

"Good plan," Mikki said. "Turns out I prefer the Gulf Coast: the water is gentler, clearer. No bad memories." She shuddered hard enough that Lark felt the shiver run through her too. "I did a two-year degree in interior design at community college. I run a little shop where I did my work-study, called Beach House Home Decor. The owner is mostly retired, and the plan is for me to take over. We carry a combination of new and secondhand stuff—I acquire it all myself and doctor it to look high end without costing high end."

"I bet you're great at that," Lark said.

"And I do design work for private clients, word of mouth. I met my husband at the college. He teaches a real estate class there. His business helps first-time home buyers get financing and all the assistance they qualify for. There's more money in upscale real estate, obviously, but he has a soft spot for underdogs." Lark heard pride in Mikki's voice. And love. "He has a daughter Dove's age," Mikki added. "We have her every other week. She's great."

"I'm happy for you," Lark said.

"I'm happy for you too. I liked Heath instantly. And no pressure to let me meet Dove, but . . . Well, you've done a wonderful job."

Again, that was the part that got her. Dove's name on Mikki's lips. She wasn't sure whether to forbid Mikki from mentioning her or to drag her off to meet Dove right now. She tried to picture it—Dove's face lighting up in recognition of the elusive, legendary Aunt Mikki—but that didn't make her feelings any less complicated. So she changed the subject. "What about Chris? He has even more to process than we do."

"Yeah." Mikki took a minute to collect her thoughts. "Now that I'm over the shock of him being alive, I really feel for the guy. But we had a chance to talk a little more, and it's funny. He said that as hard as it is to grapple with what Kim has done, it helps restore his memory of Cooper to the way it should have been. We talked about how Cooper probably would have gotten along with the new Chris a whole lot better. Cooper was someone who could appreciate living life to the fullest. He just lost sight of how to go about it after the wildfire."

"Did I imagine some chemistry between you two? Unfinished business, maybe?"

"Maybe." Mikki bowed her head. "But there's no finishing it now. I guess we have his sister to thank for that too."

Lark didn't know what was getting into her. Here she was, feeling sorry for Mikki that maybe, if things had been different, she could have had her actual Prince Charming. When the real tragedy was what had been lost between the two of them. A lifelong friendship. A feeling of sisterhood she wasn't sure they could ever get back.

"If Chris hadn't shown up," Lark ventured, "were you really never going to reach out to me? Kim had you that indefinitely afraid?"

A long moment passed before Mikki answered. "Five years," she said quietly. "That was the deadline I gave myself when I figured we could risk it. But by then . . . someone convinced me it was unfair to you at that point. That I was being selfish. Cruel."

The dinner conversation came back to Lark. "Is that someone related to you and living with me?"

"I promised not to say."

Lark was incredulous. Maybe she *did* know who she was mad at. "Didn't you tell me never to take criticism from someone you wouldn't take advice from?"

Mikki sighed. "I don't live by rules anymore," she said. "Some things are only fun with a friend." Just as she said it, she stumbled, pitching forward in a dip in the sand. Instinctively, Lark reached out and caught her by the shoulder. They stared at each other, sheepish, and then Mikki was hugging her, and they were half laughing, half crying, the way old friends did when they hadn't seen each other in years. Because this close, no number of unanswered questions could obscure the flood of emotion that here, at last, was Mikki, *her* Mikki—who cried in the corner on the first day of kindergarten, who upended her soup on a bully's head in seventh grade, who danced with Lark at prom when Chad decided the keg behind the bleachers was more fun. Mikki, who helped bag all the trash in Lark's parents' trailer after they died. Who always saved Lark the last waffle. Who scared Lark half to death when she disappeared.

Who'd *been* scared half to death when she disappeared. Lark could still feel Mikki trembling now, in relief and sorrow and yearning. She wanted to reassure her that as heartbreaking and unbelievable as all this was, it could have been so, so much worse. Lark had had plenty of time to imagine all the ways, in excruciating detail she could never forget. Because she'd always known there could never be another Mikki. Not even close.

When Lark pulled back, she still felt awkward. But she couldn't deny the connection that remained. The one that saved Mikki's seat in her life all these years—from the recurring dreams she'd never quite wished away to the photos still framed in every room.

Some things would always be too big to put in a box. Even if you were tempted to try.

"At risk of sounding childish," Lark said, "you don't have a new best friend?"

"I never wanted a new one," Mikki said.

Lark toed the sand. "You'll get a kick out of this. I made you actual bumper stickers."

"I know," Mikki said, brightening. "They're great. I have one on my car."

"You're messing with me. The CATCH YOU LATER one?"

"Would you believe I saw one? In Orlando—on the highway. This will shock you, but Nini isn't too big on conveying touchy-feely details. I ordered one from your website."

Lark didn't know what to say. "Why?" she managed.

"I guess it made me feel like there would be a later for us." Mikki's voice broke on the word. "It's about hope, right?"

When they turned to walk back, they linked arms. Lark wasn't sure what might really change for either of them—maybe everything, or maybe not much at all. They weren't the same Lark and Mikki anymore. But neither was willing to let the other go.

When you're separated by hundreds of miles of interstate, maybe that's enough.

AUTHOR'S NOTE AND

ACKNOWLEDGMENTS

The idea for this book came to me—as you might guess—on a road trip from Ohio to Florida, and I've never looked at any travel stop the same way since. Which is to say, not without imagining how it compares with Mikki and Lark's home base. So I suppose I should start by thanking my husband and children for graciously pretending it's totally normal for the grown woman in the passenger seat to approach every interstate exit as if fictional people might appear.

Becksville is not a real town in Ohio but a composite true to the spirit of many such places along I-75 (and beyond). While Amelia Island is, in fact, a lovely place, I took a few liberties with the island's geography and did indeed invent a pier as well as a resort. While the Topaz is not real, it was loosely inspired by many hours drooling over the Omni Amelia Island Instagram feed. (If you're looking for bucket-list accommodations, you're welcome.)

Sincere thanks to my friend and fellow novelist Mindy McGinnis for making introductions when I was looking for a trooper in a more rural area of our state. I can't imagine a better source than the one I met through you, further proof that fiction writers make amazing (and handy) friends. And to the aforementioned trooper, who declined to be named here but humored me with honesty and insight through countless hypothetical questions, proving invaluable in shaping not only Heath's character but also aspects of the plot: thank you for lending such good-natured expertise, for being so generous with your time, and for debunking the popular misconception that "I would not give my own mother a ticket." I have passed this along as promised, but many of my fellow Ohio drivers remain skeptical.

Kirk Barbro: Who knew I could have so much fun talking about private vehicle sales, skipped titles, and the ways everyday people bend the rules without even realizing it? Thank you for a long and entertaining brainstorming session that made Chris's car conundrum more plausible (your ideas were better than mine!), and for sharing your years of experience on the car lot.

With this, my seventh novel, I'm more grateful than ever for the talented publishing professionals who've come along on this leg of the journey. My admiration only grows for my agent, Barbara Poelle, whose positive energy knows no bounds. On the editorial side, gratitude to Alicia Clancy for championing this idea from word one and bringing a collaborative spirit to the table. Jodi Warshaw, I'm so grateful for this opportunity to have been on the receiving end of your thoughtful editorial guidance and encouragement. The two of you are a dream team, and this book is better for it. Thanks also to so many supportive talents at Lake Union, including but not limited to: editorial director Danielle Marshall, cover designer Jeff Miller (via Faceout Studio), art director Adrienne Krogh, Rachael Clark in marketing, Darci Swanson in author relations, and the production team led by Karah Nichols.

The writing life is full of untaken roads, which leaves me extra grateful for my fellow writerly travelers I'm honored to call friends, including the Career Authors team, *Writer's Digest* colleagues past and present, Tall Poppy Writers, Fiction Writers Co-Op, and the blue underwear squad (you know who you are). I'm equally grateful for the many independent bookstores (notably Joseph-Beth Booksellers, Cincy Book Bus, The Bookshelf in Madeira, Pittsburgh's Penguin Bookshop, The Book Loft of German Village, and welcome new addition Bike Trail Books) and wonderful libraries that have championed my books, as well as the book clubs who've selected my titles for their discussions and sometimes even invited me to join them. And to all my real-life friends who text me out of the blue and readers who take the time to drop me a message after reading one of my books: when I tell you I can't overstate how much that means to me, it's true.

Extra thanks to my wonderful family: Evan, Courtney, and Holly Yerega, and especially my dad, Michael, who hand-sells more of my books than I do. And to the one I married into, especially Terry Strawser and Amy Strawser, for showing up when I least expect it.

Scott and the kids: I might imagine people for a living, but I could never dream up anyone as wonderful as you three. I love you more.

READING GROUP DISCUSSION GUIDE

1. At the start of the story, are Lark and Mikki holding each other back, perhaps outgrowing their friendship? Or are they smart to stick together no matter what? When we say our close friends are "like family," do we really mean that, or are there limits?

2. Do you think Mikki was reckless in walking out of her shift and getting into Chris's car? Or was she right in fulfilling a promise she'd made to herself, no matter the risk?

3. Can you imagine anything Lark could have feasibly done to stop Mikki from leaving, even if she'd tried? Is the Becksville rumor mill too hard on Lark, or does she deserve it?

4. What do you remember about the first time you saw the ocean (or have you seen it)? If you were a child at the time, how do you think that experience would differ as an adult?

5. Regret is a powerful motivator, for better or for worse. How does regret shape Lark's character in the present day? How did it play into Mikki's decisions in 2016? What does regret do to Chris (who humorously self-identifies as "pining") and the other Redmonds? Do you think regret does more harm than good, or is that up to us?

6. Do you get the sense that Nini is closer with Lark now

than she ever was with Mikki? Do Nini and Lark make the best of things out of necessity, or is there more to it?

7. Lark is haunted by a recurring dream of searching empty cars in the Travel Stop parking lot in an endless, looping search for Mikki. Have you ever had recurring dreams, and do you interpret them as significant?

8. Dove says little on the page but plays a huge role in the story. How do you imagine things might have played out differently—then and now—if Lark had never been pregnant?

9. Given the way Lark has been treated by law enforcement, did you find Heath an odd love match for her, or a perfect choice? After Chris reappears in Lark's life, did you empathize with Heath having to tread so carefully? What did you wish he'd done differently?

10. Were you hoping for Mikki and Chris to get together, or do you think they were too different for a romance to ever make sense?

11. The Rolling Stones make several appearances in this novel's soundtrack, from the singing trucker wearing vintage concert tees to one of the novel's final scenes, when Lark notices "You Can't Always Get What You Want" playing in the restaurant at dinner with Heath, Nini, and Dove. What does that song mean to you—do you find it reassuring, or kind of a downer? How is it appropriate (or not) to Lark and Mikki's story?

12. What do you imagine the future looks like for these characters and their relationships?

ABOUT THE AUTHOR

Photo © Corrie Schaffeld

Jessica Strawser is the *USA Today* bestselling author of *The Last Caretaker*, *The Next Thing You Know*, *A Million Reasons Why*, *Forget You Know Me*, *Not That I Could Tell* (a Book of the Month selection), and *Almost Missed You*. She was editorial director at *Writer's Digest* for nearly a decade before becoming a novelist. Jessica is also a Career Authors contributing editor, popular speaker at writing conferences, and freelance editor and writer with bylines in the *New York Times* Modern Love column, *Publishers Weekly*, and other venues. A Pittsburgh native and Outstanding Senior alum of the top-ranked E. W. Scripps School of Journalism at Ohio University, she lives with her husband and two children in Cincinnati, Ohio, where she served as 2019 Writer-in-Residence for the Cincinnati and Hamilton County Public Library and received a 2024 Ohio Arts Council Individual Excellence Award. For more information, visit www.jessicastrawser.com.